# A RESPONSIBLE MAN

## ACKNOWLEDGEMENTS

For technical and professional advice I should like to thank Professor J. Rotblat of Pugwash; Ashley Jones, Senior Network Engineer, BBC World Service; Dr Marc Jordan, art historian; Eva Haraszti Taylor; Alison Samuel, my editor; and, above all, Susan Crosland, my friend.

# A
# RESPONSIBLE
# MAN

## Cynthia Kee

Chatto & Windus
LONDON

Published in 1993 by
Chatto & Windus Ltd
20 Vauxhall Bridge Road
London SW1V 2SA

A CIP catalogue record for this book is
available from the British Library.

ISBN 0 7011 5683 X

The lines from 'In Memory of Sigmund Freud' and 'Lullaby'
by W.H. Auden are reproduced from *Collected Poems*
(edited by Edward Mendelson) by permission of
Faber & Faber Ltd.

Phototypeset by Intype, London
Printed and bound in Great Britain by
Mackays of Chatham PLC, Chatham, Kent

To Sarah and Carolyn

# Chapter One

Harold's face flicked above the crowd, white, taut and fierce, between the yellow of his hair and the emerald green of his bow tie. Both were awry, shaken by the frantic animation of his conversation. People milled round him; a centre of attraction but also, apart. Victoria caught glimpses of him above the waves. She was in the thick of it too and she loved it. She loved being hemmed in by the throng, admired, enfolded by eager febrile voices and the intellectual fug. She sparkled and felt safe.

A man she knew wriggled through the massed backs, his thin face glistening and his buck teeth gripping his lower lip. 'You're the only girl I could bear any of my friends to marry,' he drawled. His eyes glinted above the rim of his glass. He took a sip from it and slipped away, still looking at her.

What an odd thing to say, thought Victoria. She smiled at him. The man standing next to her put his arm round her. She stiffened and shrank away. He was shorter than she was and she had never met him before. They were rather a scruffy lot in their hairy suits and tight haircuts, but she was pleased to be there. They were literary. They wrote books. One of them would ask her out to dinner soon. She threw herself back into the conversation.

Let me out, thought Harold, wildly. What am I doing here? Let me out. He wanted to squash someone flat. If they thought they owned him just because they paid him for editing a bit of their paper he would show them. He would walk out, resign, throw himself under a train, drive his car up a one-way street. If he did not kill himself, it would be quite comforting to be in a prison cell again. But he had not got a car. Fuckit. He looked round for someone he could make cry and saw Victoria, bright pink with a little pink hat perched on the back of her short dark hair. She wore thick make-up and looked animated, interestingly dressed and a shade too plump. I could tear her to pieces quite easily, he thought, and smiled brilliantly at the proprietor's wife.

The proprietor's wife was an heiress and not to be taken lightly. Though wispy, girlish and seductively cosy to talk to, she was a formidable gossip yielding considerable socio-political power. A mother of twins herself, she still called her own mother, an ex-Bluebell, 'Mummy'. Englishmen loved her. Mr Macmillan was a family friend, so was young Jack Kennedy. Her gardens and her parties were to be taken seriously. Giggling, she asked Harold to one of them and, flattered, he accepted. He had no intention of going. It was funny, he thought, the worse you behaved the more people seemed to like you. They found it dashing and reckless, he supposed, and he liked that. He could be conspiratorially bashful and contrite too. But really he was desperate – if only they knew, desperate. He felt panic rising in his throat and lit a Gauloise. Puffing furiously, hating the taste, he laid on the charm.

Somebody Victoria knew, a film critic which was a good thing for a man one went out with to be, had already asked her to have dinner and she was pleased enough;

safe at any rate. They were good friends. Small, dark, clever and passionately cultivated, he educated Victoria and often took her out. She had got him to write a daily lampoon in verse for the programme she worked on. They would sit side by side on the red plush banquette of a good French restaurant, not touching, and make one another laugh. Once, as he left a party in her flat, Victoria had kissed him on the cheek and he had recoiled. They knew each other just enough. She felt interested and deferential: he liked her style. They were both fastidious.

Across the room, Harold took a half-step back and shook his head hard so that a long spike or two of hair flew across his eyebrows. The woman who was talking to him took a step forward and two men at her side closed in.

'I thought Peggy was quite wonderful as Cleopatra, didn't you?' she said, intensely. She had big teeth which she kept closed as she talked and thrust her chic, cropped grey head so close that Harold could see the dark line of hairs growing along her upper lip. Her mouth was painted cherry-red.

'I'm afraid I haven't been yet,' he said, clenching his fists so the nails bit into his palms. He forced himself to smile.

'Oh, but you must,' she cried. 'Ken'll get you a ticket. We'll all go together.'

'That would be too boring for you. You couldn't,' said Harold.

'But we'd love to,' said the woman. She grasped the arms of the men beside her. 'Wouldn't we?' she said, nodding at them vigorously. She looked at Harold and their eyes, cool grey and steel-blue, clashed, locked in wordless battle for a moment or two.

'I hate seeing things twice,' said Harold.

'I adore it,' said the woman.

'Have a cigarette,' said the man called Ken. He was taller than Harold and stooped towards him as he held out a silver cigarette case with a row of Sobranies held behind an elastic band. Harold shook his head but the woman took one. Her nostrils flared as she fitted it into an ivory holder. 'How divine,' she said as she inhaled. 'We'll have supper at my flat afterwards.'

As the party thinned out, Victoria found a paunchy red-faced man beside her. He had a thick dark moustache and heavily marked sideburns. In spite of his corpulence, a sense of power came through the bulk. Victoria felt it penetrate the thin pink of her dress and it made her uncomfortable. She tried not to look at him but he took her by the elbow.

'You're a damned attractive young woman,' he said in her ear. Tufts of hair grew out of his and he held his face so close that she could see the long black hairs in his nostrils too. She held herself away and smiled at him gaily. His breath was hot and smelled of violets.

'I'd like to take you to dinner,' he said, and pressed the inside of her arm.

Victoria felt his fingers against the side of her breast. His foot touched hers. She strained and wriggled as discreetly as she could. 'I'm going out to dinner with somebody already,' she said.

'Come with me,' said the man. 'I know how to give women a good time. I'll take you to the Mirabelle and we'll go on to the Milroy.'

Victoria freed herself and stood facing him. She had never been to the Mirabelle. The man watched her. He had very small light eyes beneath black eyebrows that looked like slugs come to rest on the skin of his forehead, and the tip of his tongue showed pink between his lips under the forest of his moustache. His wide tie, Windsor knotted, was fastened with a diamond pin.

He looks like a boxing promoter, thought Victoria. What's he doing here? She could imagine him crooking his little finger round the handle of a teacup.

'My chauffeur's downstairs,' he said to her in a low voice.

Victoria shook her head. 'I'm already going out to dinner,' she said.

The man felt in his pocket and brought out a card. 'Geoffrey Champman,' he said, handing it to her. 'They tell me you're in journalism. I'm giving a private dinner for the Second Press Attaché from the Russian Embassy next Thursday. You'd find it interesting. My secretary'll 'phone you. We're on the river at Richmond.'

Richmond, thought Victoria, shocked. How could anyone live *there*? But she had never met a Russian before – no one she knew had. She began thinking about what to wear. She had a number of careful frocks designed by herself that she could wear all day at work and subtract or add to for going out in the evening. 'I'd love to come,' she said, brightly, fine grey herringbone in mind.

'Eight o'clock,' said the man. 'Just a family party.'

Victoria looked down at the card he had given her. It was heavily inscribed in Gothic script, 'Sir Geoffrey Champman', and in a smaller face underneath, 'British Press Agency'. She held onto it by its sharp corners and turned away. There were spaces now between the knots of people still bunched together, talking. She looked around among them for the tall man with the wild yellow hair and wondered whom he got to cut it like that. There was still time for him to walk over and maybe . . .

But the film critic had on his coat, a loose tweed one, at odds with his earwig body and big bespectacled head.

'Come on,' he said.

Victoria found her coat and they went out into the cold night. It was December and their breath puffed out in little clouds when they talked. The film critic waved his umbrella at a taxi and named a famous restaurant. Victoria had read about it; indeed, when working on a magazine further down the street, she used to stand above the grating of its kitchens to warm herself. They would have a seriously good dinner there, with underdone vegetables and cheese instead of pudding. He would talk to her about the *nouvelle vague* and the Method style of acting, and Victoria, her eyes fixed on his face, would deplore with him the backward and parochial state of the arts in Britain. Later, he would leave her outside her basement flat in Holland Park while he went back to his own in Finchley. He was too delicate to drive, and Victoria was dimly aware that his passionate intellectual interests were deliberately cultivated to offset the almost allergic sensitivity of his flesh.

As Victoria and her escort tucked themselves behind their stiff white table-cloth and the head waiter pointed out to them the delicacies of the evening, Harold found himself beached in the suddenly emptied room. Only the proprietor, his wife and one or two other members of staff lingered in the stationary haze. One by one they pressed him to join them for dinner. 'Come and have a bite at Bertorelli's, old chap.' But he turned them down with a lop-sided smile. Tomorrow, he would find himself back there among them at his desk.

What was he doing, he thought glumly as he let himself out of the front door. He had not got a proper coat, he despised them and the bleakness of the cold fed his mood. He had become attached to deprivation through the long years of boarding-school and prison camp. Choice and plenty unnerved him. He held his ungloved hands stiffly at an angle from his body, then dug them into his pockets. The suit was battered but sharp and one of two he owned. He walked the few streets back to his flat in Soho, past the Christmas lights, thinking of his ex-wife Clare. Little pictures of the dark-haired girl in pink kept popping into his brain, but he chased them out. The flat in Soho was lent to him by a friend who lived abroad with her husband. Women were always trying to take care of him, men too. He called out a maternal impulse in both but was attractive and unpredictable enough – dangerous even – to lend a dash of glamour to their supportive endeavours.

He could use the flat on condition there was always a room free in it for his friend's disreputable half-brother. It was on the top two floors of a dilapidated eighteenth-century house, above a restaurant and a tailor's work-room. The floors were crooked and the windows did not fit, but there were Nicholsons, Winifred Nicholsons, and Matthew Smiths on the walls.

He unlocked the door and went into the dim kitchen. The sink was piled high with unwashed crockery and glasses – the layabout brother had probably peed on them too, as the bathroom was one floor up. Harold found a piece of bread, buttered it, dropped the knife and walked into the drawing-room eating. It tasted unsatisfactory. He left it among the socks and papers on the table and went up to his bedroom. Dropping his clothes on the floor as he went, he got naked into the unmade bed. There he

7

wrestled for a while with the chilly grey sheets, trying to force them into some sort of accommodation with his resentful body. Then he turned off the light. But the switch would not work. So he turned his back on it and went grudgingly to sleep.

# Chapter Two

On Thursday, Victoria went to work in the fine grey herringbone. She wore her waspie underneath. The dress had a tight top which the waspie kept wrinkle-free, a flared skirt and a round neck, lower at the back than the front (after Balenciaga), with a pin-tucked white cotton infill press-studded in for day. For going out she removed the white cotton and put on lots of strings of pearls and tortoiseshell-coloured beads, and pearl earrings.

At the studios, the team was sitting round the table in one of the ground-floor hospitality rooms, going through the daily papers. Interviewers and the anchorman came in after lunch. Victoria already had two items in hand for that evening's programme. Robert Frost, in England for a short visit, was coming in to be interviewed and she had some clips of Ingmar Bergman films that would have to be cut together that day to make a compilation marking the opening of *Wild Strawberries* in London. Andrew, the assistant producer, wrote them down on his provisional running-order: three minutes for Robert Frost; four and a half for the Bergman films. Victoria fought him on Robert Frost and got three and a half minutes. None of them had ever heard of Frost or Bergman. They still thought of American poetry as 'Hiawatha' and, for foreign cinema, Jean Gabin.

Gregory, an ex-newspaperman lately co-opted, who had established a network of provincial stringers, was very excited about a prize pig in Northumberland; a small item he had found in the depths of the *Daily Express*. The pig ate bacon and eggs. It was agreed that the pig should be brought down and get five minutes in that evening's programme. Gregory rushed off to activate his stringers. He would be happily shouting at the top of his voice from his desk next to Victoria's in the back-bedroom offices upstairs for the rest of the day.

Owen, the producer, stocky and pugnacious in his grubby three-piece suit, was off: it was the anniversary of some battle or other, and he had launched into an unstoppable monologue on the English character compared with the Welsh. The Italians and the French – though he had never been out of the country and was too young to have been in the war – came into it too, as well as, somehow, bloody Descartes, bloody Voltaire and a lot of bloody marvellous.

Andrew shuffled and looked at his watch. It was half past nine. 'Must get on with the Programme, boy,' he murmured. His face was a greyish putty colour from exhaustion. He took the overall daily responsibility of running the Programme on his shoulders as well as the actual directing of it. Owen had been banished from the control room because he shouted too much. Andrew had a wife, two young children and a small house by the railway line to look after. His wife was often ill and some nights, when he came out of the control room, little beads of sweat stood out on his pallid forehead.

'Shut up, Owen,' said Victoria loudly.

'Sorry, boy – I mean girl,' said Owen. He looked crest-fallen for a moment but revived at the thought of having one of his pet professors come up from the university for the Programme. Few pukka academics permitted themselves to descend from the uplands of the intellect into the brief and vulgar limelight of the new popular medium. Owen was tickled pink to rub shoulders with those that did.

'Two and a half minutes,' said Victoria, sternly.

'Right, girl, right,' said Owen.

Two MPs were to discuss race relations down the line from Birmingham, Andrew's item; there was some film about metropolitan water fountains; either Andrew or Victoria was to try and get the General Secretary of the Boilermakers' Union in to talk about a demarcation dispute currently crippling Clydeside; and the day's topical verses that opened the Programme would arrive that afternoon in a taxi, written by Victoria's film critic friend. That left fifteen minutes to fill.

The four film editors took the lift up to their cutting-rooms, laughing and joking. The three secretaries went off to the canteen for coffee. Owen put his hand on Andrew's shoulder and Andrew put his hand on Owen's shoulder. Heads down, like two horses in a summer field, they walked through the corridor of the main building. Then Owen broke into a jog. Andrew let go of him and followed, up the lino-covered stairs, through the dingy passages to their offices in the taken-over houses next door.

Putting in an occasional skip to keep up, Victoria followed.

Harold came to that morning in the quiet, crooked room. Dead light, the colour of old dishcloth, hung against the window panes like an exterior curtain. For a while he stared at the Matthew Smith opposite his bed, caught up in its redness. It was crooked too and, as he stared, it crashed to the floor. Christ, he thought, looking at the time. He leaped out of bed and started thrashing to get his legs into his underpants, untangled from the blankets. They were half inside-out and no amount of effort would make them viable. He abandoned them and, grinding his teeth, made for the half open drawers of the chest of drawers. He found socks, ties, waistcoats, letters, aspirins, a shoe, a few belts, a comb or two and a photograph of his daughter. Her solemn, ten-year-old face gazed up at him unsmiling. Her fine hair fell in two thin plaits on either side of her face. She looked neither happy nor sad: she just was.

Harold went back to the bed, untangled the underpants, put his legs in the legs and went to the bathroom to shave. Most mornings when Clare was away, he took his daughter and her half-sister to school: neither a duty nor a pleasure, he clung to this daily chore partly out of conviction that to hang on to what shreds of parenthood he could must be right, and partly out of longing. He went on thinking about her as he shaved, peering at his handsome face through the condensation and seeing hers, so like Clare's that, from behind, you often could not tell them apart and yet, so essentially her own. His daughter, he thought, he was as deprived of her as he had been of his own father and the shaving brush fell out of his hand. As he fished for it in the cooling soapy water the thorough, total, cataclysmic unsatisfactoriness of his life pressed in on him from all sides. He kicked the listing wash-basin, scraped away with the razor at his face, dried it with the damp towel and plunged into his clothes: silk shirt, disintegrating round the collar but cream and silk; crumpled suit made by Anderson & Sheppard; socks, by some miracle a pair; lace-up shoes unpolished and all the more distinguished because of it; and his old ripped-up sheepskin Fleet Air Arm flying jacket.

He flung himself down the uneven stairs, out into the morning crowds hurrying sedately to their places of work and into the tube at Tottenham Court Road.

At St John's Wood, he got out and made at speed for the broad avenue where Clare lived in a house of substance bought for her by her last husband. To his surprise, she opened the door and stood there, frail and provocative in a pool of silence smiling her secret smile. He smiled back and kissed her. Most carefully now, he entered the house and accepted a cup of strong coffee which Clare poured for him, hot, into a thick, old, painted cup. The two little girls were finishing their breakfast; Flora, the daughter of the suave Frenchman who had taken his place as Clare's lover and temporary husband, and Alice, his own Alice. Joking and solicitous he helped them button up their coats, Flora's fur made specially for her by Madame Rochas and Alice's black corduroy from Harrods. Clare gave him the keys of her Bentley.

'You can keep it,' she said in her low voice. 'I'm going to Rome.'

Alice put her hand into his and Flora rubbed her cheek against his other one. 'Will you pretend you're flying us?' she said, dancing up and down in her fur-lined boots. They got into the car. Harold revved up the engine, crashed the joystick into gear and took off with a roar into the traffic. Flora squealed with delight as she slithered across the leather seat and even Alice smiled.

That evening after work Harold visited them again, on

their own by now with the au pair girl, in the big house. He hated it when Clare went away and left them, but he did not dare to say so. She often went away and he felt the emptiness on their behalf with vague unease, but Clare's spell was fast upon him. He had loved her. He still did, and her friends, her magic circle, were arbiters of his image. He tried to compensate, to keep in fatherly touch, to fill the gap, but he often went away himself. He had been sent back from the East by his own parents to boarding-school when he was five and the bleakness was still within him, as was his attitude to rules and institutions which enraged and cowed him at once. He wished he could have stayed on with the little girls and put them into bed, but he felt incompetent, disqualified; it was woman's work and in a way he was relieved that the much-resented call of social life drew him on before he could do so.

Leaving it as late as he dared, he kissed them good-night and drove fast into the night towards Richmond.

Victoria arrived by car too, driven by her friend Roderick. They worked on the Programme together; he, in front of the cameras, she, as a producer and they were very close. The Programme had been a humiliating disaster from their point of view. The great American poet had been cut off in mid-sentence at three minutes. Owen, rattled by the old man's faltering sing-song, had charged into the control room head down, fists clenched shouting, 'Wind him up. Wind him up.' Andrew wound him up as much to get Owen out of the control room as anything else. Victoria and Roderick were scandalised – such an eminent literary figure, such a distinguished white-haired old gentleman. They had not been able to make head or tail of his utterances either but his presence was an honour. Roderick, interviewing him, had dealt as deferentially with him as he could, and Victoria had been there, waiting at the studio door to congratulate the old man and see him at length into his car, leaving Owen in the viewing-room, beside himself with glee as the pig from Northumberland wandered round the studio, incontinent.

Afterwards, there was a row in the pub. The post-Programme shouting sessions were a feature of Programme life.

Ignoramus, boor, thought Victoria surveying Owen's stained waistcoat with disdain. 'You're just not couth,' she shouted, 'simply because you've never heard of him doesn't mean a thing. Even if he wasn't famous, someone of his age deserves respect and courtesy. It's a disgusting thing to do at any level. How do you expect me to get good people to come on if they get treated like that?'

'You shouldn't have done it, boy,' said Andrew at his side. 'There was enough time. We had to put on an extra song at the end.'

'Dear fellow,' said Roderick, debonair in his slate-green suit and shell-pink tie, 'you're completely out of your depth here. Not everyone – not even all Welsh men – prefers pigs to poets.'

'All right, all right,' mumbled Owen, 'have another whisky, girl.'

'Oh, Owen,' said Victoria with irritation, 'I'm on gin. You know I've been drinking gin for the last three months now.'

'It's for her figure,' said Owen, aside, to Andrew. 'No extra sugar, see? Bloody marvellous. You look bloody marvellous, girl. Come and have a bite at the Portofino.'

'Tomorrow,' said Victoria. She was going out to dinner

and Roderick, who knew all about Victoria's life – almost all – had offered to drive her. Owen offered too. As Roderick and Victoria left the dim saloon they heard him give a short bark of laughter as he settled into the bar and a session with Andrew in which praise of pigs, Plato, the Common People, BBC politics and Cardiff cocoa were inevitable ingredients.

Their leader, their grubby, belligerent, exuberant leader opening up new television territory with his devoted private army; operating on a wondrous shoe-string; working incredible hours; breaking rules, making legends for honesty, equality and truthful communication of all that was best between men and women. No talking down, no evasion, no prejudice, no pretension: on the Programme you presented what was important to you. What was important to you was enough for mankind. No question.

At dinner, Victoria sat on Sir Geoffrey's left. The Second Press Attaché's wife, a stout unsmiling woman in brown cut-velvet, sat on his right, her pudgy face glimmering behind the rows of silver and cut glass that flanked her place. Beside her, white-faced and untamed, was the handsome man who had caught Victoria's eye at the literary party the week before. His uncombed hair fell in floppy spikes across his forehead and the frayed collar of his shirt was rucked up under his rumpled suit. He had arrived late in a blast of cold air as the company's tankards, all except Victoria's, were filled with champagne for the second time.

'Ah, Fox!' bellowed Sir Geoffrey, laying a hand on his shoulder. 'One of our most promising young men. A Russian speaker too.' He clasped Harold's arm and propelled him in fatherly fashion from guest to guest, but his eyes were as hard as ice. When he got to Victoria he gave a grunt. 'Hah!' he said and left them as dinner was announced. Now they sat, eight of them, on heavy Chippendale chairs round a long oval table, all gleaming surfaces in the yellow light of two ornate candelabra as Victoria watched, while she conversed, from the corner of her eye, the Second Press Attaché's wife soften and flush in the blaze of her neighbour's blue-eyed charm.

'I see you're smitten as women always are,' said Sir Geoffrey, pausing in his description of the latest technological innovations being introduced, under his aegis, at the British Press Agency.

'Smitten?' said Victoria, flustered. 'No, I'm not.' What a funny word, my mother always says 'smitten', horrid florid toad, she thought to herself. If she could not sit next to Harold she wished she could have been seated next to the Second Press Attaché, a tall skull-headed man with thin lips, now picking his way with a fish fork through rolled-up bits of sole and mushroom, as he made conversation with Lady Champman at the other end of the table.

'Have you ever been to Russia?' she said, looking into Sir Geoffrey's pale eyes and smiling at him.

But Sir Geoffrey did not reply to her question. He fixed her disconcertingly with an unblinking stare. 'Are you a virgin?' he said in a loud voice.

Victoria's ears tingled, her composure crumbled and blood drained from her head, leaving her faint and shaky. She looked down at her plate. Virgin was a word she had never heard spoken at all before except in connection with Christmas. Under her eyelids she saw the jumble of beads round her neck wink and glow in the candlelight. A small piece of fish, speared by prongs, lay against the back of her fish fork. The steady thrum of conversation rolling round the table seemed far away.

'No,' she said, 'no, I'm not,' and looked to see if anyone was looking.

'Are you sure?' said Sir Geoffrey. 'Hmmn.' He turned away. 'Boris!' he shouted down the table, 'what are you getting lined up for us in next year's May Day Parade? Any new big 'uns?'

Victoria took tiny mouthfuls of food and chewed slowly. She was utterly thrown; besides, being thin was one of the most important things in life to her. She clung to that and kept her eyes off Sir Geoffrey, longing for the moment when Lady Champman would signal at the ladies to leave the table.

Upstairs, she spent a long time in the bathroom, all flounces, sponges and big drums of talcum powder, seeing herself reflected and magnified many times over. As she smoothed the fine grey herringbone down over her waspie and twitched at her bra, she began to feel better.

'How elegant you look,' said Lady Champman, an etio-lated blonde in a green dress splashed all over with blue roses, as she came out.

Downstairs, the men were still in the dining-room. The four ladies sat on the edges of four plush-covered chairs and sipped their coffee.

'Do you have dinner parties in Moscow?' said Victoria.

'Of course,' said the Second Press Attaché's wife with a toss of her head.

When the men came back in they were smoking cigars. Harold stood for a long time puffing smoke and talking to Lady Champman and then strolled across the carpet towards Victoria.

'How do you know Russian?' said Victoria, gazing up at him.

'I learned it,' said Harold. 'I'm pathetically bad.' He sat down.

'Oh,' said Victoria. He looked tormented and romantic. 'Sugar?' she said, handing him an urn-shaped silver container in which a pair of tiny tongs lay helplessly atop a pile of white lumps.

Harold leaned towards her. 'Let's get out of here,' he whispered.

Victoria leaned towards him. 'Yes, let's,' she whispered back.

The Second Press Attaché motioned across the room at his wife. She got up. 'Time for going home,' she said, and nodded stiffly round the room.

'Where do you live?' said Harold softly to Victoria.

'Holland Park,' said Victoria. Her eyes sparkled.

'*What* park?' said Harold creasing his furrowed brow into a cross frown.

The Second Press Attaché came up to him. 'Goodbye, Mr Fox,' he said, shaking his hand. 'It was a pleasure to see you. I thought we might never meet again.'

'Thanks,' said Harold, 'thanks very much.' He made a dart for the door.

Victoria took a step after him, but the Second Press Attaché had her hand in his. 'Goodbye, Miss Benjamin. I hope we will see you in future at our receptions,' he said. 'The vodka is very good – but I am sure we will be able to find you some gin.'

'I'd love to come,' said Victoria, 'and I've never had vodka. I'd like to try it.' He had a nice face, mournful and attenuated, with very smooth skin stretched over high cheekbones. She followed him to the door and found her coat in the hall. In the press of departing guests she managed to avoid Sir Geoffrey but said a rapid goodbye to his wife and slipped out into the black night. The Russians were getting into a big limousine. A chauffeur held the door and there was another man sitting in the seat beside the driver. How grand, thought Victoria, casting round the gravelled space in front of the house for a sight of Harold. She saw him, as her eyes grew accustomed to the dark, across the central plot of grass and flower bed, getting into an unexpectedly large car.

'Get in,' he said sharply as she ran up, and roared off as she was still closing the door; a dangerous animal, his handsome profile in dark relief against the grey square of window.

He drove fast and carelessly, screaming the tyres round corners and taking the car up violently onto the pavements of the narrow sleeping streets. The second time, Victoria said, 'I say, did you have to do that?' She felt she was meant to say something. Harold turned to her. 'What's wrong?' he said, coolly.

'Nothing,' said Victoria. Reassured, she smiled at him.

'Don't be so hypocritical,' said Harold. 'You must have meant something. You can't just say something and not mean anything.'

'Well, I just thought you were driving your car with unnecessary speed and violence,' said Victoria.

'I'm not,' said Harold, taking two wheels of the car up on the pavement again.

'You are,' said Victoria. 'That's not the usual way to drive a car along an empty street.'

'Usual,' said Harold, mockingly. 'Usual. I'm driving perfectly properly. Are you frightened?'

'No, of course I'm not frightened,' said Victoria. She smiled at him again.

'You are,' said Harold. 'There's nothing wrong with my driving.'

'There is,' said Victoria. 'It's not . . .'

'It's not what?' said Harold. 'How typical. I knew you'd be like that.'

'Like what?' said Victoria.

'Conventional,' said Harold. He was driving now with exaggerated slowness along Kensington High Street.

'I'm not . . .' began Victoria, thinking that perhaps she was. She looked out of the window seeing every crack on the paving stones as they drove at fifteen miles an hour along the deserted street.

'What an awful country this is,' said Harold suddenly.

Victoria started. 'Awful, yes, isn't it. Why?' she said.

'Midnight,' said Harold, bitterly. 'Just midnight and there's not a single place open in the whole ridiculous city where one can go and get a drink.'

'Yes, there is,' said Victoria, eagerly. 'I know a place.'

'I don't believe you,' said Harold, 'not open *now*.'

'But it is,' said Victoria. 'I promise you.'

'I'm not going to a nightclub, if that's what you're used to,' said Harold.

'It's not a nightclub, honestly,' said Victoria. 'Anyone can go there any time. You can just have a drink and a dance.' She was filled with doubt as she spoke, but optimism buoyed her up. They drove to the West End where, earlier in the week, she had been invited to the opening of a new late-night restaurant with drinking and dancing till three.

'Oh, the Golden Eagle,' said Harold, when they got there. 'A friend of mine's been here.'

Victoria felt validated; what's more, she was a good dancer, featherlight on her feet and with a strong sense of rhythm. She forgot herself when dancing; or rather, moving to music, she remembered parts of herself she had only read about in books.

'I suppose you're expecting me to dance,' said Harold.

Victoria walked ahead of him to the dance floor and turned, smiling up at the tall blond stranger. She felt rather proud to be with him. He had exactly the sort of looks she liked most. She took great trouble with her own and usually had to put up with second-best in men, holding herself in reserve for the real thing. The real thing, the most potent image of her imaginative life, was compounded from a series of heroes out of books: fairy-stories, Greek myths, *Boy's Own* adventures, travellers' tales and the works of John Buchan. She put up her arms, resting her left hand lightly on Harold's right shoulder. Harold seized her, clutching a fistful of the fine grey herringbone in his right hand, difficult because there was so little of it to spare. He pressed her to him and forced her violently round the floor, jigging energetically up and down in a-rhythmic patterns of his own. Victoria struggled to follow him, concentrating on making herself lighter than air and on anticipating his unpredictable movements. She could not see his feet, but she was more or less successful in avoiding them. Harold did not speak, for which Victoria was grateful, but, 'You're a good dancer,' he gasped once. Suddenly he stopped.

'You don't want to go on with this, do you?' he said, inaccurately.

'No, no,' said Victoria, obligingly.

He let go of her leaving her, unprotected, facing him in the middle of the dance floor. 'It's a very second-rate band,' he said.

'There's a much better one at the Milroy,' she said, hopefully, 'but that's a club.'

'Of course I know that,' he said, scathingly, 'don't patronise me.'

'I'm not . . .' said Victoria, but he was walking off the floor. She scurried after him.

'Where shall we go now?' he said. 'I want a cup of coffee.'

'There's a place by Sloane Square that's still open,' said Victoria, gathering up the flat black patent leather pochette she used for evening.

'Don't be ridiculous,' said Harold. 'There's nowhere open in London now. Have you got any money?'

'No,' said Victoria, taken aback. She never expected to use money at night. It did not cross her mind to have any with her. Men dealt with money. There was no room for it anyway in her bag. 'The woman at this place wouldn't mind. She's a friend,' she said, confused and disconcerted.

'How could you imagine I'd go anywhere without paying?' said Harold. 'We'll go to my flat.' He made for the door and started striding down the stairs.

'No,' said Victoria. 'No, no. Let's go to Sloane Square.' Things happened in flats alone with men that she did not know how to think about and there were few clues in the books she read.

'What's the matter now? What's wrong with my flat?' said Harold. They were in the street. The chilly air tasted of tin, a taste Victoria remembered from childhood as the essential taste of London which met you at Waterloo Station coming back from holidays in the country with her brother and her nanny.

'How could you possibly object to my flat when you've never been there?' said Harold, getting into the car and slamming the door. Victoria fumbled with the door on her side. Men generally – men always, even in foreign countries – held doors for her.

'What's wrong with my flat?' said Harold again crossly, as she got in.

'There's nothing wrong with your flat. It's very nice of you to ask me there but I must go home,' said Victoria.

'Home? Now? What for? How false you are, pretending to be sophisticated and then wanting to be home by two in the morning,' said Harold.

'Half past,' murmured Victoria and, raising her voice, 'I've got to be home. There's a reason.' Her mind glanced briefly away from another image, an unwelcome one of her mother and father, tightly encased by bedclothes, side by side in two high single beds with the bed table between them.

'What is it?' said Harold.

'I can't tell you,' said Victoria.

Sparring thus, they drove on until they pulled up outside the house in Soho. Victoria was timid about her body. She kept it carefully clothed but was unsure about it in . . . in other circumstances. She had a lot of men friends, seventeen of whom so far had wanted to marry her, but she usually managed to get away with hand-holding and a few kisses. Besides, tonight, poor Tom was waiting for her back at her flat. It was his last night before going home to his family in Manchester for Christmas. He loved her and, for a few weeks, puzzled at herself, she had let him into her bed. He was a philosopher.

'Bitch,' he said, 'bitch,' as he thrust his small penis in and out of her. It was strangely exciting but certainly not the real thing. Even so, she could not humiliate him on the last night he might ever spend in her flat. There would be time to make it all right if she got back within the next hour.

'I must go home. Now,' she said to Harold.

'Come in just for a minute,' he said, holding the car door open for her.

'I don't want . . .' she said, but he bent down and pulled her onto the pavement. 'Just a cup of coffee, I promise you,' he said. 'Why are you making such a fuss? Don't you trust me?'

'I'm not making a fuss and I don't not trust you, but I'm late already. I've got to get home,' she said.

He took her elbow and kept hold of it as he opened the front door. 'Why?' he said.

'I can't tell you,' said Victoria, 'but it's a proper reason.'

He shut the front door. The hall was dark and cold. It smelt sour and damp. 'I hate people who pretend they've got good reasons for things they don't really want to do,' he said. He went up the stairs. 'Come on,' he called, his voice becoming irritable. Victoria began to follow him up the creaking uneven lino-covered stairs. They got narrower and Harold stopped in front of a door set improbably athwart them. Inside, the stairs were even narrower and much steeper. They needed climbing. At the top, Harold took her hand. 'Well done,' he said, smiling his hero's smile at her and switched on a light. Ahead Victoria could see a thin seedy kitchen and a sink thick with crockery. To their right were two doors, both with inches to spare between their bottoms and the floor. Harold opened one and pushed Victoria inside. She was astonished at what she saw. There were many pictures on the wall, some of them familiar in style, all of them crooked. The mattress-ticking curtains with frogged borders were half pulled and hung in loops adrift from their hooks in places, and the floor, table, chairs, sofa and desk were awash with books, papers, open newspapers, socks, shoes, ties, crumby plates, smeared glasses and even some half-eaten pieces of bread, the teeth-marks clear in the butter. It looked unkempt to excess, offhandedly classy and desperately uninviting. But Victoria knew that squeamishness was one of her faults. 'What a nice flat,' she said.

'It's all right,' said Harold, proudly. He took hold of her, pulled hard and forced her onto the sofa. As she went down, Victoria was aware of a brown suede shoe awaiting her on the dented ticking cushions. She hoped it would not mark the skirt of her dress. But Harold's mouth was upon her. He had her gripped between the shoulder blades and was forcing his tongue into her mouth. She felt their teeth clash and she fought to keep hers closed. I must stay upright, she thought. Beyond his head she could see a pale moonlit picture of cypresses and a narrow paved way above the fireplace. It was very pretty. She wondered who it was by.

I must. I will, thought Harold. He could feel the hook of her bra under the thin material of her dress and he felt his penis rise. He let her go.

'Why are you being so unfeminine?' he asked.

'I'm not,' said Victoria, shakily, but she was afraid she was. 'I thought we were going to have a cup of coffee,' she said, making her voice as soft and – well – feminine as she could. She stood up.

'You don't really want coffee, do you?' said Harold. 'How naïve.' He stood up and kissed her again, holding her hard against him. This time, Victoria tried. She let his tongue into her mouth and it stayed there a long time. The sky in the picture was lavender-blue and beyond it was one of a blackbird, maybe by the same person. But she must concentrate. She tried to keep her mind on Harold's tongue, large and curving inside her mouth, hoping to conjure up some of the soft fudgy feeling between stomach and pelvis that she sometimes felt when Tom kissed her. Harold had his hand up her skirt and was feeling under the suspenders of her waspie for her pubic hair.

'No, no,' said Victoria as well as she could. She pressed her legs together and tried to push him away. Removing his mouth and one hand, he found the zip at the side of her dress and started to undo it. 'I've got to get home,' said Victoria, 'I told you.'

'You can't stop now. It's not fair,' said Harold. 'I'll take you straight home after. I promise you.'

'Promise?' said Victoria.

'Promise,' said Harold.

'All right,' said Victoria. She took off her dress and laid it carefully over the back of an upright chair.

'Why are you taking so long? I thought you were in a hurry,' said Harold.

Victoria did not reply. She stood there in her beads and bra, waspie, suspenders and stockings holding her stomach in. If she threw herself into it, she could be home in an hour. Harold took off his coat and his tie and his shoes. How will he ever find the right ones again she wondered as he took off his trousers. She could see a big bulge under his loose Aertex pants and she looked away. He kissed her again and then took her on the sofa, thinking of Clare as he did so. Victoria held onto him and moved her pelvis round and round, up and down. It was hard work but she was determined to keep up the momentum. The brown suede shoe dug into the small of her back and she bucked up and down faster, making large round snaky movements with her hips. Harold was grunting softly, his face buried in her collarbone. He came, lay slack on her body for a moment and then moved out of her.

What a delicious feeling thought Victoria, as his slithery penis, now quite small, slipped out of her. Her body softened and she pressed him gently to her.

Harold got up. 'I'm tired,' he said, 'let's go to bed.'

Ignoring the sweet slackness creeping into her body, Victoria got up too. 'But you promised,' she said, 'you're going to take me home. Now.'

'You can't really expect me to do that,' said Harold. 'Stop fussing. I'll take you back as soon as I've had a bit of sleep.' He made for the door. He had a nice bottom, very white under the silk shirt, which was torn, and well-shaped hairy legs. Victoria stood there, uncertain, unprotected and rather angry.

'Come on,' called Harold from above. 'I've made the bed. It's warmer here. I'll take you home in ten minutes.'

So Victoria went up the stairs, feeling extraordinarily silly and exposed and glad of her many strands of pearls and tortoiseshell beads.

The room upstairs was angular and cold. A picture of large red poppies and geraniums lay on the floor against the skirting-board. Harold was already in bed. Victoria took off her bra and her stockings and her waspie and crept in beside him. She lay on the edge on her back and thought worriedly of Tom.

'Why don't you take off those things too?' said Harold, reaching out a hand and stirring among her beads.

'No,' said Victoria, fiercely clutching them, '*no*.'

'Well, I'm going to sleep,' said Harold. His arm brushed her nipple as he turned away.

Victoria lay and stared at the ceiling and, suddenly, in a storm of twisted bedclothes, Harold was on top of her again. He took both nipples between his thin fingers and squeezed them. 'Ow,' said Victoria, but Harold only twisted them and squeezed them harder. 'Take me home,' whispered Victoria through the pain. She stiffened her body. Harold bit her tongue and clamped his lips on hers. He moved his hard body roughly on her clenched pelvis, found the lips of her vagina and went straight in. Very quickly he shuddered, groaned and came. His wet penis slid out, he turned on his side and went to sleep.

Victoria lay beside him wondering why she did not feel moved, excited. He was by far the best-looking man she had ever met. She was not sexy. She never had orgasms. There was something wrong with her, she knew; something missing. She must try harder. Then she realised, with a shock, that neither of them had used a contraceptive. Oh dear, she thought, oh dear, oh dear, but Harold was the kind of man you could not possibly ask to think about that sort of thing. Then she remembered Tom. The square of sky at the window was turning a dead watery grey. It paled as she watched. She nudged Harold in the back. 'Wake up,' she said softly, 'wake up.' He did not stir, so she dug him hard with both hands. 'Harold,' she said loudly, 'get up.'

'All right,' he mumbled. 'I'm getting up.'

She sat up in the bed holding the sheet round her. The room had a wrecked look and it was cheerless and cold. There was no sign of a fire of any kind.

'Get your clothes on,' said Harold, 'I'll be ready much quicker than you.' He got up, looked at her with the sheet clutched up to her shoulders, grinned and went naked down the stairs. Victoria began to put her clothes on. She felt horribly unwashed. Then she ran downstairs and put on her dress. She felt absurd without the white cotton infill which was back at the office in her daytime handbag. Harold was in the kitchen, barefoot in his trousers and shirt.

'What *are* you doing?' said Victoria, incredulously.

'I'm making breakfast,' said Harold. He handed her a cup of coffee.

'I don't want any,' said Victoria, furiously, 'you can't have any now. Take me home.'

'You can't expect me to take you home without any breakfast,' said Harold. He looked dangerous as he bit into a piece of toast. Victoria turned her back on him and went into the drawing-room. She tried to calm herself looking at the pictures. She heard Harold go upstairs. She followed him and found him rummaging in a drawer spilling over with nameless bits and pieces. 'I'm finding some clean socks,' he announced. Victoria sat on the bed. She watched as he discarded one sock after another and, eventually, put on two with agonising slowness. She got up, but Harold went over to a cupboard, opened the door and started selecting a tie from the dozen or so that hung there on a piece of string. He put on one, looked at himself in the mirror, took it off and went to extract another. Victoria could stand it no longer. She put on her shoes, found her coat and left the flat. Gasping, she hurried down the crooked stairs and let herself into the street. She ran towards Oxford Street, looking for a taxi. She could pay when she got home. She had a little money in the flat and Tom might have some she could borrow. There was hardly any traffic on the streets, few people and no taxis. She stood frantically on the corner of Oxford Street and Tottenham Court Road, thankful there were so few passers-by to see her scarlet shame. A few lorries rumbled by. She began to run westwards along the pavement. A big grey car drew up alongside her.

'Get in,' said Harold, sharply, leaning across from the driving-seat and opening the door. He was wearing his flying jacket and, somewhat unevenly tied, a purple bow tie with green diamond-shaped dots outlined in orange. On his face was what, in other men, would have been a smirk and on him could only be called a sardonic grin.

'What odd behaviour,' he said. 'What on earth did you do that for?'

'I was in a hurry. You knew I was in a hurry. You were being deliberately slow,' said Victoria, out of breath and trying to speak evenly.

'I was not being slow,' said Harold, indignantly. 'I was getting dressed in a perfectly normal fashion. How dare you accuse me of being slow.'

'I wasn't . . .' said Victoria and stopped. She turned her face to the window and looked out watching the bare trees in the park as they flashed past. Harold drove fast and smoothly. As they turned into her street, the milk van went by. Victoria tried to hide her face, then waved to the milkman. They drew up outside her flat which was in a house facing the gardens of a square. No one was yet about. Harold leaned across her, opened the door and kissed her on the lips. ''Bye,' he said.

As Victoria went down the steps to her own front door she realised she did not know his address, except by ear, nor his telephone number and she had no idea when she would see him again. She let herself in. Tom, in his dreadful slippers, came into the hall. He looked damp and boneless. 'I kept the gas fire on for you all night,' he said.

# Chapter Three

Once Harold turned the corner in Clare's Bentley, he slowed the car down. There was at least three-quarters of an hour to go before he could fetch the little girls. Leafless trees, pollarded limes, ugly in their deformity, lined the wide street of solid middle-class houses in which complacent families were breakfasting in gloomy dining-rooms round good mahogany tables. Damn that smug young woman with her uppity career and her elegant clothes for spoiling his morning of unaccustomed automobilised ease. Other thoughts began to surface about her in his mind, but he pushed them down. He went into a newsagent's for a paper and a packet of Gauloise. He could never quite manage smoking, but Clare smoked Gauloises, and so did most of her friends; their Frenchness made the activity something more than ordinary smoking. But the corner shop did not stock Gauloise and Harold came out thwarted as he so often was in the simplest of civilised impulses.

He hunched up his shoulders and dug his hands into his pockets but they failed to support his fists. There were holes in both, he knew. No magical repair had taken place overnight. The problem of outerwear in the English winter was insuperable as were all his problems. They crowded into his mind with sickening familiarity, overwhelming him with their urgency. There was his book which he knew he should finish, his chaotic financial situation and his interrupted career which he knew he should address, his job which he despised himself for having, Clare and Alice whom he yearned for, his mistress in her castle, and all the women of anti-fashion out to get him with their slidey eyes and their silvery laughs. There were his parents' families, his uncles and aunts and cousins, so shaming in their set ways and straitened circumstances, who made him so disagreeably impatient. There were his friends he had to behave for with their high standards. There was that mess in Geneva, all that unfinished business he had cut loose from – he should never have accepted that dinner last night. And there was Christmas. Christmas! The pressure in his head was unbearable. He knew he had a tumour on the brain. If only he were not so inexorably healthy. There must be something physically wrong with him. He caught sight of a young man and a young woman tenderly kissing farewell for the day by the bus stop. Such simple intimacy was denied him. He turned on the engine and jammed his foot on the accelerator. The clock on the dashboard said a quarter past eight. Late. He would break in on Alice and Flora, flustered and jagged, as he always did.

In the driving-mirror he saw a black Wolseley car, probably a police car out to get him. He slowed down with a jerk and drove soberly the few miles over Notting Hill to St John's Wood, where, by and by, he would have to surrender the car and take to public transport alongside hundreds of thousands of other wage-slaves indistinguishable, one from another, in their conformity.

Harold hated office life. He felt trapped by it like an unbroken horse between the traces and he loathed pubs.

The desultory, all-male chumminess reminded him of school and put the wind up in him. Too many pointless hours of his life had passed away in enforced idleness kicking his heels with the boys in common rooms, mess rooms and prison dormitories. So when the drinking-hour loomed and all good journalists started thinking about exchanging their pens for pints, he picked up the telephone and dialled Victoria's number. The little girls were going skating with the au pair girl. Victoria said she was going out to dinner but Harold steamrollered through that one quite easily. He arranged to pick her up at her flat. At least, that was what Victoria assumed he had arranged.

'Who was at dinner last night?' said Roderick in the pub after the Programme. He was wearing his dove-grey suit with a café-au-lait shirt and a mauve tie. Victoria was wearing her pleated white flannel skirt with her red cor-duroy jacket bought in Spain on holiday, a black angora beret and pearls in her ears.

'The Orlovskis were there, from the Russian Embassy,' she said.

'Oh, nice,' said Roderick. 'What a thrill. And . . .?' He looked her in the eye, smiling.

'And Harold Fox,' said Victoria.

'Harold Fox!' said Roderick. 'Women queue up to have tea with him.' He whistled.

'I'm going to have *dinner* with him tonight,' said Victoria.

'I thought you were going to have a bite with Owen at the Portofino,' said Roderick.

'Well, I was,' said Victoria.

Owen sauntered over. He leaned on the bar dropping ash over his suit.

34

'Have a fag, boy,' he said, addressing them both and holding out a packet of Players. They all smoked hard all day long.

'No thanks,' said Victoria. She took out her mother's old tortoiseshell cigarette case and lit a Players Mild which were the only cigarettes small enough to fit into it.

'It was a good programme,' he said, chuckling.

'Not bad,' said Andrew from his bar stool a few feet off. 'But that Bardot woman – I can't see what all the fuss is about.'

'Too skinny for me,' said Owen, spreading his short, nicotine-stained fingers and holding them up to his chest. He laughed uproariously. 'French, you know,' he said, meaningfully to Andrew.

'She's got a marvellous body,' said Victoria, 'narrow but full. That's what's so special about it. Didn't you see? Sophia Loren was like that too.' She had admired Brigitte Bardot even more off the screen than on. She had thought her figure in its cream woollen shift sensational, and Brigitte Bardot had given her the name of her dressmaker in Paris. She and Roderick shook their heads at each other.

'Narrow but full,' said Owen into his whisky. 'Sounds all right. I just didn't notice, see?'

'You never do notice anything but the most crude and obvious,' said Victoria.

'Crude and obvious,' said Owen staring into his whisky. 'Let's go to the theatre next week. Take me to something I ought to see.'

'Please, please, please not *Under Milk Wood* again,' said Victoria.

'Ah!' said Owen to Andrew, '*down to the sloeblack, slow, black, crowblack, fishingboat-bobbing sea* . . . Marvellous stuff.' He chuckled. Over his shoulder he called as

Victoria started to move off: 'I'll book seats tomorrow.'
He turned back to Andrew.

Outside, thin drizzle fell in the shabby street making the
lamps into fuzzy ineffectual balls of light. Victoria thought
of the moon in the picture in Harold's flat. I won't change,
she said to herself. Under the red corduroy jacket was a
sleeveless black silk blouse. She would re-do her make-up
and put on some pearls. Would they dance again, she
wondered . . . Her mind petered out and she started planning a new dress. She had got to the cuffs, double ones
with buttonholes for cufflinks, by the time she got home.
As soon as she got in she lit the gas fire in the sitting-
room.

The flat gave out onto a small garden with a raised
paved terrace outside the windows of the bedroom and
sitting-room. The bedroom was white with white silk curtains and one of the two beautiful possessions she owned:
a small gilded Regency mirror from the Portobello Road.
The other, in the kitchen, was a big grey stoneware jug
saying *Huile d'Olives* that she had bought with her best
friend, Emmanuel, in the Flea Market one joyous afternoon off from the Programme in Paris. If there were a
fire, she often wondered, which of the two would she
save?

She had shared the flat until six months ago with her
wild and sexy friend, Rosalynn, who had thoughtfully
arranged her first sexual encounter for her at the age of
twenty-five two years before. Rosalynn was now married,
pregnant and living a life of extraordinary respectability
and constraint down the road near Marble Arch.

Victoria went into the walk-in cupboard where she kept
her clothes and started doing her face. She loved putting
on lipstick, filling in her lips with tangerine, shocking pink,

scarlet shiny grease and doing her eye make-up which was modelled on Audrey Hepburn's in *Roman Holiday*. The flat was very quiet. To fill the emptiness, stark compared with Harold's flat, she went to put on a record. She had three Beethovens, two Mozarts, two Louis Armstrong and Ella Fitzgeralds and a new clarinet concerto Tom had given her. She thought the clarinet concerto might suit Harold, so she put it on. The minutes were starting to drag. The telephone rang, pulsing through the showers of notes with mechanical insistence. Victoria jumped up.

'Hullo,' she said.

'Good evening,' said a strange light male voice. 'Is Mr Harold Fox there?'

'No,' said Victoria.

The voice was heavily inflected with an accent she could not identify. 'Can I . . .?' she said. A prickle of fear flared in the pit of her stomach and shot, like a tiny flame, round her belly. She heard a long exhalation of breath. The telephone clicked and went dead. She held onto it for a moment listening to the empty purr, then she put the receiver down. Her heart was thumping uncomfortably hard somewhere in the base of her throat.

She walked to the wall of window giving onto the blackness of the night garden and drew the curtains. Then, forcing herself, because her inclination was to freeze and curl up, she went into the bedroom and, keeping close to the wall, pulled the butterfly-wing curtains before she switched on the light. She sat down on the floor against the bed and picked up her book.

Minutes of dead time spun round her. It was nearly nine o'clock. Waiting was an alien state for Victoria. She was always late, mostly to spare herself the agony of being kept waiting – or worse, of finding nothing there at all. The telephone rang again.

This time it was Harold's voice, brittle and exasperated: 'Are you there?' it said.

'Yes,' said Victoria after a while, 'yes. Where are you?'

'Somewhere,' said Harold. 'I'm telephoning to tell you I'm going to be late.'

'When will you be here?' said Victoria.

'Soon,' said Harold. 'Ten minutes.'

'Did you ring before?' said Victoria.

'No,' said Harold.

'Well, a strange man did. I wondered . . .'

'Wishful thinking,' said Harold. 'And you might say thank you.' He rang off.

Three-quarters of an hour later Victoria let him in at the door. He was wearing a strange rumpled suit, double-breasted and spiv-striped and one of his extraordinary bow ties. He had his hands in his pockets and looked curiously disarmed against the chill of the night. He smiled at her and there was a challenging innocence in his blue eyes as he looked at her. He put his icy hands round the back of her neck and kissed her on the mouth. Though, theoretically, she expressed everything he most abhorred, he felt an unaccustomed lightness of heart. Over her shoulder in the narrow dark green hall he could see a room, orderly and airy. Jubilation warmed his body through. Victoria preceded him into the room and he took in her neat figure with its short dark thick hair. Her white skirt swung at her round calves as she moved. The black bile of bitterness and regret rose in his throat. Clare's hair was fine, and fell to her waist; her voice was low and her movements slow with a droopy underwater quality to them.

'What a racket,' he said. 'I hate background music.' His savagery startled him.

'Don't you like it?' said Victoria, anxiously. She hurried to the gramophone. Why was she so damn eager to please?

'Magazines, women's magazines,' he said, scathingly. 'Clearly you get all your ideas out of them. Pathetic.'

Victoria stood by the gramophone. She did not know what to do. The notes of the clarinet floated inexorably out, one after the other. Often she hummed to them; sometimes she even danced. They sounded silly now. She wished they were not there.

'Come here,' said Harold. She stepped towards him, stiff and awkward and he took hold of her. Clamping his mouth on hers, he kissed her long and hard. Victoria returned the pressure. Her neck hurt. One earring gave a little pop and jumped off the lobe of her ear. She watched it out of the corner of her eye roll along the floor and settle by Harold's foot.

Oh dear, she thought. My skirt is getting all crumpled, all crumpled, crumpled. With all her force, she held herself away from him. 'Let's go out to dinner,' she said, unsteadily, hoping he would not notice her ears.

'You're not really hungry. You just want to be in a restaurant,' he said with some accuracy. He had eaten anyway, deliciously, of thick flakes of white fish, green bunches of watercress and yellow mayonnaise, at Clare's when he had taken the car back.

'But we're going out to dinner,' said Victoria uncertainly.

'So that's what you had planned,' said Harold, letting go of her. 'You want a man out of a magazine who'll be smarmy to waiters and order you champagne in a bucket.'

'Oh no,' said Victoria, distressed at the thought of champagne in a bucket.

'Oh, yes,' said Harold. 'I'm going.'

'Don't go,' said Victoria. 'Have a drink.' She had half a bottle of brandy Tom had brought her from Spain. Harold said nothing. He stood there looking handsome and annoyed. Victoria ran into the kitchen and poured out two brandies, one large and one small. She gave the big one to Harold. He tasted it and sat down in the armchair. 'I love Spanish brandy,' he said.

'Do you often go to Spain?' said Victoria.

'Yes,' said Harold. There was silence. The clarinet concerto had finished and the record was clicking round and round on the turntable. Victoria wondered whether to take it off, or ask him about Spain, or tell him about one of her holidays there.

He finished his brandy. 'I'll be off,' he said. 'Thanks for the brandy.'

'Have another,' said Victoria. She ran into the kitchen again and bumped into him in the hall as she came out with the bottle in her hand.

'No thanks,' said Harold, 'where's the nearest tube?'

'Tube!' said Victoria, 'but what about your car?'

'Aha,' he said, 'so that's it. You think I'm a man with a smart car like your television friends.'

Victoria thought of Owen and Andrew and Roderick with their worn old Austins and Morris Travellers. 'Honestly,' she said, 'none of them have smart cars like yours.' He stood there glowering. She put up her hand with its scarlet polished nails and touched his cheek.

'What do you want?' he said with irritation. 'You're getting me muddled. Do you want to go to bed or don't you?'

'I want to . . .' said Victoria.

'Well, come on then,' said Harold. 'Where's the bedroom? I hate grappling around on sofas.'

So they went into the bedroom, took off their clothes and spent a stormy night there grappling between Victoria's clean white sheets with the light on. She had never been taken so many times in one night before. She tried to keep count so she could get good marks when she told Rosalynn about it on the telephone, but she gave up after four. Again and again Harold grasped her, rolled on top of her, forced her legs wide with his hard knees and rammed his fighting penis inside her, while Victoria, wriggling and heaving, clung on with stubborn determination.

Each time he finished he rolled away and lay hunched in the twisted sheets and blankets with his back to her. Unappeasable sexual hunger possessed him, but he felt dissatisfied and irritable. Lying there tense, drowsing and frowning to himself, he tried to find peace but the thought of her dense wiry pubic hair seeped into his mind and made his penis stone-hard with desire. If she speaks, he thought, I'll smother her. But Victoria said nothing. She lay on her back staring at the ceiling and once reached out to turn the light off. He seized her hand, pinioned it behind her back and rose to fuck her yet again. Towards morning they both fell asleep and woke, Victoria first, to find thin sunlight falling quietly through the white curtains onto the bed. How lovely, thought Harold opening his eyes, like floating in music. He smiled at Victoria, kissed her eyes and got out of bed.

It was a nice room, light and tranquil. He put on his clothes, the underpants draping themselves strangely round his stiff cock. Victoria, watching him, caught his eye and looked away.

'What are you looking at?' said Harold.

'Nothing,' said Victoria and pulled the sheet over her head. Next time she looked, he was dressed.

'I'll ring you,' he said, and went.

She heard the front door shut quietly and his feet go up the steps into the street. She hoped that, handsome as he was, he would not meet the milkman. But then, she thought, she did not really mind.

On Christmas morning, two and a half weeks later, pale golden light filtered through the white silk curtains onto Harold and Victoria in Holland Park. At the bottom of the bed lay two parcels carefully done up in coloured tissue paper and tied with narrow satin ribbons; turquoise, green and red; white, brown and pink.

Victoria had looked at the labels inside Harold's torn shirts, located the shop in Paris and arranged for Emmanuel to put two of them on an aeroplane at Le Bourget. She had also bought him a striped tie, the most wild and daring she had ever seen, made by some friends who had just opened a shop in the King's Road. She had bought one for Roderick too. His was mauve and orange and Harold's was peacock blue and emerald green. She had seven shillings left in her purse and was filled with delight at the thought of Harold, unkempt and uncared for, in these beautiful unspoiled garments.

They had seen each other every day. Victoria, who usually went out each evening with a different man, turned down all invitations and waited for Harold's call. Sometimes it came when she was still at the office, in which case she could turn her mind wholeheartedly on work; sometimes it came far into the evening by which time, alone in the flat with all the ironing done, her stomach was tight with despair. He never told her what he was doing, though she knew he had a daughter.

Harold had taken up his book again. As he laboured over the pages so disobliging to his will, he was somewhat sustained by the thought of the warm, white bed that awaited him and the funny, sturdy little creature in it. She was bouncy and unbreakable, not that it mattered either way to anyone if she fractured, and she smelled spicy, like summer fruit. He found himself turning down Clare's murmured invitations to stay on to dinner with her friends and refusing his mistress's offers of a ticket to fly out to her castle on Lake Como.

One Saturday they had bought a bookcase together in a second-hand shop off the Portobello Road. 'Christ, where can I put all these books,' he had said one day in his flat, through gritted teeth.

'Get a bookcase,' Victoria had said, helpfully. Harold had looked at her with contempt. 'You can get one quite cheap. Really you can. I know where to go,' she had said. So they went and, to Harold's surprise, found a Victorian chiffonier without any doors which he bought for five shillings. They had taken it back to Holland Park, put it on the terrace on newspapers and sandpapered it and painted it white. She had heard him telling a friend he quite often telephoned in the country about it: 'I'm painting it in a garage in Notting Hill,' he had said.

'Happy Christmas,' said Victoria. She hopped out of bed and put on her housecoat. She loved her housecoat. It was white cotton, covered with tiny black flowers and there was a lot of it. She washed it and ironed it smooth at least once every two weeks. She sat on the bed. 'Happy Christmas,' she said.

'Happy Christmas. Oh God,' said Harold from deep in

the bedclothes. Victoria went into the kitchen and made some coffee in her old tin Napolitana which Harold seemed to approve of. Her coffee was posted to her weekly from a shop in Soho. She brought the pot, hot milk and two cups into the bedroom one by one and put them on the window-sill by the bed.

'You ought to have a bedside table,' said Harold.

'I know,' said Victoria, sadly. She had no intention of getting one as it would break into the pure lines of the room. She poured him some coffee and sat on the bed beside him. 'Happy Christmas,' she said again.

'You've said that before,' said Harold, crossly. He opened his eyes and looked at her. 'Dressing-gowns are so bourgeois,' he said. 'I can't think why you wear that thing.'

'Look, there are some presents,' said Victoria.

Harold sat up, took the cup and saw the parcels at the bottom of the bed. 'So there are,' he said.

'They're for you,' said Victoria. She was smiling, her eyes were bright and she actually looked rather pretty in the white dressing-gown all covered with flowers.

Clare wore, when she wore anything, an old Jaeger man's dressing-gown of camel-coloured vicuña. Shall I be nice or shall I lay into her thought Harold. Little sparks of irritation were shooting upwards somewhere round his stomach. It would be quite easy to fan them to scene-size. He decided against it and sighed. 'Well, let's have a look,' he said. Victoria gave him the parcels.

'I'm hopeless at doing up presents,' he said. 'You do them up well.'

'I'll help you,' said Victoria. He glared at her, undid the parcels and was quite astonished at what he found inside. Leaping out of bed, he put on one of the shirts and tied

44

the tie. He stood and looked at himself in the gilt-framed mirror on the white wall. 'Marvellous,' he said. 'However did you get them? Thanks very much.' He took hold of her by the shoulders and kissed her. 'I've got a rotten one for you,' he said.

'A present – ooh!' said Victoria, who had been expecting one, though half her instincts warned her not to.

'Don't get excited. It's really rotten,' he said, sounding pleased. Victoria sat on the bed, surrounded by tissue paper and ribbons, and waited while he went to his flying jacket hanging over a chair next door. 'Here you are,' he said, coming back into the bedroom. He held out two small bottles of Veuve Clicquot. 'Quarter bottles,' he said. 'You can drink them alone in the mornings.'

Victoria's heart sank like a small stone. 'Thank you,' she said, taking them. Tears pricked the back of her eye-balls. She hated champagne, mean thin wine with pointless prickles in it. The orange Clicquot labels meant nothing to her. She liked claret and whiskey-sours, and drink was something that came at dinner parties, bars and res-taurants. Harold was looking at himself in the glass. 'I told you it was a rotten present,' he said, retying the tie. 'Where's your hairbrush?' Clare and the children would be impressed by his get-up coming, as it were, from nowhere.

Victoria gave him her hairbrush. 'It's a lovely present,' she said stoutly. 'What a good idea. Let's have some now.'

So they toasted each other, that first Christmas morning, in champagne which lay uneasily on Victoria's stomach with the coffee and went, sparkling, straight to Harold's head.

'I'll give you a lift if you hurry,' he offered. He wanted to be in time to watch the little girls open their mountain of presents and drink more champagne round the Christmas tree in St John's Wood. Victoria was going to her parents behind the park in Bayswater and did not want to be early. 'Thank you,' she said. She went to turn on the bath.

Harold did not have baths in the morning; he had them at all times of day or night and put his clothes straight on when he got out of bed. He went into the sitting-room and switched on the clarinet concerto trying not to be irritated by Victoria's decorations which were of silvered twigs hung with red glass balls. Most affected and un-Christmassy he thought them, and had told her so. But though he could undermine her easily in general, there were some matters of visual taste on which she would not budge. A mulish expression would come over her face and she would say nothing. He would change that, he thought contentedly, looking out of the window and thinking life was not so bad after all, that is if he ever saw her again.

She came in smiling and wearing black with a back-to-front white collar and a big gold star on a chain hanging below it – like the mannequins at Dior and, sometimes, Jacques Fath. Her face was beige with make-up and her lipstick was orange. Harold's lips thinned into a snarl. 'Why . . .' he began and swallowed it back. 'You look nice,' he said and took her by the elbow and hurried her up the steps into the street.

'You've got your car again,' said Victoria.

'It's lent,' said Harold.

'Who by?' said Victoria.

'Someone,' said Harold and got in.

At the end of the empty street a black Wolseley was parked. As they drove past Victoria saw a man with a thin sallow face and dead black eyes staring at them. The

Wolseley started up and passed them cutting in rather suddenly as they drew up at the traffic lights.

'Christ!' said Harold.

The man looked round, stared expressionlessly and raised his hand, palm up, in their direction. Then he accelerated away. Harold's heart lurched and started hammering under his shirt. He tightened his grip on the steering-wheel and his knuckles went white.

'It wasn't your fault. You were driving impeccably,' said Victoria.

'You don't understand,' said Harold.

'Understand what?' said Victoria.

'You don't understand *anything*,' said Harold.

He dropped her at the top of her parents' street and drove away. Guilt and shame possessed him as he did so.

# Chapter Four

❧

Victoria spent the next day, Boxing Day, alone in her flat: something she was not at all used to doing. The telephone rang twice. Once it was her brother asking her to play squash with him and have lunch. 'How are you, sis?' he said as though he had not noticed who was pulling crackers with him the day before. They had great games of squash together and he was becoming a good and careful cook. He had a pheasant, he said. She longed to warm up and thin down bouncing round the court in her short pink shorts and slamming the little black ball, and she wanted to support his cooking. She disliked turning him down.

Once it was Roderick. 'I never expected to find you there. What's up?' he said.

Victoria told him, in part. She wished he would get off the telephone.

'I'd better get off the telephone. He might be trying to ring up *now*,' said Roderick, and rang off.

The day stretched in a shapeless loop towards night. She went to bed slowly at twelve. He still might turn up, she thought fighting to keep the demons of worthlessness and rejection from taking her over. She imagined his brusque presence in the door as she opened it to him, shivering in the cotton housecoat over her bare body. 'Hullo,' she would say casually as she slipped out of it and back into bed. 'Move over,' he would say as he thrust himself under the sheet. She put a hand over her breast and felt the nipple rise. She went over and over Christmas morning. What had she done wrong? It must be that she was too fat.

When the Programme started up again, it was better. She and her secretary had nine telephones between them. She could barely contain her irritation when Gregory leaned across and poached one of them from his desk next door. She went to a reception at the Russian Embassy in Kensington Palace Gardens and kept away from Sir Geoffrey Champman, whom she saw blustering at the other end of the big ballroom. Harold was not there.

'Have you known Harold Fox long?' she asked the Second Press Attaché.

'How do you like our vodka, Miss Benjamin?' he replied.

Owen asked her to go to Paris to oversee an item she had fixed up there. When the new Eurovision link was opened up for a big sports event the Programme took advantage of the facility and organised inserts from European cities. Victoria argued, uncharacteristically, against going over. She could just as well produce the item from her desk in London, she said. 'I thought you'd like to, girl,' said Owen, puzzled.

The item was a flop. Afterwards in the pub, for the first time in two and a half years, Owen forbore to berate her uninhibitedly.

'Sorry,' said Victoria, avoiding his eyes.

'That's all right, girl,' said Owen, avoiding hers.

At the beginning of the second week she nerved herself to telephone Harold's office. 'He's away,' said the girl on the switchboard. 'Any message?'    'No,' said Victoria, helplessly.

Next day she telephoned again. In a careful voice, she explained that she knew Mr Fox was away but as she needed to get in touch with him for work, could they say when he would be back, or where she could get in touch with him. 'Two or three weeks and we don't know where he is,' said the switchboard girl after a pause.

At the weekend she took a train down to Wiltshire where her friend Jessica had a cottage on her parents' estate. Jessica, who lived rough and careless, was going travelling and had offered to lend Victoria her van. For the first time in seventeen days, a spark of anticipation warmed her soul as she set out to drive it back, jolting and swaying through the country lanes. The hedges, bare-twigged against bedraggled fields, wound starkly under watery sky and the first tight snowdrops trembled on the muddy verges.

Back in the city, she shivered as she stepped down into the still of the Sunday night street. No one was about, there were no leaves on the trees to stir in the melancholy hush and a moisture-laden chill hung heavy on the exhausted air. With the familiar taste of tin on her tongue she ran down the cold stone steps to her own front door, her ears alert for the sound of the telephone. Someone had left her dustbin underneath the kitchen window and she pushed and trundled it to its dark place under the stairs before she let herself in. In her mind's eye, she could see Harold sitting before the gas fire in her armchair, a lop-sided half-smile on his handsome face. She willed him to be there.

An unfamiliar smell – soap on unbathed bodies? – met her as she opened the door and the bulb in the hall had broken. Dark pressed down all round her and crowded like a heavy presence at her back. She shivered again as she groped her way into the bedroom and felt for the switch. Light blazed and Victoria gave a short scream of terror.

Clothes were all over the floor, spilling out from open drawers in disgusting disorder. Her heart began to beat suffocatingly. She stood there, appalled and then tiptoed to draw the curtains – was there the glimmer of a white face at the window? With fear pricking her spine she went into the room next door, made a dash over to the windows and pulled the curtains shut. Then she switched on the light in there. Papers and books were everywhere, lying crumpled and damaged on their faces where they had dropped. Her box of kept letters lay open on the floor with all the letters from it out of their envelopes. Only one of them, from a Swiss sailing friend, appeared to have gone. In the dressing-cupboard off the hall, her clothes were on the floor, her jewellery box open and one old diamond pendant of her grandmother's missing. A powerful air of defilement, stale and menacing, hung over the whole place. Only the kitchen was untouched.

After the police had gone, Victoria sat on the corner of the bed holding herself rigid, all the lights on. Her jaws were clamped so it was difficult to open them and her stomach knotted tight. The bulb in the hall was not broken; the socket was empty.

She telephoned her brother. 'Would you like me to come round, sis?' he said. He spent the night on the floor and left, early next morning, for his office. Victoria skirted round the flat, repelled, unable to touch the alien heaps made up of her own belongings.

When the postman came, there was a postcard for her

with an Italian stamp. She could not make out the post-mark. It said, 'Here in the sun the springs in my head are unwinding. Love, Harold.' The picture was of a bicycle race in France.

# Chapter Five

It was bleak by the lake, and cheerless. The *jet d'eau* went spurting up into the sky, flat monochrome like the water, in a ceaseless display of pointless energy. Harold sat on a bench, as he had sat for the past two mornings, watching the lake water, brownish in the shallows, lap quietly against the asphalt edge of the municipal shore. A few children, well dressed and orderly, walked along the paths through the flower beds behind him, holding their nurses' hands. In the pavilion to his left, fur-collared couples were drinking chocolate and hot grog. Harold felt nothing. He thought no more of the amiable skies he had left behind him; of breakfasts on the terrace and picnics in the Alban Hills. This was his portion, this impotent grey waiting caught up in the rigid structures of other people's rules. All struggle led to this. It was a familiar place. If he moved without caution it would break up into chaos. He took the volume of Pushkin's poems from his pocket and tried to concentrate on the lines. He had started translating them in the camp as part of his self-imposed task of learning the language of the future, but the words broke up before his eyes and merged with the wavelets that ruffled the water's surface.

A woman in grey furs approached the edge of the lake.

She slipped onto the bench beside him. Without moving her head, in low tones, she spoke. The voice was husky, the inflexion urgent, the words English. Startled, Harold turned. It was Melissa.

'You must give it to me,' she said, looking straight ahead of her. 'This is not a game. This is not a battle of wills. If you're not coming too, you *must give it to me.*'

Harold gazed at the *jet d'eau.* 'What?' he said through clenched teeth.

She put a small grey-gloved hand, light as a feather from a dove's wing, on his arm. 'Please,' she said, 'please. I have to go back. It's the end. There's nothing more I can do. I know you're proud – but there's no point in keeping it. Really, there isn't. Please.'

'You're overacting,' whispered Harold, fiercely. 'Stop being hysterical. I don't know what the hell you want.'

Melissa giggled, then she gave a little gasp of fear. Soundlessly she unfolded herself and was gone. Only a faint sigh disturbed the chilled lakeside air. As it subsided, Harold saw two men in black overcoats with fur hats on, one very fat, one merely stout, pace gravely by in the thin grassy space between the bench and the water's edge.

He got up and moved off, slowly. His shoulders and the back of his neck were stiff, so were the backs of his knees. Geneva was bad news, it always had been with its manicured respectability and its international institutions insulated in self-righteousness. He felt emasculated there. The two men in fur hats passed him again. The fat one was still talking. '*Nam,*' said the other one and they both chuckled. Harold jumped on a tram. He was shivering.

So it was Melissa who was responsible for the tissue-thin notes in porridge-coloured envelopes that the concierge handed him with his key. '*Monsieur Renard,*' he would

54

say, the familiarity of his overtone concealing, Harold always felt, the hint of a sneer, *il y a quelque chose pour vous.*' And it was Melissa whose stifled voice on the telephone had directed him so compellingly to the park bench in the Jardin Anglais. Or was it?

Images overlaid themselves, one after another, on the raw surface of his mind. They went faster and faster like the little books of black and white photographs demonstrating golf strokes that his father, on leave from the East, used to have in his pocket. 'Always follow through, Harry old chap,' he would say. 'Watch carefully. Magnificent isn't it?' and his mild blue eyes would gleam, as Harold, home for the holidays, made the pages whizz: a drive one way; a putt the other. His father: that watery gleam in his eye as he stood to attention for the National Anthem or, grasping Harold's hand in his, sang 'Jerusalem' in a wavery bass, at church. But the images in the little books followed one another in quick succession to form a single perfect stroke, while the images now racing in Harold's mind added up to nothing. They gripped him with unbearable confusion. If he banged his head hard enough against a wall, maybe they would stop.

'*Rien pour vous, Monsieur Renard,*' said the concierge with an unmistakable leer.

He thinks I'm having an affair, thought Harold. He felt like taking the scrawny neck between his hands and smashing the concierge's self-satisfied face into the wall behind him. 'Bad luck,' he said with an icy glare. He left a tip, nonetheless, half an hour later when he checked out of the small hotel.

Drenching rain cut out the dawn when he reached Dover next morning. Grades of grey simply succeeded one another until the clock said it was day. The seagulls wheeled and screeched with inextinguishable ardour inexorably programmed to perpetual motion. He tried to open his mind a chink to the blue skies of the Roman countryside which he knew, scientifically, must be there in the folds of his brain. Picking up his suitcase he started the trudge for the station platform. Things were so cramped on this side of the Channel, the different kinds of writing on shop fascias, hoardings and notices so cluttered and petty with their claims for attention. England was a continual let-down, but he was committed now.

His suitcase seemed lighter than he remembered. He bought a ticket and got on the train. As he sat down, a man opposite him opened a newspaper. Harold picked up a flash of headline as the man folded it: ACTRESS DEFECTS TO RUSSIA, it said in three-inch type. Harold's heart lurched. Simultaneously a horrible thought presented itself. He hauled his suitcase down from the rack and opened it. All 119 pages of his manuscript had gone. He sat down. His knees were trembling. To his surprise, he found himself thinking of Victoria. Her bright and competent person, carefully ironed and freshly painted, would think of something to do.

As a little boy at prep school he sometimes used to imagine his mother, unimaginably far away Overseas, coming into the dormitory after lights out. The twelve small boys would be lying in their hard narrow beds fast asleep or, in Harold's case, holding himself still in the tepid patch of warmth made by his own body, his hand on his penis. The door would slide open and there would be the familiar shape of his mother in her long UK coat with a fur collar and a cloche hat pulled down over her bony face. She would glide – strange for her, such noiseless locomotion – up the lino and sit on his bed. In the moonlight he could see that her coat was blue. 'Harry dear,' she would say, bending forward, 'I've got your socks and Auntie Doris has made you some fudge. I hope you're being a good boy. Daddy sends his love and says don't forget to say "God Bless the King and Queen" in your prayers.' She would lean down, kiss his forehead and Harold would smell powder. Then before he could put out his hand and touch her she would get up and vanish in the shadows.

Knowing that his socks were there would send him peacefully to sleep. Recalcitrant mislayers of personal property were regularly caned on the hand by the headmaster, even if they were top of the class and promising members of the cricket team. In the morning, tense and awake before the others, he would have to face the fact that they were not. Would it be better to wear no socks or only one? The thought of either filled him with shame. If only someone would tell him what to do – but if anyone tried to boss him around, he would hit them. The impossibility of his situation, his absolute impotence, the totality of his isolation overwhelmed him and he would lie insolently in bed long after the bell rang partly hoping that, by magic, no one would notice him, and partly so that, when he was punished, he would be punished for something of his own choice. Such irregular behaviour was the source of some admiration to both boys and masters.

The loss of his manuscript was something Harold often went through in his mind and in reality, insofar as he frequently mislaid it. The whole process was a form of insurance, a painful non-stop game played with fate. If you imagined the worst, you would never be as ignominiously caught out as if you hoped for the best. This time the worst really had happened. The concierge's penultimate leer at the Rosemary presented itself to his mind's eye – but he had packed his suitcase himself after that. The manuscript written by hand, with manifold corrections, must have been taken on the boat, because it was only when he got off that he noticed his suitcase was lighter. This was exactly how he expected life to be: there was no hope. He could give up now and abandon the book. He felt a certain relief at the realisation, and a certain negative satisfaction that life had so exactly matched his expectations.

By the time he arrived at Victoria Station it was too late to call on the little girls. Clare, he knew, was still in Italy. He telephoned her house, nevertheless, and asked the au pair girl to say he would call round that evening. He had bought a striped silk skirt for Alice and a giant Toblerone for Flora and he knew in his heart that Flora would show more pleasure at her minor present than Alice would at hers. Telephoning Victoria would be too complicated. He caught a No. 24 bus and went straight to the office.

He worked all morning in a daze of misery, opening parcels of books, correcting proofs, deflecting enquiries, fending off invitations. He kept his loss to himself and lunched alone in an anglicised Italian restaurant round the corner where he chewed his way through a wood-hard escalope of veal with peas and potatoes to match. At one moment his feelings caught him unawares and he found himself, mouth full, on the point of tears. He chewed on, forced himself to swallow and opened his *Evening News*. There he saw Melissa's beautiful face, hair flying in the wind, laughing up at him. She was at the wheel of her Triumph convertible.

*Melissa O'Malley, sparkling new star of* Private Lives, *recently revived in the West End*, he read, had failed to turn up at the theatre the previous week. The understudy had taken over. Miss O'Malley, who had gained considerable critical acclaim as Portia, Rosalind, and Shen Te in *The Good Woman of Setzuan* had disappeared but been recognised by a ticket collector getting on the boat train to Newhaven. Her mother, a widow living in Hampshire, had received a letter from her with a Swiss postmark the previous day. The contents of the letter, which Mrs O'Malley refused to divulge, seemed to indicate that her daughter had gone to Moscow, not for a visit but for ever. Mrs O'Malley had taken the letter to the police but was too upset to be interviewed. The Foreign Office was making investigations and questions were being asked in the House. There were pictures of Melissa at school, Melissa in tights and jerkin as Rosalind, Melissa in a hard hat and white stock, riding her horse, Karl Marx.

Idiot, thought Harold, now drinking tepid liquid the colour of the water at the lake's edge from a coffee cup. He paid his bill. 'Nice to see you again, sir,' said the owner's wife at the cash desk. He gave her a smile, diffident and full of light, and went out into the street, the smell of cooked fat clinging to his clothes.

At the office there was a parcel for him; brown paper, bulky and badly wrapped as he might have wrapped a parcel himself. He took it upstairs to his desk and, towards the end of the afternoon, undid it. It was his manuscript. The pages were disordered and the first seven seemed to be missing. There was no accompanying note and nothing at all written on the outside of the brown paper.

When his heart was beating evenly enough he telephoned down to the receptionist in the front hall. 'That parcel,' he said, 'how did you know it was for me?'

'Gentleman left it. No message,' said the girl.

'What did he look like?' said Harold.

'Dunno. Wasn't on,' she replied. 'Anything wrong?'

'No,' said Harold, 'nothing's wrong. Thank you very much.' But he was not sure at all.

# Chapter Six

There were huge celebrations in the small back room of the house off the studios in Shepherd's Bush. That is to say, Owen was chuffed which meant he emitted short unprovoked chortles every three to five minutes; Andrew, watching him, was delighted to see him doing it; Roderick, beaming, dapper and affectionate, called everyone who crossed his path 'old boy'; Gregory bounded and whooped like a hyena; the film editors carrying their big circular tins of 35-mm film under one arm slapped each other on the back with the other; the rest of the team and the contributors shook one another warmly by the hands. The three secretaries pushed back from their typewriters which were red-hot from typing running-orders, interview questions and introductions for that night, leaned back in their green Rexine-covered chairs and lit cigarettes. Victoria felt detached though pleased.

Naturally, they were the best. She had always come top in exams at school, never expected to compromise her standards and never intended to work for or with anyone who was not first in their field. She assumed her colleagues felt the same. The jubilation and congratulations seemed artificial to her. She felt wary. The fact that, for the second year running, the Programme had won first prize for current affairs was merely normal in her estimation. Besides, recognition had its perils. They were to be given a better studio, more money and more staff and they did not need them. The Programme was likely to deteriorate as a result of its raised status. However, she felt confident enough that day to exclude herself from the pub at lunchtime and, while the office was empty, telephone Harold in his office. She was put through straight away.

'Oh, hullo,' she said.

'Hullo,' said Harold.

There was a long pause. At her end of the line, she went red.

'I'm rather busy, actually,' said Harold after a while.

'Well, I wondered, would you like to come to dinner next Tuesday?' said Victoria, which was what she had planned to say, though never in her life had she done anything so bold or so forward.

'Next Tuesday?' said Harold. 'I think that's all right. Thank you. See you then. Goodbye.' He put down the telephone.

Victoria held on to hers, then put it down slowly. She felt empty and shaken. She went to the small bathroom next door and looked at herself in the mirror. Carefully, she put on some more lipstick following the lines of her mouth meticulously and filling them in with bright geranium-pink. Then she went back to her desk and telephoned an elderly American friend, an ex-actress of great beauty and theatrical birth, whom she loved and who now wrote novels from her flat in Earls Court.

'Hullo, Bea,' she said, 'would you like to come to dinner next Tuesday?'

'Darling,' said Bea, 'how wonderful. I'd love to. Who's coming? Are you all right, my beautiful?'

'Harold Fox is coming,' said Victoria.

'Harold Fox!' said Bea, 'I've heard of him. How exciting. Tell me . . .'

So Victoria told her, and when she had finished Bea chuckled: 'Don't worry, darling, I'll do my bit,' she said.

Warmed by her voice, Victoria left her desk and put on her coat. It was made of grey mohair tweed with pink flecks in it and had a clip-on fur collar of straggly grey Mongolian lamb. Smoothing on her grey suede gloves she walked down the street. She would ask a second man to come and they would have pheasant, which she had never cooked before, and chocolate mousse for dinner.

In the pub, the others had taken over half the room. Watched by the regulars sitting quietly round the edge with their pints, they were making a lot of noise. They cheered her when she came in. 'Sit here, boy,' said Owen, climbing off his stool and, 'One gin and water,' he called to the barman.

On Saturday, Victoria went with her brother to buy the pheasant.

'You'll need two,' he said.

'Surely not,' said Victoria, 'with bread sauce and bacon and fried breadcrumbs and chestnut purée and Brussels sprouts and *gratin dauphinoise*.'

'Well, maybe not,' he said.

They had played squash in the morning and had lunch with their parents, the usual kind of Saturday lunch in Westbourne Terrace: roast lamb, carved on the big flowery china meat dish with a depression for the gravy at one end; crisp roast potatoes in the same flowery china with triple gold rings for handles; cabbage cut in squares in a silver dish with hot water in its base; gravy and redcurrant jelly from silver sauce-boats with silver ladles. For pudding there were pancakes with castor sugar and lemon.

'That china will come to you, Victoria, when I'm gone,' said her mother, as she always did. It was a handsome service of many pieces that her mother's mother's mother's husband-to-be had had made in Paris for his bride before they were married. Though Victoria liked it, the statement always rubbed her the wrong way and she made no reply, which was why her mother went on saying it.

Her father sat at the other end of the polished mahogany table in the dark dining-room, saying little, eating carefully and sipping occasionally from his cut glass of pink gin. He had a delicate digestion and a delicate chest and he felt the cold terribly. He wore a knitted Balaclava helmet in bed and had had the house painted more or less brown from top to bottom, so it would not show the dirt. Only the day nursery had escaped, fought for by beloved Nanny Smith, and painted primrose-yellow and bluebell-blue after Victoria's favourite woodland picture from Wool-worth's.

Victoria turned down the glorious potatoes and allowed herself one pancake which she ate very slowly.

'Go on, have some more,' urged her mother, which she did week after week with the same result.

'Eats like a bird,' said her father suddenly in his gruff voice, as he cut up his pancake into digestible, stamp-sized pieces.

After lunch he went back behind his paper in front of the gas fire which had lumps of coke threaded on wires strung across its face. Victoria's mother put her feet up on a Maples Chippendale drawing-room chair.

'Tell me what you've been doing, dears,' she said.

Victoria looked hopelessly at her brother. 'Well,

Mummy,' he said, 'this week I've been doing an audit at Buckingham Palace . . .'

They left the house at about half past two and got into Jessica's van which was parked outside. Their mother waved to them from the front door. Only the markets were open on Saturday afternoons, so they went to the North End Road. They parked the van at the Fulham end and walked up one side and down the other looking at all the pheasants hanging upside-down round the stalls like macabre Christmas paperchains. Victoria's brother examined the claws and pinched the breasts and chose a bird they had seen almost at the beginning. The stallholder plucked it for them. He was wearing a boater with a blue band and there were brown bloodstains on the front of his white apron.

'Beautiful bird, beautiful bird,' he shouted as he plucked. His red hands had fingers like sausages. Victoria gave him the money, 7s 6d out of her £12 pay packet.

'You'll enjoy it. Never seen a better bird,' he shouted as he gave her change from a ten-shilling note. She drove her brother back to his flat.

'Good luck, sis,' he said, as he slid back the door and got out.

On Monday when she got home at midnight she made the chocolate mousse and put it outside the door on the terrace covered with a cotton scarf. On Tuesday she bicycled to work and came back at lunchtime to do the vegetables and lay the table. She covered it with a white sheet, put some ivy and twigs from the lime tree in the garden in a glass in the middle with four candles in saucers round it. She left work as soon as the Programme was over.

'Hey, where're you going, girl?' shouted Owen, as she dashed away.

'Home,' said Victoria, laughing at him over her shoulder.

'Aga Khan coming to see you, then?' he shouted after her.

Back at home, she worked hard in the kitchen, buttering the pheasant and covering it with bacon as she had seen her friend Rosalynn do, crumbling the breadcrumbs, sticking an onion with cloves and boiling it in milk, slicing potatoes and emptying chestnut purée out of a small tin into a saucepan. The chocolate mousse on the terrace had firmed up and she sprinkled it with Nescafé. She put the pheasant in the oven and went to change. She put on her red flannel circular skirt with a black jersey top and a wide black elastic belt, and changed her lipstick. As the bell rang, she sprinted back to the dressing-cupboard and put some *Mouche* behind her ears. It was Bea, in furs and pearls, pigeon-shaped with a big bosom and fine ankles, her grey hair scraped back from her cheekbones and fastened with tortoiseshell combs.

Good, thought Victoria, he won't get the wrong impression.

'Darling,' said Bea, kissing her, 'turn around. You look wonderful. I came on time so he wouldn't get the wrong impression.'

She had brought a small bottle of brandy and stood in the kitchen doorway while Victoria, trembling a little, basted the bird. She had no idea how long to cook a pheasant. Her ordinary dinner-party dish was leg of lamb or else rice with onions and raisins and Fray Bentos corned beef.

The bell rang again. It was the second man in an embarrassingly loud checked country suit with a waistcoat. Tall and confident he folded himself down and poked his head in the oven.

'Put a spoonful of water inside,' he said in a tone of authority. Victoria struggled with the bird slipping about in the roasting tin. Fat spat up at her as she put the water inside. The smell of cooking would drown out the *Mouche*.

She had two bottles of Spanish wine called Perequita which had cost six shillings each. The second man opened one of them and put it masterfully in front of the gas fire. But first they had whisky from the half-bottle Victoria had bought on her last trip abroad.

'How pretty the table looks, darling,' said Bea. 'You are a clever girl.'

'You should never have ivy in the house. It's bad luck,' said the second man.

How silly he is, thought Victoria, uneasily, but she deferred to him. He was a man.

Bea sat in the armchair; Victoria sat on the floor, her skirt spread round her; the second man sat on the divan, his long lean legs loosely crossed as he held forth in his deep baritone about coursing. Victoria took the details without flinching and hoped Bea would not be upset, which was undoubtedly what she was intended to be. She hoped to get the conversation round to more cerebral subjects before Harold – where was he? – arrived. When the second man started to describe the cooking of hares once they had been killed, she stood up. 'I think it sounds disgusting,' she said, 'I'm sure you're making it up.' She went into the kitchen and turned off the Brussels sprouts. She did not know whether to drain them or leave them warm in the cooling water. The *gratin dauphinoise* was beginning to turn black at the edges and the pheasant looked brown and small in the big roasting tin. She turned off the oven.

'Maybe we'd better have dinner,' she said, going back into the room. It was nine o'clock.

'Telephone him, darling,' said Bea. 'Maybe he's forgotten.'

The other man raised an eyebrow, which he could do remarkably well, and looked at Victoria with his staring pale blue eyes. Once she had gone to bed with him in the afternoon in his damp Chelsea flat. She felt puzzled about it now, a disturbing and unremarkable half-hour. She had felt like a duck getting up and ruffling her feathers and then waddling off. Not even a quack. She went into the hall and dialled Harold's number. It gave a half-ring and he answered. Victoria's heart jumped, it was a horrible feeling.

'Where are you?' she said, keeping her voice low, 'we're waiting for dinner.'

'So sorry,' he said, 'I fell asleep.'

'Fell asleep?' said Victoria, nearly crying, 'but it's all cooked. We're waiting for you.'

'I forgot. Too late now, I'm afraid. I'll ring you tomorrow,' he said and rang off.

Next day, he did telephone; early in the afternoon.

'Hullo,' he said, 'how are you?'

'All right,' said Victoria. 'What happened last night? It was awf—'

'Oh, that,' he said. 'Look, I'm taking my daughter to a pantomime on Saturday. Would you like to come?'

'Oh, yes,' said Victoria. Her heart gave a leap from

where it had lodged in the pit of her stomach. 'But where have you been?'

'Away,' he said. 'Abroad. Where shall we meet? Palace Theatre at two fifteen?'

'I've got a van,' said Victoria. 'I could pick you up.'

'A van! Alice'll like that,' he said. 'How did you manage it?'

'Well,' said Victoria, 'a friend of mine who lives in Wiltshire is going abroad, so . . .'

'All right,' said Harold. 'No, don't pick me up. We'll meet there.' He was going to have lunch at Clare's.

'How old is your daughter?' said Victoria.

'She's ten,' said Harold, 'and her name's Alice.'

What a plain name, thought Victoria, a very plain name for anyone, especially a child. If she had a little girl she would call her Jennifer or maybe Christobel. She tried to imagine what Alice would be like; dark, lively and stout? She herself had been a fat child. Alice would like fairy-stories or stories about girls and their ponies and she could invent games for them to play which would involve a lot of shouting and chasing and jumping out at each other. Harold would play too. They could bounce about on cushions in his flat, act bits from the pantomime and then, maybe, read to each other. She would put some of her own favourite books in the van, just in case.

'Vick,' said Roderick, softly, 'Vick, time is passing.' He was sitting by her desk with the blank cards for that evening's programme in his hand. Victoria had to tell him the questions and introductions she had worked out for his interviewees, and go through them with him. That evening she had a young playwright for him, whose work she did not think much of, called Osborne, and a mad

Irish lord, who had just come back from Moscow, both lightweight items she had had to fall back on in a lean week.

'Never mind,' said Roderick, 'we can have some fun with them.'

He chuckled as he read through the questions she handed him. 'You're a genius,' he said. 'I thought you were getting past it.' He turned his chair to the wall, put his hands over his ears and started studying the questions and writing notes on his cards.

# Chapter Seven

❧

In the tawdry foyer of the Palace Theatre, Alice stood silent and white-faced on the margin of the matinée crowds. Harold held her hand which lay lifeless in his own. He kept squeezing it, longing, in an unacknowledged way, for a reciprocal sensation of pressure from her woolly-gloved fingers. Victoria saw them standing there, Harold in his ripped-up flying jacket and the pale child in a black corduroy coat with silver buttons. The coat was exactly the same shape as she herself had had to wear: double-breasted and vaguely fitted with a half-belt at the back, only hers would have been hairy wool, in a colour – mid-blue or dusky pink – considered suitable for children, a new one every two years and two sizes too large to allow for growing into.

She saw the two of them from far away and waved but she had to go right up before Harold saw her.

'Hullo,' she said, pleasure and excitement drowning out her apprehension.

'Oh, hullo,' said Harold and kissed her on the cheek. 'This is Alice.' He gave the child's hand a little pull.

'Hullo,' said Victoria, smiling at Alice. Alice stared but said nothing.

'Say hullo,' said Harold, giving Alice's hand another pull.

'Hullo,' murmured Alice. They pushed their way through the crowd to their seats. Harold kept smiling at Alice and making funny faces. They sat on either side of her quite close to the front.

'Thank you for your postcard,' said Victoria to Harold over Alice's head.

'Daddy sent me a postcard,' said Alice without turning. She spoke so quietly that Victoria had to bend down to hear her.

'What was your picture?' she asked. Alice said nothing, so Victoria said, 'Mine was a bicycle race. Have you got a bicycle?' but Alice made no reply.

Harold said, 'Victoria's got a van. Won't that be fun?' He smiled at his daughter.

'Mummy's got a Bentley,' she said, impassively.

Immediately Victoria felt deflated. 'It's not really very different from an ordinary car,' she said to Harold, who glared at her.

The heavy puce curtains, all tarnished swags and tassels, went up and the pantomime began. Victoria had disliked pantomimes as a child. She had preferred plays with stories like *Bucky's Bears*, or *Bluebell in Fairyland*.

She was not surprised that Alice made no reaction at all as the audience bellowed and roared around them. When the lights went up for the interval, Harold said, 'Let's get some ice-creams.' He spoke with unfamiliar gusto, rolling the 'r' of cream. They got up. 'Take off your coat,' he said to Alice. But Alice stood mute and unmoving.

'It's a very nice coat,' said Victoria. 'Where did you get it?' She did not expect a reply, but after a time Alice said, 'Mummy got it.'

They moved off to the foyer, Alice buttoned in her coat.

'Get some ice-creams,' said Harold to Victoria, 'I'm

going to the lavatory. You'd better take Alice to the lavatory too.' He disappeared.

Victoria looked at Alice. She felt intimidated as she had never felt intimidated before with a child. 'If you would like to go to the lavatory, it's over there,' she said, 'and if you would like me to come with you, I will.' She waited, then she said, 'What kind of ice-cream would you like?'

By and by she got two choc-ices. 'Which ugly sister did you think the ugliest?' she asked. Alice unwrapped her choc-ice without speaking. When Harold came back they were both leaning against pillars on opposite sides of the corridor and staring at the shifting throng of chattering families, the air between them heavy with defeat.

Victoria gave Harold his choc-ice.

'Did you take Alice to the lavatory?' he asked.

Victoria shook her head.

'Why not?' he said. 'Speak, can't you?'

'I don't think she wanted to go,' said Victoria.

'How hopeless,' said Harold. 'Alice, do you want to go to the lavatory?'

Alice nodded her head. Harold gave her his hand and together, they moved off towards the ladies' toilet. Victoria pressed up against her pillar and felt the hard plaster bumps of its plinth dig into her back.

After the play, they walked through the darkening streets to find the van. Harold had Alice's hand in his and, to her surprise, Victoria felt Alice take hers. She let it rest there, not daring to respond and glanced to see if Harold had noticed, but his eyes were on the way ahead.

When they reached the van, Victoria let go of Alice's hand and slid back the door. Pulling the driver's seat forward, she said, 'Hop in, or would you like to sit in the front?'

'Isn't it fun, Alice,' said Harold.

Alice climbed silently into the back and sat on the bench along one side. Harold got in beside Victoria and they set off. As they drove down Oxford Street she noticed in the driving-mirror the hint of a smile on Alice's face. She speeded up. 'Left or right, Alice?' she called. 'Which way?'

'Right,' said Alice, almost inaudibly. Victoria swerved right. 'Now where? Quick!' she said. Going down one-way streets and, once, up on the pavement, they arrived in Trafalgar Square. Victoria drove twice, fast, round the square and then, soberly, back to Harold's flat. Nobody spoke. Alice clambered up the stairs ahead of them. When they got there, Harold stood among the wreckage. 'There's nothing much for tea,' he said.

'Have you ever had Raspberry Ripple?' said Victoria quickly. 'It's ice-cream with wriggles of raspberry in it.' Alice shook her head. 'But she's had ice-cream already,' said Harold.

'Does it matter if she has more?' said Victoria.

'I suppose not,' said Harold. Victoria ran down the stairs and out into the street. She found a newsagent's and bought a packet of Raspberry Ripple, some custard creams and a bottle of orange squash. There was sixpence left in her purse. She bought the *Dandy* and ran back. Harold and Alice were sitting on the sofa, Alice still in her coat, and Harold was showing her photographs in an album. She had two helpings of Raspberry Ripple, and a glass of orange squash and, when she had finished, took the *Dandy* to an armchair where she unbuttoned her coat and sat turning the pages. Harold made some coffee and sat hunched in a chair, eating custard creams until the packet was finished. Victoria drank her coffee sitting on the edge of a chair and explored a hole in the loose cover. She felt anxious, alert and very unsure of herself. The spidery, thin-ice feeling Harold's presence so often induced in her began to paralyse her limbs. She jumped up.

'You're Korky and I'm a dog!' she said, going down on all fours and barking at Alice's chair.

Alice squealed and climbed over the back. 'Meeiouw!' she said fiercely from behind it.

An hour later, dishevelled and pink, the three of them got back in the van. Victoria drove across the park to St John's Wood.

'Wait here,' said Harold, just past Lord's. He and Alice got out. 'I won't be a minute,' he said, as the two of them walked off. Alice turned to wave and Victoria waved back. She sat in the van smiling to herself, then she looked at her face in the driving-mirror and began redoing her make-up. She did not want Harold to catch her at it, so she worked fast. As she finished she half noticed a black car draw up and park behind her. She started brushing her hair. The spidery feeling was coming back. She got out of the van and walked towards the corner round which Harold and Alice had disappeared. She imagined him hurrying back to her down the street, his collar turned up and the ripped coat, buttonless, flapping. But there was no sign of him. She went back to the van. The man in the black car was lighting a cigarette. He looked familiar. She got back in and misery swept over her. Abandonment, though she did not know it, was what she most feared.

By the time Harold reappeared three-quarters of an hour later, she was beyond speech. As he opened the van door and got in, she stared at him, wordlessly.

'Well, it's quite clear you've got no idea how to treat children,' he said, as he slammed the door.

# Chapter Eight

Victoria tried to argue with Harold, but he kept switching tack. Every time she felt she had made a good point, one that would appeal to his superior intellect, about the psychology of children or the rationality of her intentions, he took the wind out of her sails, leaving her flapping and adrift. He made her feel personally responsible for a web of lies distorting childhood, and the way he combined passionate concern with personal invective unnerved her. She struggled to stick to her points, dealing seriously with the accusations as they came at her from all quarters.

'Why do you wear all that stuff on your face? Basic insecurity . . . You're so false,' he said, as she battled to save something of the afternoon, now collapsing in painful particles around her.

As a child, she used to have a dream. She sat on the floor in a classroom at school with the other girls crowded round her in a circle. They threw a netball at her head as she, bewildered, tried to fend it off and take it like a good sport. She strove to take on his argument through the fog of misery and self-doubt that blotted out her mind.

Enraged, Harold cursed her in his. Women were to be broken – all his instincts told him – before they broke you. Only Clare, with her low laugh and her wiry body which would never give, made him feel safe.

'Hullo,' she had said, as she opened the door. She shook her fine, straight hair back from her face with a slow familiar movement and fastened it back from her forehead with a wide ivory band. 'Did you have a good time?'

She laid her narrow hand on Alice's shoulder. She made it her business to have only good times in her own life; golden times of long lunches in leafy sun-filled gardens off tables straight out of a Bonnard painting. Alice nodded her head.

'Come and have a drink,' said Clare, moving ahead of them through the hall. Her house was always full of roses; deep crimson blooms that arrived in huge bunches on her doorstep at all times of year.

'Just a quick one,' said Harold, following her. He stifled a needle of guilt and stepped into her drawing-room where three or four people sat laughing in pale silken-covered armchairs around a wood fire, glasses in their hands.

'Where have you been?' they cried, as he entered. 'Why weren't you at Tees last weekend?' 'Come to Spain next week – we're going to see the gypsies!' Accepting a Campari, he sat on the arm of a chair in his flying jacket and, with charming diffidence, parried their questions, half promising to come to Spain too. When the conversation moved on, he got up to go. Clare and Alice came with him to the door and stood there in silence watching him as he walked away, Alice with her big eyes and her straight face; Clare smiling her half-smile. By the time he got back to the car he was out for blood.

Of course, Victoria cried. Half-way through dinner in the restaurant that had, until then, been one of her favourites, she found it impossible to get the food past the lump in her throat. Tears started to run down her cheeks. Suspended in time she saw Harold's face, lips tight, glaring at her. She wanted to escape. The door, far, far away across a no man's land of chattering diners and clattering waiters, seemed unattainable. The scene blurred and wavered in front of her eyes. She put her head down on the white table-cloth and wept.

'Sit up,' she heard his voice hiss in her ear, 'sit *up*. They'll think you're drunk.' Shocked, she sat up and caught the eye of a man sitting at a table across the floor. He was staring at them with dull eyes in a sallow face, a forkful of spaghetti half-way to his mouth.

'Look!' she said shakily. 'Who's that?' But she knew. It was the man in the black car.

'Don't try to get out of it!' said Harold, fiercely, looking nevertheless. He started violently. 'Christ!' he said. 'Don't look. Get on with your food. I don't want him to see us.'

'But, of course, he's seen us,' said Victoria. 'Who is he? Do you know him?'

'In a way,' said Harold, 'maybe.' His voice was suddenly drained of rancour and he spoke quietly, hesitantly even.

'Why don't you say hullo?' said Victoria.

'It's too embarrassing,' said Harold, looking at his plate. He finished up his food and paid the bill, saying little. Victoria said nothing. She finished up the food on her plate. As they left the restaurant, the man from the black car followed them with his eyes. There was almost a pleading look in them. Harold took Victoria's arm and gave it a little squeeze. That night in bed he did not make love to her.

Volnicek went back to his room. It was small and bare at

the top of a house in a dismal North Kensington square. Shivering, he lit the gas fire, but it sputtered and died out. He had no money left for the infernal British machine that consumed his shillings so remorselessly, denying him the warmth he craved. The Italian restaurant had been much too expensive. His affiliation, the Co-operative of Responsible Scientists Against the Development of Nuclear Weapons, had little money to spare for its workers. They were all, like himself, eminent professionals; men of science who had cast themselves off from the busy honeycomb of everyday life to work for their Cause. Like him, they had severed all ties: to nation, to institution, to family, to friends. They were solitaries belonging, like Einstein, to the human race alone; members of the species, Man.

He sighed and sat on the bed which bounced and squeaked beneath his weight before its thin springs settled down into temporary equilibrium. Soon, he would have to move on. He put his head in his hands. The bald light from the central bulb that he had taken from Miss Benjamin's flat shone through his fingers. He rather liked Miss Benjamin. It was a shame he had had to raid her flat in such an ungentlemanly fashion. He would like to have invited her to go to the Opera with him. In the old days, he would have done. Janáček! Smetana! Unheard of in this strange uncultured land. Upright, in white tie and tails, the Order of St Vaclavski on his breast, he would have given her his arm. White-gloved hand on his sleeve, her long black cloak sweeping the ground, they would have entered the National Theatre in his native land to the murmured greetings and bows of the assembled intelligentsia and nobility. Miss Benjamin would have looked well amongst them. She had style, unlike her fellow countrywomen in their dreadful hard colours and boxy tweeds. Even the trinkets he had been obliged to take from her dressing-room – well, hardly a dressing-room – and sell for such a disgracefully low price in their wretched flea market had been pretty pieces of their kind. His own grandmother, in her palace high above the town, had worn just such pieces on a black velvet ribbon at her throat.

But such thoughts were forbidden. The past was a figment, a dangerous indulgence that leeched away resolve. He had sworn a solemn oath to surrender it for ever. And time was closing in on him. The other side – both other sides, East and West – with the full secret weights of their governments behind them, were stirring into action and would catch up with him soon. Terrifyingly soon. Caught up in a mad unwinnable race with each other, they were beyond the reach of responsible thought. He had weeks, maybe only days, in which to find the lost configuration and destroy it. His own co-operative, he knew, carried no responsibility for those who failed. There was no hierarchy; rather, it was an affiliation of equals. He supported that.

Fox was a brute, the product of a barbaric educational system. Volnicek could never make out how much he knew. Was he a principal in the service of the East, in the service of the West or a double-agent? Was he playing a deadly game with him or was he a bungler from somewhere low down in the ranks caught up in strategic complexities of which he had no understanding? Whatever he was, he was not to be trusted. Ignorance itself was dangerous.

Volnicek smiled wanly to himself. Trust! It was a word from a bygone age. He stood up and the bed whined an accompaniment of protest. He saw his own face, yellow and gaunt, reflected in the chipped mirror above the gas fire. It looked so very unhealthy. His mother and sister would not recognise him in the cheap black suit and nasty rayon tie he wore these days. He would never see them again anyway, even if they had not perished in the camps.

He forced his brain back to the present. Trained intellect, clarity of mind, independence of thought, and knowledge of the science of psychoanalysis from his studies in Vienna could not fail to outwit Fox in the end. For now, there was nothing for it but to go to bed. Tomorrow, he must address himself to the unappetising business of investigating the man's flat.

Watchfully, he opened the door onto the dark landing. Nothing stirred and no sound came from behind the other doors opening onto it. Volnicek, Count Dr Alexandr Volnicek, slipped into the bathroom and, without switching on the light, cleaned his teeth. His sensitive nostrils picked up the smell of cheese and tomato on his fingers, but he did not wash them. To have done so would have meant turning on the hot tap which, in turn, would have meant a flash of blue light and a ghastly explosion from the machine called 'geyser' above the bath. He returned noiselessly to his room, locked the door and, after placing a pad of paper and a pencil carefully beside the bed, he undressed himself and got in. Maybe resolution would yield itself up to him in dream.

Victoria almost never had dreams, she slept badly on the whole, but Harold was prone to violent starts during sleep. He would give one or two wild jerks as if at the hand of some unseen watchmaker and start thrashing about muttering and then shouting an incomprehensible stream of words. Victoria would lean worriedly towards him.

'Harold,' she would say softly, then louder, 'Harold.' She would touch him gently on the shoulder, straining to make out the words and feeling impertinent as she did so. His torment was so private and so compulsive that she hesitated to disturb him, but she longed for a clue into the world he kept so determinedly locked away from her. He would wake up shuddering. Victoria would try to put her arms round him, but he would shake her off and fall back into sleep, pulling the bedclothes with him.

'Why didn't you wake me? What did I say?' he would ask in the morning.

'I don't know. I couldn't hear,' Victoria would say.

'What, nothing?' Harold would say.

'Some of it seemed to be foreign,' she would say, 'German, or maybe Russian.'

He would turn irritatedly away. 'How hopeless,' he would say.

They were going away for the weekend to stay with friends of his in Sussex. Ever since he had told her, she had been packing and repacking her suitcase.

'Will they mind if I wear trousers?' she asked, intending to do so anyway.

'For Christ's sake!' Harold said.

'Do they change for dinner?' said Victoria.

'Don't be ridiculous,' said Harold.

She decided to go to the office on Friday morning in her white pleated skirt with a black polo-necked sweater and a caramel-coloured suede blazer. Harold was to pick her up after the Programme in the Bentley, which seemed to have appeared again. With gold jewellery the white skirt and black sweater would do for dinner anywhere. On Saturday, she would wear the black trousers her brother's tailor had made for her, with a loose striped top converted out of an old pair of her father's thick woollen pyjamas. For dinner she could put on the black polo-neck under an orange corduroy sailor-top and on Sunday she would wear her new pale blue Italian trousers with an olive-green Shetland sweater. She washed and ironed until the clothes were as smooth as ivory, folded them with sheets of tissue-paper and put them carefully in her flowered carpet-bag with a couple of empty scent-bottles still smelling of *Mouche*. For the first time, she was going to leave before the Programme went out on the air.

'Don't worry, girl,' said Owen abstractedly. He and Andrew were hunched round his desk with Gregory going through the itinerary of one of the contributors filming in Scotland. There was a salmon-fishing dispute, a piece about the construction of the Forth road-bridge and another about the Edinburgh tailor who made kilts for the Royal Family, little people's stuff that Victoria was uneasy with. She knew she should have been in there with them. She felt she was missing the tide. She stood for a moment on the fringe, uncertain where she belonged.

'Have a fag, girl,' said Andrew, holding out a packet without raising his head. Victoria shook hers and went back to her desk. She had one item for that night, a filmed story about an exhibition of Georges de La Tour opening at the Royal Academy. The Secretary there had become a friend. 'Miss Benjamin' he called her in his quavery teasing voice. He had told her about the show and Victoria, excited by this confidence from the uplands of high culture, had persuaded Owen to let her go ahead and do a story. It had not been very hard, though art, shot in the way Victoria intended with the picture filling the whole frame, had never been shown like that before on television.

She had gone to the galleries with a cameraman as soon as the pictures were hung, and shot the still, luminous centres of the major works under the Secretary's guidance.

She went up now to the cutting-rooms to have a look at the footage on the editing-machine and saved a vital frame or two from the bin. She was surprised at how good it looked, the candlelight of the paintings somehow enhanced by black and white. The Examiner-General of the Queen's Paintings was coming in at three to dub a commentary. Back in her office, she sat down at her type-writer and began writing it for him. He was called Sir Christopher Sharpe.

She was bad at film commentary and Roderick, already around, helped her with it. They went up together to the dubbing-theatre at lunchtime, where that evening's film was being dubbed. Roderick had two commentaries to read.

At exactly three the Examiner-General of the Queen's Paintings was shown in, stooping in the dark. He was very tall and immensely distinguished with a long, lined, handsome face and silvery hair. His beautifully cut grey flannel suit hung loosely on his gaunt frame. Victoria greeted him in a whisper – they had already talked to each other on the telephone – and showed him to a seat. Nobody bowed or made a speech, so she sat down beside him. She gave him her commentary: 'I don't know whether you'll be needing this,' she said. 'It's quite difficult saying just the right amount of words to go with each shot. Have you ever done this kind of thing before?'

The Examiner-General of the Queen's Paintings gave her a charming smile. 'Actually, I haven't,' he said, 'this is quite an adventure for me.'

The lights went up.

'Victoria, is your speaker ready?' called the chief editor from the glassed-in box at the side of the theatre where he sat at his dubbing-table.

'Yes,' Victoria called back.

'We'll give him a run-through first,' called the chief editor.

'That's very thoughtful of you,' said the Examiner-General of the Queen's Paintings, 'but I don't think it'll be necessary.' He spoke with immense courtesy in a deep melodious voice.

'Go straight for it, then? Are you sure? Right,' said the chief editor.

The lights went down and the first picture came up on the big screen. It looked beautiful. The Examiner-General of the Queen's Paintings started speaking and continued without faltering, matching his scholarly, perfectly worded comments to each shot until the film finished four minutes later. Victoria turned to him as the lights went up.

'That was brilliant,' she said. 'It's unheard of to dub something straight off like that, let alone sight unseen.'

'Beginner's luck,' said the Examiner-General of the Queen's Paintings, diffidently.

'Perfect. No complaints. Ask him if he wants a job,' called the chief editor.

'Is that all you want of me?' said Sir Christopher.

'All!' said Victoria. 'What you've just done would have taken an ordinary mortal half the afternoon. Thank you very much.' She smiled up at him. 'I'll take you down to your car. The driver will be surprised to see you so soon.'

Sir Christopher had come in a Programme car. He did not drive. Together they went down to reception and found his driver. Victoria went to the door with him and waved as he got into the car. Sir Christopher inclined his

85

head and raised his long El Greco hand. There was some-one else already in the car. Sitting in the corner of the back seat hunched up against the maroon leather of the old Austin Princess was the man from the black Wolseley. He looked, Victoria thought, quite terrified, as the car drove away.

# Chapter Nine

ॐ

At half past five, full of regret, Victoria picked up her carpet-bag and left the team as the evening rush for the studio began. Only Roderick noticed her slip away.

'Have fun,' he said, softly, as she passed him on her way out. He was wearing his slate-green suit with the tie she had given him for Christmas.

'Let me know how the de La Tour goes,' she said back. She had a feeling that the box with its own interior glow would pull out the special slow quality of light in the paintings. She felt a private and satisfactory glow herself at the notion that television, the medium in which she worked, did not necessarily diminish art. Her friend, the Secretary, had told her of a major Italian exhibition coming up in the summer. She would do the same with the Piero della Francescas come May. She smiled at the girl behind the desk in reception who smiled back.

'Leaving early?' she said.

'Yes,' said Victoria, 'I'm going away for the weekend.'

The girl bent down over her work and Victoria hoped she would look up again when her incomparably handsome lover arrived to take her away. Forty minutes later she was still there, head held high, well-being draining out of her, as the first familiar bars of the Programme's signature tune came out from the viewing-room close by. How awful it was to be hearing it like an ordinary member of the public.

'Oh, hullo. There you are. Hurry up. We'll be late,' said Harold, rumpled and jagged, appearing suddenly beside her. He was wearing blue trousers and the jacket of his sharp striped suit with one of his dolly-mixture bow ties. His appearance startled her on a number of levels. He picked up her bag. 'What on earth have you got here?' he said, peevishly. 'We're only going for a weekend, you know.' He disappeared through the doors into the street. Victoria hurried to catch up with him.

'Why were you so—' she began.

'We're going to get the worst of the traffic,' he said, accusingly. 'I hope you know the way to the Brighton Road.' The Bentley was parked askew from the pavement, its front end sticking well out into the street. They got in and Harold jerked the car straight out into the traffic. Two cars screeched to a standstill behind them and the drivers stuck their heads out of the windows and began shouting. 'Bloody English,' muttered Harold, gripping the steering-wheel and putting his foot down on the accelerator. They shot away and were round the corner at the end of the street before Victoria had settled the pleats of her skirt beneath her.

Speeding west along the Uxbridge Road, she made a tentative comment. Sometimes she found it hard to decide what tone and emphasis to give the simplest of phrases in Harold's company. 'Isn't this the wrong way?' she said, mildly, giving each word equal weight.

'I don't know,' said Harold, crossly. 'This is your part of the world. You're meant to be map-reading.'

'Well, this is west surely, and Brighton's south,' said Victoria, as evenly as she could.

'Don't be so intelligent,' said Harold, 'map-reading's exact. You're either right or you're wrong. Look in the *A to Z*. It's on the floor by your feet.' He wrenched the car left and roared south along a small domestic side-street. 'What's the name of this road?' he demanded as they reached the end of it and were faced by three more grey-brown ones of equal uniformity and anonymity.

Victoria wound down the window and peered out. 'St-Ethel-something, I think,' she said, unsteadily.

'Look at the map!' shouted Harold. Without slowing down, he took the middle of the three roads and surged along it. 'Here, you take the wheel,' he said suddenly, abandoning it and bending towards the *A to Z* lying open on Victoria's lap.

'You haven't even got the right page,' he said, furiously, as she struggled to hold the car steady above his head, dug hard into the caramel suede. He stopped the car and seized the book. 'We're *here*,' he said, stabbing his finger at the mass of thin grey lines wavering incomprehensibly across the pages. 'See? *Here*. Don't look at me. Look at the map.' He started up the car again. Victoria put her finger, painted an iridescent pearl for the country, on the place his finger had seemed to be and attempted to relate the tiny letters and congested threads of print to the lines of houses and corner shops flashing past her. She kept her head down and looked through the window out of the corner of her eye, praying for the traffic lights to be red.

'Where are we?' shouted Harold every now and then.

'Notting Hill Gate, Hyde Park Corner, Buckingham Palace,' said Victoria, wildly in reply. At last one of her surreptitious glances informed her that they had reached

Clapham Common. She knew the road to Dover all right and she knew where the road to Sussex branched off it. She lifted her eyes from the map and sat back in her seat with a little sigh.

'Right or left?' shouted Harold, ignoring the sign to Brighton south across the Common and veering left along the top of it.

'No, no,' shouted Victoria, 'we should have gone right back there.'

'Don't shout at me,' shouted Harold. He wrenched the car round into a U-turn and drove back towards the sign: BRIGHTON – A23, it read.

'How do you know this is the right way if you're not looking at the map?' said Harold, turning to stare at her accusingly.

'It says it on the signpost,' said Victoria.

'Never trust signs,' said Harold, 'the map is always right. Show me where we are on it.'

Victoria began to laugh. Giggles rose from her diaphragm like bubbles and came up her throat and out of her mouth in waves; wave after wave of them spilled round her in the charged atmosphere of the car. She tried to suppress them, saw Harold glowering at the wheel and failed. His attitude of extreme suspicion struck her as irresistibly comic. He glared at her, removed his right hand from the wheel and struck her hard in the face.

There was silence in the car after that; silence whose weight grew ever more oppressive with the charge of unspoken words massed like storm clouds piling up round their heads. Victoria felt frozen, her only impulse one of flight. Somewhere round Croydon when the car stopped at a red light, she opened the door. Harold leaned across her and pulled it shut.

'Don't be such a fool,' he said. Fury, despair and self-righteousness kept him upright at the wheel. He smelled the smell of his mother leaving him again in the dormitory at school and wished to be alone, shut away in a small room with bare walls where no emotion could reach nor hope tease him. Am I mad? he thought, gloomily.

He stared ahead into the gathering dark. He wished the person sitting motionless beside him would speak, because then he could turn on her and loose off some of the disquiet coiled so uncomfortably within his head. He tried to empty his mind of her presence. Perhaps he should have gone to Spain with Clare and her friends. They would have walked in the mountains, stayed at small inns, drunk large quantities of hard red wine, and danced with the gypsies under the moon. But it would not have been like that. He would have felt uneasy, out of place, trapped like a performing animal in a circus of good times. Clare lived for pleasure and her bonds of enchantment were insidious and strong. He had to free himself from them.

Or he could have gone to Italy. A ticket had arrived for him in the post earlier in the week with a note: *Villa Castagna* said the letterhead in thick embossed script and, underneath, in his mistress's big blue scrawl: 'Darling, Do come. The house is full of all the people you like best and I long to see you. All love.' He had not replied. There was nothing to say. He must work, write, get back into the mainstream of life.

And Melissa, what an idiot she was, taken in by all that communist claptrap. *'From each according to his abilities, to each according to his needs.'* A seductive notion! He had become perilously close to being taken in by it himself, led on by Melissa's soft voice and mocking smile daring him to take the next step, like a jump on the hunting-field.

God knew how free he was of them even now. They probably had him on their files for ever, the bastards. He drew his breath in sharply and put his foot down on the accelerator, in flight before a howling host of demons.

They were driving through country roads now, the bare line of the Downs dark against the dark sky outside. Victoria stirred beside him. She was looking at herself in a pocket-mirror and dabbing bits of this and that on her face.

Just as well, Harold thought, she's probably been blubbing away there to herself in the dark. He would not want Guy and Vivien, sharp as needles, to think badly of him. It was enough of a risk bringing her anyway. They had almost certainly never met a working woman before, certainly not one who worked in television. Come to think of it, they had almost certainly never seen a television set. He would have to explain; a kind of wireless with pictures.

He swung the car into their drive, a short stretch of rutted mud with tall trees on either side. A long flint house lay low in the headlights at the end of it, yellow lights in some of the lower windows. Shabby was the word that came to Victoria's startled mind. As they got out of the car the front door opened and a woman called 'Hullo' to them. She was wearing shapeless trousers, a top of indeterminate cut and colour and a necklace of what looked like dull silver teeth round her neck. Her face was creased, her eyes round and brown and her grey hair thin, wispy and short. Behind her stood a big burly man with a red face and a rumbly voice. They were both laughing and clucking as they greeted Harold with pats, hugs, handshakes and kisses. Their educated voices had an unusual lilt to them in which the stress seemed to come fairly frequently but on unexpected words. Speaking seemed to be a sort of game to be played with initiates; an odd word here or there, a cue for general amusement.

Harold introduced Victoria. Guy and Vivien shook hands with her. Guy picked up her bag and they moved ahead of her into the dim wide hall. There, the floor was bare wood with a threadbare rug or two on it and many pictures on the walls. There was a uniformly static quality about the pictures as well as an air of not so much childishness as left-handedness. Hefty women in bathing dresses played with beach balls beside the sea, or draped their seal-shaped limbs over mauve and orange rocks. At the end a door with a fanlight, through which Victoria could see the line of the Downs, led out into a garden.

The party ahead turned right into a big room filled with worn chairs and sofas. There was a piano, several low-watt bulbs in wonky painted parchment shades, more of the left-handed pictures on the walls and several big painted jugs full of daffodils and horse chestnut buds. A fire flickered in the grate which was surrounded by painted tiles showing a group of people arrested in contemplation before a fireplace. And above, was a strange picture of a very long thin man in a yellow suit lying back and holding the tips of his attenuated fingers together before him.

Vivien detached herself and addressed Victoria. 'Have a drink, my dear,' she said, lowering her voice on the third word and lengthening it by a second or two.

'I'd love one,' began Victoria, but Vivien had turned away again and was laughing with the others over the drink itself, Chianti, which had come by some complicated means of personal import-export direct from a remote village in Tuscany. Suddenly they all turned on her. 'You haven't got a drink!' they cried.

'But I *asked* you, my dear, some time ago,' said Vivien.

'Victoria, have some vino,' said Guy, solicitously, pouring her some from an unlabelled bottle. He handed her a glass with a nice twinkle and fell to again describing the semantic pitfalls attendant upon bringing a barrel of wine into the country from Italy. They seemed to view Italians with a mixture of reverence and patronage and they seemed to know the country well. Victoria took a sip from her glass. She felt it slip sourly down her gullet and trickle round the sad sore places in her stomach. Gin would have burned them out. It was getting colder and colder, and she wondered if she could move nearer the fire. She took a step or two towards it. No one took the slightest notice of her. She moved boldly right up to it and felt with relief faint heat warm her knees as she carefully examined some boxes and pictures made of shells on the mantelpiece, her mind far from them.

'Have some more vino, Victoria,' said Guy, coming over to her with the bottle. She shook her head and smiled at him. He looked nice but not very and was obviously less important than Vivien and Harold.

'Supper soon. Come and talk to me in the kitchen while I get it, Harold,' said Vivien.

'What is it?' said Harold, moving off beside her.

'Toad-in-the-hole,' said Guy, dropping his voice conspiratorially on 'hole'. They all laughed and Guy left the room with them to lay the table. Left alone, Victoria bent over the fire. She would have to get warm enough to take her coat off and display her black and white as planned at dinner. She wondered where her bag was and how she could get at the gold star and bangle that would take her into evening. She had no idea what the others would wear for dinner. They did not appear to have changing for it on their minds, but you never knew. She had failed to assess such situations before and been caught out in country trousers in a company of rose-patterned prints and black velvet. A bell tinkled somewhere at the far end of the hall and the fire began to die away. Victoria wondered if she dared put another log on: there was a heap of them, rather damp, in a wicker box beside a pair of tiled feet. She had just done so when Harold appeared in the doorway. He was in his shirt-sleeves and waistcoat, a napkin in his hand and his mouth full.

'What the hell are you doing? We've started supper. Come on,' he said. He moved off into the hall.

'Where's my bag?' said Victoria, following him into its dim shadows.

'I don't know,' said Harold, brusquely. 'Come on. It's rude to keep people waiting.'

Victoria made out the shape of her bag near the bottom of the stairs. She went over to it.

'Come *on*,' said Harold.

Victoria closed her lips tightly. The mulish expression came over her face. She went over to her bag, opened it and put her hand straight onto the gold jewellery lying neatly coiled inside a sock among the layers of folded tissue-paper and clothes. She took off her suede jacket, laid it carefully on top of the bag, hung the gold star round the neck of her black sweater and slipped the bangle on her right wrist. Then she fluffed up her hair with her fingers. Harold stood with his hand on the door knob, his teeth clenched and his lips pulled back from them in a thin line.

'What are you *doing*?' he said. 'Come on.' He opened the door.

The room inside was square, its walls covered with pictures, and long french windows opened from it onto a verandah overlooking the garden. Vivien and Guy were sitting on either side of a round table with an amaryllis in a pot in the centre of it. They were eating toad-in-the-hole, Brussels sprouts and fried potatoes. Guy had a napkin tucked into his collar. He half rose as Victoria came into the room. Harold sat down in front of a plateful of already-begun food and Victoria slid into the vacant chair still tucked into the table. It had a rush seat and a ladder back which threw her weight forward, so she balanced herself on the edge.

'I'm so sorry,' she murmured.

'My dear,' said Vivien, 'help yourself.' She pushed some brown pottery dishes towards Victoria. Guy filled her glass with wine from a china jug. They resumed their conversation. They were talking about someone called Madame le Cul, who, it seemed, was a funny shape and rode a bicycle. Madame le Cul had somehow failed to do something she was meant to do because someone in her family was poorly, which they should not have been, and which meant that Vivien had had to cook the Brussels sprouts. She seemed put out about this, but the whole subject caused general merriment. Victoria, hoping her lipstick was intact, smiled too. She had taken more sausage than batter, though she loved it, when helping herself, and none of the potatoes.

'Tell us about yourself, my dear,' said Vivien suddenly, turning to her.

'Victoria works in television,' said Harold.

'Television,' said Guy as though he was tasting an early strawberry and lowering his voice several registers on the third syllable.

'It's a sort of wireless with pictures,' said Harold. 'Like

the cinema. It comes out of a box and people watch it in their own homes as if they were listening to the wireless.'

'How very fascinating,' said Vivien. 'Tell me, what news of Clare and the children? We had a letter from Italy yesterday, but we haven't seen them since we came back in January.'

'Alice is going to a new school next term,' said Harold.

'Can it be *good* for her, changing schools again?' said Vivien, frowning a little. 'One's at one's wits' end with these wretched schools.'

Victoria thought of the frozen little girl in the corduroy coat she had met at the theatre with her expressionless face and her wary, wide-eyed stare.

'I know a very good school for children up to about eleven,' she said. 'It's in Roehampton.'

They all stared at her for a moment.

'The first rhubarb for pudding,' said Guy, jovially. 'Monsieur la Touffe picked it this morning!'

After dinner they had coffee out of a Napolitana like Victoria had herself at home.

'*Too* queer about Melissa, isn't it?' said Vivien, stirring hers.

'I saw her actually a few weeks ago. She seemed as dotty as ever,' said Harold.

'There but for the grace of God . . .' intoned Guy, wagging his finger at Harold.

'Victoria's in the forget-me-not room opposite the North Pole,' said Vivien quickly. 'There's a hot-water bottle in the bed.'

'I'll take her up,' said Harold. He got up and held open the door for her.

'Breakfast at nine. Sleep well, my dear,' said Vivien.

'We stored ice in the bath there in the war,' she heard Guy say from his armchair, as she left the room.

Harold took her bag up the stairs. It was cold in the hall and colder on the stairs. He led her across a wide landing, along some narrow linoleum-covered passages, up and down short flights of stairs and stopped before a door.

'Here you are,' he said, putting down her bag. 'Sleep well.' He kissed her and walked back down the corridor they had just come along together. Victoria opened the door. The room was indeed covered with forget-me-not sprigged wallpaper, peeling in places and browning in patches. There was a single bed against one wall, a wash-basin, a green-painted chest-of-drawers, a green-painted cupboard and a bedside table with a lamp on it. The lampshade was handpainted with a pattern of dots and tadpole-like dashes and a window with striped curtains looked out over the garden. There was no heating of any kind and as Victoria, shivering in the penetrating chill of the narrow room, unpacked her clothes an owl hooted in the moonlight outside. She cleansed her face and cleaned her teeth in the wash-basin, and then slipped across the passage into the bathroom opposite. It was dim and cavernous and there was a bath in it, up some steps and big enough indeed for a small igloo, but no lavatory. She slipped back across the passage, hitched her leg over the wash-basin and peed into it. Whatever will I do in the morning she thought desperately. She climbed into the bed and lay on her back, staring up at the ceiling. The sheets felt clammy against her skin, the blankets weighty and the hot-water bottle – a real bottle in a flannel case – burning hot against her freezing toes.

Bott, she thought suddenly, Mrs Bott! As she did so the

door knob began to turn. The door opened and Harold stood there in his underpants and jacket.

'Move over,' he said as he shed them on the floor and clambered in beside her. He squealed as his limbs touched hers. 'You're so cold!' he said accusingly, and drew himself away. Then he put a hand on her belly. 'Show some human response,' he said as he moved it down between her legs. His lips, wet and warm, found hers in the dark and fastened on her mouth.

Victoria's lips felt odd to her. They felt like rubber and her body was dry. There was no sensation in it at all.

# Chapter Ten

Sixty miles away in London, Sir Christopher Sharpe sat at his desk in the elegant office he occupied on the top floor of the building in which he worked. As Director, the Institute would have expected him to settle into one of the nobly proportioned rooms of the first floor with their fine plaster ceilings. But Sir Christopher preferred to be above the crowd. He had chosen a charming room on a level with the tree-tops in the square beneath from which he commanded a spectacular view out over central London and the park beyond. All his art books were there, ranged in comforting proximity on the bookshelves he had had constructed, and there was a single picture on the cool grey walls, a small masterpiece by the English painter, Joseph Wright of Derby. It was a work he loved, its luminous interior light, not unlike the marvellous effects achieved by the Frenchman, Georges de La Tour, whose work he had been instrumental in assembling – and thereby introducing to a public insulated too long from the civilising influence of European culture – for an exhibition at the Royal Academy.

His secretary in the next room had long since gone home to the benighted suburb – Pinner he believed it was called, or was it Purley – in which she lived. The building was deserted. Only the night-watchman, Mr Tyson, dozed in his braided uniform by the single bar of his electric fire in the hallway five floors below.

Sir Christopher removed Ruskin's *Stones of Venice*, all three volumes bound into one, from the shelves and placed it upon the tooled leather surface of his desk. Its thin wafery pages concealed amongst their numerous treasures a small but powerful wireless-set. He placed the earphones over his ears and tuned in to the control centre in Kensington. His instructions, as expected, came tapping through the crackle of the resistant airwaves. He decoded them and sat back in his chair, pensively, the tips of his long fingers placed together before him. Then he bent forward and dialled a number in Holborn where he knew his opposite number, Sir Geoffrey Champman, would be awaiting the call. Sir Geoffrey, in black tie and preposterously cummerbunded, no doubt with one of the monstrous cigars he was attached to in his mouth, would have popped into his absurdly pretentious office on his way back from an official reception at Lancaster House, leaving his chauffeur in the Rolls waiting in the street below.

Sir Christopher thought, with nostalgia, of his old wartime colleagues in SIS and MI5, amateurs and gentlemen to their fingertips. Those of them, idealists like himself, who played the double game, were all gone now, though he still received an occasional postcard from P in Beirut. One was obliged to work with persons of a very different calibre these days, defective characters with grudges to work off, chips on their shoulders and old scores to settle with the ruling class. He heard Sir Geoffrey's jarring voice at the other end of the line: he would probably be required to address him as 'Geoff' any moment now. He shuddered.

'Evening, old boy,' said the voice.

'Geoffrey, dear, is that you?' said Sir Christopher, languidly. He repeated the mandatory crypted phrase required of him.

'Good to hear you,' boomed Sir Geoffrey in reply. He smacked his lips round his cigar and went on: 'Neat little coup you pulled off with the actress – damned attractive woman, what . . .! Anything to report on the Bohemian?'

'Thank you, Geoffrey,' said Sir Christopher. The defection had been a minor triumph in its genre and he felt some satisfaction at its conclusion, but Volnicek and his co-operative were more problematic. They operated in an entirely different sphere and according to an unknown set of rules. 'I'm afraid the second is proving more obstinate,' he said, 'putting us to a lot of trouble, y'know. I get the impression he's onto something, however, and his knowledge, imperfect though it may be, is clearly unhelpful. I feel the moment may have arrived at which we have to er . . .' He gave a little cough and went on: 'He drives a dreadful old car. The steering-wheel must be somewhat inefficient.'

'How unfortunate,' said Sir Geoffrey and sighed. He was reluctant to turn his mind, warmed by the excellent brandy the government provided these days, onto such taxing details. 'You know what a stir these things cause, however insignificant. I take it it's considered to be a necessity?'

'Absolutely. Regrettably,' said Sir Christopher. He could detect through the baffle that Geoffrey was in one of his disgustingly mellow moods and he mistrusted his loose dedication to good living. Asceticism was the aesthetic he adhered to. Sir Christopher's voice tightened, but Sir Geoffrey's rumbled on: 'One of my chaps from Bush

House . . . or I've got one or two young correspondents coming along nicely here at the Agency.'

'Geoffrey!' said Sir Christopher sharply, his voice edgy with distaste. Sir Geoffrey, he could hear, was becoming maudlin, a state of mind – if you could call such crude apparatus as he had assembled within his thick head a mind – in which his affinity with bloodshed became positively Caligula-like. 'Geoffrey!'

'I know, old boy, I know,' said Sir Geoffrey and sighed again. He would have to get his chauffeur to deposit him outside the Bag of Nails and expend his aroused carnal appetite on one of the young women available there on the dance floor. Women were all the same in the dark. 'It'll have to be one of my mechanic chappies. I'll get someone onto it immediately,' he said.

'NV 2648, black Wolseley,' said Sir Christopher. They exchanged codes and Sir Christopher, alone again in the lamplit serenity of his office, turned a few pages of the Ruskin, calming his ruffled nerves in their ordered prose before putting the contraption away.

'*Wherever the workman is utterly enslaved,*' he read, '*the parts of the building must be utterly like each other; for the perfection of his execution can only be reached by exercising him in doing one thing, and giving him nothing else to do. The degree to which the workman is degraded may be thus known at a glance, by observing whether the several parts of the building are similar or not; and if, as in Greek work, all the capitals are alike, and all the mouldings unvaried, then the degradation is complete; if, as in Egyptian or Ninevite work, though the manner of executing certain figures is always the same, the order of design is perpetually varied, the degradation is less total; if, as in Gothic work, there is perpetual change both in design and execution, the workman must have been altogether set free.'*

Soothed, he replaced the book on its shelf, took down his Homburg hat from the peg behind the door, looped his covert coat over his long arm and loped down the stairway which grew ever broader, shallower and more magnificent as he descended. Tyson, in his shirt-sleeves, was sleeping mouth agape before his electric fire, an enamel mug full of orange-coloured tea at his elbow. Van Gogh, thought Sir Christopher, one of the early drawings. He inserted his key into the door and let himself out in the night.

At Heathrow Airport, the two professors fell into one another's arms.

'Pisti!' 'Gyuri!' they cried, as they flung their briefcases around each other's necks and embraced with loud smack-ings of the lips across the wide expanses of astrakhan-collared coating that separated them. Their guttural exchange provoked a raised eyebrow and a smile or two from the few passengers around at that hour of the morn-ing. 'Fancy seeing you here!' 'Where have you come from?' they cried in Hungarian, having separated three hours earlier at Cointrin and boarded, one, a Swissair, the other, a BEA flight to London. They moved off together, arm in arm, carrying their stomachs before them, resolved to share a taxi and breakfast again off scrambled eggs and sausages at the Royal Court Hotel before returning to their families in Cambridge and Oxford. Both had spent fruitless hours in expensive restaurants, Professor Kús at La Perle du Lac, Professor Nagý at La Bonne Auberge, endeavouring to coax the beautiful Miss O'Malley not to desert her native culture for an alien land. Both had hugely

enjoyed this exercise in the service of their adopted homeland.

Wiping the corners of his lips with his napkin, cocking
his bald head to one side, and exposing Miss O'Malley to
the irresistible twinkle of his bright brown eyes to which so
many women had succumbed, Professor Kús had pleaded:
'Don't go. Such a beautiful country. So deliciously deca-
dent. How can you leave it for such a horrible place?'

Serious for a moment, Melissa thought of Karl Marx in
his stable, bay coat gleaming with health and good groom-
ing, and the glorious gallops along the short, soft turf of
the Ridgeway as larks tossed about above them in the blue
spring sky. How can I, indeed, she thought and laughed
back at him, showing perfect pearly teeth within a rosy
mouth and mocking him with her wide grey eyes. Professor Kús felt for her hand under the table-cloth. 'You
are the essence of England!' he cried, deciding to forgo
the luxury of picking his teeth with one of the delicious
little paper-clad quills tempting him from their silver container beside his place on the table. 'The flower of the
most vunderful country in the world. Think of all those
teeny-weeny houses along the railway lines, each one with
its own pocket-handkerchief garden. Think of Dicey's
*British Constitution*. Think of roses, violets . . .' He faltered, unable to think of the names of any flowers other
than carnations, which were what he usually sent ladies
who had captured his attention. 'Think of our policemen,'
he continued lamely, 'and think,' his voice gathered passion, 'think of our incorruptible system of justice, our
judges in their wigs. Incomparable in the world!' Tears
gathered in the corners of his eyes and he dabbed at them
with the hem of his table-napkin. Melissa removed her

hand from the urgent clasp of his small paw. 'I'll think about it,' she had promised.

Professor Nagý's approach had not been dissimilar. He had removed his spectacles towards the end of the long meal and gazed at her with his soft black eyes until Melissa felt a warm blush creep up her neck and a faint melting sensation round the tops of her thighs.

'Dear child,' he had said, softly, 'sweet brave child. Ah, the wild madness of youth! You are bewitched by a noble philosophy in the hands of unscrupulous bureaucrats. Believe me, these men are not what you suppose. They care nothing for the faceless mass of common people, labouring without rest for the merest cabbage leaf to put in their miserable soup. Life in the Soviet Union is unbelievably tedious; their theatre a kind of prison system, limited to the work of a few nineteenth-century writers and some ponderous myths. No Shaw, no Fry, no Williams Tennessee, no Miller, no *Salad Days*, no *Oklahoma!* . . .' He paused. He had not actually been to the theatre since his wife had insisted he take her to *Oedipus and the Critic* at the New Theatre in 1947. But he heard about these things from his students and, sometimes, colleagues at unspeakable meals round chilly tables in North Oxford. 'No fun!' he continued. 'My dear child, how can you?'

Melissa trembled a little. She had indeed been offered a part in *The Crucible* alongside Ralph Richardson, no less. She thought of the cramped dressing-room at the Haymarket Theatre, the bright lights, the rows and rows of Leichner face paints and the door with her name, all on its own, on the outside of it. 'Don't,' she whispered, looking up at him from under her lashes, 'don't.' Without taking his eyes off her, Professor Nagý raised his arms and summoned a waiter. 'Two Armagnacs,' he said in heavily accented French, 'or would you prefer marc?'

'Armagnac's fine,' said Melissa, smiling at him. She thought of the foul Georgian brandy, fiery and sweet, which was the best she could hope for from now on and chased the last crispy caramelised crumbs of *vacherin glacé* from her plate. Professor Nagý smiled back at her, a slow, intense, deliberate smile. Leaning towards her he lowered his voice. 'And your mozza,' he said, impaling her on his burning stare, 'alone in the world. It will break her heart.'

'Don't!' said Melissa, angrily. 'D'you imagine I haven't thought about that, you capitalist toady, you economic pervert?' White as the narcissus petals in the centre of their table she pushed her chair back, flung the grey fur round her shoulders and swept out of the restaurant, looking neither to right nor left.

# Chapter Eleven

❧

In Sussex there were primroses in the woods, and a few violets. Patches of them grew on the banks at the edge of the big garden where it merged into field, and along the sides of the drive.

Victoria, in black trousers, gum boots, striped overshirt and Fair Isle gloves, had gone out on her own after breakfast and wandered among them. They always reminded her of her nanny, Miss Florence Smith, whom she had loved and whom she still wrote to. Smithy had taught her and her brother about 'the country', superior in every way to London or abroad. They loved it through her. When Victoria's parents proposed holidays in Houlgate and Menton, Smithy fought to take her charges to farms in Sussex and Hampshire and, at weekends, to Kew instead of Kensington Gardens. There they lay on a rug beside the big lake, reading books about fairies or working-class children like Ameliaranne Stiggins, and watched the birds, learning their names as they ate paste sandwiches and drank milk while Smithy drank tea, unfit for children, out of a Thermos.

These were important days; real life to Victoria and her brother, free of the restrictions and obligations of nursery life. Smithy laughed as she watched them climbing about on haystacks or feeding crumbs to the robins. They caught tadpoles and newts and brought them back to Bayswater and fed them little bits of meat on sticks.

Victoria's father was disgusted when he climbed the stairs to the nursery. 'Dirty things,' he growled, short of breath after the long uphill trek, as he peered through his thick glasses into the murky waters of the jam jars. Her mother feigned interest, but she was really more concerned with bowel movements and invitations to tea with her friends' children in their houses in Kensington and St John's Wood. Clean gloves on their hands, they would set off after rest on a No. 73 bus and play in top-floor nurseries with children in Daniel Neal clothes like their own. The point of these excursions for Victoria was cake, only permitted in the Benjamin nursery on birthdays. She never really wanted any company other than Smithy's, who read to her, taught her to make paper boats or to sew with jewel-coloured threads on pieces of canvas with big holes in them, and told wondrous stories of her own childhood with her four sisters and two brothers.

'Can we go and see your mother, Smithy?' the children would ask, holding her hands and jumping up and down in their spoon-toed Start Rite shoes. Mrs Smith was getting on for a hundred and lived in a dark flat in Kilburn. There was something wicked about flats. Proper people lived in houses with a cook in the basement and children on the top floor below the maids in the attic. Mrs Smith lived on one floor and the rooms were close together. She had an ostrich egg in a glass case above the mantelpiece and lots of books in dark green and maroon-coloured covers with stories in them about little girls and boys who picked bunches of wild flowers and, guided by God, gave them to old gentlemen dying in workhouses. There were always pink meringues for tea. Victoria, who was going to be a ballet dancer when she grew up, worried about being fat even then, but she ate her cake and had it in those days, in her dreams which were entirely satisfactory and filled with princes and maidens and gossamer dresses, summer and winter; pink, turquoise and yellow.

She was cold now, though a thin sun glinted from a watery sky. May, the great turning-point of the year, when she was allowed to change her scratchy Chilprufe vest for an Aertex one, had not yet arrived. She smiled to herself, lifted her head, waved her arms about like wings and breathed in the damp mushroomy air. She started picking primroses, keeping her knees straight to exercise her waist. They smelt faintly of honey and the petals, if you sucked the pimple at their base, tasted of honey too. She forgot the time and went on picking primroses, humming 'April in Portugal' to herself. Amalia Rodriguez, the great Portuguese *fado* singer, was one of the Programme's steadies. They had shown a clip of her singing in the first Programme and once, interviewed her down the line from Paris.

Alone on the moss, Victoria danced to the music through the bare trees, shaking her shoulders, swaying her knees and turning round and round. The bunch of primroses was getting untidy, the ones she had picked first straggling out of the middle. If Smithy had been there, she would have had a ball of green wool in her handbag to tie them up with. Vivien's face, with its creases, was not unlike Smithy's. Perhaps she would have some green wool. She had better give them to her anyway, though she would love to take them back to Holland Park and place them one by one in cups and egg-cups around the flat. She turned back towards the flint house and felt a sick flutter in her stomach. She had left the others round the breakfast table locked in conversation. Guy was reading out a letter from an old friend in foreign parts. They discussed his behaviour in such intimate detail that Victoria was slightly shocked. She had wanted to go to the lavatory and looked at Harold across the table for help.

'Do go on,' he was saying, salaciously. So she left, in terror of being noticed and tiptoed upstairs to a small closet she had found at one end of the passage. Then she had let herself out of the house into the clean cool air and her heart lifted, as it always did, under wide empty skies.

Harold was vaguely conscious of her absence. He wondered where the hell she had got to. So far she had not been too much of an embarrassment and, thankfully, had kept her mouth closed when Vivien asked after his new bookcase. He would not have put it past her to chirrup up with some ghastly clodhopping statement about its provenance. He knew that Vivien, with her exclusive and idiosyncratic view of the world, would be likely to resent her and he felt uneasy about exposing her to such a rigorous – and rigged – initiation into his inner circle. But some aridity at its heart had compelled him to do so. He hoped she realised what a privilege it was. She appeared now, holding a large bunch of primroses and his heart hopped with pleasure before he pushed it down again into its proper place.

'My dear, how lovely,' said Vivien, accepting them. 'It's been a wonderful primrose year. The house has been full of them for weeks.'

'Sit down,' said Guy, thinking how pretty she was. He pulled out a chair and offered her a newspaper. '*Melissa O'Malley. Foreign Office Enquiry Reveals Secret Spy Network*', she read, over and over again, trying to appear absorbed by its contents. Silence fell on the table. Guy studied the shares columns in the *Financial Times*, Harold turned the pages of the *New Statesman* and Vivien went off to play the piano. It was only eleven o'clock in the morning.

That night Victoria lay among the ageing forget-me-nots trying to think lascivious thoughts. She had put touches of *Mouche* under her arms, between her breasts, in her navel. She could not bring herself to go further.

The day had not been without its pleasures. As the sun prevailed over the clouds and smiled down on the nut trees in the copse, Guy and Vivien had decided to go for a picnic. A Spanish basket, just like the ones in seventeenth-century paintings by Velázquez, had been packed, and Guy had backed his old Rover out of the garage. Carrying rugs and bottles of wine, they had settled themselves into the car which Guy drove as if he were riding an upright bicycle, and climbed in low gear to the top of the Downs. There, in the clean wind, Victoria's spirit soared.

They walked for a while along a blunt, bow-headed ridge and settled on the grass in a windless hollow. There had been cold omelette to eat, home-made bread, cheese and apples. Guy had poured wine into real wineglasses. They were clearly practised picnickers. After lunch they had walked down the smooth green curves and Victoria had started running. Breathless, in the wind, she had lain down on the turf and rolled. It was pricklier than it looked. She had picked herself up at the bottom feeling more ruffled than she would have wished and very foolish, but her action had passed without comment. In the evening they had driven out to dinner with a neighbour and friend, whose amorous adventures provoked much beady speculation of an indulgent kind on the way.

Lady Rose Stewart was a small stocky woman with a pointed face, its skin as creased as a tortoise's neck, and twinkly blue eyes. She wore jeans on her sturdy legs, an amazing many-coloured mohair sweater and a diamond necklace. She wore lipstick, too, and cooked a delicious dinner which they ate at a scrubbed wooden table in a big kitchen with a stone floor and an Aga cooker. Lady Rose admired Victoria's scent and seemed familiar with the Paris house from which it came. She also seemed to know some of the actors and directors Victoria had on the Programme from time to time and, in between long stretches of conversation about a cavalcade of unknown characters, including Clare, made chuckling asides to her about them. She called her 'darling' and asked her to carry the plates.

Back at the flint house under the Downs, Victoria had climbed the back stairs to her room alone in the dark. She knew if she tried harder she could do better and she lay now under the blankets with the night air blowing in on her from the open window, hesitant fumes hinting at unthinkable caresses and intimacy under the bedclothes unfurling themselves in her cold body.

It was a long time before Harold turned the knob and stood in his odd garb in the doorway. Victoria held out her arms and shut her eyes. When she opened them again she saw that he was pacing the room, pausing now and again to peer at himself in the maple-framed mirror above the basin. He shed his jacket and sat on the edge of the bed, his head in his hands. Victoria put out a hand and gently scratched the hair under his armpit. When it provoked no response, she slid it round the loose soft skin of his upper body and scratched under his other armpit,

gently pressing and circling with her fingertips. She felt
bold and wanton like a courtesan pleasuring a sultan. A
book by a new French writer had recently come onto her
desk. It was called *The Law*. A scene from it had impressed
itself on Victoria's consciousness. Naked, she crouched
beside Harold's seated body, reached down and started
stroking his legs, first one and then the other, very slowly,
upward towards his groin. The caressing motions she was
making, though they made her arms ache, seemed irresistibly lascivious to her and she was thrilled to hear Harold
give a deep groan. She crept her fingers towards the opening in his underpants.

'Don't,' he said and pushed her with his elbow between
her breasts back onto the pillow. 'Don't.' He lifted the
bedclothes and lay on his back beside her, one arm over
his face. 'It's too embarrassing,' he mumbled.

Victoria turned to him, her breasts rubbing against each
other in the dark. She felt for the waistband of his pants,
slid her hand underneath it and moved her fingers slowly
down towards – towards – she did not like to think . . .

'Ouch,' said Harold.

Victoria was startled. This was not the response the
book had led her to expect. Suddenly he rolled away,
turned his back on her and curled himself up into a ball:
'It's no good,' he muttered. The house, container of so
many of his aspirations and failures, held him like a silent
witness in a network of reminders and reproach. 'It's not
right. I can't,' he said. He clenched his hands and drove
them hard against his eyeballs.

'What's the matter? Oh, Harold, what have I done
wrong?' whispered Victoria.

'Help me,' said Harold. 'Help me.' He swung his legs
out of the bed and sat on its edge. 'I must see a psycho-

analyst.' He got up, picked his coat from the floor and left the room.

'Harold,' called Victoria, 'Harold, Harold, Harold!' But only the moon, now on the wane, looked in on her and cast a silver shadow as it sailed across the night sky and faded into dawn.

# Chapter Twelve

%

'What seems to be the trouble?' said Dr Lemaitre. He put
the tips of his fingers together and stared gravely at Harold
from under his bushy eyebrows. Harold sat facing him, a
few feet away in an upright leather chair with wooden
arms. He had put on his best suit, plain dark blue, for the
occasion and was wearing an ordinary tie of dark red
foulard with one of his cream silk shirts. He had polished
his shoes. Dr Lemaitre's chair was bigger and squashier
and had padded leather arms. He was wearing a bow tie
of navy blue with white spots. His room, in the quiet
South Kensington house, was lined with bookshelves and
there was a couch covered with a sort of carpet against
one wall, a small hard-looking pillow at one end of it.

Harold's mind broke up in confusion and particles of
thought milled round inside his head. They went faster
and faster and his heart beat uncomfortably hard. Camp
commandants, headmasters; he knew the situations well
and was accustomed to beating his way out of them with
a mixture of charm, disdain and counter-attack. This time
he was trapped, of his own volition, for an hour and a
half – the length of a first consultation: subsequent sessions, should he opt for them, to last an hour.

There was a long silence in which the particles subsided

somewhat. As they settled, Harold gathered his wits and looked sharply at Dr Lemaitre, waiting for a clue. But Dr Lemaitre said nothing, continuing his grave regard, his face perfectly still. Harold began to get angry. He was paying the fellow twelve bloody guineas. He was damned if he was going to do his work for him. He stared impudently back at the doctor who, according to all Victoria's assiduous research and his own few casual enquiries, he had been assured was the best man in the entire psychoanalytic establishment for his case. Minutes ticked by. He could hear them on his own chunky Rolex watch acquired during his last visit to Rome from a street vendor, who had approached his table in the Piazza Navona. The watch had later turned out to be an R *punto* Olex. He squirmed at the memory, but it had made a good story.

But what was he doing? He rearranged his stare, making it fiercer and more menacing. The fellow did not flinch. He seemed rock-like, positively monolithic. Harold sneered mentally and a biting remark formed itself in his mind but no word came to his lips. It would be a giveaway. He must preserve perfect composure at all cost. He glared at Dr Lemaitre, tightened his grip on the arms of his chair and found himself in the cockpit of his Blackburn, enemy flak sputtering all round as his own aircraft juddered sickeningly from the force of machine-gun fire emitting from its own tail. His heart thumped in his throat and he clenched his teeth. One day, he knew, he would crash. He glanced nervously at Dr Lemaitre, grateful momentarily for his solid presence and the Turkey carpet, unmoving in its pattern beneath their feet. He felt furious with the doctor for failing to protect him.

'I'm so unhappy,' he blurted out, and the room disintegrated around him; books, couch, carpet, the good doctor and his own self all swimming around in a tidal wave of unexpressed emotion. Harold let go of the chair arms and clasped his hands between his knees. They were trembling. He gripped them together and forced the panic, for he knew it was that, back to its customary location in a tight black knot at the back of his head. He looked the doctor in the eyes, willing him to put his foot in it. A suave remark, an empty generalisation, a figurative pat on the shoulder, a softening of the face was all that was needed and he could file him away under 'phoney'. But Dr Lemaitre remained unmoving; his face, showing neither approval nor disapproval, turned attentively on his client. Harold shifted his eyeline and allowed his gaze to wander round the room. It was remarkably conventional, the titles of the books on the shelves betraying little but predictable professional interests. There were sets of Freud, Klein, Anna Freud, even Jung, some authors unknown to Harold in the pale almond dust-jackets of the Hogarth Press and a number of art books. He thought how nice it would be to lie down. Maybe that's all there was to psychoanalysis: a prone hour guaranteed on the hour every day of the week. He began to feel at home.

Dr Lemaitre cleared his throat. He looked at his watch. 'That seems to be it,' he said. 'I have a vacancy. Nine o'clock on Mondays and Wednesdays: a quarter to eight on Tuesdays and Thursdays. The cost will be ten guineas a session and I will send you the bill monthly. Will that be convenient?' He stood up. Harold shuffled awkwardly to his feet. He turned and made for the door. It seemed an awfully long way away. When he got there, greatly daring, he turned his head. The doctor was standing exactly as he had last seen him, still, solid and unwavering in his regard; a monolith in human form.

He let himself out of the room feeling as if he had swallowed a dose of shrinking medicine from *Alice in Wonderland*. The walls of the passage leading from the room he had just left to the door with the fanlight into the street seemed, from the corners of his eyes, to be made of shifting molecules. He heard the sound of a buzzer and a door to the right and ahead of him opened. A shadowy figure slipped out and murmured an apology or greeting as it slipped by. Something about the thin vowels and clipped consonants stirred an uneasy note in Harold's brain.

Light and the living warmth of the day struck him as he stepped into the street. He squared his shoulders and dropped into it, running down the steps with his hands in his pockets like an impenitent schoolboy dismissed from an inconclusive interview.

Why – Volnicek! he thought, as he walked down the street in the May sunshine. Volnicek, that pathetic Czech, who had hung round Melissa with his sad dog eyes in hopeless courtship in Geneva and followed them everywhere. Volnicek, of course; still floating on the ebb-tide of war, rudderless, round Europe. He knew too much about Harold's own flirtations, political and personal. How embarrassing.

'How did it go?' said Victoria. 'What happened?'

'Nothing,' said Harold. 'It's private. Have a drink.'

They were in his flat and he had laid a table in the drawing-room for dinner, covering it with a white cloth and decorating it with some fairings from the mantelpiece. He was informed by an acute sense of narrow escape but on sufferance only. It was an uncomfortable feeling. He had shaved again and greeted Victoria with warmth and a tender embrace. Victoria was encouraged. It's going to be all right, she thought. She herself had been to two psychoanalysts and told them, with tears in her eyes and some omissions, of the distressing events in the flint house under the Downs two weekends ago. One analyst had been able to see her almost immediately. A youngish man, dark and fleshy with a rose in his name, he had come out so clearly on her side, that she discounted him at once. He looked at her as men usually looked at her, with admiration, and offered to take her on as a regular patient and to see Harold as well. Victoria had left his Hampstead consulting-room uncomforted and distraught, her feelings of hurt and confused desperation as acute as ever.

The other, whom she had gone to see in Harley Street, charged her twelve guineas. He was an elderly man, small and dapper with a sharp bird face and a quizzical expression in his eyes. He had asked some shrewd questions which went some way towards stilling the frightful turmoil round Victoria's waistline, and used cricketing similes. But he, too, had patted her on the back as she rose to leave. 'I think your boyfriend needs a trick-cyclist,' he had said, lifting an eyebrow. As he shook her hand he had made no further offer.

Victoria knew he was right about Harold, but suspected that both were wrong about her. She tried, however, to believe them. She had taken time off from the Programme to see them, sending her secretary out to choose clips from old Bing Crosby films, because Roderick was due to interview the star on a golf course the following week. She had also missed a morning conference. It had been strange to be at large in the city by day. She had forgotten about children going to school and women with shopping baskets. She found she was wearing less make-up these days and leaving the Programme early to buy food for the dinners with Harold on which she was spending all her money. Her secretary had returned from the film-viewing saying stolidly, 'I didn't choose anything. I didn't know what to do.' Victoria had had to take what the film company offered which she knew was second-best. There were more staff on the Programme and Victoria felt sometimes that she did not know what was going on.

Harold looked at Victoria standing in front of the electric fire in the fireplace in his drawing-room and decided to kiss her. She was wearing a white shirt patterned with orange flowers and an orange woollen suit with a rather short skirt. He found her outfit disturbing, so he grasped her to him, shut his eyes and brought his mouth down on hers. Victoria, unprepared, accepted the embrace as enthusiastically as she could. She kept her eyes open and counted the seconds. When she got to a hundred and twenty-one Harold let her go.

'He kissed me for three minutes,' she told her friend Rosalynn on the telephone next day. 'That's very good,' said Rosalynn, an expert on sex.

Harold put a Beethoven quartet on the gramophone, poured wine into glasses and lit the candles. He had bought supper: salami, mortadella, hard-boiled eggs, Greek bread and two cakes from the grocery down the road.

'What did you do today?' he said, as they sat down to eat it.

Oh, how lovely, thought Victoria, laying her napkin over her knees. With shining enthusiasm, she answered him. 'We had Bing Crosby on film from Sunningdale Golf Course. Roderick interviewed him. And we had clips from some of his films. And we had Dr Azikiwe from Nigeria.

121

He came in amazing white robes over his suit. You could see he had trousers and shoes on underneath, and—'

'But what did you *do*?' said Harold. 'You're just making a list of the boring people you had on your boring programme.'

'They're not boring,' said Victoria before she could stop herself and added quickly, 'What did *you* do?' Harold glared at her. 'Oh, yes, of course. I mean, what else did you do?'

Harold sighed. 'Haven't you got any gossip?' he said in a disappointed voice.

It was a question, Victoria found, that he quite often asked and she was not sure what he meant by it. Did he mean titbits of information about other people's private lives? If so, she knew very little of what Owen did — apart from trying to take her out to dinner, or Andrew or Gregory, who both had wives and children, out of Programme hours. There were not many of them left in the day anyway. She knew more about Roderick's extra-marital romances, but that was confidential. She was sure he did not want to know about her brother or Rosalynn's new baby son, and she hardly saw anyone but him any more.

'I don't think I have,' she said, apologetically.

'Oh for Christ's sake,' said Harold, pulling a piece of salami rind out of his mouth. 'You're such a prig.'

Victoria sat tight. He must like her to have kissed her so long. She smiled at him. 'Can I have the salt, please?' she said.

'Don't be so hypocritical,' said Harold.

'Salt, please,' said Victoria.

'Don't be so bloody domineering,' said Harold.

Victoria took a mouthful of hard-boiled egg. 'Please,' she said, 'could you let me have the salt?'

'You're so affected,' said Harold. He munched on in silence. After a while Victoria said, 'I say, Harold!'

'Yes,' said Harold.

'I want some salt for my hard-boiled egg. D'you think you could pass me some? It's by your plate.'

'Can't you speak naturally?' said Harold. 'You sound just like a schoolmistress, all prissy and spinsterish.'

'Harold,' said Victoria, 'salt, please. Salt.'

'Don't bully me,' said Harold.

Victoria gave a little whimper of supplication. 'Please,' she said softly, putting her head on one side. 'May I have the salt?'

'Stop trying to manipulate me,' said Harold. He reached out for the *Evening News* lying on the button-back velvet chair nearby and started reading it.

Victoria tried to mix salami and egg together in her mouth. But she would have liked some salt. She leaned forward and stretched out her hand. Harold lowered the paper and scowled. Victoria began to cry. Harold felt calmer. Behind the paper, a sense of composure settled on his chest. She could sweat it out there, he thought, on the other side of the table. He read the paper thoroughly. There was only one item referring to Melissa, a small paragraph saying that Mrs O'Malley had been admitted to a gentlewomen's retreat in the New Forest. An uneasy thought oscillated at the back of his mind: Dr Lemaitre. He almost looked over his shoulder. He was not altogether sure he could handle him. He wished Victoria would bring him some coffee. That was what was needed now to go with the Greek bun. 'Show a sign of life, can't you?' he muttered.

123

But Victoria was in the kitchen. She had started on the pile of dirty crocks piled in the sink with her fingertips, trying not to get her hands wet in the soapy water, and she had put the coffee on. In a few minutes the tin pot was at his elbow and Victoria back in the kitchen, drinking hers at the sink. Gulps and sniffs shook her from time to time as she worked and she shut the door, fear surmounting hope, but it was lonely in there all by herself and she opened it again. She had left her cake on the plate, so, abstractedly, Harold reached out a hand and put it on his. He was reading the paper through again, this time from back to front and it was beginning to bore him. They could make it up in bed, he thought, where all proper communication between men and women took place. He would like to have heard more about Zik, as the Nigerian leader was called, but he was damned if he was going to hear about him from a woman; from Victoria at any rate. Her place in television rattled him: he would have to dislodge her from it if they were going to go on seeing one another and they might as well. She would lead him back into normal life.

Victoria came into the room and started to clear the table. Harold put down the paper and yawned. 'I'm going to bed,' he said, 'don't be too long.'

At least he wants me to stay, thought Victoria, and her heart gave a feeble hop.

The bedroom was in its habitual state of chaos, doors and drawers open and bedclothes heaped on the bed in an unyielding mound. The window was open too, letting a waft of sharp night air in from the rooftops. Harold sat on the bed in his underpants, leaning on his knees. He groaned as Victoria came into the room.

Keeping her eye on him for signs of disapproval, she

closed the window. 'We can open it later,' she said softly, slipping her feet out of her shoes and immediately stumbling on one of his, lying on its side on the carpet. 'Ow!' she squeaked and clapped her hand over her mouth. Harold raised his head, teeth bared and dropped it again, in dejection, on his chest. Victoria started heaving at the sheets and blankets. She shook them out, arms aching with their unhelpful weight and laid them on the mattress, making the bed round Harold as best she could. There were papers under the bed, letters and pages of typescript, but she left them there. She began to take off her clothes; laying them over the top of a cupboard door. She did not like to disturb the strewn surfaces of the other possible alternative spaces.

Harold caught a glimpse of her in her satin slip. He wriggled out of his underpants as fast as he could and rolled into bed. Victoria opened the window and jumped in beside him. She had a habit of bouncing onto the bed before getting in under the bedclothes and making violent nesting motions as she settled them round her. Vestiges of the habit obtained on this bleak night even. Harold paused a moment or two, his rampant penis lifting the sheets and blankets, before throwing himself on top of her.

Why can't she respond, he thought, as he wrestled with her passive flesh.

What's wrong with me, thought Victoria, as his penis drove into her. She turned her head to avoid his lips.

Fuck it, thought Harold, fuck her. Fuck. He liked it better this way really, when there was no fear of drowning. He knelt up and forced her head up and down. Lips compressed, smothered in the dark den of moving flesh and pubic hairs, Victoria struggled to breathe. She opened her mouth for air and he was in, rammed right up to her throat and making her gag. Good heavens, she thought. Next moment she was flooded with warm sticky fluid. Whatever was she meant to do? Then she swallowed – it seemed politer, wondering if it was fattening. The taste was yeasty. It must have some nutritional value, maybe you could live on it on a desert island. Harold subsided onto the bed, turned on his side, pulled a blanket round his shoulder and, holding it there with one hand, settled for sleep. Victoria tapped her lips up and down and rubbed her tongue against her teeth. The seminal fluid lay thick in her gullet. She got up to get a drink of water to wash it down. Harold tightened his grip on the blanket and bored his head into the pillow. Victoria put the glass of water on the floor beside the bed and pulled the sheet up round her neck. She edged closer to the warmth of Harold and he jerked away. She pushed her pillow as close to his head as she dared and lay on her back. Salt, she thought, salt. Perhaps there's another word for it I should have used. She closed her eyes and lay still.

And as she lay there, she became aware of a strange sensation like a tickle just outside the range of her consciousness, beyond the quiet and regular hiss and blow of Harold's breathing, apart from the slow seething of her own bruised thoughts. She caught a sound and froze. A faint dry scratching noise was coming from the direction of the window. She lay still on her back, alert and tense, and felt with her elbow for Harold's spine. Something else was breathing out there in the night. Victoria dug her elbow slowly into Harold's back and held her breath. Cold fear hardened in the pit of her stomach and sent chilly fingers prickling up the back of her neck. Her scalp contracted like a mouth at the taste of raw lemon. It was a horrible feeling. Harold stirred, grumpily.

'There's someone there,' Victoria breathed in his ear, 'outside the window.'

'Don't be ridiculous,' mumbled Harold, shifting his position.

'But there is,' breathed Victoria again. 'Listen!'

The noises had stopped. An image of Dr Lemaitre's unblinking eyes, steady under his bushy brows, passed across Harold's mind. 'Wishful thinking,' he whispered, viciously.

'What do you mean?' Victoria whispered back.

'You want someone to come in and rape you, that's all,' said Harold. He hunched himself into the bedclothes. The blankets were scratching his chin and he fumbled for the sheet twisted somehow limply round his waist from the recent amorous skirmish.

'Please go and see, please,' whispered Victoria. 'I know there's someone there.'

'Speak properly,' said Harold, testily. He gave an eloquent yawn or two then threw back the bedclothes, and swung his legs to the floor. 'I suppose I'll have to,' he said. 'You are a bore.' He made his way to the window, pushed it up and looked briefly to right and left. Then he came back to bed.

'What did you see?' said Victoria, still whispering.

'Nothing, of course. Now shut up and go to sleep,' said Harold. He turned his back to her again and pulled the bedclothes round him. Victoria lay on her back staring at the window, then she turned and fitted herself round the curve of his back, pulling her pillow as close to his as she could. I'll never go to sleep, she thought.

*

Outside, in the gully between the slopes, Volnicek pressed himself against the slates. He had been on the roof for hours. 'Peaceful use of nuclear fusion . . . peaceful use of nuclear fusion . . .' he kept repeating to himself. Sometimes, he murmured it out loud through chattering teeth. He was frightened and miserable, though misery was not an appropriate emotion for someone in his position. Science had made it possible for the human race to commit suicide. Scientists – and psychoanalysis, his discipline, based on systematic investigation into the infrastructure of human behaviour, was a science – were responsible for preventing it doing so.

He looked up at the sky and tried to consider the terrible effects on that sky and the unthinkable consequences for all mankind below if he failed in his quest, but all he could think about was his socked foot, sopping and icy cold from the little pools of dirty rainwater lying in the gully. He lifted it carefully now and rubbed it tenderly against his calf. The movement gave him little comfort and only made his right leg colder. He would have to stay up there at least until the seedy restaurant below opened in the morning and he could slip out the way he had come, via the lavatory window on the second floor.

He shuddered at the memory of the short climb thence onto the roofs, his feet scrabbling on window-ledges, his thin hands clutching at old drainpipes. At least two small pieces of plaster had become dislodged and crumbled with a hideous clatter into the darkness below on the way up.

The sound reminded him of pebbles tumbling down steep slopes in the Tatras Mountains where he and his sister, warm and singing at each other with elation, had so often hiked in his days as a young doctor before the war. He had been clothed, then, in the finest Loden, reliable and waterproof, his feet in stout Swiss Bally boots, a good sleeping-bag in his rucksack.

Maybe he should climb down now before first light. A few hours on the lavatory would do him no harm. But he should go back. His search was not yet complete, though he had one promising page of a letter in his pocket. '*My dear Harry,*' it read, '*Mummy and I often think of you and the rabbits in the cornflowers. Last week it was her poppy red birthday. We went to a show in town and the roof of the theatre was full of buttercups. Afterwards, we had supper at the Trocadero. We gave in our white rose coupons and had soft roes and antirrhinums on toast, followed by shepherd's pie and thistles . . .* '

The style was familiar and he knew enough to recognise the encoded symbols standing for details of construction, materials and positional relationships essential in the development of a new generation of thermonuclear weaponry. But he ought to return. He dared not leave any trace behind for the others to find. The least clue would set either of their mighty atomic institutions on track. They would get there in the end, of course, but time – and time alone – could provide the space for openness and sanity to prevail over the deluded excesses of the Cold War. It was the only hope.

Besides, on a pitifully mundane level, Volnicek needed his shoe, not that Fox would ever notice anything amiss in the disgusting pigsty in which he lived. His heart went out to Miss Benjamin lying so sweetly coiled in the bed beside him just a few feet away. What scenes he had witnessed! Spying was a poor way to describe his activities these days: scopophiliac would be more accurate.

Volnicek thought he detected a faint paling of the sky behind the chimneypots. He collected his straying thoughts and resolved to stay where he was until the couple left the flat. He hoped they would leave early for work. Ever so cautiously he edged further along the gully to where a group of king and queen chimneys provided him with some cover, though heavens knew, not much, and started playing through *From the House of the Dead*, from its first plaintive notes to the final crushing climactic bars, in his head.

Lying in the bed on her back, Victoria put her hand on her stomach. It was nice and flat. She sucked it in further so she could feel her hip-bones and wished she could keep it like that all day. Soon she would have to get up and go to work, calling in at her flat on the way to change her clothes. Should she have her bath here or there, she wondered. Both ways there were disadvantages: if she bathed here she would have to put dirty clothes on her clean body, and if she bathed there, she would have to dress without washing which she hated. She decided to bath in her own flat and supposed she would be late again at the office.

Harold had left ten minutes earlier for Dr Lemaitre. He had put on a suit and a clean shirt without washing. But he had shaved with great care and selected a very dark tie with dull stripes in it and run off down the stairs without any coffee. Victoria had offered to drive him in the van, which she was going to have to give back soon, and Harold had refused with disdain, clicking his tongue and frowning as though she had made an indecent suggestion. Victoria felt sure Dr Lemaitre was going to do him good and she looked forward to feeling the benefit of his treatment soon, herself. She would have liked to talk to him and hear what he had to make of Harold's behaviour:

was it unusual or did he think, as she did, that it was all her fault? She had faith in him and the magical process of psychoanalysis.

It was a wet grey morning and she watched drops of rain running into one another and making long irregular streaks on the outside of the window. They were slowed down versions of rain patterns, flattened by speed against train windows. As children, she and her brother would lick at them from inside as they rushed, hyni-minoosh hyni-minoosh, across Europe, and the black smuts swept by against a changing landscape.

A scratch, a rustle, a dragging sound and a tap. She lay still, her eyes and thoughts transfixed. Once as a little girl, but old enough to have her own bedroom, she had woken at first light in a farmhouse where the Benjamin children and their nanny were spending the summer holidays. Getting up early was not allowed, even waking was a minor sin. Outside the window, muddled up in the ivy, she could see the thick black body of a boa constrictor. Rigid with terror, she had lain there for a nameless age, watching in the silence and not daring to move. 'Get up, Vicky-Ticky,' Smithy had said cheerfully, as she came in at half past seven. Life and hope came in with her. 'Ssh,' said Victoria mouthing the words, 'there's a boa constrictor outside.'

'Oh, Vicky-Ticky,' Smithy had said, going over to the window. 'It's the drainpipe. Look!' She had opened the window wider and touched it. Then she came over to the bed and hugged Victoria. 'Put on your clean liberty bodice quick and come down,' she had said. 'You can have mushrooms for breakfast.'

It could not be a boa constrictor now – though the Zoo was not far away, and the faint slithering could come from the movement of a long black eel-like form snaking across the slates. Don't be ridiculous, she thought in Harold's words.

She sat up but held the sheet round her with one arm. The hands of her watch on the floor were nearly at eight. When she raised her eyes again, a pale face was pressed against the glass. She caught a glimpse of it, a single frame, and it was gone. She gasped and her heart beat so hard in her throat she could not breathe. Her legs were trembling and as she forced them to the ground, her body seemed to slip away from her down towards the floor, leaving her head pin-sized and detached. Dragging the sheet with her she went to the window and looked out. Nothing was there. And then, from the corner of her eye, she caught the flash of a trousered leg disappearing round the corner of the roof behind the chimneypots. It was impossible but the image was printed on her mind's eye. She leaned her head right out of the window and called loudly, 'Is anyone there?' Her voice came out as a squeak. She waited an instant, then closed the window and pulled the curtain across it. She turned back into the bedroom and picked up the shoe lying on the floor between her and the bed. It was rather more pointed than the ones Harold usually wore. She dropped it in the narrow wall-cupboard on top of the others lying higgledy-piggledy in a bumpy cliff at the carpet's edge and pushed the door shut. Then she went over to the telephone and dialled her brother's number. She was shaking.

'Hullo,' she said, when he answered. 'Hullo, sis,' he said in his deep, measured voice, 'I haven't seen you for a while. How are you?'

'I'm all right,' said Victoria.

'Are you at home?' said her brother. 'Ring me at the

office if you want a chat. Nice to hear your voice.' He rang off.

She could imagine him, already dressed in dark suit and tiny-patterned tie, getting on with his serious breakfast at the hinged flap that was his kitchen table, the *Financial Times* open beside him. His voice had steadied her heart. She made the bed quickly, keeping her eyes on the window as much as she could, dipped her face in cold water and put on her clothes. Then she ran down the stairs, waited till the street looked empty and made a dash for the van.

As she drove across London, the clouds broke up and patches of palest blue showed behind their drifting mass. She could miss the departmental meeting and go straight to her desk. She would wear her red corduroy jacket with its own matching skirt, gold earrings, black angora beret and – black polo-neck or cream Viyella shirt?

# Chapter Thirteen

ૐ

'Daddy's always late on Thursday,' said Alice. She was kneeling by the window looking down on the street and picking paint off the frame. She got her best fingernail, the one next to the little finger, inside a small blister and a most satisfactory strip peeled away.

'Mummy says he goes to a psychalist,' said Flora. 'What's a psychalist?'

'Dunno,' said Alice. She did not like thinking and hated being asked questions. Something was making her feel sad. She often felt sad, but mostly she felt bored.

'They put things inside your head,' said Flora. She was lying on the floor in her coat, colouring in a picture in her homework book. The picture was of a house with three people, a small one between two big ones, standing outside it. The house had a chimney on top, a path leading to a gate and flowers in the garden. She had just finished doing the sun yellow. Alice always drew stick-people and never coloured them in – well, sometimes she did little blue or red triangle skirts on the ladies. Flora wormed her way across the carpet to the window-seat, where Alice was now sitting with one leg folded under and the other dangling. Flora seized the dangling leg and rubbed her cheek up and down against its fawn sock.

'Darling, darling, darling, darling,' she said.

'Stoppit,' said Alice, giving her a mild kick. 'I'm not Mummy.' She turned to the window and began breathing on it. Flora scrambled up beside her and drew a face with her forefinger in the misty patch. For a few minutes they played a game, infused with some animation, of blowing and drawing on the window-pane. Alice stopped. 'I'm bored,' she said. Flora stood up and tried to puff enough air onto the glass to do a whole person before the patch faded. There had been a new car parked in the road since yesterday, a black one, outside the railings opposite their house. Flora tried to draw a car but it was a waste of time and she went back to people. 'Mummy's coming back tomorrow,' she said.

'No, she isn't,' said Alice.

'Yes, she is,' said Flora, 'I heard Heidi say so. She told Mrs Macguire, "Mrs Richardson's coming home tomorrow, so you'd better clean her bathroom", I heard her. Heidi has baths in Mummy's bath with Ivan. Soppy Heidi. I hate Ivan.'

'I know,' said Alice, 'and Mummy isn't coming back. I heard Heidi telling Vivien on the telephone. She said, "Mrs Richardson will be back early next week".' Flora stopped drawing and sat beside Alice on the window-seat. She started drumming her heels against the wood. 'Stoppit,' said Alice, 'you'll make a mark. Mummy'll be cross.'

Flora went on drumming. She began to giggle. 'Mummy says Harold's got a girl friend.'

'I know,' said Alice, 'I've seen her.'

'What's she like?' said Flora. Her own father often brought ladies with him when he came to see her. They were all different but some were French in high-heeled shoes and fur coats.

'All right,' said Alice, 'she's got a van.'

'Does she wear lipstick?' said Flora. She was still drumming.

'Lots,' said Alice.

'D'you think they'll get married?' said Flora.

'Of course not,' said Alice.

'Only in fairy-stories,' said Flora, 'people in fairy-stories get married.' She turned back to the window. 'Here he is!' she said, excitedly. 'He's coming!' She slid off the window-seat and dashed down the stairs. 'Harold! Harold! Harold! Harold!' Alice heard her call.

Her father's voice said, 'Where's Alice?' He came up into the room, put his hands on her shoulders and kissed her forehead. 'Come on,' he said, 'we'll be late. I've got a taxi waiting.'

They sat either side of him on the back seat. Alice looked out of the window, and Flora chatted away telling him about her homework. Newly introduced that term, she was enormously excited by it. She undid her miniature initialled satchel and showed Harold her book and the words she had copied with the pictures she had made beside them: dog, cat, sun, man, hat.

'Where's *your* homework, Alice?' said Harold. Alice shrugged. She went on looking out of the window.

'She's forgotten it!' said Flora. 'You did, didn't you? You left it. Oh, Alice.'

'For Christ's sake,' said Harold, turning on Alice, 'can't you do anything properly? It's because you're so disorganised. You should have a routine in the morning. I gave you a satchel. Why can't you remember it? Why?' Hopelessness overwhelmed him. They were late already. He dared not be angry with Clare to whom school was optional and incidental, nor could he give orders to the

136

au pair girl. It was his fault, anyway, for having failed in his marriage. The future filled up with deadly black, and despair engulfed his soul. 'Do you want me to go back for it? Do you? Speak,' he said, angrily.

Silently, Alice began to cry. Flora abandoned her satchel and books on the seat and crawled across the hairy mat on the floor of the taxi. She put her arms round Alice's knees and hugged them. 'Darling, darling,' she said.

Tears rolling down her face, Alice went on looking out of the window. She had not done her homework anyway, not so much because she did not want to as because she could not. She did not understand what was wanted. She did not know how to do it. She hated being late and she hated arriving by taxi. The tears ceased, mysteriously reabsorbed and she found, as usual, that she felt nothing. So she said nothing.

The taxi stopped outside the school, an ordinary-looking four-storey house in Hampstead, and Harold asked the taxi to wait. He put his hand on Alice's shoulder. Flora gathered up her things and he took them both up the steps to the front door, now closed. There, he rang the bell and kissed them goodbye. Schools made him uncomfortable.

Left alone on the doorstep Alice knew that, sometime round the middle of the morning, her satchel would turn up, its arrival in the middle of class embarrassing her further. A long, boring day stretched out ahead.

Harold ran to the taxi. He told the driver to go back to where they had come from. He hoped the silly little au pair girl would still be there; Mrs Macguire at any rate. As he left the taxi to fetch the satchel he, too, noticed the black car opposite the house and, behind the wheel, a man soundly sleeping.

*

Down in Sussex, the first bluebells were brushing the woods with dim indigo haze. Vivien had put on a straw hat to go out into the garden. She had a long flat basket in one hand and scissors in the other. She was cutting tulips and narcissi and some branches of horse chestnut with their limp leaves of tender green just now unfurling. She loved nature and the quiet pleasure of garden and field. Next she would go to the kitchen garden and cut some young chives to go with the salad she was making for lunch: tissue-paper shop lettuce, of course – all one could obtain these days, their own not yet being ready.

She and Guy had had some lively moments discussing Harold's young woman, a strange little creature from an alien world. They had not found her very amusing, but, of course, one must support dearest Harold in his curious adventures. Dearest Christopher was coming over that day from Brighton, where he had been on some semi-official expedition to the Pavilion connected with whatever work he now did in his Institute. An old friend from Cambridge days, his presence was always delightful.

She would prepare the salad, put the flowers she had gathered into some of the big majolica jugs she and Guy had collected on their travels and, perhaps, play a little on the piano before he arrived. The visits by members of their large circle of close friends were a continuing source of sustenance and texture in the humdrum life they led, tucked quietly away in the country with only the odd month here and there in the year spent in France, Italy and Spain; the journeys up to London to see an opera or a play at the theatre; the dinners and weekends passed at other country houses round about or further afield; the many letters received and written, and the evenings at home spent listening to BBC concerts on the wireless and reading aloud to one another before going up to the big bed in the long room overlooking the Downs.

Guy came out onto the verandah, his burly shape filling the window-frame, the shrimp-pink pages of the *Financial Times* flapping at his side. He raised his arm in a ho-ho-ho gesture of greeting and her heart quickened with affection. How she worried about his health. The warmth of the English sunshine could be deceptive in May and she was glad that they would be, before long, safely strolling together under the more reliable and mild skies of the Italian lakeside.

Guy went into the pantry, a cool room with a flagged floor. He poured a bottle of wine into a jug and upon reflection, added another. It had been a hell of a job siphoning the stuff from its barrel into the bottles. They had had to lie on the floor sucking on hosepipes for the best part of a day. He hummed 'The Chorus of the Hebrew Slaves', his big bass voice rolling agreeably round the room and among the stone shelves on which reposed rows of apples, Cheddar and Stilton cheeses, and eggs in baskets. It was nice to have the place filling up again after the rigorous austerities of the war and post-war years. He bore the jug into the dining-room, where the table had already been laid by Madame le Cul. Christopher was certain to have some amusing gossip with which to regale them. He relished the prospect. He was bringing some financial chap from the newspapers along with him, who, Guy trusted, would not interrupt the flow of anecdote too gravely.

Outside in the sun a midnight-blue Rolls-Royce turned into the drive and purred its way noiselessly to the front door. A heavy red-faced man, profusely whiskered, got out followed by Christopher, whose lean and elegant form unfolded itself and descended gracefully onto the sparsely gravelled space before the house beside him. Vivien was already at the door and Guy joined her in the hall. They greeted their guests with some warmth and Christopher introduced his companion, Sir Geoffrey Champman, who was wearing a double-breasted blue blazer with naval buttons, and sharply creased grey flannel trousers. Christopher himself was in ancient tweeds.

Champman, a greedy fellow it seemed to Guy, downed his sherry in a gulp and held his glass out for more before they had even sat down in the drawing-room, where intermittent sunlight playing through the windows lay in occasional pools of light on the worn and faded patches of the old rugs.

Guy warmed to Champman. He was interested in finance and dabbled in stocks and shares himself. He looked forward to a quiet word or two with him after lunch, and found his swaggering manner not unattractive. Vivien, however, he could see, found his presence odious and was struggling with her distaste.

'Do *tell* us, Sir Geoffrey,' she said, turning to him over the fish pie, '*what* it is ex*act*ly that you do. It must be so fascinating. We country mice lead such *dull* lives.' She turned away immediately, but Sir Geoffrey, impervious to such delicate nuance, boomed across the table. 'Dull! My dear Lady . . . er . . .'

'Mrs,' said Sir Christopher, quietly, 'Mrs Hammersley.'

'My dear Mrs Hamilton, dull would be the last word I could apply to your charming little place down here – an excellent cook too. May I help myself?' He heaped his plate with more fish pie covering the mound with a thick blanket of mashed carrot, and his voice bounced on making the very petals of the young narcissi in their painted jug shiver in its robust vibrations. 'So convenient for the great wen, ha, ha, ha. Under an hour, would you say, eh? Rhoda and myself have been thinking of buying a country place – something larger than this with a few acres.' He filled his glass from the rapidly emptying jug. 'Can't cost more than a few thou to run. We could set it off against tax. Rest and repose, y'know. Round here would be ideal for us. The boys are at Harrow. Make a nice little bolt-hole for them at weekends. We could get a few horses, build a swimming-pool. Mustn't let the young get bored.' He gave a rich laugh and his colourless eyes, light, bright and darting, took in the room. 'One of these new decorator chappies could set the place right in a trice. Give the little woman something to do. How much—'

'Geoffrey,' said Sir Christopher, 'Vivien and Guy are very interested in old books. Why don't you tell them about your first editions before we go?'

Guy got up to refill the jug, chuckling as he left the room. Vivien smiled at Sir Christopher. 'Tell me,' she said determinedly, 'what are you planning for the Pavilion? Such an exuberant construction. I've become quite *fond* of it over the years.'

Leaning backward in his chair and extending his lengthy legs under the table, Sir Christopher gave his old friend a selective account of the restorative work under review for the Royal Pavilion by the Fine Arts Commission. She had been a luminary of his undergraduate days, a great beauty and with her short hair, her boyish outline and her bold unconventionality, not unlike one of the androgynous figures of Florentine painting that had so entwined themselves with his young heart.

Guy filled Champman's glass and embraced him in discussion. He tried to lead him towards South Africa and the gold mines of the Rand where his own speculative interests lay.

At precisely half past two, Sir Christopher looked at his watch, a paper-thin Patek Philippe, and began to murmur his adieux. Whilst Sir Geoffrey went to the bathroom, as he called it, the three of them, standing in the hall, made a quick run-through of absent and mutual friends.

'And Clare?' said Sir Christopher, finally.

'In Italy again,' said Vivien. 'We expect her and the children for a week in June.'

When Sir Geoffrey reappeared amongst them, he grasped Vivien's hand in his. 'Most enjoyable, Mrs Hamilton,' he said.

Guy clapped him on the back. 'Guy and Vivien,' he said, heartily.

'Call me Geoffrey,' returned Sir Geoffrey. 'You must come up for a boardroom lunch. We've got a splendid new chef from Alsace – and I'd be most obliged if you'd keep your eyes open . . . something modest and Georgian with about eight or ten bedrooms . . . a stable block . . .'

Sir Christopher led him off towards the Rolls-Royce where the chauffeur, cap in hand, stood holding the door. As the car turned smoothly into the ruts of the drive, Sir Christopher raised his hand in a languid gesture of farewell and Sir Geoffrey, leaning back into the soft leather, felt in his breast pocket for his cigar case. Ah, the yeomen of England, he thought with some contentment.

For a while, the two men sat in silence as the big car rolled through the narrow lanes. Shades of green, inimitable in their tender newness, clothed the trees reminding Sir Christopher of his friend Stokes, an amateur who, notwithstanding, had a way with light and leaves in English landscape that was very beguiling. He opened the window a little, as much to bring in the exquisite greenness as to let out the not unpleasing smell of Sir Geoffrey's cigar. The wind ruffled his silver hair, but made no impression on his companion's dense cap, plastered as it was to his head by the application of expensive pomades. Beneath that well-maintained carapace, he knew, his colleague's mind would be working with acuity and speed, calculating chances, balancing risks and exploiting possibilities in abstraction.

'What Centre has discovered,' said Sir Christopher, in a barely audible murmur, 'is that the wretched Bohemian believes the only remaining trace of the material we require to be in the possession of a young man named Fox.'

'Who is not unknown to you, I take it,' said Sir Geoffrey, 'nor to the charming couple we have just left . . .?'

'Precisely,' said Sir Christopher.

'That means,' said Sir Geoffrey, 'that the first is immediately expendable and the second must be persuaded to hand over what we need before he, too, becomes expendable. Hah!' He spoke with gathering relish.

'More or less,' said Sir Christopher. He sighed and held his face to the narrow beam of air rushing in at him through the window.

'Procedures for the first are in hand, a word will set them going. But the second. What do you suggest?' said Sir Geoffrey.

'He has a daughter,' said Sir Christopher, his words scarcely perceptible from the breeze that filled the car, 'to whom he's very attached . . . intimidation . . . a little sharp pressure applied . . . a swift well-ordered operation . . .' His voice faded into the wind.

'Clare and the children – ah!' said Sir Geoffrey. He chuckled. 'Say no more, old chap.' The long ash on his

Havana trembled slightly in his hand but held as he took another slow puff.

The lanes had given way to double carriageway and the hills had flattened out as the fields were swallowed up by row upon greedy row of dull brick houses. Croydon, Purley, Streatham, Clapham. It was from deep in their midst that Sir Geoffrey's father, a dentist, had pinched and saved to educate his only son, thereby implanting in him deep loathing for petit-bourgeois values along with a thoroughgoing hatred for all things intellectual. He glanced at his colleague's fine profile. Arrogant turd, he thought. The early days of his service when, as a young recruit, he had penetrated SOE only to be cold-shouldered out of it by the effete upper-class bastards who ran it, flooded his mind with painful memories. He put out a thick hand and let it rest, with its manicured nails, on the bony tweed knee so sharply angled next to the triangular slab of his own grey worsted one. In the New Order there would be no elite: men of Sir Christopher's calibre would labour in the potato fields, or, at best, collect rubbish from the streets. Removing his hand and making a small flourish with it in the air he said, loudly: 'The News Agency will support your work of restoration in the Historic Buildings field, have no fear. I shall bring it up at the next meeting of our Charities' Committee. And now, where would you like to be dropped off? We can take you to the door if you wish.'

'No, no, no, dear Geoffrey,' said Sir Christopher, shuddering imperceptibly at the thought of such an ostentatious arrival upon the doorstep of his own discreet Institute. 'Hyde Park Corner, a No. 73 bus will do me very nicely.' Or, he thought to himself, a walk through the park. The blazing tulip beds and the swing of his own long legs would cleanse his mind and settle his thoughts down into scholarly working rhythms.

The car slowed down and paused outside Apsley House. Before the chauffeur could open it for him, Sir Christopher was out of the door, into the crowd and moving with rapid easy strides under the great stone arches of the gates. He crossed the road and disappeared behind the statue of Achilles. Anonymity was the vehicle he preferred.

# Chapter Fourteen

Professor Kús emerged from his rooms in college. He adored his rooms in the college with their crooked floors, their cosy fireplaces and their view over the sweep of the Great Quadrangle and the low grey sixteenth-century buildings with the Chapel soaring away to the left that surrounded it. He adored trotting the quiet pathways in his billowing gown with its scarlet hood to the lecture hall, and he adored the attention paid to his dazzling mind by the brilliant young men – and, happily these days, sometimes women – who came to him for tutorials.

It was not only tutorials that he was able to conduct so satisfactorily from the shelter of his Turkey-carpeted rooms with their leather sofas and armchairs, but many a pleasurable intrigue. He had just made an assignation with a young woman who had caught his eye at a reception in London the previous week. Clearly flattered by his academic eminence, she had agreed to meet him for a drink at the bar of the Royal Court Hotel that evening. He adored his beautiful wife and their children too, but they belonged on the other side of town across the river and beyond the city. But now, he must hurry to catch the train to London for lunch and the meeting with Pisti – or Steve as the English would have it. The two of them had their next moves to plan in detail.

Nimble on his small feet, he descended the dark staircase and came out into the light; sunlight for once. It was all so ordered, so unpretentious, so English. He adored England.

'Message for you, sir,' called the porter as he passed through the lodge. He came out from his room and handed the professor a piece of paper. 'Beautiful weather, sir. Exceptionally warm for the time of year,' he said.

'Vunderful,' said Professor Kús. He mounted his bicycle and pedalled slowly off down Trumpington Street, wobbling slightly and keeping firmly to the middle of the road. Other cyclists, speedier than he, swooped round him and the few cars on the streets hooted furiously as they slowed down and lined up behind him. Professor Kús peered around as he always did in perplexed surprise in search of the offender. What could be the cause of such untoward kerfuffle this sunny morning, he wondered. The movement caused him to wobble further and a lengthening queue of Austin Sevens and Morris Minors crawled at his back, their drivers changing down to first gear in resignation. A Volkswagen Beetle, greatly daring, nosed past him. 'Get a move on, prof,' shouted the driver through its open window.

'Vunderful day!' called Professor Kús, removing one hand from his handlebars in a dangerously unstabling gesture of reciprocal greeting. Arriving at the station, he dismounted and handed his bicycle to a porter. 'Nice day, sir,' said the porter as he wheeled it to the stationmaster's office.

'Vunderful,' agreed Professor Kús.

The train was already in the station and he opened the

door of the third-class carriage immediately facing him – he avoided walking wherever possible – and settled down in a corner seat with his back to the engine. He had at least an hour ahead of him in which to work on his next public lecture before he need sharpen his mind for the main business of the day, of all his days, in fact. He took out his pen and some folded paper from his pocket. There was another slip unexpectedly amongst them. 'Your six o'clock appointment is unavoidably cancelled,' he read, with increasing dismay. What a disappointment. Such a handsome young woman. If he remembered aright, she was fair-haired with remarkable breasts. He must telephone one of his other London girl friends as soon as he reached King's Cross. He began making notes in his tiny hand on the wad of paper on his knee, but the exertions of the morning soon overcame him and before the train reached Royston his head had dropped onto his chest and he was fast asleep, snoring comfortably to the rhythm of the wheels.

Professor Nagý arrived at the restaurant from Oxford in his car. He had driven the whole length of the A40 in third gear, his mind wrestling with physical conundrums of great complexity, as the car proceeded with extreme slowness along the smooth tarmac wandering, sometimes, across the white line down its centre. Every now and then, he pressed his foot hard on the accelerator and the green Riley leapt forward in a burst of exhilarating speed. At these moments, Professor Nagý, who thought of himself as a capable and experienced driver, lightened his grip on the steering-wheel, leaned one short arm casually on the window-frame and imagined himself to be in the company of a beautiful young woman – Miss O'Malley for instance

– whose cheeks went pink as the needle of the speedometer touched seventy mph, while her long hair and silk scarves drifted in the wind.

There was clearly something wrong with the engine, however, and he must return the car to his garage, whence it had so latterly come, upon his return next day. Much as he loved England, his chosen foster country, its workmen lacked the dedication of those in Europe. He avoided the word German, since its use as a model brought with it so many qualifications. Never again must this precious planet on which he so relished being alive get sucked into war through the dementia of a totalitarian regime. His eyes behind their thick spectacles moistened with emotion and the speed of the car dropped abruptly to twenty-five mph as his mind refocused. His work in the secret service of his new homeland caused him incalculable pride.

The restaurant where he was going to meet Gyuri – George as he was called these days – was tucked away behind St James's, a cosy club of which they were both members, and where the food was of a vague garlicky Frenchness. They both loved its red-checked table-cloths and its zinc bar. There was a definite Europeanness about it which made them feel delightfully conspiratorial, which was, after all, exactly as it should be. He parked his car within walking distance, in his case not more than fifty paces from the door, and hurried down the street, a busy figure in his brown suede brogues and his brightly checked tweed suit. He loved the Englishness of tweed.

Rapidly approaching from the other direction, he caught sight of Gyuri, his stout figure smartly encased in black and white chalk stripes, traces of that morning's breakfast and, no doubt, yesterday's dinner and lunch too, staining his jolly paisley-patterned tie.

'*Servusz!*' they cried as they collided in the narrow doorway. '*Hogy vagy?*' In England, one did not embrace so they shook hands and clapped each other on the back in true gentlemanly fashion. They had known one another since childhood when, along with the atomic physicist Jenö Wigner, the three boys had captured between them every prize at the Berzsenyi Gymnasium in all subjects, year after year. From opposite sides of the Atlantic the three of them were now ranged with their pugnacious compatriot, Teller, in immutable opposition to another old schoolmate, Leo Szilard now turned against the development of nuclear weapons alongside Bohr and Kapitsa. Nationality of origin had no meaning in the nuclear world order.

At the zinc bar, perched on stools, they ordered Pernods, consuming several as they waited for their table. Not until they were upstairs and tucked in behind the red-and-white cloth did they lean closer and begin the intense exchange of information for which they had come. Across the room, Victoria, lunching with a pale publisher, noticed them and thought how comic they looked.

'We have some urgent decisions to make,' said Professor Kús in his own language. 'Jenö informs me that it will take years for the laboratories in Arizona to work out all aspects of the configuration from scratch.'

'I, too, have something of interest to communicate,' said Professor Nagý. His eyes narrowed and his voice dropped. 'The office in Gower Street has informed me that the details we are searching for are in this country.'

'You know where they are!' said Professor Kús.

Before them were set little white porcelain dishes of hors d'oeuvres: sliced tomatoes, sliced eggs in thin salad cream, *cornichons* and tinned sardines. He helped himself to his third sardine.

'An ex-prisoner of war received them in coded form in his mail,' muttered Professor Nagý, withdrawing a fragment of sardine spine from the side of his mouth. 'The Camp Commandant who censored them was an anti-Nazi, a very great man of science who was working for us. The ex-prisoner lives not a mile or two from here – in Soho.'

'British?' asked Professor Kús.

'Fleet Air Arm,' said Professor Nagý.

Professor Kús whistled through his teeth, exhaling particles of egg as he did so. 'What makes you think he still has the letters?' he said.

'The British have a sentimental streak, especially the officer classes,' said Professor Nagý, shaking his head. 'It comes from their terrible system of education. Deprived as they are of natural affection, they cling to every crumb.' Professor Kús shook his head in sympathy. Both men were silent, overcome for a moment or two at this shortcoming in the nation they so admired in every – almost every – other respect. 'Besides,' continued Professor Nagý, 'I understand that the misguided Volnicek has been trailing him for some weeks. His co-operative is meticulous in such matters.'

'Indeed,' said Professor Kús. He had caught sight of an extremely pretty young woman on the other side of the room. As the waitress removed the plates, he gave her a long unblinking stare. Feeling his eyes, Victoria shifted in her chair. She half turned, her companion was extremely dull, but she turned dutifully back to him. Professor Kús noted her brown eyes. She was even prettier in full face. When the waitress, charmingly dressed *à la française* in short black skirt and saucy white apron, had placed their *gigot* and *flageolets* in front of them, he said, 'Can you be sure this air-seaman is the only source?'

'The Camp Commandant destroyed everything before he perished in the Russian advance,' said Professor Nagý. 'I knew him. We were research students together under Bohr.'

'Poor fellow,' said Professor Kús. Remembering that he had run out of carbon tetrachloride, he tucked his napkin under his chin and then, invigorated by the thought of action after so many arid weeks, and the failed mission to save Miss O'Malley for the nation, he said, 'One of my recruits shall be directed to enter the home of this man. I have a young graduate in the School of Anthropology who is most promising. A fiend of fitness, too.' He thumped the table with his fist.

Professor Nagý shook his head again. 'Hit and miss,' he said.

'Better still,' said Professor Kús, 'we will make friends with him. What is his circle? England is so small.'

Professor Nagý passed on to his old friend all that their Control at MI5 had told him of Harold: the profession of his father, the schools he had been to, the newspaper he read, the names of his lovers – they both sighed at the mention of Melissa – the address of his ex-wife, the size of his shoes. Both noticed Victoria as she left and their eyes met in unspoken comment over their mock-cream éclairs, as they continued their discussion.

By the end of the following week, they decided, at least one of them should be on friendly terms with Harold. They went through the names of friends and acquaintances whose circles touched his. When they left the restaurant, Professor Nagý turned east towards the London Library of which, as they knew, Fox was a member, and Professor

Kús turned north, making for the British Academy where that snake, Sharpe, was due to give a four o'clock address in front of the learned audience assembled there. He could sleep safely through such discourses, he knew, while his brain recorded in faithful detail every item pertinent to his mission, rejecting those of mere academic or aesthetic interest.

# Chapter Fifteen

Victoria put her face in the lilac and breathed deeply. To her delight, Harold had presented her with a bunch the previous evening. His self-deprecating smile, as he thrust them at her, went straight to her heart. She would have preferred white; it was more spectacular than mauve, which reminded her, anyway, of the thin tree straggling bravely out of the mean patch of earth beside her parents' front door steps.

'This is proper,' Harold had said, 'I hate white. It's so pretentious.'

Victoria was not sure which she ought to like best now. She had put them proudly in her vase, a two-pound jam jar.

'Haven't you got anything proper?' Harold said, tightening his lips. 'A real jug or something?' He opened the doors of the two cupboards in the kitchen and looked briefly at their contents: some plates and cups, a tin of corned beef, a packet of rice, three onions, olive oil, coffee, a few sheets and towels. 'You haven't got much, have you?' he said, turning away and leaving the doors wide. Victoria closed them. 'You must bash the stalks,' he had said, seizing a branch from the water where she had stood them, one by one. The lilac in the jar collapsed inwards, forlornly, and one branch fell out scattering tiny four-petalled florets on the draining board. Harold put the stalk in his mouth and chewed. 'You need a hammer, really,' he said through the leaves. He took off his shoe and hammered hard at the stem. More florets fell. Victoria took up a branch herself and chewed. It was woody, hard and tasted of London. Biting and battering, they had worked their way through the six stalks. Once Victoria had restored them to their container she carried them to the next room where she placed them grandly in the middle of the table.

They drove up in the van, flat out, to Soho, where they were to meet an old friend of Harold's and go out to dinner.

'Have you got any money?' he had asked on the way.

'No,' said Victoria. She was wearing a thin black alpaca dress with a pleated skirt and a big white piqué collar. Her gold star hung on a chain just below the collar as she had seen the mannequins at Dior wear their jewels, and she carried her flat black patent leather pochette.

'No?' said Harold. 'No! How do you think we're going to pay for dinner? Who do you think you are? You behave as if the world was made for your convenience.' He turned away from her and sat staring gloomily out of the window, hunched in his sharp pin-stripe which was buttoned lop-sidedly across his chest, his hands deep in his pockets. Victoria had said nothing. She hoped that if she made herself unobtrusive enough, he would change his mind. She drove, making as little movement as possible and they arrived at his flat, silently, just in time to open the door to Harold's friend.

The friend was a man with a legendary literary reputation and a limited number of slim volumes to support it. Small and tubby with babyish features inside a soft fat face, he spoke in fits and starts in a high, lisping voice dotted with occasional velvet chuckles. He and Harold spoke intently together about mutual friends, some of whose names Victoria was beginning to know. Then Harold, mystifyingly, had left them to hurry ahead and make sure of their table. Not one word had passed the friend's lips, despite Victoria's efforts, until they rejoined him in the restaurant some twenty minutes later. Nor had she spoken during dinner except once, when, reminiscing about great meals they had enjoyed, Victoria had said, 'Who's the best cook you know?' and the friend, turning to her, had said, 'Clare.'

Afterwards, in the street outside, Harold had said good-bye to Victoria in a friendly off-hand way, so she had gone back to the van and driven home. Now in her schoolgirl jodhpurs, riding-coat and yellow jumper she was waiting for him to arrive and drive off to Richmond Park. They had taken, the last few weeks, to going for a ride at eight o'clock on Friday mornings. It was a glorious idea but a terrible rush, and she was getting later and later for work and more and more tired. She laid her black and white Donegal tweed suit with the scooped-out neck and the gored skirt out on the bed, ready to change into when she got back, and a white ribbed sweater to go with it. Then she went into the kitchen to wait, taking a look at the mauve lilac on the way. It was twenty to eight.

Harold came clattering down the area steps in his blue suit jacket, his striped suit trousers, silk shirt, and bow tie. He had a conviction that unmatched meant informal, sporty even. He put his hands, trembling slightly, on Victoria's shoulders and kissed her diffidently on the lips. Then he took her hand and ran back up the stairs. 'Hurry,' he said, opening the door for her, 'we'll be late.' Victoria hopped up into the driving-seat and the van trundled off, rumbling and swaying as she pushed it on. The little team of three, poised in concentration, intent on the co-operative effort of getting there on time.

An unwelcome thought hovered on the corner of Victoria's brain: what would happen next week when she had to give the van back to Jessica?

'I'm going to get a car,' said Harold, as they crossed Kew Bridge.

'How wonderful,' said Victoria. 'What kind?'

'Don't think it's for you,' said Harold.

'I'm not . . .' said Victoria, and stopped. As she did so a fleeting image of herself in the passenger seat sitting beside Harold at the wheel of an open – what? – as they drove, laughing through summer lanes, passed across her mind. She changed gear with a jerk, cringed, glanced at Harold, but the hiccup passed.

They were in the park now, rolling down a long sweep of hill where clumps of pale deer grazed in new-sprung bracken, and the old chestnut trees bore their great candles of newly opened white, and sometimes pink, blossom with grave majesty. They turned into the stables on the edge of the park. Their horses were ready for them and the owner, a small man with short legs and a red weather-beaten face, all hard muscle and loud jokes, shouted a greeting. Honoured, they fetched their own horses from their loose-boxes and, with huge effort, mounted from the ground. The horses were polo ponies, lively, well-schooled and sensitive. Victoria's Polly was as fluid as water and, as she hitched her leg over the saddle to tighten the girth, Polly flexed her brown neck and played, in her soft mouth, with the silver bit. Chinking and springing, they moved off, Harold ahead on big black Turpin.

'Don't you bring those horses back sweating!' shouted the owner, pausing on his bow-legged way across the yard.

Victoria, tense and upright on dancing Polly, kept her knees in, her toes carefully up and her hands down light on the reins. Harold, his knees flapping, slouched. They trotted up the hill and Victoria, squeezing her legs and shortening the reins, sat down in the saddle as Polly melted into a canter. She felt frightened and excited. Harold looked round at her, raised an eyebrow and grinned.

They crossed the riding track and followed a path through the bracken. The park lay before them, still in the cool morning air, a sea of rolling green, the spires and towers of the distant city massed and misty grey at its edges. Walking alongside Turpin, Victoria concentrated on her seat. She had had a short, horsy patch in her teens when she had hung around the local stables all day, studied books by authors with names like 'Snaffle' and 'Huntsman' under the bedclothes at night and saved up her pocket money for rides. Harold, the sands at Bognor apart, had first sat on a horse at his mistress's castle in Italy and, daredevil that he was, hung on and let rip. He had found the technique perfectly adequate.

Seeing a long level strip ahead, he pumped his arms and kicked his horse in the ribs. Turpin leaped forward, stretched his sleek black neck, laid his ears back and raced ahead. Polly leaped too, but Victoria gathered up the reins and fought with her a moment or two before she settled her into a light canter, comfortable and controlled as a cat's purr. They caught up with Harold under some trees. He had let the reins drop and his horse was eating grass. Victoria was shocked as she so often was at Harold's disregard for convention. It was absolutely not allowed, for some reason she knew not, to let one's horse eat grass while one was riding. She tugged determinedly at her own horse's head and managed to keep it aloft.

'Come on,' said Harold. He hauled on his reins, turned Turpin into the trees and cantered off. Victoria put her head down on Polly's neck, shut her eyes and followed. Branches brushed against her legs and scraped the top of her head. 'Let's walk for a bit,' said Harold, gasping a little, and they walked side by side in the sun, Turpin's head drooping low and easy; Polly's head held high as Victoria, hands low, heels down, sat primly erect in the saddle. Polly shied at a fallen branch, Harold laughed, squirrels raced in clockwork bursts across the grass and up the trunks of trees.

'Let's gallop,' said Harold, faced with a long, grassy incline. He kicked at Turpin's sides and was away. Let's, thought Victoria. She bent forward, loosened the reins and urged Polly on. As the little mare's stride lengthened into a gallop, she stood up in the stirrups. One leg was wobbling wildly. She felt breathless and out of control. They passed Turpin and careered up onto the crest of the slope. There, she reined in and, panting like Polly, turned to smile at Harold. He came thundering up behind, slowed down and walked past.

'Wasn't that great?' she called, relieved to have stayed on board, her heart beating hard. Harold made no reply. Victoria trotted up alongside him. He stared straight ahead. Victoria's heart sank. She walked beside him in self-conscious silence. A man taking his dog for a walk raised his cap and said 'Good morning.'

'Good morning,' said Victoria. The park lay spread out around them, serene and green, silent in the sun. A massed bank of cloud that had sat low on the horizon rolled up and sailed across its face.

'Let's have a last canter,' said Victoria as they neared the gate from whence they had entered. She knew it was not done to canter on the way home, but Harold remained unmoved. They walked through the gate and entered the lane that led back to the stables. Victoria dropped behind, let her feet out of the stirrups and crossed the leathers in front of her. A stable girl came out to meet them and took hold of Turpin's bridle. Victoria dismounted, led Polly to her box, unsaddled her, slipped her halter on, leaned her cheek against her warm salty neck and carried the saddle and bridle over one arm, as she had been taught, to the tack room. Her knees were weak and shaking. Harold gave the stable girl a pound. 'Shall I book next week for you?' she asked. 'I'll telephone,' said Harold. He went over to the van and got in. Victoria got into the driving-seat and started the engine. They drove back to Holland Park in silence, the air between them thickening with every mile as the first fat drops of rain plopped soundlessly and dribbled down the windscreen.

By the time she got to the studios, the team, nowadays greatly swollen, had broken up and was dispersed among the warren of offices in the houses next door. Their intense activity seemed slightly unnatural to her and she felt alienated. Owen and Andrew passed her in the passage muttering to one another. Owen gave a short bark of laughter followed by a similar sound from Andrew, mirthless and more subdued. Neither of them spoke to her, but Owen turned and held out a stubby-fingered arm. 'Where have you been, girl?' he said.

'I've been . . . I've been . . . riding,' said Victoria.

'Horses,' said Owen, his tone midway between expletive

and query, 'bloody nobs. Pit-ponies . . .' He continued on his way, Andrew tacked close to his side.

She went into her office. Gregory was shouting excitedly down the telephone; her secretary was talking quietly into another, an unhooked receiver lying on the desk in front of her. At her own desk sat an unknown young man reading a newspaper. Victoria stared at him frostily. He had fair hair and a rather high white collar above his black suit, giving him an old-fashioned, clerkly air. He lowered the newspaper. 'Is this where you usually sit, then?' he enquired, mildly. He got up holding the paper open before him. 'I'm looking for stories,' he said. Victoria ignored him.

'I've done your letters, Victoria, they're on your desk,' said her secretary, a receiver now at each ear, the mouth-pieces tucked under her chin.

The young man edged out from behind the desk and Victoria took her place. The chair was warm. She began signing letters. The young man stood in the small space left between the three desks and the wall. He did not seem at all put out. Lost between outrage, pity and guilt at her own disloyalty to the Programme, Victoria said without looking up, 'There's a wastepaper-basket over there.' The young man looked round and spied a wastepaper-basket with less inside it than some of the others. It was made of dark green tin. He transferred its contents to one of the other baskets, turned it upside down and sat upon it. There he remained reading and occasionally making a note in a small black book which he took out of his pocket, until five minutes to one when he said, 'I think I'll go out for a spot of lunch now.'

Victoria stayed at her desk. She had one rather weak item for that evening's programme, but she was not at all sure that it would have been remembered in her absence. Her mind was only half on it, the other half preoccupied with dinner. She and Harold were going to a party at the paper where she had first seen him and where, presumably, he still worked.

'If only I could ask some people back to dinner,' he had said, wistfully. 'If one led a proper life it would be easy.'

'I'll cook it,' Victoria had said, eagerly. 'I can leave the Programme a bit earlier and buy some food on the way.'

'Impossible,' Harold had said, scornfully. 'Of course you can't. It's much too difficult,' and sunk into deep gloom.

'I can, I can,' said Victoria. 'It'll be no trouble at all.' But she was not certain now that she could. Avocado pears, roast veal, *haricots verts*, new potatoes and . . . and – crème caramel, that was easy. And then there was bread, butter, olive oil, garlic, milk, sugar and eggs. Harold had nothing in his flat. Panic pricked her armpits.

She shook her head violently to clear it and bent down over the introduction she was writing. Her guest was an extraordinary writer-explorer, whose new book, *Men of the Sands*, had greatly captured her romantic fancy. He stood little chance without her advocacy, she knew, against the pit-ponies. The item was a scoop in its way. Another lunatic writer-explorer now at large and whooping in a publisher's office had sent her the book. Victoria was swept away by it, caught up in the nobility of adventure. The publisher had given her the author's telephone number and warned her that he was very shy. A man's deep echoing voice had demurred at the suggestion of – television? – and invited her to come round and meet his mother. Victoria had gone, carefully dressed in sugar-pink and pearls, to a small dark Knightsbridge flat in a red

Edwardian block. The author himself had opened the door; a looming craggy figure with a great beak of a nose and a hesitant lop-sided stride, he had led her into a drawing-room where, across a waste of occasional tables, a severe grey-haired lady had sat, with a pious air, in a wing-chair. For twenty minutes they had made conversation and then the old lady had offered Victoria a glass of sherry. With their sherries in their hands, the author had taken Victoria into his narrow bedroom where they had sat on his high single bed and looked through his boxes of photographs. The pictures were marvellous. Victoria had selected half a dozen and brought them back to the office. She had meant to have them blown up so that the interview could take place in front of them. Now, they would just have to be used as cutaways.

The office was filling up again and Andrew came in. 'Anything for this evening, girl?' he said. 'Didn't you have something?' He was on his rounds, calling on the offices, filling up spaces in the running order. Victoria gave him the photographs and explained the cues in the introduction and questions. 'Take it seriously,' she pleaded with her eyes.

'He's an amazing man,' she said, hopefully, 'and a very good writer.' The item needed her attention and she would only have time to greet her guest and introduce him to the interviewer.

'Who's interviewing him?' she said.

'It had better be Roderick,' said Andrew. He raised his eyebrows, smiled his bleak smile and hurried on.

'Burn three spoonfuls of sugar in a saucepan' – was there a saucepan? – 'pour it into a dish' – no dish either, probably – 'beat three eggs and some sugar in a bowl' – a jug would do – 'add a pint of milk, pour it into the dish and put it in the oven, very low.' Matches! She must remember matches, but she had a cigarette lighter. And rubber gloves.

Roderick came in. He had two small cylindrical tins of bubble mixture in his hand. The lids, when unscrewed, had pieces of wire curved at the ends into circles attached to them. He handed Victoria a tin. They unscrewed the lids and blew bubbles.

Beautiful iridescent bubbles floating in the air filled the office and burst on the corners of filing cabinets. Victoria leaned back in her chair and gathered a fat quavering stack of them on her wire; Roderick darted round the tiny space catching them as they fell on his. They tossed them back and forth to each other. The secretary dodged them as she typed, without looking up. Gregory screamed instructions to his stringer in Wales for all the world as if the telephone had never been invented. The fair-haired young man opened the door, said, 'Excuse me,' and sat down on his wastepaper-basket. When the tins were empty, Roderick said, 'What have you got for me this afternoon, Vicky-Ticky?'

'A treat,' said Victoria, handing him *Men of the Sands*.

# Chapter Sixteen

ℰ

Harold had chucked it in. He felt relieved. He also felt guilty, but he would not have to tell Dr Lemaitre until Monday, if then.

Maddened by constriction and mindful of his image as an untamed free spirit, he had drawn his golden brows together and erupted, as he had been longing to do, in one wild burst of fury, scattering papers, kicking desks and hurling insults at the assistant editor, a mild fellow who had come in in his braces, galley-proofs in hand, to query one of Harold's editing marks. Now he was out of it and he would never go back. The small problem of the evening's party prickled uncomfortably at the back of his mind. Victoria was sure to want to go. He would let her drag him there and smoulder against a wall, letting off flashes of bashful charm at those worthy of it. It was their fault, anyway.

He sat at the table in his flat with a tin of small cigars, a whole afternoon in front of him. He was going to finish his book. Papers lay in stale disorder round about him. He picked up his pen and drew a sheet of fresh paper towards him. It was very good paper, thick, watermarked and inviting. He had bought a stack of it on the way home. He should have bought a new pen too, and a fresh bottle of Quink. He lit one of the little papery pale brown cigars and wreathed himself with bitter smoke. The first mark was important. Perhaps he should read something through; the characters had become strangers to him. Perhaps he should have gone to the British Museum and read up some background. He got up to fetch a saucer, stubbed out the cigar and wrote: '*At 12.45 on the morning of the 12th May, 1930 the District Magistrate of Surat, two Indian police officers, armed with pistols and some thirty policemen armed with rifles, silently and suddenly came into the peaceful little compound where Gandhi and his Satyagrahis were sleeping.*'

He had been thinking about the sentence for weeks. Its rhythms were familiar to him. He had never seen it before. The blue marks looked good on the white. He crossed out the second '*armed*'. They did not look so good now. He groaned and gritted his teeth. Forcing himself to go on, he wrote: '*They immediately surrounded the party and the English officer going up to the bed and turning a torch-light onto Gandhi's face, said: "Are you Mohandas Karamchand Gandhi?" "You want me?" said Gandhi gently. "Please give me time for my ablutions." He began to clean his teeth and the officer, timepiece in hand, stood watching him . . .*'

Overcoming the urge to give up, Harold covered a page. When he got to the bottom he threw it on the floor, wrote '2' at the top of another one, finished the sentence and stopped. It was not '2'. Maybe it was '92' or '102', or even '3'. He shuffled through the papers around him. They were in baffling disarray. He should have a secretary, but she would only get in the way: the effort of explaining would drain him. He was hopelessly unfitted for such a task, for any task, come to think of it. There should be a butler now silently at his elbow with a silver tray of strong coffee and, perhaps, a few delicious biscuits. There should be someone to wash and iron his shirts, to brush his suits and hang them up, to clean his shoes and place them side by side in pairs on the floor of the cupboard. He craved order, but all he got was chaos. He undid his tie. Creative thought was impossible on such a foundation of mess. Life was impossible.

He sat back in his chair, pushing impatiently on the table with his hands, and the bottle of Quink, half balanced already on a rubber, tilted and fell over. A few drops spilled out and gathered against the edge of the stack of paper. He took out his handkerchief, dabbed and dropped it on the floor. His mother and father had been a neat couple, everything had had its proper place in the houses of his childhood. Spoons, knives and forks lay in sets in baize-lined boxes; newspapers were folded and laid, overlapping one another, on footstools; on his mother's dressing-table, the initialled silver-backed brushes, the hand-mirror, the button-hook and the shoehorn were set out, maddeningly, in a fan-shaped pattern, even when travelling. Where had it all gone wrong? They had done their best, damn them.

He summoned his will. First, he would get his manuscript in order, starting from page one. Much of it was upstairs, still in the brown paper in which it had been delivered to his office – his ex-office – that bleak February day. That was a queer episode, and one he did not wish to think about too much. Infused with purpose, he rushed for the stairs. The door handle came off in his hand. With prudence and self-restraint he placed a telephone directory in front of the open door, and dashed on. In the bedroom, more chaos. All this was going to change. He pulled up the bedclothes, tucked them into the mattress, shook the pillows and drew the bedspread over them. It did not look right and he patted at some of the lumps with his hands which, he noticed, were shaking slightly.

The drawers, as usual, were open. They stuck in places when he tried to push them, but he battled with them and won. A tie or two hung insolently out over the edges, but he ignored them. His manuscript was in a top drawer and he remembered the missing pages. They were the ones concerning Mr Gandhi's comments to his disciples, in 1946, on the atom bomb. He would have to write them again, that was all. He felt the eyes of Dr Lemaitre upon him. Was that a faint inclination of the head he detected? He nearly glanced over his shoulder. Bills, postcards and letters lay strewn over the bottom of the drawer. There were even some stuffed into an envelope he had received from his mother and father when he was a prisoner. Most of them had been burned in the camp stove but some remained. Such odd, stiff, parochial communications they had been, like all interactions with his parents always had been. Now they were gone and there was no communication at all.

The past rose up and hit him in the face. He sat down on the bed, gasping. Then he stood up, straightened his hair in the mirror, tied up his tie, put the brown paper parcel under his arm, marched down the stairs and straight over to the table. Grasping his pen firmly, he began to write and thus Victoria found him two hours later, when she arrived, breathless, shining and laden with packages.

She saw the room before she saw Harold and was appalled. It was already ten to six – but one thing at a time, nothing was impossible. 'Hi,' she said. Harold gave an exaggerated start which offended Victoria.

'It's you!' he said, turning round.

'It's ten to six,' said Victoria.

'Christ,' said Harold, automatically, and then, with some interest, 'what are all those parcels?'

'Dinner,' said Victoria. She went into the kitchen, cleared a space with her elbow and lowered them onto the draining-board. Harold followed her. He looked peculiarly unkempt. 'Anything to eat?' he said. Ready to cry, Victoria kissed him on the cheek and began putting dirty dishes into the sink. She felt like the Solent at the turn of the tide when four strong currents all meet at once: in her sea of conflict, misery, irritation, hopelessness and determination. 'You couldn't give a hand, could you?' she said, brightly. Harold was peering into the brown paper bags. Raw meat, raw beans, raw potatoes, French butter and a long loaf of granary bread. He opened the butter and broke off a piece of bread.

'No-o,' wailed Victoria.

'Don't try and dominate me,' said Harold. Spilling crumbs he went back to the table.

In the kitchen Victoria washed up in her rubber gloves. She unwrapped the long roll of veal she had bought in Soho and, with it still lying on its paper so as not to dirty the draining-board, made slits in it and inserted bits of garlic and rosemary. Then she salted and buttered it and put it in a tin pan. She topped and tailed the beans, hundreds of them, and washed the potatoes. Then she made the crème caramel and, with great caution, crouched and held her lighter to the jets in the ancient oven. It lit with a bang and jumped out at her. Shaking, she placed the dish of milk and eggs in a pan of water and put it in the oven. The shelves slanted and some slopped out. She closed the door and turned the gas right down. Then she

169

went into the drawing-room and started making little piles of shoes, socks, papers and books round the edges of the room. Harold felt her busy presence and it grated. 'You're behaving like a wardress in a concentration camp,' he said.

'Have you got a table-cloth?' said Victoria.

'We're not going to the party,' said Harold.

'What!' said Victoria. 'Not going to the party? What do you mean?' She went on tidying.

'We're not going. That's what I mean,' said Harold.

'But we've asked all those people back to dinner. Why?' said Victoria.

'I've asked some people. They're my friends. And I can't go, that's why,' said Harold.

Victoria sat down on the edge of an armchair. She was wearing a cream-coloured nunsveiling dress with a pin-tucked bodice and a pleated skirt, its back folded down into a low V. 'Why aren't you going? We must go. Why can't you go?' she said. It was twenty-five to seven and the party would have begun.

'I can't go, that's all. How typical of you not to understand,' said Harold.

Victoria was determined not to spoil her make-up. It would only waste time. 'Please,' she said.

'Don't manipulate me,' said Harold, shortly.

Victoria felt her eyes moisten and her throat constrict. She got up hurriedly and fetched a pretty lace handkerchief – it had belonged to her grandmother – and wiped it carefully under her eyelashes. 'Please,' she said, going over to Harold and touching him on the shoulder.

He shrugged violently. 'I don't work there any more. I've chucked it. That's why,' he said through gritted teeth.

'Oh,' said Victoria, 'but I'm sure you could still go.

They'd love to see you. And I'm invited. You could come with me.'

Harold leaped up from his chair. His face looked dangerous. He seized her by the shoulders. 'All you care about is using me for your own social ambition,' he said. 'Of course I can't go. It's much too embarrassing.' He raised his arm. Victoria ducked. She went over to the table and straightened the fallen Quink bottle. Where was the lid?

'You go,' said Harold. He left the room and went upstairs. With great care, reverence even, Victoria collected the papers on the table together and put them on the floor. She divided up the rubber bands and the paper clips and the Sellotape and the stamps and put them in separate cups which she brought in from the kitchen. She found the cap of the ink bottle and screwed it on. Then she flicked the bits off the table with her handkerchief and laid it for eight, using an odd assortment of implements and glasses. It looked very squashed but not too bad. She started hunting for chairs.

'What the hell are you doing?' said Harold, thrusting his head round the door. 'It's seven o'clock. We're late.' He was wearing his sharp striped suit and the tie she had given him for Christmas.

'Sorry,' said Victoria. She took a pocket mirror from her handbag and licked her mascara brush.

'You can't do that now!' said Harold. 'Hurry. Come on!'

'Sorry,' said Victoria. She finished putting on mascara and sidled past Harold in the doorway, bending to pick up the telephone directory as she did so.

'Don't,' said Harold, furiously, 'the door'll shut.'

'Oh,' said Victoria, 'sorry.' She looked in on the crème

171

caramel, it was still liquid, and ran down the stairs after Harold. He was striding down the street.

'We can go in the van,' called Victoria, getting out her keys.

'We can't go in that thing!' he shouted back over his shoulder. 'How naïve you are.'

'Sorry,' said Victoria, running to catch up with him.

From a shop doorway across the street, Volnicek, who had been studying the electrical goods on display in its window, felt his heart go out to her. What a barbaric way to conduct a courtship, he thought sadly. Melancholy, anguish for the whole of humanity swept over him as he watched them reach the end of the street and disappear round the corner.


'Hullo, darling,' said a little man in the doorway. He pecked Victoria on the cheek and waved his glass at Harold as if they were standing on opposite sides of a football field instead of pressed together on the fringe of a crowded London party. Harold nodded at him briefly. His frown deepened. He had walked the whole way there at top speed without speaking and had strode up the stairs, two at a time, without waiting for Victoria and he was a little out of breath.

Victoria, hurrying to keep up with him and putting in an occasional running step, was out of breath too. The little man squeezed her elbow. 'How are you, darling?' he said. Victoria shrank in her arm and pressed closer to Harold, who turned rudely away and stared into the crowd. 'Go away,' he muttered, 'it's embarrassing.' Victoria's heart sank. She had nearly cried so many times that day, these last months indeed, that the ache in her midriff

and throat was becoming a familiar element in her repertory of daily physical feelings.

'Harold, my dear fellow, how are you?' called the proprietor, catching sight of him from not far off. 'Come on
over here, I want you to meet the Duchess of Middlesbrough.' Harold gave a diffident smile and the proprietor
pushed his way towards him propelling a light woman
with laughing blue eyes before him.

'I've heard so much about you, Mr Fox,' Victoria heard
her say, before Harold vanished from view, talking ani-
matedly with a group of people that closed in on him. She
was left with the little man who was opening and shutting
his mouth and shrugging his shoulders up and down. She
could hear nothing for the blood singing in her ears and
the thump of her heart drumming in her chest. He drifted
away and she caught the eye of a young man buried deep
in the thick of the room. He edged towards her. It was
the fair-haired young man who had appeared in her office
that day.

'Have a drink,' he said, holding out his glass. 'It's
whisky.'

'Thank you,' said Victoria and swallowed some.

'Cheer up,' said the young man, 'it's been a hard day.
That chap of yours was great, a real find. I've put in an
order for his book.'

Victoria looked at him and laughed. 'Was it very
uncomfortable on the wastepaper-basket?' she said.

'Not at all,' said the young man. 'I've always wondered
what Miss Muffet felt like. I may bring a cushion tomorrow. Would that be in order?'

'I expect so,' said Victoria, distractedly. She was looking
for Harold and she could not see him anywhere. She

looked back at the young man and tried to smile. 'Why are you there?' she said.

'Well,' said the young man equably, 'they send chaps down to Cambridge to find chaps and I was one of the chaps they found.'

'Oh,' said Victoria.

'I'm going to get another drink. I'll be back,' said the young man and disappeared.

Left on her own, Victoria sought a friendly face. She knew that parties were work and you had to throw yourself into them, but she felt rooted to the ground and her legs would not work. She backed towards the wall and leaned against it, sipping the whisky which was warm and watery. The noisy throng she had so much relished on previous occasions seemed alien and impenetrable. A long elegant back caught her momentary attention. It had a familiar cast, but she felt too weak to pursue the connection in her mind. She finished the whisky and slipped out of the room.

'Where's the lavatory?' she asked a waitress, making her way in with a tray of glasses.

'Just up the stairs on the right, dear,' said the waitress.

Victoria took one of the glasses, a tumbler, and swallowed the drink in it as she went up the stairs. It was too insipid for comfort. She sat on the lavatory lid and put her head on her hands, struggling to control her tears. Then she stood up and slowly brushed her hair and put on new lipstick. The room was too dark and the mirror too small to see as well as she would have wished. She turned up the collar of her dress and smiled at herself experimentally. When she got to the bottom of the stairs again a short fat man came out of the double doorway to meet her.

'I have been waiting for you. Where have you been?' he said in a thickly accented voice.

'I've been in the lavatory,' said Victoria.

The man, who had a bald head and small bright brown eyes with creases at the edge, took out some spectacles from a case in his pocket, put them on and stared at her. 'You look quite beautiful,' he said, putting them away again.

'You were in Le Maquis the other day at lunch time!' said Victoria.

'And you were having lunch with a terribly boring man. I have been waiting for you ever since,' said the short fat man. He chuckled and took her hands in a warm clasp. 'Now we have been waiting so long for each other, you must come and have dinner with me,' he said. 'Why do you go around with such boring men? Life is an entirely pointless journey except for the friendships you make on the way. It can be very beautiful.' He patted her hand and dropped it. 'Come,' he said, 'I know a dear little restaurant tucked away down a teeny-weeny street. Not far from here.' He looked at his watch. 'Come,' he said, and took her hand again. This time, his grip, though small, was forceful and he tugged at Victoria quite hard.

'No, no, no,' said Victoria, pulling back. 'I can't. It is very kind of you but I can't.' He was ridiculous but she was beguiled. His sturdy, wise and worldly air and his open admiration offered a prospect of solace to her sore soul. The man came up to her close, and his round protruding stomach covered in black chalk-striped waistcoat almost touched hers. He gave her a long unfaltering look, then he put his head on one side. 'Please,' he said, 'you will not regret it.'

'I'd love to,' said Victoria, 'but I'm having dinner with

175

someone else.' She thought of the veal. It would take at least an hour to cook. She looked anxiously into the room of which they were still on the threshold. It was less crowded now and she saw Harold, the blue-eyed Duchess still at his side, at the centre of a group on the other side, their heads together, all laughing. 'I must go,' she said.

'I will come with you,' said the short fat man. He stuck with surprising agility to her side as she moved through the room. Harold failed to catch her eye as she reached the edge of his group, but the Duchess smiled at her. 'Introduce me to your friend, Mr Fox,' she said gaily. Harold frowned at Victoria. 'Go away,' said his eyes. 'This is Victoria Benjamin – Daisy Middlesbrough,' he mumbled as fast as he could.

'And I am George Kús,' said the short fat man, in his impossible accent. Benign, twinkling and tubby, he shook hands with everyone in the group.

Victoria moved closer to Harold. 'We must go,' she whispered, 'the dinner will take at least an hour.'

'Don't blackmail me,' muttered Harold, hardly moving his lips. Victoria felt the kick in a place already sore, but she smiled. 'Give me the keys. I left mine,' she said quietly. 'You come on later with the others.'

So that was who her short fat friend was! The famous left-wing sociologist, Professor Kús from Cambridge. She had tried once or twice to get him to come on the Programme. She looked at him with respect. Harold felt in his pocket for the keys and held them out to her, without looking, behind his back. Victoria took them and moved off.

'See you later!' called the Duchess.

'Vunderful, vunderful,' said Professor Kús, rocking backwards and forwards on his toes.

He's like one of those balloons with cardboard feet, thought Victoria – a red one.

'See you later, all!' said the professor, cheerily. He moved off, clamped to Victoria's side. At the door, he took her arm and pressed it warmly. 'You are very beautiful,' he said in her ear.

When they got to the door of Harold's flat, Victoria paused. 'Well, goodbye,' she said.

'Wait,' said Professor Kús, 'I will get you something vunderful.' He darted across the road to a wine shop, its windows crowded with bottles and cardboard labels proclaiming prodigious discounts in large handwriting. A few minutes later, he darted back holding a paper-wrapped bottle. 'This is Tokay,' he announced, handing it to her. 'You have never tried it. It is the drink of pure life.'

'How exciting,' said Victoria, 'thank you very, very much.' She opened the door and went in. Professor Kús went in with her. As she climbed the stairs, he climbed them too, close behind her. Before the door into the flat itself, Victoria stopped. 'I'm afraid you really can't come any further,' she said. 'We're having a private dinner party.'

Professor Kús was puffing. 'Phew, phee-uw,' he said, patting his chest. He smiled at her with his head on one side and his eyes, so brown and bright, touched the sore place at her heart. 'Just one teeny little drink,' he said.

'Oh, dear,' said Victoria. 'All right. Just one.' She opened the door and the smell of burnt sugar and warm custard floated down to meet them. She went straight to the kitchen and opened the oven. The crème caramel was just set, wobbly but not liquid. She took it out in its pan of steaming water. 'You go into the room next door and

177

sit down,' she said to the professor, whose big tummy was taking up most of the narrow space, 'I won't be a minute.'

'Just one teeny-weeny kiss,' he said, grasping her hard round the waist. 'Just one. It can do you no harm.'

'Go away,' said Victoria, pushing him back. 'It's too much. Go away.' But he made her laugh. It was good to feel wanted. Professor Kús let her go and, with extraordinary acuity, put his hand on a corkscrew. Still puffing and making phewey noises, he uncorked the bottle, found two glasses and poured them each a drink.

'*Egeszegeve*,' he said, lifting his glass, 'you will like this,' and went into the room next door.

Victoria took a sip. The drink was golden-coloured and not unpleasant, sweet and musty at the same time with a not unsatisfying kick to it. She turned up the oven and put in the veal, a tea-cloth tucked into the neck of her dress. It was twenty minutes to nine. She heard a bang, the building quivered and there was the sound of voices and many feet on the stairs. Harold and at least six people, the Duchess among them, poured into the flat, talking and laughing. Victoria went to meet them, the tea-cloth in her hand. 'Hullo,' she said. 'Hullo.' Harold, animated and deferential, was pretending to be a butler and took their coats.

'Hullo,' one or two of them cried back. They crowded into the drawing-room.

Harold came into the kitchen. 'Where's the wine?' he said, urgently. He looked desperate.

'Wine?' said Victoria, 'I don't know.'

'You don't know!' said Harold. His voice had a dangerous edge to it. 'You don't know,' he sneered. 'This is your do. Where's the wine?'

'I never thought about it,' said Victoria.

'Christ,' said Harold, he closed his eyes and screwed them up. 'Have you got any money?' he said through his teeth.

'Not much,' said Victoria. She went to her bag and took out three pounds. 'There,' she said, giving it to him. 'That's all there is.'

Harold drew in his breath and held it. Victoria stood, transfixed.

'Hu-llo, hu-llo,' said Professor Kús. He was standing in the doorway, the bottle of Tokay in one hand, an empty glass in the other. 'Your very good health, sir!' he said pouring some into the glass and handing it to Harold.

The Duchess appeared in the doorway behind him. Her eyes sparkled and her face was pink. 'Your delightful learned friend has been giving us the most interesting foreign drink,' she said. 'We've been having a lovely time, haven't we?'

Harold gave her a dazzling smile. 'I've just got to go down and buy some wine,' he said.

'I'll come with you,' cried the Duchess. 'I love shopping.'

Harold swallowed his Tokay and left the kitchen. 'Get that oaf out of here,' he said, from the corner of his mouth, as he left.

As soon as they had gone down the stairs, Professor Kús poured himself another drink, filled Victoria's glass, gave her an almost-wink, and disappeared up the stairs to the bedroom floor. He hummed to himself as he went, still holding the bottle by the neck, and his stumpy legs and solid tread made surprisingly little noise on the creaky boards. First of all he went into the bathroom, banged the door and turned on the tap. Then he went into the bedroom whose door was ajar and drew in his breath. Was it always like this or had Volnicek got there before him?

Someone, certainly not the spick-and-span Victoria Benjamin, had made the bed after a fashion. He sat down on it for a moment: the depression made by his weight would be imperceptible among the many lumps and troughs. His bright eyes made a rapid survey of the room. He got up and moved swiftly to a top drawer in the chest of drawers from which some thin pieces of paper protruded beside a couple of drooping tie-ends.

From outside the window, whose catch had been secured from inside, Volnicek watched him in pale despair. Professor Kús rifled quickly through the papers in the drawer, scanning and rejecting them at speed. He found an envelope with two or three pale-blue airmail letters inside it and read them quickly through. Chortling with delight, he put all but one in his pocket and closed the drawer, wiping round the places his fingers had touched with the end of his silk tie. He made sure to leave a few papers hanging out. He tiptoed lightly to the bathroom, turned off the tap, pulled the chain, banged the door and descended, effulgent with self-congratulation. As he bounded into the drawing-room on the floor below, he collided with the Duchess. 'Goody, goody,' he said, beaming at her, 'my dear lady, my very dear Duchess.'

'Oh goody, goody,' said the Duchess, 'my name's Daisy. We've got lots of bottles of lovely wine, but I'd like some of your delicious drink, Professor.'

'Georgie,' said Professor Kús, pouring her some. He clasped her elbow as she held out her glass. Beyond, he saw Victoria perched, tense, upon the arm of a chair. She was alone and around her, people in twos and threes were talking to one another. Harold moved among them flourishing a bottle in each hand. He wore a teasing smile which became his clean-cut romantic features with their few deep lines round mouth and forehead: people's faces lit up as he approached. Professor Kús, still holding onto the Duchess, motioned towards Victoria with his head and, together, they moved over to her.

'Now we can have a nice chat,' he said, with a plump air of triumph.

'You look so nice sitting there,' said the Duchess. 'I do like your dress.'

'I must go and look at the dinner,' said Victoria. 'I've got to put on the beans.'

'Oh, you are clever. I do admire people who can cook,' said the Duchess.

Victoria smiled at her and laughed. 'I'm sure you can, really,' she said. 'I can't do it properly either. It just takes time.'

'I have just bought a dear little machine for my London flat,' said the professor, patting his pocket contentedly. 'You can boil eggs on it and cook steaks.'

'Just what I need for my upstairs flat in the country! Do tell me about it,' cried the Duchess.

Victoria slipped away from them and went into the kitchen. She felt paralysed. Those people back there did not need her and there was so much to do. She did not know where to begin. The veal was done, the potatoes soon would be. She put water on to boil for the beans and started cutting the avocado pears in half. They were perfect. She had to lay another place and find another chair. She took the jug of vinaigrette she had made earlier and some more knives and forks into the next-door room and pushed her way through the people. They were talking hard.

'I told you to get that oaf out of here,' hissed Harold, as she passed him. Victoria gave him a pleading look, but he had turned his back. She put the things she was carrying on the table and went back to the kitchen for the avocado pears. When they were all on the table, she said, 'Dinner's ready.'

No one heard her, so she gave a big smile, cleared her throat and said, 'Dinner's ready.'

Harold gave her a kick on the ankle. 'For Christ's sake, it's nearly ten o'clock. Do something,' he said in her ear.

Victoria tugged at the sleeve of the man nearest her. 'Dinner's ready. Please go and sit down,' she said to him. She said it three times before he looked at her. 'Dinner!' he said. 'Capital. I'm jolly peckish.'

'Please get the others to sit down,' she said, and went back into the kitchen for the butter and the hot bread. When she came back they were all standing around the table.

'What's the placement, Victoria?' said Harold. He spoke heartily in a way she had never heard him speak before.

'Placement?' said Victoria. 'You mean where should everyone sit? I don't know. Wherever you like.'

Harold shot her a look of what could only be described as hate. 'Daisy on my right,' he said, 'and Sandy next to her . . .'

Professor Kús approached Victoria. 'Vunderful, vunderful, vunderful, I have so much enjoyed myself,' he said. 'Next week we will have a cosy lunch together. Now I have my train to catch.' He gave her a warm smacking kiss on the cheek and pressed her hand. 'Dear Mr Fox,' he called, 'thank you for your kind hospitality. Please do not disturb yourself.' He waved.

'Come and stay,' called the Duchess, now seated, as he left the room.

Victoria watched him go, thankful – at least she would

not have to hunt for another chair – and homesick at the loss of her champion. She sat down and said, 'Don't wait, and please have some dressing.'

# Chapter Seventeen

Waiting at King's Cross for the suburban line train, which was all there was left at that hour, Professor Kús went into the buffet.

'Time, gentlemen, please,' called the barman. The professor interrupted his call. In a voice of authority he said, 'Two double viskies.'

The barman glanced at him. 'Too late, sir, I'm afraid,' he said.

'Two double viskies,' repeated the professor. He pointed to the time on his watch. It was one minute to eleven. The barman put two double measures into two glasses and banged them on the bar. 'Anything with them, sir?' he said with exaggerated politeness. The professor shook his head. 'Three crisps,' he said.

'Three what?' said the barman with a snarl.

Professor Kús, head down between his shoulders, leaned forward on his toes. 'Three crisps,' he bellowed. The barman reached beneath the bar and slammed three packets of Smith's crisps in front of the professor. 'No drinking off the premises,' he said as nastily as he could. Professor Kús, unperturbed, downed the whiskies in two unhurried draughts and hoovered up the crisps. What an excellent inventor this Smith was, he thought. Crumbs spattered his waistcoat and clung there like specks of golden snow. With his fingers he extracted three carbon-blue coloured twists of tough paper from his mouth, along with a lot of saliva, and deposited them in an ashtray. The barman averted his eyes. 'Foreigners,' he muttered under his breath as he wiped the bar. Professor Kús put two half-crowns and a sixpence on the counter. 'Keep the change,' he said, and hurried off to his platform. How he would love to have been sitting at a candlelit table alongside sweet little Victoria, his knee pressing hers, at the end of a cosy dinner at which they would have exchanged confidences of reckless intimacy. He would telephone her tomorrow.

His train was completely empty, and as it trundled off into the night Professor Kús felt in his pocket for the thin paper of the letters he had so resourcefully succeeded in obtaining. Wide awake, his mind clear and alert, he calculated how and when to transfer the information to his friend Pisti and to their control in MI5. How fortunate that Gower Street was so conveniently situated within walking distance of the British Museum. His mind dwelt reluctantly, as it sometimes did late at night, on the horror from which Europe had so lately been delivered. He was British now, an honoured member of the establishment, and tears came into his eyes at the thought of the dear, brave country of which he was a loyal and devoted citizen. No other nation must ever gain the upper hand in preparedness for war. The West had right on its side; in order to overcome the forces of evil ranged in opposition, it must also have might. Within his pocket lay the key to nuclear superiority. For a brief space of time the safety of the world was in his keeping.

On Cambridge station his bicycle stood outside the stationmaster's office. He had no lights, so he pushed it for a while, mindful of his status as a law-abiding member in the community of his adoption. But soon his legs got tired and he mounted and pedalled off in the direction of his college. There, the night porter greeted him with familiar deference. 'Will you be needing it again tonight, sir?' he asked, as the professor handed him the bicycle.

'How kind,' said the professor. 'Ten minutes, maybe.'

He climbed the staircase to his rooms, let himself in and poured a tumbler of whisky. Then, reaching up to the limit of his short stature, he removed Dicey's *Law of the Constitution* from its place on an upper shelf. Inside were concealed some brilliantly devised cryptographic conversion tables which he had been taught to use during a weekend at Ditchley, plus some other ingenious bits and pieces. He adored the paraphernalia of his second profession – his spy-set. It included a one-time pad and a set of hollowed-out coins for transferring messages. With boyish enthusiasm he settled down to transform the contents of the letters in his pocket into a mass of detailed information containing the names of materials unfamiliar to him as well as precise instructions for the making of a drawing of particular size and disposition. It was a laborious, time-consuming exercise. And he had to repeat the process in facsimile, making two copies – one for Pisti's experienced eye to assess and one for Control – in tiny writing on thin slivers of rice paper. But he was excited; even with his limited knowledge of atomic physics he could appreciate that what lay before him on his desk made young Teller's hydrogen bomb look like a pop-gun.

When he had finished, he took out two florins from the inside pages of the Dicey. These, he prised apart and, into each hollowed-out centre, inserted the wisps of precious paper. He pressed the coins together again, making sure that the ridges matched and made a mental note of their dates. Then he went over to the gas fire, took a box of matches off the mantelpiece, struck the match and held the letters, one by one, to the flame. He dropped them onto the hearth where they glowed like balls of wire worms before collapsing into black fragments. With some difficulty, Professor Kús awkwardly, on his knees, gathered them into his handkerchief. Humming to himself a tune resembling 'Mack the Knife', he went into the bathroom and shook the fragments down the lavatory. He returned to his room and, using a chair to stand on this time, put the book back on its shelf. Seated comfortably at his desk he finished his whisky and poured himself some more. 'Just a nightcap,' he told himself, but before he could finish it he fell into an abrupt and deep slumber to wake as the clock struck three.

'Hu-llo, hu-llo,' he said to himself kindly, 'where can I be?'

With a feeling of great satisfaction, he recognised his own college rooms. He left them, locking the door behind him, and collected his bicycle from the porter. As the sky paled from inky black to deepest midnight-blue he pedalled away across the river to his cosy nest on the outskirts of the city, where lay his beautiful wife and their six clever children, sleeping in their Heal's beds – By Appointment to Her Majesty the Queen.

Volnicek had no advanced technology to assist him. Laboriously, working letter by letter and from memory, he had decoded the encrypted details contained in the sole document he had had time to remove from Fox's flat. The information it yielded was incomplete; he had enough physics to see that, but it was, nevertheless, a vital fragment in the missing jigsaw. He would have to pass it on to Piotr Kapitsa in Russia, and Leo Szilard in America, both key members of the Co-operative of Responsible Scientists, before destroying it. But they could not rest, none of them could rest, until they were satisfied that no trace of the information remained for the forces of insanity abroad in the world to put to use. He doubted whether he would live to see their work completed.

He had changed his address and was now living in even seedier and more transient lodgings in Paddington, but he knew that that would not deflect the agents on his heels for long. Sharpe and Champman, for the Russians, would stop at nothing and the two professors working for the British – in other words, for the Americans, their masters – were not to be underestimated, amateur and innocuous as they might seem. All of them were in the grip of irrational, unconscious forces. The emotional need to build up an external enemy and to dehumanise that enemy, transforming it into a monster in which all evil was located, exerted a strong pull on societies whose energies had so recently been concentrated in the pursuit of a justifiable war. Primitive fantasies of evil sucked both sides into an insane arms race of which death, destruction and untold suffering could be the only winners. Moreover, the lure of secrecy, of suppressing unknowable knowledge in favour of digestible fragments, had a mystic fascination for much of the human race. It brought with it so many agreeable sensations of superiority that openness withheld. The evasion of thought about the unthinkable was practised at so many levels.

Sanity, the area inhabited by men of responsibility, was a cold and lonely place to be; the world of delusion so much easier to surrender to. Volnicek sighed deeply.

Denial was a mental process unavailable to him. Since he could not embrace the illusions that bound his fellow men, one to another, he was compelled to walk alone, though he longed for company.

He went to light the gas ring, one of the few amenities with which his unprepossessing room was furnished. He must not ignore those of his physical needs to which it was possible for him to attend. It had been a ridiculous self-indulgence to allow himself the visit to Dr Lemaitre whose paper 'On Paranoia and the Unconscious' was well known to him; unforgivably expensive as well, although the doctor had reduced his fee for a fellow professional. That hour on the couch had been a nostalgic as well as a therapeutic one. Nostalgia was a luxury he had to resist although psychotherapy could, legitimately, be considered essential to his mental stability. He made himself a cup of instant coffee and sugared it profusely. Together with the last two digestive biscuits from the fat roll he had bought only yesterday, it would be his supper.

The coffee was hot and restored his resolve. He locked the door, put the chair under the handle and sat down on the bed. Pulverising pieces of digestive biscuit between tongue and palate and sucking the sweetness from them, he set to work. The essential information from the letter had to be re-encoded and demanded absolute concentration. He worked far into the small hours and as the deep midnight-blue of the receding night paled into colourless dawn, he sat on, wrestling with letter-substitution patterns of intense complexity.

When the work was done, he copied it again onto the thin cheap paper he used, and put the original to the flame. Blackened motes drifted onto the linoleum and he mopped them up with his handkerchief, dampened in water from the kettle. There was a hand-basin in his room and he washed the handkerchief under the cold tap, patting it to dry flat on the wall. Then, after carefully combing his hair and straightening his tie, he let himself out.

The sour brown smell on the dark landing assailed his nostrils and he put his hand over his face. Holding his breath, he crept down the stairs. The whole place was in an extreme state of dilapidation, but since he had tested out and memorised the weak places in its structure he was able to avoid the creaky patches. He eased open the front door and stood at the edge of the deserted street. A cat regarded him with suspicion from the rim of a dustbin. Gently, Volnicek closed the front door and prepared himself for the long walk ahead. His goal was Finsbury Park, where two empty houses designated by his control centre provided posting places in the curious system of communication for persons in his position known as Dead Letter Drop. There he would deposit the information now in his possession and pick up whatever new indications for action might await him.

That evening, Sir Christopher Sharpe had looked in at the party in Bloomsbury too. He penned an arcane comment for the paper now and then, more out of affiliation with the proprietor's wife, whose mother had been a boyhood acquaintance, than for intrinsic scholarly reasons. He had had a word with Daisy Middlesbrough – there was a superb Claude in the collection at Tees House; he had nodded at the proprietor, failed to spot his wife and noted, with a keen eye, those who were of interest to him among the company. Then he had moved on without touching the contents of the glass in his hand, parrying the greetings of those impressed by his presence in an agreeable mellow voice.

In the cool of the lengthening evening, he strode through the stilled streets towards the Royal Academy where a reception was taking place to mark the opening of the great Italian Exhibition. His attendance there was a mandatory function of his professional position: he had already escorted the monarch, a surprisingly well-informed young woman for whom he felt some affection, on a private visit there the previous afternoon. He would slip in again from time to time during the next weeks after the galleries were closed to the public. Champman was there with his wife, he remarked without acknowledgement and the Secretary, of course, whom he embraced in the cool and courteous manner of a civilised European. As soon as he could, he disengaged himself from the proceedings and walked back through Bond Street to his Institute. Tyson, in his braces as usual, saluted him. 'Chilly for the time of year, sir,' he said, respectfully. 'Can I offer you a cup of tea?'

Sir Christopher declined and then changed his mind. 'Well, perhaps I will, Tyson, that's very thoughtful of you,' he said, and gave the man one of his rare, memorable smiles. Upstairs at his desk, the tea cooling beside him, he rearranged the furniture of his mind: he had eleven minutes in which to do so. Then, with *The Stones of Venice* open before him, he extracted the little Stoneleigh receiver, smoothed down his silvery hair and placed the headphones over his ears. On the appointed second, the dots and dashes came tapping through the crackle. He noted them down and decoded them with the aid of his one-time pad. Centre, as he had suspected, was becoming impatient. Though it was risky, he had to communicate with Geoffrey at his home. He would be there by now, half expecting the call.

'My dear Rhoda,' he said, when Lady Champman answered, 'you looked very striking tonight. Crimson becomes you.'

'I'll get Geoffrey,' said Lady Champman, a plain Yorkshire woman, not unpleased.

'He'll take it in the study,' she said, a moment later and added, 'I haven't worn red since I was a girl.'

Before Sir Christopher could make an appropriate response, Sir Geoffrey cut in. 'This is a very bad line,' his voice boomed in Sir Christopher's ear. 'I'll ring you on the other 'phone.' The two men hung up and, reconnected, began to speak in low unhurried voices.

'A very pleasant and instructive outing. Many thanks. When can we make another expedition?' said Sir Geoffrey.

'I've had to make some alterations in my diary. There are some pressing engagements,' said Sir Christopher.

'I could fit something in within the next fortnight,' said Sir Geoffrey.

'I'd be most obliged if you could,' said Sir Christopher.

'My secretary will be in touch. Night night, old chap,' said Sir Geoffrey.

'Good-night, Geoffrey,' said Sir Christopher.

Down in Surrey, in his house by the towpath, Sir Geoffrey twirled in his chair and rubbed his hands on his knees in anticipatory glee. This was the part of the job he relished most.

Up in London, Sir Christopher put away *The Stones of Venice*. His mood was sombre. He switched off the light and left the building. In the square outside, he hailed a taxi. He had no heart for physical locomotion and the pleasures of aesthetic reflection. He needed all his powers to keep the demons of self-doubt at bay. When he reached his flat in Chelsea on the river, that same river that ran past Sir Geoffrey's house like a silent ever-flowing reproach, he undressed and went straight to bed. He prayed to the God of his childhood for dreamless sleep, the no man's land where all action was suspended and the conscious self extinguished.

# Chapter Eighteen

Sir Christopher dreamed of horses, of mares and long-legged foals, drifting in fields of eighteenth-century tranquillity. The fat white horse from the Chagall in Hradčany Castle in Prague with the circus dancer slid under its belly slipped into his dream and he struggled to the surface, shuddering.

Victoria and Harold were gripped in a living nightmare and could not break surface. Half-way through dinner, when Victoria was in the kitchen, draining beans and transferring the slithery roll of veal from roasting tin to china dish, Harold burst in. His face was contorted. 'What the hell are you doing?' he hissed and stood over her, a circus master with a whip.

'I . . . I'm getting the next course,' said Victoria. Her spine crawled with alarm.

'It's embarrassing,' said Harold, grinding his teeth, 'you should be there.'

'I've got to get the next course ready,' said Victoria. Her whole being shut down and shrivelled to a tight nut in the pit of her stomach.

'It's blackmail,' said Harold. 'You're a cheap little blackmailer.' He raised his arm. Victoria faced him, frozen in fright, the dish in her hands. 'Don't look at me like that,' said Harold. 'You're blackmailing me.'

Victoria ducked under his arm and put the dish on the draining-board. She wanted to run or hide. All she could do was go on doing what she was doing, minimising activity to the rigid confines of immediate necessity. Harold refrained, with an effort of will, from smashing up the kitchen. He returned to the drawing-room.

Blackmail, thought Victoria, blackmail? The word lodged awkwardly in the small section of her brain still operating. Kidnappers, ransom — what can it have to do with me? The concept got in the way of the task immediately confronting her, like a bone in the throat, and she had to hurry. There was some truth that, on this uncomfortable evening amidst an alien tribe, the kitchen was a haven; the function of cook, a protection. She felt uneasy about that. She must try harder. She swallowed the word whole and carried the veal on a dish to the table. Silence fell on the company as she did so.

'How delicious!' said Daisy Middlesbrough. 'You are clever. I wish you'd come and tell my cook how to do it.'

'I'll get the plates,' said Victoria. Harold followed her into the kitchen. 'You can't expect me to carve that thing,' he said, furiously. Victoria looked at him in wordless amazement — men always carved, it came packaged with their gender at birth. It was true, her own father never did, but she did not think of him as a man.

'Oh,' she said.

'You've got such second-rate bourgeois ideas, straight out of magazines,' said Harold, his face dark with outrage. Victoria ignored him. She took beans and potatoes to the table and brought the veal back into the kitchen and attacked it with a knife, sawing away and burning her fingers as she withdrew bits of string. Harold breathed over her shoulder. The veal disintegrated into lumps. She seized a bottle of sherry and poured some over it. She gave everyone at the table a plate and came back into the kitchen. Harold was still there.

'I'll hand it round,' she said to him.

'I'm not going back,' he said. He turned his face to the wall and stood there, napkin in hand, as Victoria carried the sliced meat back to the table and handed it round.

'It's all ready,' she said, coming back into the kitchen, 'the dish is in front of your place. I didn't know how much you'd want.'

'I'm not coming back,' muttered Harold and started banging his head against the wall. Victoria watched him in horror. The whole sore area from her throat to her entrails felt as if it had been mashed with a sharp fork. He looked much too frightening, intense and concentrated, to touch.

'Don't,' she said, 'please don't.'

Harold went on banging.

'Come on,' said Victoria, 'please come on. Everyone's waiting. Do come. It's all ready now.' She touched him on the arm.

'Don't,' snarled Harold, shaking her off. He swung round to face her, his face livid with aggression. Victoria took a step back and found herself pressed against the draining-board. She stared at him completely paralysed.

'I can't,' said Harold. 'You don't understand,' and ran upstairs.

Victoria stood in the kitchen fixed in a vacuum of indecision. She felt as if she was in a glass snowstorm bubble. The pull of social obligation drew her, still encased in thick glass and snowstorm, to the drawing-room. She took

196

her place and started eating her meat. 'Can I have the beans, please,' she asked the man next to her. Knife and fork, cut, chew, swallow: the food was perfectly cooked and tasted delicious. Conversation round the table came and went in fits and starts. From far away, Daisy Middlesbrough said, 'You work in television, don't you? I love television. It must be so interesting.'

'Not really,' said Victoria. Her office, the team, her work were caught in a bright circle at the wrong end of a telescope, distant and inaccessible. 'Do you do anything – I mean apart from being a . . . a . . .?' she said.

'Oh, my life is frightfully dull,' said Daisy Middlesbrough. 'I'm not clever like you. I never went to school, you see. I can't do anything at all.'

Victoria smiled at her, shakily. 'I think you're frightfully clever,' she said. 'What do you mean, you never went to school?'

'My father didn't believe in education. I've never even read a book,' said Daisy Middlesbrough. Her blue eyes laughed and the hint of a giggle tangled in her last word.

'My father didn't believe in education either,' said Victoria. 'He's only ever read *Bulldog Drummond* and Rider Haggard.'

'Two of a kind,' said the Duchess.

'What did *your* father do?' Victoria asked the man next to her.

'My father?' said he, looking out over the table. 'My father was the Sheikh of A-ra-bee.'

There was an outburst of laughter and a rush of talk, incomprehensible to Victoria, punctuated by shrieks and cries of merriment. They died away and Victoria began collecting plates. It seemed an impossible task and some people had left a lot on their plates. She carried a pile in aching arms to the kitchen and ran upstairs to the bedroom. There on the bed, entirely covered by blankets and bedspread, lay a hunched form curled into a ball. Victoria surveyed it, switched out the light, drew the curtains and ran downstairs. She did not understand. She went into the drawing-room for more plates.

'I simply must be going,' cried the Duchess, 'Chelsea in the morning. Mr McGregor's got a new rose there. It's called Daisy. Isn't it a scream?'

'I'll drop you,' said the tall man called Sandy.

'Oh, but there's pudding,' said Victoria. 'Don't go. It won't be a minute. I'll get it.' She hurried to the kitchen, ran a knife round the crème caramel in its dish, put a plate on top and reversed it. A few drops of dark sugar liquid fell on the floor, otherwise it looked impeccable. She took it to the drawing-room.

Daisy Middlesbrough, followed by the Sandy man, was half-way to the door; the others, pushing their chairs back from the table. 'Crème caramel,' she cried, 'oh, you are so clever. How I wish I could stay! Thank you so much.' She left the room.

'Thank you so much,' said Sandy, bowing across the crème caramel at Victoria. 'Delicious dinner.' He followed the Duchess from the room.

Victoria put the dish down. The table looked wrecked; strewn with bits of bread, crumpled napkins, half-finished glasses of wine and gravy stains. The four remaining guests were on their feet. 'So late all of a sudden . . .' 'Perfect *haricot verts* . . .' 'Early start . . .' 'I'll drop you at Earls Court . . .' they said, retreating towards the door. They vanished and Victoria heard their voices and their feet growing fainter on the stairs.

All was silence; palpable populated silence. She sat on

a chair, her arms round her legs, and hugged them tight into her chest. Then she started clearing the table. It took an hour and a half before everything was washed and dried. She left the crème caramel on the table. She had not got the heart to remove it. As the velvet black of darkest night softened into deepest blue and the red night-haze over London receded, she went up to bed, carrying her shoes in her hand. She slipped carefully into the edge at Harold's back and lay beside his inert form staring at the ceiling, pain and confusion choking her throat and tears trickling past her ears onto the pillow.

# Chapter Nineteen

❧

Harold turned the pages of the *Illustrated London News*, several at a time. He was still getting his breath back. He had caught the six o'clock train from Sussex where the children had been spending the weekend, taken a taxi from the station to his flat, thrown himself into his best suit, buttoning fly buttons and tying his tie at the same time; burrowed in his pile of shoes like a dog throwing up earth behind it, taken the tube to South Kensington, and dashed up the steps of No. 52 at three minutes to nine. Was that Mrs Lemaitre who opened the door? She looked not unlike a headmaster's wife. Was he married? It could have been his sister or a secretary. He had beamed her one of his diffident smiles just in case. Did analysts have wives? He found the thought disturbing. Did Dr Lemaitre have sexual relations with her? His mind shied from the thought, but he found himself imagining Dr Lemaitre in pyjamas. He would wear pyjamas. He must wear pyjamas.

The door of the waiting-room opened and Dr Lemaitre stood there as the clock in the hall struck nine. He was wearing a suit and a bow tie as he always did. Harold stood up and the *Illustrated London News* fell to the floor. He bent to pick it up. He felt extremely foolish. 'Good morning,' he said. Confusion descended, making every simple movement a decision of great import. Dr Lemaitre, as he knew he would, said nothing. He preceded Harold down the short passage to the consulting-room and seated himself on his chair at the head of the couch. At least, Harold supposed he did so, because he did not look. Keeping his eyes averted he laid himself down and felt, with gratitude, its hard surface meet the length of his back.

He lay there looking at the ceiling. It was painted cream and there was a plaster rose in the centre; rather crude Victorian plasterwork but quite pleasant. Why had Dr Lemaitre chosen this house? It was a substantial one in a conventional upper middle-class area – not Hampstead. He could not have gone to an analyst who lived in Hampstead. He must be quite rich. Was he being asked to pay too much? Maybe his wife was rich? Maybe he had a mistress? No, he could not. Did he have children even now, at this moment, somewhere in the upper storeys of the house? They must have been begotten somehow. Dr Lemaitre cleared his throat and Harold heard his own voice say: 'Did my parents fuck me up?'

'Did your parents fuck you up,' said Dr Lemaitre evenly and without emphasis from somewhere behind his head.

The sound of the doctor's voice saying the word 'fuck' gave Harold a shock. His reverie smashed and the room twirled, shattered into a thousand circling particles. 'Fuck?' said Harold, wonderingly, as they began to subside.

'Your parents fucked. Maybe I fuck,' said Dr Lemaitre's deep, measured voice.

No, said Harold to himself. It was much better to say nothing. He lay there and tried to think about the room again. He would love to have looked round at the unseen presence athwart from his head. Did he dare? He lay still. Hour-long minutes went by, one after the other, in innumerable succession, pressing down on him with intolerable weight. This man was meant to relieve him. Why didn't he? That was what he was paid for. He would tell him off, demolish him, wrong-foot him, trip him up. The idea of Dr Lemaitre sprawled on the floor upset him. 'Help,' he said in a small voice. Suddenly, he felt like crying. He had noticed a box of paper handkerchiefs on the floor beside the couch. On no account would he touch them. He tightened his body and gritted his teeth. To his surprise a harsh sob came up his throat and escaped from his mouth making a loud and ugly noise. It sounded like a donkey braying. It hurt and Harold struggled with the pain, forcing it back down his aching gullet. His jaw hurt. His ears hurt. He found it difficult to breathe.

One day, when he was about seven, his dog, the family dog, had been run over. Harold could see its body now, stiff, helpless, paws in the air, dear brown eyes open. It was unbearable. Another sob racked, literally racked, his whole body. 'Rex,' he said. He had loved Rex. Something had gone for ever with his death. Don't be so disgustingly sentimental, he told himself fiercely. Something had gone for ever! How trite. Dr Lemaitre was a charlatan, a phoney trading in cheap clichés and trapping his clients into false second-rate revelations.

'You are angry with me,' said Dr Lemaitre from his bastion a little to the north of Harold's right ear.

'I'm not,' said Harold, angrily. 'I wouldn't be angry with you. You're not worth it.'

That'll get him, he thought. He took a deep breath and prepared himself to launch a devastating attack on

psychoanalysis, theory and practice, and on this psycho-
analyst in particular.

Dr Lemaitre cleared his throat. 'That seems to be it,' he
said.

Rage curled Harold's innards. A flame sprang up and
died away. He smouldered with resentment. This was
cheating. Just as he was about to touch his innermost
feelings, to trust the man with precious revelation, he was
turned out. Habit found him stumbling obediently to his
feet. Without looking at Dr Lemaitre, he made the doorway. He turned the handle, a slowed-down, dreamlike
action, and glanced back. The doctor's steady gaze,
unmoved, unmoving, met his own. He fled: along the dark
passage, past the clock trembling on the last stroke of ten
in the hall, to the bright fan of light above the front door.
There were wallflowers in the tubs on either side of the
steps. Their sweetness stung his nostrils cleaving a thread-
like pathway through the thick congestion in his head.
Some lines of Auden came into his mind:

> Only Hate was happy, hoping to augment
> His practice now, and his shabby clientèle
> Who think they can be cured by killing
> And covering the garden with ashes.

As he pressed the buzzer for his next patient, Dr Lemaitre thought:

> He wasn't clever at all: he merely told
> The unhappy Present to recite the Past
> Like a poetry lesson till sooner
> Or later it faltered at the line where
> Long ago the accusations had begun . . .

*

'I didn't do it, Mummy. It was Daddy's fault,' said Alice, nearly crying. It was not fair. Nothing was ever fair. She was not going to say any more. She lowered her head and looked at the carpet, herringbone matting with little ridges going this way and that. Flora slipped a small hand round her unresponsive fingers and held on tightly.

'Never worry, madam,' said Mrs Macguire, 'Mr Macguire will come down of an evening with his pot of paint. He'll fix it in a jiffy. You'll see.' She looked at Clare and made a clicking noise with her tongue. 'Now run along upstairs, girls,' she added, 'there's some nice clean things on your beds. Start your packing like dears. Mummy's upset. It's all this travelling in foreign parts. A week in the fresh air will set you all as right as rain.'

'Come on, Alice,' said Flora, tugging at her half-sister's hand, jigging towards the doorway. Alice allowed herself to be pulled, slowly, keeping her eyes on the herringbone and dragging her feet along the lines. She wanted Mummy to kiss her before she went. She never kissed her like Daddy did. She was always too busy. She knew she loved her better than Flora. She knew.

Upstairs in the bedroom, little piles of clean clothing were set out on the beds: folded vests, folded knickers, small balls of socks, shorts, checked shirts and Fair Isle sweaters. Alice sat down on a pyramid of socks. The rug by her bed had a sheep with horns on it and a palm tree. Mummy had brought it back from Egypt. Flora's rug had a camel. Children at a special school on the River Nile had made them, Mummy had said. Any school would be better than hers. She was always going to different ones. She could never keep up, never knew where she was. When they asked her if she would like to go to a new school, she just said nothing. Sometimes she nodded her head: it seemed to be what they wanted. She wished she could stay now. There was a girl who had asked her to tea. She had a puppy at home. The country was as boring as London.

Flora was jigging, up and down on her bed. '*Je t'aime, tu m'aimes, il m'aime*,' she chanted and jigged in time. '*Nous vous aimons, vous nous aimez, ils nous aiment.*' The jig became a bounce. She held her legs out stiff in front and pushed with her hands, pigtails flying. '*Je t'aime.* Come on, Alice,' she sang.

'Stoppit,' said Alice, 'it's silly. Stop showing off. I don't know French.'

'*Il m'aime*,' sang Flora. She was getting giggly and breathless. 'Yes, you do. It's easy. Just say "*Il m'aime*" and bounce. It's lovely.'

'*Il m'aime*,' said Alice, slumping on her pyramid of socks. It made quite a nice knobbly feeling on her bottom. Socks were rolling off Flora's bed and falling on the floor and Mrs Macguire's neat piles of clothes were getting rumpled up with the bedclothes.

'You'll get sick,' said Alice. She got up and went to the window. A nanny with a pram was walking along the pavement. She had a dachshund on a lead. The black car was there again. A man got out of it and stretched. He locked the door and walked along by the railings looking up at the trees as he went. There was a blue car behind the black car. A man in a mackintosh got out and got into the black car. Alice turned. Everything was boring.

Flora was doing standing bounces, gasping for breath and singing through the gasps. Alice made a dive for her legs and Flora came down on top of her. 'Beast,' said Flora. Alice held on to her and Flora thrashed with her legs. She was much smaller and Alice sat on top quite quickly and began bouncing on her. Flora squealed and wriggled out and began bouncing beside her sister on the side of the bed. 'One *two* buckle my *shoe*,' she panted.

'Three *four* knock at the *door*,' said Alice. They looked at each other and grinned, bouncing up and down in time to the rhyme.

'Well, well, well,' said Mrs Macguire from the doorway. 'Well, I never did in all my born days. You two will be the death of me. Come along and do what you're told.'

Alice stopped bouncing and looked at the floor. Flora lay back on the bed. Her cheeks were bright pink and her breath was coming in short gasps. She felt a bit sick. Mrs Macguire was on her hands and knees picking up socks.

'Where's your suitcases, girls?' she said. 'Flora, come over here. Your plaits is all come undone.' She sat on the bed. Flora stood in front of her between her knees.

'Where's that Heidi, I'd like to know,' said Mrs Macguire, undoing Flora's plaits and replaiting them.

'She's in her bedroom putting on make-up,' said Alice, making a face. 'Soppy Heidi.' She lay on her stomach and pulled a suitcase from under the bed.

'Ow!' squeaked Flora, 'you've got a bit of hair. What's my born days?'

'When I was your age . . .' said Mrs Macguire.

'Tell us about when you were little. Please, Mrs Mac,' said Flora.

'Please, Mrs Mac,' said Alice.

'Whatever next. I haven't got all day,' said Mrs Macguire. She finished Flora's plaits and gave her a pat on the bottom. 'There's a good girl,' she said to Alice. 'Shoes on the bottom, socks in the corners. Where's your hairbrush? Come along now.'

Flora stood on a chair in front of the cupboard. 'My case's on top. I can't reach,' she said.

'There, lovey, I'll get it,' said Mrs Macguire. She fetched down Flora's suitcase, brown leather with initials on it, and the three of them worked away. '*Savez vous planter les choux*,' sang Flora, dropping crayons in one by one.

'I don't want to go to the country,' said Alice. She could not find her toothbrush. She had not cleaned her teeth for several days. She did not know what to do.

'There, lovey, it's a shame,' said Mrs Macguire, 'it's a shame missing school. You come home and have tea with me and Mr Macguire when you get back.'

'What's it like being married to Mr Macguire?' said Flora.

'Get along with you, Flora. Any more of that and I'll smack your bottom,' said Mrs Macguire.

She waved to them from the top of the staircase. 'Be good. Do what Mummy tells you. Send Mrs Mac a post-card,' she called, as she watched them go down. Poor mites, she thought, as she turned back into the bedroom and started straightening sheets. Still, the fresh air'll put roses in their cheeks. She looked forward to a nice cup of tea in the quiet kitchen by and by. The place could do with a good spring-clean, she thought, as she withdrew a toothbrush from between the sheet and the underblanket on Alice's bed.

Guy and Vivien were in despair. They sat on the lop-sided wicker chairs padded with faded cretonne on the verandah and discussed the situation with some gravity. Mrs Bott had given notice. The quiet curve of the Downs, still, under scudding clouds, lay in momentary sunlight before them. The familiar view with its harmonious proportions never failed to give pleasure.

'Typical,' said Vivien.

'Sheer panic,' said Guy.

Mrs Bott, almost in tears in the dank flagged kitchen only half an hour before, had informed them that, owing to the indisposition of Mr Bott, she would no longer be able to bicycle up from the village to clean for them and cook. 'I don't know how we'll ever manage,' she had said, between sniffs, still in her shapeless coat. Her big red hands, strangely divorced from the rest of her body, protruded helplessly from the frayed sleeves.

'This is a terrible blow for us, Violet, you must understand,' Vivien had said, appalled. 'We have visitors arriving today. You know that.'

'I know, madam, I feel terrible,' Mrs Bott had said, 'but Mr Bott can't do nothing for himself no more. The doctor says. He can't lift a thing. I'll see if I can find a girl in the village for you.' She rubbed her sandpapery hand back and forth against her nose.

'Come, come, Violet,' Vivien had said, 'take off your coat. Make yourself a cup of tea or whatever you need – cocoa, perhaps. We'll discuss it later in the week.'

'No, madam. I can't stay,' Mrs Bott had said with uncharacteristic firmness. 'Mr Bott's not to be left. He had another attack at the weekend . . .' Her voice had faltered. 'He's very poorly. He can't be on his own. The doctor said.'

'But this is most inconvenient,' Vivien had said, sternly. 'You are being very inconsiderate. You know that Mr Hammersley's health is not all that it should be, and I am not strong myself. Surely you can find someone to stay with Mr Bott while you are out. One of your daughters . . .?'

'No, madam, I'm sorry. Truly, I'm sorry. Mr Bott needs me. I'll see what I can do about someone else,' Mrs Bott had said. She had wiped her nose again with the back of her hand, buttoned up her coat and cycled away down the drive, pedalling slowly, her lumpy figure overlapping the old black frame like ripe Camembert cheese.

'And the beds aren't even made yet,' said Vivien. She had her watercolours out, but had quite given up the attempt to concentrate on the Queen Anne's lace before her. She was vexed beyond bearing.

'What people!' said Guy. 'It's their terrible diet. Even Monsieur la Touffe won't eat anything from the garden except cabbage.' He shook his head. 'Poor old Bott. He can't have had much of a life what with being gassed in the war.' He shook his head again. He was looking forward to Clare's arrival as he knew was Vivien. The little girls and the au pair were another matter. He did not want to consider them too much, but tucked away in the back of the house near the North Pole they need not be too much of a problem. What glorious times they were going to have with Clare all to themselves. 'What about Rose?' he said suddenly.

Vivien looked up at him sharply. Rose! The perfect solution. 'Dearest Guy,' she said, fondly. She reached out and touched his hand. He clasped hers reassuringly in his big firm one. There were little brown marks on the back of it. They were all getting on. 'I'll go and telephone her now,' said Vivien. She must not fuss him. Peace of mind was the least one could provide for one's mate. She went off into the house.

Relieved to see her spirits restored, Guy felt for his pouch. He packed his pipe and leaned back puffing. The clouds, piling up in the sky, layer upon fat layer of white, grey and stormy black, still let through a patch of pure blue. The sunlight, now on the Downs, would be with them soon.

'Of course, darling,' said Lady Rose at the other end of the line, ever her cheerful, irrepressible self, 'what a catastrophe. Bad luck. I'm off tomorrow for a few days, but they can have the attic. The beds are all made up. I'll tell Huggins to leave milk and eggs. I won't be there myself when they come – I've got a party in London – but you can tell the girl about the Aga. Door open as usual. Don't let them go into my study.'

What a sport, thought Vivien, dearest Rose. 'Dearest Rose,' she said affectionately. 'We were at our wits' end, I can tell you.'

'I bet you were,' said Rose with a chuckle. 'How's Guy?'

'Well,' said Vivien, 'he's lost five pounds and he hasn't had indigestion since we got back from Italy. Where are you off to, may one ask?'

'Kentucky,' said Lady Rose, gaily, 'the races. In my new Lanvin. Isn't it lovely?'

'What a wonder you are,' said Vivien. 'We'll be longing to hear all about it when you get back.'

'Blow by blow,' said Lady Rose. '*Ciao* for now.'

'*Ciao*, dearest Rose,' said Vivien and replaced the receiver. She walked back through the house, settled down around her again into its still, tranquil self and went out on to the verandah.

Guy, deeply filling the old wicker chair, was puffing on his pipe and watching the clouds roll by. 'Marvellous,' he said, his head tilted to the sky. 'They never cease . . . Well?'

'Rose is going to Kentucky. They can have the attic,' said Vivien.

'Splendid,' said Guy. 'Who's she off with?'

'Who in*deed*. I *won*der,' said Vivien. They looked at one another, their social palates titillated.

'She can't be paying for herself,' said Guy. 'It must be a millionaire of some kind.'

'One can't keep up with dear Rose these days. Could it be one of her new film friends?' said Vivien.

Lost in pleasurable speculation, they chatted until lunchtime, when Vivien went to open a tin of quenelles – a little rich for the middle of the day, but it would have to do in the circumstances. Emergencies were what tins were for. She put them in the oven to warm through.

'What are we to do about supper?' she said, returning to Guy on the verandah. 'We were going to have cutlets and rhubarb crumble. Children like pudding.'

'What a problem,' said Guy. He was preoccupied with his pipe which had gone out.

The telephone rang. It was Rose. 'Just off to London,' she said. 'I've left some supper for the girls. The remains of some *foie gras* and a dish of *oeufs à la tripe*. They can do without pudding for one night.'

Guy and Vivien sat down to luncheon with serene minds. Afterwards, Vivien would make the bed for Clare, the fourposter in the best front room. She could manage supper for three for a few days, and Clare was an accomplished cook. For now, with the prospect of a delightful week ahead, they enjoyed their lunch, the two of them together across the table.

# Chapter Twenty

ℰ

Professor Kús jiggled the coins in his pocket. There were two of them, both two-shilling pieces and both with the head of the old king on one side; crossed sceptres and the shields of England, Ireland and Scotland on the other. One was dated 1933, the other 1935. He was on his way to London again, first to meet Pisti in the Reading Room of the British Museum, and then to have lunch with Victoria Benjamin. In the afternoon, he was due to give a talk at the British Academy. He would spend the night in his London flat where he hoped to persuade his lunchtime companion to join him, and the following morning at nine o'clock he was going, his Control had informed him, to buy a new tie in Harrods. There, in the clothing department, he would hand over the 1933 florin to an unknown gentleman wearing a purple tie decorated with yellow dots who had run out of small change. His spirits were high. Things were going to plan and his paper on 'Social Trends and Trading Patterns in Thirteenth-Century Kum and Yas Society and the Tatar Influence' was a winner, a work of pure originality brushed with genius.

The low domestic roofscape, spread out on either side of the railway in unending monotony as the train sped past, dreary to some, charmed his heart with its modesty.

How many stout British housewives in flowered pinnies hung out the washing, contentedly, to dry in the little gardens bordering on the line: how many oak-hearted British working men set out from their own front doors each morning, free from fear, to practise their chosen trades protected from exploitation by Union rules. A paid-up member of the Labour Party himself, he felt at one with his world.

As he hurried under the towering portico of the museum, a trifle late, he felt in his wallet for the little square of cardboard that permitted him to enter the Reading Room – the noblest hall of learning ever constructed by man. The photograph on his ticket showed a young man in his prime gazing with alert eyes into the camera. He had more hair then, but his attractiveness to women seemed undiminished.

Nagý was to be sitting at S1. Professor Kús caught sight of his checked tweed back bent over his books, spreading well out into oS and S2. He went and collected his own books, ordered up the week before, and sat down at S2, to Nagý's right. He set his own books in a pile to his left. Nagý did not raise his head. Professor Kús put on his spectacles and began to read; a frightfully dull and pedestrian account by T. Dömitör of the principal problems in his investigation into the ethnography of the industrial working classes in Hungary. After ten minutes or so of tedium, he felt in his pocket for his handkerchief and brought out with it two coins, two two-shilling pieces. He turned them over in affected wonder, remarked the one dated 1935, transferred it to his left hand and placed it on the open pages of *The Hungarian Academic Quarterly* vol. xxiv. He returned the other florin and his handkerchief to his pocket, yawned, leaned back in his chair and closed the book. He pushed it to his left and picked up a bound dissertation by I. Katona on 'Types of Work Groups and Temporary Associations of Seasonal Labour in the Age of Capitalism'. Then he frowned, searched among his papers and sauntered over to the enquiry desk.

Without taking his eyes from the book he was reading, Professor Nagý felt abstractedly among the books on his right. His hand closed over the topmost one and pulled it towards him. He smoothed out the pages and raked in the florin. Putting his hands in his pocket, he leaned back and stretched, looking up at the glorious blue dome above him apparently deep in thought. The hands of the clock were both on the XII. He glanced at his own watch, gathered up his books and took them over to the circular desks in the centre. On the way, he bumped into Gyuri. In piercing whispers, like children who believe they cannot be seen because their eyes are closed, they greeted one another patting each other on the back, their heads close together bobbing with cordiality. Then Professor Nagý made for the exit while Professor Kús went back to his seat. Half an hour later he, too, gathered up his books and deposited them at the central desk. He strolled out, through the pigeons in the forecourt and into Great Russell Street.

At the top of Shaftesbury Avenue, he caught a bus to St James's. Such was his mood of elevation that he climbed to the top deck and, since the front seat was free, lurched the length of the bus to gain it. From this position of irresponsible command he surveyed the drab grandeur of the urban monuments as they passed by: the theatres, the churches, the fine equestrian statues, the galleries, the clubs, and the palaces. From time to time his hand closed in his pocket round his handkerchief and the small silver disc within it.

Victoria was late. It was an absurd exercise – a day's work – to come for lunch into central London. Lunch was a meal she avoided anyway. In the early days her excursions into the outside world had been justifiable. Nowadays she was no longer the exclusive source of cultural information she had been: there were others. She barely knew their names. The hours she spent at the studios were getting fewer and the reputation on which her authority in the Programme rested was becoming historical. She had begun to feel out of touch, ill at ease, a stranger in the studio and a fraud in her own office.

Professor Kús – Georgie – had been irresistible on the telephone, persuading her with a forceful mixture of charm, flattery, persistence and logic. She ran down St James's Street in her suit, all summer-grey flowers on white linen. She liked running and her skirt flapped, dancing above her knees.

Professor Kús was standing rather belligerently in the hallway of Le Maquis. He was balanced forward on his feet, planted stoutly apart, his lower lip thrust out, his hands in his pockets. 'Tutz, tutz,' he said, looking at his watch as she flew in the door.

'Oh dear,' said Victoria.

He beamed and took her arm. 'The best things in life are always worth waiting for,' he said, giving it a confident squeeze. 'What is the clock but a confection of man's making? A little drinkie at the bar before we go up?' He looked at his watch again. Victoria shook her head. 'Do you want one?' she said.

Upstairs, they waited in the narrow doorway between

two rooms. Their table had gone. Waitresses holding platters aloft pushed past them and sang out orders down the lift shaft. The lift trundled up and down the shaft on a rope, and white porcelain dishes of *petit pois* and *entrecôte* sped before their noses. Victoria felt guilty, but Professor Kús's equanimity seemed unruffled. He kept tight hold of her arm and stood forward on the balls of his feet.

'There's a dear little table in the corner,' he told a waitress suddenly, and propelled Victoria towards it before he could be waylaid.

Seated among the crumbs, he gave the room a long proprietary stare while Victoria, embarrassed, put on the most aloof expression she could manage.

'Why do you waste your life?' he said, fixing his eyes on hers at last.

'I beg your pardon?' said Victoria haughtily.

'Tutz, tutz,' said Professor Kús kindly. 'This man is no good to you. You need someone to appreciate you, to give you little presents, to take you out to cosy dinners in nice restaurants, to admire your beautiful clothes and your clever mind. A woman like you needs someone to look after her.' He cocked his bald head to one side.

'Like you?' said Victoria, half melted.

'Exactly!' cried Professor Kús. 'We would make a vunderful couple. Life is so short. We will have such fun. You will bloom. I will be good for you!'

'What about your wife?' said Victoria.

'Ah, she is the most vunderful woman in the world,' said Professor Kús, sighing.

'Tell me about her. Where did you meet?' said Victoria.

So Professor Kús told Victoria how and where he had met his wife, what she had said to him and what he had said to her: how he had proposed to her, how she had

replied and about his six wonderful children. He told
her about his first precocious sexual encounter and his
schooldays in Budapest and his brilliant successes at university. He told her about his second girl friend and his
third and about how women, contrary to his expectations,
found him continually irresistible. 'There must just be
something about me,' he said modestly, 'I don't know
what it can be.'

'I don't know either,' said Victoria.

Professor Kús put back his head and roared with laughter. Victoria laughed too. He put his hand over hers, lying
on the red-and-white checked table-cloth and pressed the
fingers, one by one. Victoria felt the faintest thrill of
response creep into her heart. 'You and I were made for
each other,' he said, leaning forward and gazing intensely
at her. 'Soon you will be married. A married woman
always needs a friend. It is not good for the marriage,
unless. I have the sweetest flat in Fulham. You can cook
me little dinners. I have delicious wine. I will buy some
candles from Harrods. I will show it to you tonight.'

'Certainly not,' said Victoria, withdrawing her hand
which felt lonely without his. 'I must go. It's terribly late.'

'I will pay for you to go by taxi,' said Professor Kús
triumphantly, making it sound as if he had just invented
Christmas. 'Now, some brandy with your coffee. It is
essential for the digestion. You will feel sleepy at your
desk without. Tonight we will be together again.' He lifted
his arm and said, in a voice that made the whole restaurant
look up, 'Waitress!'

A waitress, puzzled, hurried over.

'Two brandies,' said Professor Kús.

'No, no, no,' said Victoria.

The waitress hesitated.

'Two brandies,' said Professor Kús, 'and the bill.' He took her hand again. 'Love is the best medicine in the world,' he said. 'Brandy is good but love is better. Today we will have both.'

'Oh, stop it, please,' said Victoria. 'I must go.'

The waitress brought the brandies in big balloon glasses and a bill on a plate. Victoria took a sip of hers and pushed it away. Her nose was red already. She got up to go.

'I will come with you,' said Professor Kús. 'Wait.'

Victoria waited. She had five shillings in her purse, hardly enough to get back to Shepherd's Bush by taxi. Professor Kús put on his spectacles, wrote out a cheque, swallowed down his brandy as well as hers and put a two-shilling bit on the plate with the cheque and the bill. He hurried after Victoria, grasping her arm above the elbow. 'I will write the address for you on a piece of paper,' he said in her ear.

'Thank you,' said Victoria. She felt frantic. It was after half past three.

In the sunny street, Professor Kús stood blinking for a moment or two still holding her arm. Then he let it go and sprinted along the pavement waving both arms. 'TAXI!' he bellowed.

A taxi swung round the corner and drew up beside him. 'Take this lady to Shepherd's Bush, if you please,' he told the driver. He held open the door and gave Victoria a pound note. Then, with great dignity, taking his time, he sat on the edge of the cab and tore a leaf from his note-book. He wrote an address on it in his tiny hand and gave it to her.

'I won't come,' said Victoria. 'Thank you very much for everything. I can't come, though, it's impossible.'

'Who knows?' said Professor Kús.

He stood in the street blowing kisses after the taxi and the sunlight gleamed on the pink dome of his bald head.

As soon as Victoria and Professor Kús left the restaurant, Volnicek lowered his *Figaro*, which the management provided for solitary customers, and let his eyes flick round the room. Having failed in his subsequent essays on Fox's flat, he now had to intercept the information that others had succeeded in obtaining from it. He glanced swiftly at the coin left on the empty table next door and felt in his pocket for a similar one. He had been at his table since half past twelve, eating his way very slowly through *omelette fines herbes* and *frites*, succeeded by cup after cup of black coffee, and he had followed the exchange between his neighbours with interest. He felt he understood the dynamics of Miss Benjamin's unconscious rather well by now and put her down as an anorectic type. He agreed with Professor Kús that she needed someone to maintain her self-esteem.

Only two or three customers remained at their tables and the waitresses were changing table-cloths and re-laying for the evening session. When no one was watching, he put out his hand and exchanged florins. The one from his pocket, he noted, was embossed with the head of the young Queen; the one from the plate on Professor Kús's table, he dropped into the inside breast pocket of his cheap suit, with the merest glance. It had the head of the old King on it and the date 1933. A second florin dated 1935, Centre had indicated, was now in the keeping of Professor Nagý and would also have to be intercepted within the next day or so. He paid his bill and left the restaurant, keeping to the shadowy side of the street as insubstantial as a spirit of the night, as was his custom these days.

When the taxi bearing Victoria back to Shepherd's Bush had rounded the corner, Professor Kús switched his mind into working gear. He put his hand in his pocket and the horrible realisation of what he could have done dawned on him. He explored the pocket further and found, along with his handkerchief, some shillings, a sixpence and a threepenny bit. He felt in his other pocket. He shook out his handkerchief. He felt in his breast pocket and turned the pockets of his trousers and his coat inside out. With mounting irritation, he turned on his heel and hurried back, remarkably fast on his feet, to the restaurant. He took the stairs two at a time and arrived at the top amidst a cluster of waitresses. They scattered with cries of protest as he elbowed his way through them and made for the table. It was bare.

He sat down heavily on his recently vacated chair.

'Monsieur, the restaurant is closed,' said a waitress sternly, appearing at his side.

'One double brandy,' said Professor Kús in a loud voice.

'Monsieur, I regret, the restaurant is closed,' she repeated. There was a touch of frost in her voice.

The professor looked up. He let his eyes rest on her for some time. Then he said gravely, 'Mademoiselle, you look charming in black and white. What style. What chic. How is it that Frenchwomen always lend such distinction to whatever they wear. Such allure!'

The waitress rested her hands on her hips and swayed them a little. 'Monsieur is very kind,' she said, 'but alas the restaurant is closed. I may be able to persuade the barman to permit you a little glass.'

Still gazing at her, Professor Kús leaned closer and beckoned. 'I have a little problem and I would like to confide in you,' he said. 'Earlier I left a small gratuity here for your delightful colleague. It was a two-shilling piece. Now, I have a young son who is making a collection of these coins. It is very important to him. He has 1930, 1931, 1932 – there is no 1934; 1935, 1936 and so on. Tomorrow is his birthday and I obtained the 1933 piece which will complete the series. By some unfortunate oversight, this was the coin I left for your colleague. Please, mademoiselle, I can tell from your beautiful eyes that you have a beautiful nature, you must help me to recover this coin. Its value is beyond price to me at this moment. I have many others with which to replace it.' He jingled the coins in his pocket, and the waitress regarded him doubtfully. Keeping his eyes on her face, but inclining his head to one side, the professor went on, 'You have young brothers, mademoiselle. I can tell from your sweet features that you come from a fine family. What is your name?'

'Yvette,' said the waitress and sat down on the edge of a chair. 'How old is your son?' she asked.

'He will be eight,' said Professor Kús, taking a chance, 'and his name is Nicholas.'

'Mon Dieu!' said the waitress, putting her hand to her throat. 'The very name of my youngest brother. I will see what I can do, monsieur.' She got up and hurried towards the service lift crying, 'Fifi! Marie-Claire! Odette!'

'The matter is of the greatest urgency, dear Yvette,' the professor called after her. He got up and began searching the room, lifting table-cloths, shaking them out and dropping them on the floor; unfolding napkins, displacing chairs and crawling on hands and knees to peer under benches.

Yvette came back and bent towards him. 'My friend Marie-Claire remembers the coin, monsieur,' she said. 'You were one of the last to leave the restaurant and your companion was wearing a very pretty white suit with a pattern of grey flowers. Alas, she has put it in the special compartment of the till – we share our gratuities in this establishment. It will be impossible to find now.'

'Nonsense,' said Professor Kús, clambering to his feet. He strode determinedly to the cashier's desk and started pulling at the drawer of the till. Yvette followed him. 'No, monsieur,' she cried, 'it is not allowed!'

Professor Kús ignored her. He held out a handful of coins. 'Put one of these in and open it. The patron is a friend of mine,' he commanded. Waitresses surrounded him, twittering like birds in agitation. One of them, giggling, took a coin and opened the till.

'Now,' said Professor Kús in a masterful voice, 'we must search through all this money and extract the florins.' He swept up a pile of cash and carried it to the nearest table. 'Bring it all,' he directed over his shoulder, 'and you sit here, you sit here and you sit here. I will never forgive myself if my son has to forgo this precious gift. And, my dear Yvette, a little digestif would held us all – Chartreuse, Cointreau, Benedictine . . .'

He started sorting through the pile of coins before him and one by one the three waitresses joined him. For ten minutes there was no sound but the chink of coins, and then Yvette got up and came back with a bottle of *crème de menthe*. She poured out four glasses and the professor patted her hand before swallowing his down. At the end of twenty minutes there was a large pile of florins in the centre of the table.

'Replace the rest in the till and now assist me to search

through the two-bob bits, if you please,' said the professor. 'We are looking for one with the head of King George V and the date 1933. Another liqueur, Yvette, my dear.'

The three waitresses bent over their task like seamstresses sewing pearls onto a bride's train, only lifting up their heads for an occasional sip of *crème de menthe*. Yvette leaned over them.

'I have it!' cried the girl who had opened the till.

There were only five florins left in the centre of the table.

'Bravo!' cried Professor Kús.

'Bravo, Marie-Claire!' cried the girls, clapping their hands. Yvette turned over the last coins and shook her head. Marie-Claire rose and presented the professor with the two-shilling piece. 'With my love to little Nicholas,' she said, curtseying. Professor Kús kissed her on both cheeks. 'You are a jewel beyond price,' he proclaimed solemnly.

Yvette took the coin from him and returned it wrapped in a scrap of white paper. 'Take care of it, now,' she said, wagging her finger.

The professor looked at his watch; he had five minutes in which to get to the British Academy. He took a sheaf of ten-shilling notes from his wallet and handed them round with a kiss on both cheeks to each girl. Then he hurried away down the stairs leaving the four waitresses, pink-cheeked from *crème de menthe*, to set about clearing up the restaurant. Yvette slipped off her shoes with a sigh and thought of her brother, even now on his way home from school in his pinafore. She would send him a postcard of a London bobby tonight, on her way home.

Professor Kús's paper was well received by the handful of

people who came to listen to it: a few historians, a sociologist or two, an anthropologist; no Sharpe. After sherry and some salty biscuits, which were as boring consumed by the handful as one by one, he set off for Fulham. He wondered what on earth to do about dinner. There was little in his flat but shredded wheat and sugar, the perfect food for after, but even his optimistic nature could not envisage the circumstances in which it would be appropriate in Victoria's case, were she to turn up. She would need candlelit wooing over oysters and Chablis. He reached his flat and let himself in.

Looking at its unlived-in interior, he felt some element was lacking – flowers maybe. It would have to be the restaurant down the road. There were candles there, at least, in Chianti bottles. He made some telephone calls to his family and settled down to wait. He had plenty of work to attend to but he kept falling asleep over it. At eleven, he decided to dine alone off shredded wheat. There was no milk so he put plenty of sugar on and chomped away, but it tasted like dry straw and kept getting stuck in his throat. He had a brilliant idea and doused it with whisky. Sublime! He had invented a great new dish, combining the innocence of the nursery with a touch of adult sophistication. He emptied the packet, poured on most of the whisky left in the bottle, mashed it all up and covered the lot with a thick coating of sugar. All by himself, he had concocted a most satisfactory supper. In high good humour, he went happily to bed and dreamed of the lunch boxes his mother had filled with delicacies for mid-morning break when he was a boy at school in Budapest.

Next morning he went, breakfastless, to Harrods. After the transaction was completed he would buy himself a magnificent repast such as the English excelled in. Sustained by the thought, he entered Harrods with the first customers as the doors opened.

In the gentlemen's outfitting department he was alone except for a few smartly dressed assistants, whose ties sprang out from under their stiff white collars with a life of their own. They converged on him, discreet but implacable. Professor Kús shook them off explaining that he needed to concentrate in uninterrupted contemplation before making a decision. They retreated and he fingered foulards and club stripes, plains and paisleys, tweeds, checks and spots. He rather fancied himself in a plain knit made of some heather-coloured wool. It would bring out a county life aspect of his personality hitherto neglected – just the thing for a weekend at Tees House. Absorbed, he failed to notice that another customer had joined him at the counter.

'I say,' said a voice close beside him, 'you haven't got any change you could let me have? I've only got notes and this tie costs 27/6d. I'm in rather a hurry.'

He looked up and saw a young man, fair-haired, in a dark suit with an old-fashioned look to it. He was wearing a purple spotted tie. Professor Kús put on his spectacles and peered at the spots. They were yellow.

'Certainly,' he said, 'by all means.' He fished in his pocket and brought out a pound note, a florin wrapped in white paper, two half-crowns and a sixpence.

'I say, thanks awfully,' said the young man. 'What do you think of this?' He held up a brown tie with pink and yellow flowers woven into it.

Professor Kús had never seen a man's tie with flowers on it before, let alone pink.

'Jolly good, super,' he said, rising to the occasion.

'I'll get it then,' said the young man. 'I thought it might

225

be rather egregious. Thanks for your advice.' He took the tie to an assistant and paid for it with two pound notes. Professor Kús decided against the heather-mixture knit and took the lift up to the restaurant, the taste of kedgeree already in his mouth.

# Chapter Twenty-one

Volnicek walked slowly to the end of the avenue, past the solid polished knockers, the window-boxes, the bay trees and the well-kept tubs full of wallflowers; past the area railings and the steps down into basement kitchens where cooks were preparing cutlets for their ladies' light luncheons. Mid-morning respectability lay soundlessly upon it, the roar of traffic remote and generalised.

He listened for a particular sound; for the gruff purr of a powerful engine. He did not turn his head, but looked up along the speckled trunks of the elm trees and into the leaves which alone stirred in quiet profusion above.

At the end of the square he turned and saw, from the corner of his eye, a front door open not far from where his car was parked. Two children, one dancing on her toes, one dragging her feet, a woman and a young girl came down the steps carrying suitcases. Still walking, he watched as they put the suitcases into the boot of a big grey Bentley, got in and drove off. It was the sound he had been waiting for. A woman in a sleeveless overall waved from the front door and closed it behind them. As the car turned the corner at the end of the street away from him, another car, a blue Ford Consul, drew out from the pavement and followed it. Volnicek gave a shudder.

He squared his narrow shoulders and set off on foot for the Embankment, a slight figure in a dark suit; a bank clerk merely, out from behind the counter for an early lunch. He merged, shadowless, with the shoppers in Oxford Street and Knightsbridge.

As he crossed Sloane Square his long thin fingers worried at the florin in his trouser pocket. Word had come that the information he had already forwarded was a part of what he — what they all — had been searching for and which must be destroyed. At Royal Hospital Gardens — London was full of trees — the florin came apart and he felt the tiny wad of tissue-thin paper, no bigger than a button, from its hollow centre. Pinching it tightly, he quickened his pace. He was on Chelsea Bridge now, a key to the death of the world compressed between two fingers of his right hand. In the middle of the bridge, he paused and leaned against the iron parapet. For a minute or two he watched plumes of smoke rise, white in the white-grey sky, from the soaring chimneys of Battersea Power Station. Traffic streamed past his back. Then, delicately, almost reluctantly, holding it in thumb and forefinger, he took the paper button from his pocket and let it fall, floating down weightlessly into the thick steel-coloured waters that rushed and gushed and sucked at inexorable speed below.

There it went, the poisoned fruit of the world's best brains assembled, as they had been during the war, in unique concentration in laboratories throughout the United States, lost from sight now and for ever.

Volnicek walked on and entered the Festival Gardens. Beneath the leaves, slow-moving high overhead, he sat down on a bench for half an hour, his eyes closed and his face held up to the diffused warmth of the unseen sun. He found that he was trembling slightly, his knees and his hands watery weak. Loss, he thought to himself, depression and loss. How strange. The emotion he would have expected was triumph.

Since he could not afford to fill the empty space symbolically, so to speak, with lunch, he filled his mind with thoughts of the task ahead of him. He must get to Oxford without delay, and on the way he would buy himself a KitKat, or maybe a Crunchie. Cadbury's Fruit and Nut, though less immediately gratifying to his mood, would be more nourishing, he decided. Mustering himself with the thought of this meal-in-itself, he rose and, varying his route, headed back to St John's Wood via Vauxhall Bridge and the Edgware Road. He took his briefcase from his car and walked across Regent's Park to Paddington Station where he caught an early afternoon train. By playing with the little squares of chocolate in his mouth and rolling the raisins and nuts round his tongue before he bit them, the sixpenny bar, paid for with a hollow florin now in innocuous fiscal circulation, spun itself out until Didcot. He closed his eyes and rested his head against the prickly plush that clothed the back of the seat. The afternoon with its inhuman demands lay ahead. For now, there was nothing but the journey.

That morning, Pisti's wife had come to the door to kiss him goodbye. This was an unusual move on her part. Generally, she made straight for the telephone after breakfast and immersed herself in committee work. She was an indefatigable voluntary worker. Professor Nagý was faintly surprised.

'You're not going to London again today?' she asked in her fine strangled sing-song.

He blinked up at her. 'No, no,' he said vaguely, 'no,

not today.' He padded off towards the garage, patting the pocket of his houndstooth jacket as he went. Beside the precious coin there was something smooth and square. He felt inside and withdrew a bar of KitKat. Touched by this attention from his mate of twenty years, he turned and blew a kiss in the direction of the closing door. He must make a more energetic effort to persuade her to accompany him to his next academic meeting overseas. It was a long time since they had had a holiday together.

He backed the Riley out of the garage and was startled to find it leap forward with a convulsive hiccup. Watering cans and garden brooms clattered down onto the bonnet. His brogued suede shoe hard on the footbrake, he eased the gear into neutral and climbed out of the driver's seat to inspect the scene. There appeared to be a few more dents and scratches on the green coachwork, he could not tell. Nothing of substance actually blocked his retreat. Resolving that his next car should be one of the marvellous new American automatic models, he inched with exaggerated caution backwards down the short gravel drive and manoeuvred himself out of the garden gates and on to the tarmac. With the open road before him, he depressed the accelerator firmly. Forward was the direction that suited him best.

He had a ten o'clock lecture that morning and then, after a tutorial in his rooms and maybe a modest lunch in the Senior Common Room, he would devote himself to the study of the information so neatly contained within his pocket. He looked forward to this exercise with the keenest anticipation.

The lecture went well. Professor Nagý enjoyed himself. Negotiating the concepts among which he moved with such masterly ease in a foreign tongue still lent an added edge to what was, for so many of his etiolated colleagues, a day-to-day chore. The tutorial, with an earnest young woman of great promise and provincial background, found his mind wandering. The bulges beneath her buff-coloured jumper claimed his attention. By what physical means could they be attached to the main bulk of her gawky person, he speculated. He went to lunch preoccupied with the problem. The college food was indifferent, but the college claret was superb. After a glass or two and the merest drop of port in the Smoking Room, Professor Nagý felt his mind ready to gallop for kilometres, like white horses across the open *puszta*. He was annoyed when the porter informed him that a visitor awaited him in his rooms.

'Whatever made you let him in, Large?' he asked, frowning.

'He seemed to know you, sir,' said the porter. 'He said you'd be sure to want to see him. A foreign gentleman, sir. Very persistent.'

'Tzutz, tzutz,' said Professor Nagý. Shaking his head, he walked purposefully across the lawn and climbed the stairs to his rooms on the first floor. They commanded a fine view over Addison's Walk and the meadows beyond drifting deep in long grass now that the fritillaries were over.

The slight black figure of a man with his back to him stood at the window. There was a static quality about the shadowy form that grated on the professor, buzzing, as he was, with expectation. He coughed loudly. He was profoundly irritated by the interruption and intended to deal summarily with the intruder, whoever he might be. The small serrated disc lay beside the smooth oblong block of chocolate. He fingered them impatiently in his pocket.

Both pleasures would have to be postponed. The figure turned slowly, a dark outline against the bright panes of old glass.

'Kindly tell me what you want of me,' said Professor Nagý as politely as he could. The figure before him sighed but said nothing.

'Come, come. I have a great deal of work to get through this afternoon,' said Professor Nagý grandly. 'Please tell me your business and then leave. I have many pressing and important commitments to attend to.'

The figure sighed again, deeply this time as if all the cares and evil humours of the world were contained on the slow breath he expelled. He took a step forward.

Professor Nagý blinked. He took off his spectacles and wiped them with a corner of his tie. Then he put them on again and narrowed his eyes. There was something faintly familiar about the cast of the form before him. The features of the face were becoming clearer. Unease stirred a remote leaf buried in the layers of his mind.

'Please,' said the figure softly, 'no blood. Peace.' He held out his left hand. The hand, strange for the time of year, was wearing a black glove.

'Peace – please – blood?' said Professor Nagý. His equanimity was disturbed. He peered more intently towards the figure in the window. But after all, this was Oxford, an English university town in full term: 'Kindly be so good as to tell me your business and leave my rooms,' he said sharply. 'I shall have to get the porter to throw you out.'

'The coin,' whispered Volnicek, 'the two-shilling bit, the hollow florin. Now. In peace. There is no other way for you.' The sibilants fell into the air like small stones into a bottomless pool.

Adrenalin flooded the professor's brain. His hand went

to his pocket. He took a swift step and moved to his desk, his big mahogany Fellow's desk. With his eyes like slits now, and fixed on the other's face, he felt for the drawer where he kept his gun.

Volnicek raised his right arm. There was a gleam of blue steel. 'I'm sorry,' he said sadly, 'so sorry.' He pressed the trigger and the force of the soft, muffled pop as the gun exploded jerked him backwards towards the wall.

Professor Nagý staggered too, but sideways and during the course of a long, measureless moment his figure crumpled. He made a horrible sound; part harsh rasp, part thin scream; the sound of a soul being flayed of its life. His head hit the desk with an ugly thud and his fingers clutched ineffectually at its corners as he slid to the floor. He lay there, a shrinking figure in a loud checked jacket, grey flannel trousers and brogued brown suede shoes, blood pumping sickeningly from the back of his head and making a dark sticky pool on the old carpet. There was absolute silence and the room filled up with the stillness of death.

Leaning against the wall, Volnicek knew he must move before the tide carried him away. With a colossal effort he stood upright and made for the body. He wiped his gun, pressed the dead man's fingers round the butt and dropped it beside him. He searched through the desk, found the professor's gun at the back of the third drawer down and slipped it into his own pocket. Then he knelt by the figure on the floor and felt gently inside its pockets. His fingers closed shortly on the expected two-shilling piece. He took it to the window, saw on it the head of the old King and the date, 1935. Without a backward look, he made softly for the door. His hands were steady and his step, though featherlight, firm. At the door, he paused. His eyes clouded a little. Clenching his teeth he tiptoed back to the body and extracted the bar of KitKat from its pocket. Then he closed the door firmly, walked unhurriedly down the stairs and out, across the lawns, under the arch and into the street outside, past the porter's lodge. He nodded and half raised his hand as he went by. The muffled buzz of urban summer peculiar to England met him as he emerged: the toot and rattle of small cars, the murmurous current of subdued voices absorbed by ancient stone, the quietening touch of lukewarm air, the veiled sun. He had no place in this alien land of muted colour and blurred edges: no place at all, now his work was almost done.

On the bank of the river by Magdalen Bridge there are boats for hire. Volnicek waited his turn and took out a rowing-boat. He rowed for a long while down the silver stream. And when at last the rhythmic motion of oars pulling against water had steadied the dissonant tumult shrieking silently within his mind and his body, he came to rest in a quiet place. There, drifting beneath a willow, he picked the florin apart, extracted the wad of compressed paper slivers and dropped it into the flowing stream.

Further down, he thought, this little river joins the Thames. Maybe the current will bear it down to London and, together, these two little wads of paper containing the most fearful knowledge the world has ever known, will be washed out to sea.

A great sadness descended upon him. Violence was so simple; the line between life and death so fine as to be almost indecipherable. Alone under the leaves, he wept salt tears of anguish for love of the human race.

# Chapter Twenty-two

❧

'Dearest Clare!' said Vivien, enfolding Clare, for the briefest moment, in her arms. She was not too keen on physical contact. Sex was one thing, very much so, in its place with one's chosen mate, but indiscriminate touching, hugging, patting – let alone the embracing of virtual strangers – she found irrational.

Guy kissed Clare warmly on both cheeks and held her to him. 'Splendid, splendid,' he said, his ruddy cheeks aglow.

Alice looked at the floor. She saw the old wooden boards; the corner of a needlework rug the colour of *petit beurre* – the dullest of biscuits – in which, she knew, a big lady with a fish's tail played among a pattern of shells; and her own, lace-up, brown school shoes.

Flora stood still, pink and solemn, holding her satchel with its precious homework inside; and Heidi, simpering and sly, looked around for a telephone. There was an upright one with a separate receiver attached by a cord to its side on a table down the hall. She had already noted the telephone box in the lane not far from the end of the drive.

'Good afternoon,' she said meekly, and gave a little bob as Guy shook her hand.

Flora wiggled her feet edging closer to Alice. She took hold of her limp wrist. Guy patted their cheeks. 'How are you two? Grown again,' he said heartily.

Vivien was talking to Clare in a muted voice. They were laughing together. Both children understood quite clearly from the conversation overhead that they were not to be staying with their mother after all.

'You're going to Rose's,' she said, coming over to them. 'You'll have the attic all to yourselves with Heidi. Isn't that lovely?'

Flora broke away from Alice. She threw her arms round her mother's thigh and clutched it. 'Darling, darling, darling,' she said, rubbing her face up and down against its cotton whipcord ridges. Far above, Clare went on talking to Vivien and Guy. They were chuckling in low voices. The whole party moved slowly out onto the sparse gravel in front of the house again.

'Hop in, my chickens,' said Clare, opening the back door of the big grey car. The children and Heidi climbed in. Flora made a dive for the smooth leather back of the front bench seat and clambered over. She slithered across and laid her head on Clare's lap, looking up at the underside of her chin. '*Savez-vous planter les choux. Avec le menton, avec le menton*,' she sang as the car moved off over the crunchy pebbles after Guy and Vivien in the old black Rover.

They drove slowly over the winding downland lanes. Alice stared out of the window. It was green, nothing but green: black and white cows in the fields, sheep on the hillsides, pink roses in the hedges and wispy white clouds in the washed blue sky. Heidi thought of Ivan: as she was going to be on her own with the children maybe she could conceal her lover in this attic, somewhere. After all, that was what girls left their families and came to England for.

Twenty minutes later they drew up before a red rambling manor. There were farm buildings to one side and a huge lawn giving way, gradually, to field, undergrowth and untidy copse at its distant edge. They all went in through the old porch to a high, beamed hall hung with many large and vibrant oil paintings.

'Up you go, girls,' said Guy, handing out suitcases. He patted Heidi on the bottom.

'Supper's in the kitchen,' said Vivien. 'Come down soon and we'll wait while you start.'

'I'll come up with you,' said Clare. She took Alice's hand. As she led the way up the wide wooden staircase a cry came from Vivien, now in the kitchen down the stone passages on the far side of the hall. 'Dearest Rose,' she called, her voice drifting and fading high in the rafters. 'She's left us a bottle of champagne!'

'How *lovely*,' said Clare.

'Goody, goody,' called Guy, his voice rumbling with relish.

On the first floor there were many rooms. Clare took the girls to a door at the end of a corridor. They knew the house well. She lifted the latch. Wooden stairs led up to a maze of attic rooms all opening in and out of one another. There were white bathrooms with sloping roofs and hawking pipes, worn rag rugs over threadbare flowery carpets and bright striped bedspreads on the beds. At the head of one lay a battered china-headed doll; on another, a hairless, one-eyed teddy bear.

'My darling Ted!' cried Flora, throwing herself on the bed. She hugged the bear and licked its empty eye-space. Alice stood at a window. A slanting view gave out onto the drive, the round patch of grass at its centre before the house and a long row of beech trees with a farm cottage or two on either side. Beyond that were meadows, woods and the rolling line of the Downs, soft now and clear, in the low light of evening.

'Is Daddy coming?' said Alice.

'Tomorrow,' said Clare, 'he's coming on the train.'

'Can he have breakfast with us?' said Alice.

'He'll come over in the afternoon. He can borrow my car,' said Clare.

'Where's he sleeping? Can I sleep with him?' said Flora.

'In the red room downstairs, I should think,' said Clare. 'Come on, I'm longing for champagne.'

'Champagne, champagne,' sang Flora. She took her mother's hand and pulled her towards the stairs. 'Will you play with us after supper?' she said, tugging. 'Come on, Alice. Come on, Heidi. Champagne!'

'I don't like champagne,' said Alice to no one in particular. The low rooms were silent and empty. She did not like dolls and she did not like teddy bears. Down at the bottom of the drive where the trees went round a corner, she could see a blue car. It turned round and drove away. She wondered if her father would bring a present. From far away, she heard her name being called. Slowly, she went down the stairs. She hoped no one would say anything to her when she took her place at the kitchen table.

# Chapter Twenty-three

Victoria had an eye infection. She had woken from a broken sleep with her right eye gummed closed. She had prised it open and lain there blinking. It felt scratchy as if there were a cinder under the lid. She had pulled the top lid over the bottom one but it was no use. When she got up and looked in the glass she saw tiny yellow crystals round the edge and a yellow slug of phlegm-like stuff lying along the bottom of her eyeball. The lid was red and swollen. She extracted the slug with the corner of her handkerchief and bathed water over it, but another one appeared immediately. She put on her make-up: at least the eye was clothed that way, and kept it shut. It felt better that way, but the cinder under the lid had increased in size. Her nose was red and kept watering. She felt scratchy all over. As she washed and dressed, hysteria welled up inside her; self-pity and rage. It was so unfair! The affliction interfered with her thinking. She felt mad.

Harold had gone early to the British Museum. Victoria drove back in the van to her flat. On the way she called in at a chemist's. The white-coated man behind the counter shrugged. It was conjunctivitis, he told her. There was nothing to do but to wait till it got better. 'Some people say this helps,' he said, and sold her a tube of Golden Eye

Ointment. The ointment made it even more difficult to see. She groped in her flat for country clothes, found her dark glasses and changed into her pale blue Italian trousers. With her bag neatly packed, she got back into the van and set off for Wiltshire.

She ached for Harold. She was held in an area of conflict where no movement was possible. Every alternative brought with it unendurable anxiety. Even now, the telephone might be ringing in her flat. She would never know. She should have cancelled the weekend; arranged to hand over the van in London. She would leave in the afternoon on Sunday as early as she could. The thought of the resounding silence in her flat, where each moment passed heavy with unfulfilled expectation, repelled her, but that was where she wanted to be – now. Any other encounter lacked substance, yet the burden of waiting in it was intolerable.

'Are you in love with anyone?' Jessica said.

What an odd question, thought Victoria. 'Well, yes,' she answered, 'I suppose so. Yes.'

'What does he do?' said Jessica.

'He's a writer, I think. I don't really know,' said Victoria.

'Have you been to bed with him?' said Jessica.

'No,' said Victoria. She went red and the bench on which they were sitting outside Jessica's cottage in the sun seemed to disintegrate while the air in front of her eyes filled up with a slow-moving pattern of dots and threads. Like tadpoles in dirty water, she thought.

'Are you in love with anyone?' she asked.

'Yes,' said Jessica.

'Have you . . . have you been . . .?'

'Oh yes,' said Jessica. 'He's coming tonight actually.'

240

Victoria was impressed: how casual, how daring, how
– improbable. Jessica, in her baggy rust-coloured trousers
and her loose bold-patterned shirt, belted at the waist with
a man's belt, got up. 'More coffee?' she said. She went
into the cottage.

Victoria shut her eyes and lifted her face to the sun. She
took off her dark glasses. Iliotherapia, she thought.

'I feel I'm being visited by a film star,' Jessica had said,
coming out to greet her in her floppy sun hat and her
flapping brown sandals when she arrived.

The cottage was in a quiet fold of the Pewsey Vale. It
occurred, suddenly, amid the fields deep in cow parsley
and buttercups. Inside, it was knee-high in junk; old armchairs listed on three casters in sporadic disorder, old
chairs half broken but usable and spattered with paint lay
about; old kettles black with time; new pictures, bright
with oil; no telephone, and Jessica's painting things everywhere. She brought out an enamel pot and two mugs. She
was weak on cooking but strong on coffee. 'Black?' she
said. The mugs made more brown rings on the table-top
beside the bench. Jessica had put it together herself and
painted legs, feet and shoes on it. They drank in silence,
the smell of coffee slow in the warm air.

'I'm going in. It's too hot,' said Jessica.

Victoria, just thawing, lay down on the bench. Her eye
felt terrible. She patted it experimentally with the padded
tips of her fingers. When the slats of the bench dug into
her back she turned over, pulling up her trouser legs and
pushing up her sleeves to meet the sun, and lay on her
stomach. The heat built up on the back of her neck,
burning out thought. She felt listless, lapped in lethargy,
caught beyond time.

Jessica had the wireless on; music, strange dissonant

music pinged from another world through the open window. She put her head out. 'You all right?' she called. Victoria sat up and blinked. 'Yes. Thanks,' she said. The world swung round and steadied. Her eye was full of yellow slime. She wiped it away and wandered down to the stream, took her shoes and socks off and put her feet into the speckled water. Mud squidged between her toes and a brown cloud swirled in the shallows. She stood and, placing her feet tentatively one in front of the other, walked upstream. Reeds and rushes in thick floating clumps dragged against the current. The water flowed in patterns of perpetual motion round them. She rolled up her trousers till they were tight above her knees and watched her legs, white as the water cleared, in the running brown stream. It was cool down there under the trees. Ahead, the little river ran in sunlight through open fields. Victoria found a dappled spot on the bank and lay down with her face on her arms and her feet in the water. There, in blessed and impersonal tranquillity, she fell asleep.

Juggling with regrets, Harold battled to keep doubt at bay. Perhaps he should have given in, cut the thread, leaped in the dark and gone, leaving all this behind; burned his boats, turned a new leaf and gone. Gone to where the struggle was clear and the choices were few; to where he had no past to trip him up, to where the page was unmarked. Followed Melissa, and gone.

As he stumped the short distance between his flat and the museum he slouched purposefully under the weight of his manifold burden. He almost felt his lungs grinding on his stomach.

Sit up! he heard his mother's voice say in his ear. Sit up! said the matron at school. Sit up! said Victoria. It's not good for you... not good for you... good for you... The voices echoed and floated away into the thick air above the roar of buses, all too familiar in their redness, as they thundered and blundered past him up and down Oxford Street. He slouched more determinedly. At the corner of Tottenham Court Road, the armpit of London, he paused to cross and envy swamped him, sour and sterile: envy for all these people surrounding him in shifting patterns, going about their business, secure in everyday preoccupations, propelled by normality. He hated them for it and yet – he envied them. He was the man in the crowd with an arrow pointed at his head, dogged with a question mark that would be attached to him for ever; a man apart in a space – an uncomfortable space – of his own making, a space whose edges were invisible to all but those who knew, always.

He crossed the road in his bubble. A man bumped into him.

'Sorry,' said the man.

'Sorry,' said Harold.

He put his head down and quickened his step watching the cracks between uneven paving stones pass as the toe-caps of his shoes, miles off, ate them up in silent gulps. There had been lines all round him in camp; solid, unbreakable lines and flat routine within them. He had taught himself Russian, forced himself to learn in half-hope of a better fairer future which might never come. He was in that future now, well in, and it was all broken up round him in meaningless dots: loose ends, false starts, high half-hopes, broken commitments; rage, shame, despair.

He would be safe in the Reading Room. But there was

a price to pay, a colossal effort and a commitment to make.

*Every farthing of the cost*, he thought gloomily,

> *All the dreaded cards foretell*
> *Shall be paid . . .*

He must get there. He hurried on, holding his breath and his hands, stiff; through the gates, across the forecourt, up the steps two at a time, under the heavy portico, through the cavernous hall. He gained the Reading Room. There, under the blue dome, he let out a long, slow breath as the great book-lined space enclosed him in blessed and impersonal tranquillity. He unclenched his fists and walked, an orderly man, to ask for his books at the central desk.

# Chapter Twenty-four

That night at supper, inexpressible sadness enclosed Victoria. They sat outside the cottage, three of them, at the painted table surrounded by buttercups and eating lamb chops in the lamplight from the open window. Victoria's eye was drying up and she took off her dark glasses keeping her face carefully averted from Jessica's lover. He was extraordinarily good-looking and his long hand lay now, easily, over Jessica's unkempt one on the stained table-top. He got up to take in the plates and open a tin of peaches for pudding and the two of them smiled at one another in a matter-of-fact, intimate sort of way. Victoria tried to see her friend as an object of romance and failed; she had not even made-up her face for his arrival and was in the same rumpled, ragbag clothes she had worn all day. Victoria looked at her in wonder. She felt herself to be many miles away, an outsider within the soft circle of light and prowling, wan, at its periphery. She yearned for Harold. Would he ever put his arm comfortably round her shoulders and help with the washing-up?

'I'll dry,' she said, jumping up.

'Oh, leave them,' said Jessica, 'I never dry up anything.' She put her hands deep into the pockets of her shapeless old trousers and strolled out again into the night: 'I'm going down to the wood to see if I can hear the nightingale,' she called from the open doorway.

'Coming?' said her lover, smiling at Victoria.

'Just a minute,' said Victoria. She ran into her room and looked at her face in the shard of mirror leaning against the chimney-breast: What's wrong with me, she thought as she saw her reflection in the half-light. She put on fresh lipstick and fluffed up her hair with her fingers. Then she ran down the hill to catch up: 'What an amazing night,' she said brightly.

'And how beautiful you look in it,' said Jessica's lover. His own arm was round Jessica's waist and he picked up her hand to put firmly round his own, keeping his fingers entwined there with hers.

In bed, the sound of panting came through the wall, regular, urgent, gathering in intensity like a train approaching and thundering by; grunts, a deep groan, a high thin squeal and silence. Then another train approaching.

Victoria put the bedclothes over her head, and a pillow. 'What's the matter with me,' she moaned to herself, 'what's the matter with me . . .? Why aren't I like other people?' She worked herself up into a fine old frenzy there under the bedclothes but no Florence Smith appeared out of the shadows to reassure her. Instead, as her muffled sobs gave way to sniffs and hiccups, a faint pure note of birdsong felt its way to her through the enclosing sheets. She lifted her head and heard the nightingale sing from the wood nearby.

The faraway sound was ineffably sweet but she had to concentrate hard to hear it. Was she too miserable to manage? Her bruised and battered heart dragged her further under the bedclothes and she settled down to give herself up to the misery which kept her close to Harold.

But the tiny, limpid notes impinged on her brain. It's June. It's a nightingale. I can't not listen to a nightingale, she found herself thinking. Go on – it's experience. It's too exciting to miss.

She threw back the sheets and slipped out of bed to the window. Golden fragments of song, like a bell on the night air, floated up to her, stopped and started again. Victoria had never heard a nightingale before. She felt very pleased.

When the song ended finally she went back to bed. To her surprise, she felt quite cheerful when she got in. She flapped the sheet smooth over her body and manipulated the pillow so it made a supporting bump under her neck. I must use my brain to think with more, she told herself. And with this resolve comfortably in place, she drifted down into sleep.

# Chapter Twenty-five

In the British Museum, Harold's head fell, with a snap, on his chest. The sudden movement penetrated the fog of thick lethargy drifting in his head, but feebly. I may be the first person to die of a broken neck in the Reading Room of the British Museum, he thought, hazily. Would it be murder or suicide? But sensation and thought, both, petered away before they had attained the activating centres of his brain. His eyelids, leaden-weighted, remained closed over his eyes. A good stock of books walled him in. They tottered in teetering piles and sombre cloth covers at the perimeters of his section of the desk, a reassuring buffer between pen and virgin paper – of which he also had a substantial supply.

He had the distinct impression that Dr Lemaitre, however neutral his silences, did not accept that he was organically brain-damaged. A glow-worm of irritation flared in the sludge of his mind. He would fire the fellow for incompetence and get a proper doctor, a professional, who would take his symptoms seriously, and attach wires to his head, reading off figures from dials whose needles hovered dangerously in the red. White coats, white rooms, white-aproned nurses with sympathetic blue eyes, white beds. But Dr Lemaitre did let him lie down! He gave a petulant grunt, sat up and ground his teeth. Seizing his fountain pen, he uncapped it and stabbed the nib at the top sheet of paper. It spluttered and splodged. Summoning all his reserves of self-control, he took up one of the red pens with which he had thoughtfully provided himself for underlining sentences of particular insight and circled the blot. What would a really good psychiatrist make of it, he wondered, turning the paper this way and that. A flying horse, an explosion, an insect, a mess? That's what he was: a mess.

Next door to him, an old gentleman, frayed and frail, bent diligently over his books, his pen scratching urgently away at the lined pages of the exercise book in which he was working. He had a well-ordered life, no doubt about it; a subdued and supportive wife, regular meals, a neatly mown lawn. Harold averted his eyes hastily. He was not really interested in him of course. He was too ill-used by life to be interested in anything. Nonetheless, his gaze wandered to the neighbour on his left, a fair young man in a black suit of old-fashioned cut, who caught his eye, smiled diffidently and bent back to his book. One book, Harold noted; a single tome of encyclopaedia-like proportion. A feeling of shame tingled at his fingertips. He stifled an urge to push back his chair and stride out in search of brain food, a bar of Cadbury's Fruit and Nut, from one of the cafés in Great Russell Street, and looked back at the clock. It was midday already. He would permit himself a break at one. He crumpled up the spoiled piece of paper, put it in his pocket and pulled the open book before him closer. '*Our usual experience is that in most cases non-violence is the real antidote of violence, and it is safer to infer from it that the highest violence can be met with the highest non-violence'*, he read. How fascinating. He made a note and read on.

'I'm sorry, the second bell has gone. I'm afraid you must return your books now,' said a low voice at his ear.

Harold started and looked up. A female face swam into focus, stern and unsmiling. 'Just a minute,' he said, 'I only want to copy this bit out.'

'You must return your material to the centre desk immediately. The second bell has gone,' said the woman severely. She pushed in the chairs on either side of him, which, to Harold's surprise, were empty. He looked up at the clock. It was just after ten to five.

'I say, I'm dreadfully sorry. I had no idea,' he said. He gave the woman a rueful smile, bemused but full of charm. 'I say, let me help you,' he said, getting to his feet.

'Just take your books back to the centre desk, please,' she said, coolly.

'Of course,' said Harold, 'terribly sorry. I do hope I'm not being a nuisance.'

The woman glanced at him from under greying eyebrows but made no comment. Harold gathered up his books in an unwieldy jumble and unloaded them awkwardly on the centre desk. He reserved them and made his way out through the station-like cavern of the front hall, down the broad steps and across the forecourt. Pigeons, disturbed, fluttered in droves and settled down again behind him as he passed. As he gained the street everyday life seeped back into his veins.

Christ, he thought with a jolt and looked at his watch. The hands stood at half past two. He put it to his ear. No sound. He started to run. As he did so, he was aware of a presence keeping pace with him at his side.

'Do forgive me,' said the young man who had been sitting next to him earlier, 'I wonder if you'd mind awfully if I ran with you?' The voice was educated, cultured and amused. Harold glowered at him, turning his head, and ran on. The young man loped alongside. Every time Harold looked at him he gave a companionable smile. His dogged attendance felt vaguely spaniel-like.

'This is rather fun, isn't it?' he said, once.

Harold's feet began to hurt and his breath came in painful gasps. He struggled to control them and would have slowed down, but the young man showed no sign of distress. Six minutes' hard run away they arrived at Harold's shabby Soho front door.

'Do let me help you,' said the young man as Harold, panting, fumbled for his keys.

'Go away,' said Harold shortly, reaching out and pushing.

The young man stepped neatly aside. 'I've simply got to speak to you,' he said amiably. 'You see, I'm a friend of Melissa O'Malley's.'

'Press!' said Harold, closing his hand at last over his keys. 'Beastly little gutter pressworm. Get out!' He put up his fists and swung out at the bland young face before him. The young man stepped aside again and Harold, impelled by the force of his own empty blow, fell painfully to his knees as the keys flew with a clatter to the pavement beside him. The young man picked them up and put a hand under Harold's elbow.

'No, no,' he said, dusting him down. 'You've got it all wrong. Truly. I'd just like a few words with you. Please don't get upset. I only want to know how she was. I'm in love with her, you see.' He inserted a key into the lock, opened the front door and handed Harold his keys.

'Damn you,' said Harold, uncertainly, as he started up the stairs. 'You'll make me miss my train.'

'I won't, I promise you,' said the young man, stepping lightly at his heels. 'We'll get a taxi. Six twenty-three from Victoria Station, isn't it?'

Harold glanced at him, puzzled. His presence was unaccountably soothing.

When they got into the flat the young man drew in his breath. 'I say, what a spiffing place,' he exclaimed, gazing across the sea of flotsam to the chimneyscape beyond. Harold dropped his papers onto the floor and sprinted for the stairs. 'I've got to pack,' he said, breathlessly.

'I'll make a cup of tea,' said the young man. 'You must be famished.'

In the bedroom Harold burrowed. Like a dog after a rabbit, shoes, socks, underpants, pens, paper flew up behind him. Some he retrieved and stuffed into a small cardboard suitcase. The young man appeared in the doorway. He had a cup of tea in one hand and a saucer full of crème caramel in the other. 'I've brought you this,' he said. 'You must eat something.'

Harold sat down on the bed. He did indeed feel a little dizzy. The young man sat beside him. 'It's awfully good,' he said, 'but drink up the tea first while it's hot. I didn't know whether you took sugar, but I put some in. You must need it. Don't worry about the time. We've got forty minutes.'

Harold drank the tea. It pulled his brain together somehow and the crème caramel slid down his throat like a blessing, creamy and soft.

As he ate, the young man spoke; his voice, this time, hesitant and very boyish. 'I just think she's the most wonderful thing on earth,' he said. 'She's what made me want to go on the stage. All through drama school I worshipped her. I've dreamed of getting a part, ASMing, anything, in the same play. And now she's gone . . .' He sounded so forlorn that Harold put down his teaspoon and patted his knee. 'You were about the last person to see her. What did she look like? What did she say? What was she wearing?'

'Oh Christ, I don't know,' said Harold. He got up. 'She looked like – Melissa,' he called from the bathroom as he peed. He looked at his own lined face and dishevelled hair in the glass above the wash-basin. Frowning, he searched for Melissa's face in the reflection. 'Something fluffy – grey, I think,' he called above the sound of running tap-water.

In the bedroom, the young man was at the top right-hand drawer of the chest of drawers. He sifted through the contents, his amiable features sharpened to a point. His white teeth gripped his lower lip, tautened now into a thin, grim line. He looked like a whippet, every fibre of his body tensed in urgent pursuit of its prey. 'I know – grey fur!' he called as he slipped two or three letters into his pocket beside a sickeningly solid florin. 'She's got the most marvellous silver fox. It's about my favourite thing of hers. How exciting!'

'Look here, I've got to go,' said Harold coming back into the bedroom.

'I know, I know,' cried the young man, composing his features into an expression of eager compliance. 'You've been most awfully kind. Let me help you. I can't tell you what a thrill it is to hear you speak of her.' He sat on the suitcase while Harold forced it shut and then picked it up. 'No, please!' he said. 'It's the least I can do.'

Together they ran down the stairs and into the street.

'Taxi!' cried the young man as he hurled himself into

253

the oncoming traffic, and, 'Come on!' he called waving from a cab on the other side of the street.

Harold picked his way through the press of cars. 'We'll never make it at this time,' he said, as he got in beside the young man. Pessimism infused his being and he sat slackly, his legs thrust out in front of him, his head hunched on his chest, as he parried one image of doom with another.

'Oh yes, we will,' said the young man cheerfully as the taxi coughed its way forward in spurts and the minutes ticked by.

Round about the Army & Navy Stores they had a clear run.

'Wasn't she amazing as Portia?' said the young man as the taxi rolled down the side-street of the station. 'I went seven nights running.'

It was twenty past six. He opened the door while the taxi was still moving. 'Run!' he said, and held out the suitcase.

Harold took it and ran. He sprang, ticketless, onto the train as it drew away from the platform.

I felt like that about Melissa a thousand years ago, he thought, as he eased his throbbing knees into the most comfortable position available among the sixteen legs in the crowded carriage.

Outside the station, the young man retained the taxi. 'Kensington Palace Gardens – the corner where it goes into Bayswater Road. Fast,' he commanded, his tone of voice quite changed. He leaped in and slammed the door.

The taxi-driver glanced at him. 'Right, guv,' he said. The world was full of lunatics and a fair proportion of them seemed to travel by cab.

The bowels of the embassy in Kensington Palace Gardens

rumbled uncomfortably that Saturday evening. The Second Press Attaché, his thin lips curved downwards, paced, soft-footed, between the desks where three clerks were bowed over the contents of Harold's old letters. Slaving at their oars, the whip of his unspoken authority drove them on. K. himself had been on the telephone from the Kremlin earlier in the day, his curt voice tight with menace, but so far the gleanings from Fox's flat turned in by the idiot novice had yielded nothing but domestic claptrap. The two indolent bunglers who had recruited him, Sharpe and Champman, were to be removed, but not before they had been forced into action; incisive, surgical action that would clean up the board and settle some scores. The weakling, Fox, was too prominent in British social circles and his connection with O'Malley too well known to be eliminated without raising suspicion, but some accurately applied pressure would bring him to heel. Volnicek could be obliterated without a ripple, and none too soon. They had seriously underestimated him.

That a single individual, working wild from some crazed perspective of openness and non-violence, could thwart the entire might of the Soviet Socialist machine – to say nothing of MI5 and CIA – caused him extreme disquiet. Idealism was the most refractory of motive forces, to be crushed wherever it manifested itself. It was well under control within the Soviet Empire: capitalism – material greed – would take care of it in the West.

He bent impatiently over one of the clerks, causing the man's spine to contract with apprehension. A call came through and he straightened up to take it. The most senior of his undercover agents, all native Russians, expert English speakers and employed at menial level by the British News Agency, was reporting for instruction. The Second

Press Attaché briefed him precisely and went back to his arid task of surveillance. There was little more he could do that Saturday evening and he wondered, fleetingly, if it would be enough.

# Chapter Twenty-six

There was one more thing Volnicek had to do before they came for him. He had made his drop at Finsbury Park the day before and spent his last night in the rooming-house in Paddington. It was Sunday. He walked wearily back to the avenue where the black Wolseley was still parked and leaned against the bonnet for a second or two. It was nearly dusk and a tremendous twitter and flutter was going on above him in the leaves. It had been swallows that swooped noiselessly round the turret room in his grand-mother's palace where he slept as a child, wheeling and darting at the level of his eyes in the fading indigo sky. These urban birds kicked up the most fearful fuss at the onset of nightfall. They were immune from intimations of mortality, mercifully incapable of prediction except at a mechanical level, yet they became extraordinarily agitated among themselves at the approach of darkness.

He saw, in his mind's eye, birds by the thousand million dropping out of a dead sky onto a withered earth that was arid and defiled beyond words; a world inhabited by a few creatures barely recognisable as human. One such creature, a young man barely the age he had been when, whole in mind and body and alight with confidence and hope, he had entered medical school, lay heavy on his mind; a sinless young man who had already suffered the consequences of the abomination whose development he, Volnicek, had sought so hard to subvert.

And, he thought to himself, to some extent, succeeded. He got into the car, set it in gear and slid out into the roadway. A blue Ford Consul slid out behind him. His right shoulder still ached from the recoil of the Beretta, but the car was as light on the tarmac as a ping-pong ball – he had forgotten how light – and put no strain on it.

He drove up to Swiss Cottage, Finchley Road, Golders Green and onto the Great North Road, the old road that led, calmly at this hour of the evening, through the shires to Scotland. But his journey took him only the best part of two hours. He was going to Peterborough to see a young ex-aircraftman and he did not look behind him.

On the outskirts of the city, he stopped at a public house and spent most of the money in his pocket on a small bottle of brandy and a packet of ten Players. A hollow florin remained and he fingered it like a talisman knowing that the coming encounter would be hard to bear. By degrees he found his way to a thin street of terraced houses and rang the bell of one of them. A small worn woman in a pinny, her hair held back with kirby grips, opened the door.

'Alexandr Volnicek,' said Volnicek holding out his hand.

'Why, you're no bigger than my—!' said the woman and clapped her hand over her mouth: 'I do beg your pardon. It's just that I thought you'd be a big gentleman. It's ever so nice of you to come. I'll take you straight up. He's been a bit better this week.' Volnicek followed her up the narrow stairway and braced himself for what was to come.

In an upstairs bedroom a young man of about nineteen lay, face down, on a bed. His bandaged arms were spread-eagled awkwardly at right angles to his head, the backs of his hands covered with raised red blotches. For the moment, Volnicek kept his eyes on the boy's face. His ears looked touchingly young under the RAF haircut.

'Mr Volnicek's come to see you, lovey,' said the woman. She stood for a moment at the bedside, her hands folded in front of her, and her eyes filled with tears: 'I'll go and get a cup of tea,' she said and turned away.

Volnicek approached the bed and bent so that he was in the young man's line of vision. 'Hullo,' he said.

'Hullo, sir,' said the boy and smiled at him with one side of his face.

'Would you like a cigarette?' said Volnicek, holding up the packet.

'Not half,' said the young man.

Volnicek lit a cigarette and held it in the boy's mouth; 'A little brandy?' he said, showing the bottle.

The boy shook his head on the pillow: 'It seems to make it worse,' he said.

'When it gets better, then,' said Volnicek knowing that it might never do so. He put aside the bottle and let his eyes travel further down the bed. The boy watched: 'Mum cleans it up a bit every two hours,' he said, 'it's probably better for her when I'm in hospital.'

Volnicek felt sick. He compressed his lips and swallowed but his mouth had gone dry. The narrow back was a mass of white pimples, open abscesses, raw black flesh, hard red lumps, pus and blood; a horrible fleshscape of eruption and putrefaction. He closed his eyes. 'I am . . . so . . . sorry . . .' he murmured and anger hardened his senses. He leaned forward again and, in an even tone, asked the boy to tell him what he could.

But Volnicek was familiar with the scene. It was one he had gone through many times in his mind's eye: the island in the Pacific, the thousands of young servicemen ludicrously unprotected, lined up in rows with their knees drawn up to their heads and their hands obediently covering their eyes; the explosion, apocalyptic in its might high overhead and the unending flash so violent that it made flesh transparent, so intense that blood boiled in the veins and naked eyeballs melted in their sockets – and then, the blast and the tiny toiling figures running, running as it hurled them flat before it and bent the palm trees to the ground.

The young voice, steady at times, finally faltered and faded away. 'Nobody mentioned it for the rest of the day,' whispered the boy at last, 'nobody mentioned it . . .'

Volnicek waited, then he said: 'When did this – this trouble of yours begin?'

'Well, it was two weeks later,' said the boy, 'I was flying home with the squadron when my back came up all over in white pimples and then they turned into abscesses and hard cysts. It was over a year ago now and they haven't been able to do anything for me. I've been in and out of hospital ever since. They say it's got nothing to do with what happened out there, but I don't believe them. What happened out there wasn't human – no more than what's happened to me.'

There was silence in the room. Volnicek could not speak. There were no words. He struggled to keep his head and, after a few moments, he said: 'You are quite right, do not believe them. You will have to keep fighting, maybe for years. They do not want to know. No one

260

wants to know. They will make you feel isolated, aberrant, mad – but it is they who are insane. They live in a world of delusion and obsession: your experience is real. You are not out of your mind. Be quite sure of that, always. You and I will not meet again, but there are others like me who will stand with you. Be true to the knowledge that comes from your own experience. You *know*.'

It was what he had come to say.

The boy on the bed gave him a long, level look: 'I *know*,' he said and nodded.

Half an hour later when Volnicek left the house, it was quite dark. He noticed the blue Ford Consul up the street but with detachment. It was from another world, a world that he had stepped out of a lifetime ago, two days gone by. Clock time was an irrelevant concept in terms of human experience. He drove off and noticed, too, how loosely the steering-wheel of the worn old Wolseley, normally so solid, moved under his hands. He hoped to make the open road. He felt immensely serious: light but steady. A responsible man. He reached the highway and turned towards London. The road, raised above the flat fenland fields, stretched ahead. The headlights made a tunnel in the dark. Volnicek thought of *The Song of the Earth* and Miss Benjamin's bright face came into his mind. He smiled to himself.

At the first bend, he swung the wheel but the car did not answer. Instinctively, he swung in the other direction. The car sped on, skidding across the road out of control, and careered screeching down the bank; a metal box whose complex arrangement of wires and tubes and internal combustion were quite impotent beside the two great forces that collided in him at that moment. He felt their presence: Life and Death.

261

As the car crashed into the trees Volnicek saw blue sky. The sky was his mother's face. He reached up to embrace her and the metal box crumpled like tinfoil around him.

The tremendous noise of the crash that ruptured the night died slowly away. The leaves on the trees trembled and lay still. Quiet crept back from the stars and made the night its own again. Two men got out of the blue Ford Consul and ran across the road. They dragged Volnicek, limp, from behind the wheel that had crushed his breastbone. Accomplished professionals, they laid him on the ground. One searched his car, the other his person. His neck was broken too. After ten minutes of intense, methodical work they ran back to their car again, put it in gear and drove at speed towards London. They had with them a gun, a bar of chocolate and a two-shilling piece – hollow and empty at the centre.

# Chapter Twenty-seven

'Rhoda, where are my shooting trousers?' shouted Sir Geoffrey Champman from his dressing room that mid-afternoon. He was in a fury and the fact that there were no trousers under the Norfolk jacket hanging in his cupboard exasperated him still further.

'On the hanger, dear, in your cupboard,' said Lady Champman hurrying into the dressing-room. 'All clean. They're just back from the cleaners'.'

Sir Geoffrey glared at his wife. He held out the jacket on its hanger: there were indeed no trousers hanging beneath it. Lady Champman put her hand to her mouth and drew in her breath. 'They must have fallen, dear,' she said. She got down on her knees and started searching on the floor of the cupboard, a handsome Georgian piece from Mallets, terrible doubt at the back of her mind. The hanger had seemed oddly light when she carried it up from the hall.

'You think I'm an oaf,' shouted Sir Geoffrey, 'what makes you think I haven't been through all this myself. There are *no* trousers, I'm telling you.'

He had had an appalling day. B himself had been on the telephone from the embassy, his thin sneering voice cutting through the thickened carapace that surrounded

Sir Geoffrey's heart and making it contract with fear. 'We should have the coverts drawn at least by tonight,' he had blustered through his whiskers. B was a frequent guest at the clay pigeon shoots organised by the British Press Agency for top officials from foreign missions.

'Should?' said B and hung up.

Sir Geoffrey hurried angrily out to the Rolls, taking short, rocking steps. He was wearing his double-breasted blazer and grey flannels. The chauffeur held open the door of the driving seat for him and took his suitcase to put in the carpeted boot.

'I'm so sorry, dear,' wailed Lady Champman from the front steps. She came running down them to put her head in the window and fondle his sideburns, but Sir Geoffrey wound it up and drove off without looking at her. 'I'll be at Achille Serre's when they open on Monday,' he heard her cry. His fury at the incompetence of the idiot young man, a Cambridge protégé of Christopher's naturally, selected for breeding rather than brain, made him tremble with fury.

'It all went exactly as planned only the coin was solid. It had the right date and everything,' he had said in his impenitent cultivated voice.

'Well, get hold of the information by this evening,' Sir Geoffrey had growled, his face turning purplish red and his neck bulging over his stiff white collar. Deep in the cellars under Kensington Palace Gardens, the cryptographers were even now working on the letters the young man had eventually turned in, but so far they had revealed nothing but platitudes and pleasantries. Sir Geoffrey amused himself by taking a meat cleaver to the young man's head; should he slice through it from top to bottom or sever it at the neck? Either way there would be a gratifying amount of human blood. He decided to sever it at the neck; that way, the expression of righteous innocence would be preserved for a few hours. Rhoda could join him. He knew all her expressions too well to want to preserve any of them.

Having externalised, at least in fantasy, some of the primitive drives raging within him, Sir Geoffrey felt calmed. He reached for the glove compartment and felt, beneath its walnut veneer, for the silver hip flask. He took a swallow of whisky and swung the car into a Clapham side-street. He parked it outside a small ruined house in a cobbled mews and saw the corner of a net curtain lift. Two expressionless eyes caught his and Sir Geoffrey nodded briefly. He locked the doors of the Rolls, dropped the keys into a dustbin and walked half-way across the Common. He made a turn round the pond and walked back, his weight compressing the hard earth beneath his expensively shod feet. He had worked his way ruthlessly to the top trampling down all who stood in his way. He was a man of power. No one could touch him and those thugs in the Kremlin were, after all, thousands of miles away in Moscow.

In the mews again he made for the run-down garage where one of the blue Ford Consuls with 3-litre engines awaited him. He let himself in. There should be some good sport tonight and he, in his mobile headquarters, would be at the heart of it.

Whilst ebullience and self-deception buoyed up Sir Geoffrey Champman, a mood of extreme melancholy overtook Sir Christopher Sharpe. Alone in his office dread and foreboding held him in their grip and suppressed all his carefully cultivated aestheticism under a grey blanket of dejection. The black dog had shadowed him all his days, holding him aloof from his fellow beings since childhood. Isolated and ill at ease, he had retreated behind the boundaries of his own intellect and found solace and passion there in the marvellous world of art to which he had been profoundly attached since his schooldays at Eton. He gazed at the glowing gem by Wright of Derby on the ash-coloured wall of his office and willed it to enter into his consciousness to flood him, as it unfailingly did, with its vitality and sensuousness. But though he concentrated with all his power it remained just a picture, a small flat square of painted canvas behind a pane of glass.

He knew he had failed. He knew that, whatever the outcome of the approaching night and the next day's operations, the descent from the uplands of abstract thought to the vulgar plain of brute force was a failure for him personally and one that filled him with distaste. He had initiated the plans and he doubted their efficacy. Though Geoffrey concerned himself with their actual execution, he was responsible for their conception and it was an aesthetic downfall he abhorred. His young protégé, a graduate of his own college, had discredited him. He had been outwitted – they had all been outwitted – by an insubstantial amateur working for a loose affiliation of anarchic outsiders. Disorder was anathema to Sir Christopher: order, his god. He was a fastidious man. At best he would have to live now carrying an ugly mark like a wart on the body of his mind with him for ever. At worst, he would be forced to follow Melissa, not on his own terms, but disgraced, leaving an unseemly tangle of loose ends, incomplete endeavours and unfulfilled expectations in his wake.

He lowered his silver head down onto his desk and let

266

himself be swept on a sea of disgust. And by and by, an image swam into his mind. Indistinct at first, Sir Christopher clung to it as to a raft. As it clarified he recognised the image itself as one of a raft, a great raft in the history of painting, a seminal image of the nineteenth century: one in which men betrayed and abandoned by their fellows were elevated by the art of a great master into a composition of transcendent beauty.

Géricault, he thought, 'The Raft of the Medusa' and as he contemplated the work in his mind's eye, its noble rhythms filled his being with harmony. He raised his head, sat back in his chair and looked round his office. The room was occupied with paraphernalia relating to the great Italian Exhibition. That had been an achievement, an undertaking accomplished in entirety, complete and unblemished. He must do what he had to do now with dignity and aplomb. Before addressing himself to his work, however, he should telephone Sussex. He lifted the receiver, dialled o and gave the operator the Hammersleys' number.

'Vivien, my dear,' he said in his languorous baritone, 'I find myself in your part of the world on Tuesday. May I impose myself upon you for an hour or two in the evening?'

# Chapter Twenty-eight

꩜

It was Monday afternoon. Harold, a little girl in either hand, was waiting on the platform. He felt sad. A sense of futile yearning enclosed him, so he jumped up and down and pulled some faces. He wished he could think of a funny song. Flora squealed.

'Don't!' she cried and stuck out her tongue. She held on to her satchel and jumped up and down too.

Harold started marching. 'It's a long way to Tipperary,' he sang. Alice detached herself. She went and leaned by the chocolate machine which stood still, narrow and red with Nestlé written in gold upon its brow, near the footbridge over the line. Her face was pale, the two plaits of uncombed honey-coloured hair falling down either side of it.

'Let's have some chocolate!' said Harold. He fished in his pocket for pennies and held Flora up to put hers in. Alice put in her own. During the moments between the disappearance of the pennies and the magical arrival of the chocolate far below on its metal tray, a gleam of animation warmed her eye. As she picked up her thin red bar a train rounded the curve of the line.

'She's coming – she's coming!' cried Flora and hid herself behind Harold's legs. Alice bit into the condensed milkiness of the chocolate and stared. There were wire baskets of flowers hanging from iron columns on the platform and some flower beds marked out with white-painted stones from the beach. Red salvia, white marguerites and blue lobelia. She liked the colours.

Victoria stepped down from the train, dragging her big bag and a suitcase behind her.

'What on earth have you got there?' said Harold angrily. She looked ridiculously smart in dazzling white trousers, a bright pink top and big, square gold earrings. Her lipstick, thick and pink as coconut ice, exactly matched her top. Stifling an urge to smear it all over her face and push her in the dirt, he kissed her gingerly on the cheek and picked up the suitcase. 'Christ, what's in this?' he said.

Victoria kissed him lightly, careful not to leave a mark. Her heart sank. 'Hullo, Alice,' she said, 'I've brought you some bubbles – and here's some for you,' she said to Flora. She gave the children two tin cylinders of bubble mixture and took one out from her handbag herself. 'Look,' she said, and blew. A flock of iridescent bubbles crowded out of the tin holder. They floated lazily through the air before they popped and disappeared.

She unscrewed the cap for Flora and bent down. 'Put your mouth close and blow – gently,' she said. Flora puffed. Nothing happened. Slowly, with her back turned, Alice unscrewed her tin and blew; a minimal experimental breath. Bubbles flew out and surrounded her head.

'Well done, Alice,' cried Harold. Victoria swooped forward and caught two or three on her own holder. She waved them in front of Flora. Tiny spheres of rainbow-coloured soap danced about the little girl's face. She spun around among them and some of the mixture slopped out of her tin onto the grey stone of the platform. Alice

269

grinned. She waved her holder above her head and released a stream of bubbles. Maybe the whole world was a bubble blown by God, a huge bubble full of little people that might collapse and fall apart when He was angry or tired and stopped blowing. Perhaps He would make her His assistant when she grew up. 'Look, a whopper!' she cried.

They got into the car, opened the windows and blew trails of bubbles into the sky as they drove across the Downs. A woman by a cottage gate waved and a boy, riding no-handed on a bicycle, put two fingers in his mouth and whistled. Driving beside her on the front seat, Harold thought how nice Victoria smelled. He accelerated over a hump-backed bridge and the two little girls hit the roof with squeals of joy.

'Don't be so unfeminine,' he had said to her on the telephone. 'You're turning into a bossy office dyke.'

'What's a dyke?' Victoria had said, trying to deflect the painful impact of his words.

Down in Sussex, at the other end of the line, Harold howled. 'How can you be so hypocritical,' he yelled, 'you pretend to be so innocent and you're as hard and ambitious as nails. You know perfectly well exactly what I mean. Everybody knows what a dyke is.'

'I don't,' said Victoria, sticking to her point. It was the only one she felt she had.

'I-don't-know-what-it-is,' crooned Harold, 'just because you don't read about it in your second-rate magazines, you pretend it doesn't exist. You're pathetic. Everyone says so. Anyone who was a proper feminine woman would put human relationships first. You're just interested in office politics and your career. You're unnatural.'

Was she? thought Victoria. Probably. She had always

felt deficient in some essential element of sexuality. She had not even kissed until she was twenty-five. Her hand shook on the telephone. Harold had discovered her secret. 'I can't just not go in on a Monday,' she had said in a faltering voice, and thought, Who's *everyone*? I must think they like me when they don't.

'Everybody else does,' said Harold. 'Everybody who has a proper instinct for life.'

Victoria thought of the team: Owen and Andrew and Gregory and Roderick, her trail-blazing companions from whom she was becoming more and more estranged; they all worked twenty-four hours a day without thought and they were proud of it.

'Just because you're surrounded with second-rate hacks who haven't got anything else in their lives . . .' came Harold's voice in her ear.

Perfectly true, thought Victoria uneasily, they really don't seem to be interested in anything except the Programme.

'Say something,' said Harold. 'I'm not going to stand here with an empty telephone in my hand.' He looked round the vast empty panelled hall. Virginia creeper flapped at the mullioned window in the evening breeze. There was too much emptiness altogether. Outside on the lawn Alice and Flora were sprawled listlessly in deckchairs. 'What shall we do?' they said every time he went near them, and Heidi was – where was Heidi? She was useless, anyway.

'I've got Edith Sitwell coming in on Tuesday,' said Victoria's voice in his ear.

'Another dyke!' Harold had shouted. 'I'm going to put down the telephone.'

'Oh no, don't. Please, please don't,' said Victoria. She

had waited for this call an interminable weekend, her mind going round and round in the same worn groove. She had left Jessica's cottage in the country on a sunny Sunday afternoon in early June just as wild roses opened up in the hedges. She had panted and fought to save seconds as she struggled to her flat and waited in the crashing silence where every torturing minute that passed took an unendurable age. She could not think of anything else. She did not want to think of anything else. She could not return to that place. 'I'll come,' she said doubtfully.

'Don't sound so off-putting,' said Harold without much effect. A weight off his mind, he had just thought of French Cricket. He genuinely could not wait to put down the telephone and saunter out onto the lawn with this brilliant new entertainment.

'It'll be lovely,' Victoria had said, determinedly. This was the first step on a new path, a pathway to where she had always wanted to be. Thus she would gain her spurs and enter the realm of Real Womanhood.

It was with this expectation in mind that she stepped down from the train at Arlington Halt.

'Victoria will brush your hair — Victoria will sew on the button,' said Harold. He was leaning back on his elbows on one of the beds in the attic. Flora, on her haunches on the floor between his legs, hugged them close round her ears. Victoria was at the window brushing Alice's hair just as Florence Smith had used to brush hers in the upstairs nursery in Bayswater: a hundred strokes night and morning with plaits on weekdays and curl-papers on Friday nights, so that all weekend she could have lovely fat ringlets bouncing like glossy brown springs all round her head.

Victoria could not imagine Alice enduring the lumpy

discomfort of curl-papers, nor could she imagine her sitting on a stool, adoringly, at Florence Smith's knees in front of the nursery gas fire as they were applied: the bowl of water in front of the gas fire, the canary in the cage, her brother hammering pegs in the corner, Radio Malt or Syrup of Figs yet to come and then, the supreme pleasure of the day, bedtime reading.

'Shall I read to you in bed?' she said, and regretted her presumption. There was a long silence and then, 'Haven't got a book,' said Alice tonelessly.

Victoria was shocked. She glanced at Harold. Harold's forehead furrowed into a black frown: she dreaded the expression. 'But I'm always giving you books,' he said. 'What happened to that big book of Hans Andersen? It was extremely expensive.'

'I'll tell you a story, if you like,' said Victoria quickly.

It had been a hard day. They had spent the afternoon in the woods with packets of jam sandwiches that Victoria had cut. She had passed a lot of time on all fours being a bear and a bucking bronco. The knees of her trousers, Harold observed with some satisfaction, were covered with green and brown stains. They had played endless games of hide-and-seek and tag and lain on their backs, looking up through the leaves to eat the sandwiches. Gradually, grudgingly, gratitude and a faint sense of validation seeped into a locked corner of his heart. 'Have a sandwich,' he said.

'No, thank you,' Victoria had said.

'Don't be such a prig,' said Harold.

Victoria had nibbled her way, very slowly, through a whole marmalade-filled white triangle which was what real women, she supposed, did. She had made daisy-chains on the lawn and had been rewarded, as they went in for the children's supper, by Flora slipping a hand into hers. It had been a strange supper of *foie gras*, sausages, orange-ade and ice-cream and now, when the children were settled, she and Harold would have their own alone at the kitchen table.

'May I walk down to the village, Mr Fox?' said Heidi, putting her head round a door.

'I'm afraid it's rather boring,' said Harold, 'but do go if you want to.' He felt annoyed but gave her a big smile.

'I shall not be bored. I love the mountains,' said Heidi with a prim smile.

Desperately regretting her reckless offer, Victoria was trying to think of stories. It would have to be 'Moses in the Bulrushes', she thought. 'Do you know the story of David and Goliath?' she said. The two girls, in bed now, stared at her above the sheets. Flora put a thumb in her mouth.

'Once upon a time,' said Victoria, 'there was a shepherd boy in the land of Israel . . .' She sat on the end of Alice's bed.

'I'm going down for a drink,' said Harold. Victoria was relieved: the lacunae would pass. He kissed the children and left the room.

When Victoria joined him twenty minutes later he was sitting in an armchair reading *Horse & Hound*, a glass of whisky balanced on the arm. 'What's for supper?' he said. He looked contented, domestic even, almost like a hus-band. 'I'll go and get it,' said Victoria fondly and hurried to the kitchen.

After supper, they walked in the moonlight and Harold kissed Victoria. The night was light and very still, the sky round the moon a deep and luminous royal-blue like the little satin cushion on which her nanny's favourite scent from Woolworth's, 'Midnight in Paris', used to nestle in an Eiffel Tower-shaped bottle. He tumbled her to the ground and struggled to take her trousers down.

This is what real lovers do, thought Victoria. She sucked in her stomach and hastily pulled down the zip.

'Why do you always wear things too tight for you?' gasped Harold, an edge of annoyance in his voice.

Victoria wriggled the trousers down below her bottom. The grass was damp and prickly. She hoped there were no insects crawling in the stems. She had never made love out of doors before. She squeaked behind closed lips. 'There's an ant up my bottom,' she whispered.

'I'll sting you,' whispered Harold back. He rolled her over and dug his fingernails into the soft flesh of her behind. Victoria's face was pressed into the ground. She could not breathe. She put her arms up behind her back and tried to get her fingers into Harold's ears, caressing the lobes. Her knees, constrained by the trousers half-way down her legs, were trapped. She was ashamed of the discomfort she felt when she should be carried away by romance. Harold pinched her several times, rather sharply.

His penis, big and hard, was between her buttocks. Victoria heaved and turned over. She kicked her trousers further down her legs.

'Hold me tight,' whispered Harold. He thrust his penis between her thighs and Victoria squeezed. It was better on her back: she could see the moon, and she could breathe and she knew more or less what to expect that way up. From far away in the house she heard a thin childish scream. Her scalp pricked and goose-pimples came up on her arms. 'What's that?' she said and sat up.

The scream on a high, inhuman note pierced the night

275

and lingered in the roots of her hair, making it stand up on end like aroused nipples.

'Hold me, hold me,' grunted Harold. He pushed her down, gripped her legs with his hands and pumped up and down. Victoria, still shuddering, pressed her legs together with all her might. She hoped he would not look at her face which was contorted into a tight grimace. Harold groaned and sticky liquid trickled out between her thighs. She held him close. He breathed deep and slow. From somewhere across the fields she heard a car start up and roar into the night.

# Chapter Twenty-nine

On the Monday morning the team sat round the table going through the newspapers. They yawned, scratched themselves and lit cigarettes.

'A bush baby's escaped from the zoo,' said Gregory.

'Let's get the keeper,' said Andrew.

'And a bush baby . . .' said Owen, without lifting his head from *The Times*.

Gregory stood up jerking the table so that Corporation tea slopped into Corporation saucers. He gave one of his hyena-like laughs and bounded for the door. He was on the scent.

'Seven minutes?' called Andrew after him.

There was silence among the rustling newspapers for a few minutes.

'Here's something,' said one of the newcomers lately recruited onto the Programme in a timid voice.

Owen bit his fingernails, his bullet head hunched between his stocky shoulders. 'One of those bloody foreign professors been shot in bloody Oxford,' he muttered. 'Victoria, follow it up, girl.'

'Victoria's not here,' said her secretary. The secretaries sat back from the table against the wall, notebooks on their knees.

'Not here?' said Owen, looking up. He frowned. 'Where the bloody hell is she, then?'

'She's taken a long weekend,' said her secretary.

'Weekend?' said Owen wonderingly. It was a concept unknown to the team. 'Gone to bloody Windsor Castle has she, then?' He gave a brief glance round the table. 'You'd better follow it up then, boy,' he said to the newcomer who was a girl.

'Gosh, thanks, Owen,' said the girl and hurried from the room.

Owen grunted. 'Bloody wops taking over the country,' he said. 'What's happened to Victoria? She's never here.' He turned to the back page and held the paper up so that his face was hidden. Her absence disturbed him.

'I think she's in love,' said Roderick, who had come in early as he did more and more often these days. He spoke so quietly that only Owen and Andrew heard him.

'Love!' said Owen. He threw down his paper. 'I'm going for coffee,' he said and stood up. He dug his hands in his pockets and left the room. Andrew caught him up in the corridor. He put his hand on the back of his neck and together they set off for the canteen at a fast jog. The rest of the team pushed back their chairs, abandoned the newspapers and trailed behind in a ragged file, heads down, shoulders hunched, hands in pockets. The secretaries gathered up the papers and pushed the chairs in. It was quarter to ten. There were 480 working minutes left before transmission.

The team sent a Programme car to Cambridge for Professor Kús who, it had been established, was a childhood friend of Professor Nagý's. Kús and Nagý; little and large; Gyuri and Istvan; George and Steve; Cambridge and Oxford; European refugees taking over great British institutions. Owen was in a rage. He kept sending the questions back to the trembling newcomer. He relied on Victoria for this sort of item. She knew about abroad.

'Get a photograph of their bloody school,' he shouted. 'These questions are bloody feeds.' The suicide had made front-page headlines in the early editions of the evening papers, but no one had yet got onto the relationship between the two Hungarians. The car was despatched early. 'And tell the driver to take the bloody longest way round,' yelled Owen, biting his bitten fingernails.

When Professor Kús arrived at the studios he asked eagerly for Victoria. She represented the sum total of his knowledge about television, though one or two of his more disreputable colleagues occasionally made off to London to appear on the mysterious box. He was familiar, of course, with the BBC through the wireless.

'She's away today,' said the new girl, escorting him to the hospitality room where chromium jugs of coffee and plates of sandwiches under greaseproof paper were set out on low Formica-topped tables.

Professor Kús was upset. 'Terrible, terrible,' he kept saying. 'Poor, poor Pisti.' He took off his spectacles and wiped his eyes with the back of his hand. He seemed overcome with emotion. The new girl floundered, all at sea. She had covered pages and pages in her notebook with points and reminders all numbered and neatly under-lined in red Biro.

'We only want to ask you about your boyhoods in Budapest,' she said sitting anxiously on the edge of her chair. 'Did you ever notice a depressive streak in his nature?'

'That's not the way!' yelled Owen hurtling through the door. 'Here, you take over, boy,' he said to Roderick.

'Would you like a whisky?' said Roderick in a sympathetic voice, leaning towards the professor. He offered him a sandwich. 'What kind of sandwiches did you have at school?' he asked. It was a technique he had picked up from Victoria. Professor Kús took three of the little white triangles and popped them into the black cavern behind his teeth.

'Goose liver,' he replied mournfully.

'Goose liver?' said Roderick softly.

Professor Kús nodded. 'Dear little sandwiches of soft bread with caraway seeds and thick slices of goose liver,' he said. 'Every morning my mother packed me a little box. I carried it on a strap over my shoulder. *Tizoray.* "Tenses". You have "elevenses".' His eyes twinkled at the memory, and he sat up.

'And Professor Nagý?' said Roderick gently.

'Cabbage and pickled cucumber,' said Professor Kús, shaking his head. 'He was never as clever as me though he had a brilliant mind. He was a moody little chap. We used to walk home from school together through the snow and do our homework at my house. My mother gave him warmed milk with honey and a splash of Tokay. He was always shivering. We wore shorts, you see, until we were twelve – and little braces. Poor, poor Pisti. He was very fond of my mother.'

Although Professor Kús presented an appearance of unworldliness and helplessness bordering on imbecility, his mind was keenly tuned in to the proceedings. His Control at the Ministry had given him the go-ahead: his mission was to disinform. He was, indeed, distraught by the murder of his old friend who had paid the ultimate price for dedication to his new motherland. He himself had spent the weekend with Pisti's shattered family, and his wife had left her own bed to sleep on a camp-bed beside poor Pisti's poor wife. But he was also intent upon building up a picture of a deprived and unbalanced personality susceptible to unpredictable changes of mood. Ingenuously, when his time came to be questioned on the Programme, he gave a most convincing rendering of a man dazed with grief by the loss of a loved but unstable colleague whose defective personality could well have been liable to suicidal impulse.

Owen was delighted. 'Well done, boy,' he said to the new girl as she led the professor, blinking at the sudden change of light, from the studio after the interview. Three or four press photographers and reporters were waiting in the street outside. Once again, the Programme had made news.

Professor Kús stumbled along the corridors, removing his spectacles from time to time to pass the back of his hand over his eyes. He kept shaking his head and sighing deeply. The new girl escorted him at a respectful distance. As he stepped into the street the pressmen closed round him. The driver got out of the waiting car and pulled him inside.

'Give my love to Victoria,' called Professor Kús as the door was banged shut behind him.

'I will,' called the new girl as she turned to face the press, crowing at the successful conclusion of her first independent contribution to the Programme.

# Chapter Thirty

❧

'I want Mummy,' said Flora and was sick on the floor. She had never felt more miserable, not even when she had had her tonsils out.

The floor seemed to be made of very hard earth; dark and smelling of oil. Alice was sitting on it, hunched up, her head on her knees by the bed. The bed was iron with rusty, broken springs – the sort of bed that looks right at the bottom of a canal – and there was a thin dank mattress upon it. It was the third or fourth time Flora had been sick. 'Mummy,' she whimpered. 'Mummy. Why don't you come . . .'

They seemed to be in a sort of garage or shed. There were cars without wheels, cars without bonnets, nameless car parts, tools, tyres, all coated with oily, black grime. It was the oily smell that was making Flora sick, it was sticking in her throat and she could not swallow it down. She half opened one eye, closed it and gave a little whine. Where was she and why didn't someone draw the curtains?

Light filtered in through the gap between some big doors and the ground, through cracks between the boards that made the walls, and through a dirty pane of glass in the roof. It was gloomy, cool and soundless, though from far away came the distant, steady roar of traffic.

'Ugh,' said Alice, and Flora began to cry. The tears made marks on her cheeks like roads on a map. Both children were grubby and unkempt. It had taken but a night, plucked from their cloistered environment, to transform them into white-faced urchins of the street.

'I 'spect she'll come. She always does in the end,' said Alice. Things happened, you never knew why or when, you just had to wait. 'Just a minute' grown-ups said. Sometimes they were cross with you, sometimes they did not seem to notice. She scratched a pattern in the dirt with her finger and then began to pick it out of the nail. It came away in nice thick black bits like snot, and she rolled it between her thumb and forefinger.

Their abduction had had its moments of stifled terror. Alice had woken in the moonlight. A tall dark figure cast a black shadow on her bed. Where there should have been a face was blackness. She caught a gleam of eyeball like boiled egg-white in the black, and she opened her mouth and screamed. All the unspoken fear of many nightmares was in the scream. It came up her throat, out of her mouth and spilled into the night, a thousand needles of primeval fear. Victoria, fucking on the lawn, heard it and shuddered. Then it was snuffed out by a big hand. She bit the hand, but there was something in it choking her. It felt like the time she had had her tonsils out in a nursing home. She had struggled against it with all her might but slipped away into nothingness. The figure picked her up, slung her over its shoulder and hurried, on stockinged feet, down the wooden stairs.

In the bed next door, Flora had not woken at all. A

wad of cotton over her mouth and nose and she had slipped simply into a deeper dream of sleep.

Fighting up through it, fathoms of thick black, she had come to in this place, on this bed in thin watery light where nothing but her body was her own. Her sister sprawled, snoring, beside her. She dug at her with her elbows. 'Wake up,' she had said, giggling, 'look where we are. And you're snoring!' Alice went on snoring and Flora had been sick. She began to feel frightened.

Now, there was a rattle of locks and a clatter of chains and a man came in through a little door cut in the big doors. He slipped in sideways carrying a tin tray and he had something black all over his head that squashed his face up, and there were slits for eyes. Flora gasped.

'He keeps coming,' said Alice, who had surfaced dimly, several times, before sinking back into bottomless dark. Eventually, she had woken up properly and tried sitting on the floor.

'Are you a robber?' said Flora. She sat up, fascinated.

The man approached their corner, started at the sight of the sick and almost dropped the tray. He laid it on the bed, put out a black-gloved hand and patted Flora on the head. There he stood, rather hesitant. Then he put his hand in his pocket and held out a tube of fruit gums to Alice. Alice sat motionless, her face expressionless. The man put the fruit gums on the tray. On it were: a box of cornflakes, a bottle of silver-top milk, a carbon-blue packet of Tate & Lyle sugar with a picture of Mr Cube on it, some slices of white bread, thinly buttered in floppy squares, and a half-empty jar of Robertson's Golden Shred marmalade. There were two cups of tea, two bowls and two spoons besides.

'I want to go to the lavatory, please,' said Flora, sitting

on her hands. The man gave a muffled groan and then beckoned to her just like a burglar in a picture. He unlocked a door into a little office and led her through, up some dirty stairs to a doorless room where there was a lavatory without any seat, a chain without any handle and a grimy basin without any plug. Flora took down her pyjama trousers and sat on the lavatory, hooking herself on with her knees. Much as she wanted to, she could not make anything come out.

'My bottom can't think with you there,' she said.

The man moved down a couple of stairs and sat with his back to her. Then it was all right. She hopped over to the basin and stood on tiptoe to turn the tap. A trickle of water came out and turned a lovely dark grey below her hands. She rubbed them together and tried to splash some on her face, then she went out and touched the man on the shoulder. 'I've finished, kind man,' she said. The man led her back, through the office, to the garage. He stood in front of Alice and jerked his head towards the stairs.

'Go on, Alice,' said Flora, 'it's lovely, with cobwebs and dead flies.'

Alice sat, immobile. The man shrugged his shoulders and locked the office door. Flora sat on the mattress, away from the sick end and shook a mountain of cornflakes into a bowl. Nobody told her not to. She struggled to scrape the silver top off the milk bottle with her teeth. The man held out a black hand. It was obviously difficult for him too, in gloves and with no teeth available. Eventually, he turned his back and put the bottle between his knees, dropping one glove on the floor, and prised off the top with his nails. He brought it back and Flora, holding it in both hands, sloshed a bluish-white stream all over the bowl and the surrounding tray.

'Cheerio,' said the man through squashed black lips.

'Cheerio,' said Flora.

It was a word she loved saying, a word Mrs Mac sometimes said as she left for the shops with her string bag. The man walked away towards the door.

'Thank you for our breakfast,' called Flora and kicked Alice's shoulder.

'Thanks,' mumbled Alice. Her back hurt from sitting in the same position so long.

As soon as the man had locked the door behind him, she got up and sat on the bed the other side of the tray. Flora poured sugar from the packet. She poured and poured.

'Stoppit,' said Alice and put her spoon in the stream. White granules jumped off the back of it like a fountain. She reached out and grabbed the packet and poured sugar into her own bowl. Flora shook in cornflakes again, a golden stream beside the white one.

They started to eat. The cornflakes were crunchy at first and soggy underneath, like wet cardboard. They floated bits of aerated bread beside them in the sugary blue-grey milk. What were they going to do after breakfast?

'I suppose Daddy knows we're here,' said Alice.

Harold supposed that the girls had gone out early to play. He attributed this to embarrassment or tacit disapproval at his relationship with Victoria, who was carefully quartered in a different section of the house from his. Heidi, coming in at half past eight to wake them for breakfast, had found their beds empty and supposed much the same thing. She had gone straight back to her own bed and the arms of her lover. Around ten Harold's alarm system started tingling. He roved round the house shouting, lifting curtains, peeping into closets. 'Al-ice! Flo-o-o-ra!' he called, expecting them to pounce out at him round every corner. He stopped at Victoria's door. 'Where are they?' he demanded. It was an impossible house – and garden – to search, packed with nooks, nests and cubbyholes in any of which they might be peacefully playing, miserably imprisoned, lying helpless and hurt, or gleefully hiding. He did not want to make a fool of himself.

Victoria, bent forward with her back to him, was making up her eyes, intent on her reflection in the looking-glass. She was wearing grey this morning; grey trousers with a white stripe down the sides and a grey and white striped top. They had already had a restless cup of coffee together in the kitchen: Harold, edgy and unshaven, Victoria in her billowing white dressing-gown all covered in tiny black flowers. She felt pale and shaken after an uneasy night with Harold beside her under the big patchwork eiderdown in her room. From time to time he had put out a hand and patted her. At dawn, he had left her bed with a guilty start and padded back to his own, the thin light of early morning glimmering on his naked body.

But now, she was irritating him. He strode across the room and removed the mascara brush from her hand. 'You've got what you want,' he said, 'you don't care about anything else. You've got no normal human responses.'

Victoria blinked at him. 'Do they often run away?' she said.

'Run away!' said Harold. He found the suggestion preposterous and quite tangential to his own preoccupations. He threw the mascara brush at her with all his force. Victoria ducked to miss his hand, ignored her thumping heart and scrabbled for the brush in the curly-haired rug round the dressing-table. 'I quite often ran away when I was a child,' she said. 'I'd put the cat under one arm and my money-box under the other and march out of the house. My nanny always came to get me. They're probably at the end of the drive now, waiting to be found.'

Her tone failed to meet Harold's mood. He glared at her. 'How typical of you to think of yourself,' he said as harshly as he could, and went.

As Victoria finished off her eyes, she heard the car start up and drive slowly down the long beech avenue to the front gates. She jumped up and thought for a moment, then, rather tentatively – this was not her territory – she went up the staircase into the attics and knocked at the door. 'Breakfast time!' she called bravely, though her flesh shrank somewhat at the prospect of another boisterous and draining morning. There was no reply, so she knocked again. 'Come on!' she called, 'I'll show you how to fry eggs.' She turned the handle and went in.

The bedroom that Alice and Flora were using was just as she had left it the night before; their clothes were in two little piles at the ends of the beds where she had picked them up off the floor and folded them, their shoes tucked under the ends where she had put them – only it was empty. It had an uninhabited air as if it had been unused for some time.

Victoria stared. 'Oh my God!' she said with a sharp intake of breath. Her entire scalp prickled and her skin crawled with horror. The forgotten scream, lodged in her tissues, bored its way into her consciousness with a corrosive surge. It felt as if sticking plaster was being wrenched from the inside of her veins. She stood as if being electrocuted, magnetised to the floor while charges of current went through her. Then she pulled herself free and ran. She ran to the banisters. Her legs would not work. The joints of all her limbs were loose and useless. 'Harold,' she screamed, 'Harold.' She collided with him on the first-floor landing.

'They weren't there,' he said gloomily, 'I went right to the end.'

'They've been kidnapped,' said Victoria. She clutched his shirt, she clutched his arms, she shook his body with the force of her own agitation. 'They're gone – taken – *kidnapped*!' she shouted into his face.

'You needn't shout,' said Harold, disengaging himself. Victoria took hold of his wrist and pulled him up the stairs. 'No need to drag the whole world into your own paranoia,' he grumbled as he allowed himself to be drawn, lagging, upwards to the attic.

In the empty room, he picked up Alice's folded cotton shirt from the end of her bed, lifted it to his face and sat heavily down. A nagging thought ticked in his brain too; a stifled memory of disquieting sounds in the moonlight that he had pushed out of consciousness. Victoria sat down too. As they faced one another on the two beds in the attic room, wrangling, Heidi entered.

'You've got to have it your own way,' Harold was saying fiercely. 'How is it you're the only person in Sussex that heard this – this scream?'

'Telephone for you, Mr Fox,' said Heidi, her eyes downcast.

'I can't take it now. Tell them to go away,' said Harold.

'Maybe it is of the children,' said Heidi.

'Who is it?' said Harold.

'A man,' said Heidi.

'I said *who*,' said Harold, showing her his teeth.

'He would not give his name. He said you would want

to speak to him,' said Heidi. 'Take it, Mr Fox. Maybe it is important.'

Harold clutched his head in his hands and plunged down the stairs. The telephone, a rather fast new white model, was in the hall. The only other one in the house was out of bounds, in Lady Rose's study.

'Yes?' said Harold brusquely into the receiver.

'Is that Harold Fox?' said an educated voice at the other end.

'Yes,' said Harold, 'what do you want?'

'I believe,' said the voice, a deep and resonant one, 'that by now you will have discovered the absence of your daughter and her half-sister. They are in very great peril. Their well-being depends on you. If you will now, when you have heard this message, walk straight out of the house and down to the end of the drive, a blue Ford Consul will meet you . . .'

'Where's Alice?' shouted Harold. 'Tell me where my daughter is and stop playing ridiculous Bulldog Drummond games. I'll have to call the police.'

'If you call the police, you will never see your daughter again,' said the voice, evenly. 'Do what I have told you. Go alone. Do not speak to anyone. You have five minutes.'

There was a click and the line went dead.

'Who are you?' shouted Harold into the receiver. 'Who are you?' He shook it and jiggled the contact points up and down, but, although he used all the force in his body, the machine remained lifeless. He was cut off, pushed into a waking nightmare, alone.

'I heard,' said Victoria coming up behind him. She looked into his eyes.

'How?' said Harold.

'Upstairs,' said Victoria, and went red.

'I'd better go,' said Harold. The voice of command had touched a reactive button in his brain. Thrash about as he might, he was conditioned to respond.

'You can't,' said Victoria, shocked.

Harold thrust his face close. 'Don't order me about,' he said between his teeth. He used the consonants like expletives.

Victoria backed away. 'But there must be something else. How do you know the man was telling the truth? Why don't we make a plan?' she said.

'How typical of you to undermine me just when I need support,' said Harold bitterly.

Victoria felt a strange impulsion. She took a step forward and raised her hand. She wanted to hit him. 'You can't just go on like that when your children are in danger. Out of touch. Children, Alice – your daughter.' She spat out the words and surprised herself.

'You don't understand,' said Harold, spitting back.

'Well, tell me!' shouted Victoria. 'Who is this man? Who are these people? Do you know them?'

'I might,' said Harold. He turned abruptly away from her. 'I'm going,' he said.

Victoria ran round in front of him. She felt possessed with energy. 'Please,' she said, mouthing the word with exaggerated emphasis, 'you can't just march off into nothing like that. It's absurd.'

'Who the hell are you to tell me what I can and can't do?' said Harold. He pushed past her and wrenched open the front door. As he took his first steps across the gravel Victoria caught hold of him. 'Give me the car keys at any rate,' she shouted, 'I'll come after you.'

'Don't you dare!' shouted Harold. He shook her off and felt in his pocket. 'There you are!' he yelled and flung the car keys on the ground. Victoria picked them up. She ran after him again and stood in front of him holding onto both his elbows. 'Harold,' she said gravely, 'Harold.' She stood as straight as she could and looked hard into his eyes.

Harold grinned at her. He put his hands on her shoulders and kissed her. 'I'll be all right,' he said.

'All right?' said Victoria, raising her eyebrows.

'All right,' said Harold firmly. They looked at one another for a moment and then, together, they both laughed.

'You stay here in case Alice and Flora turn up,' said Harold. 'I expect they will.' He kissed her again, put his hands in his pockets and sauntered down the drive, whistling.

He found to his surprise half-way along that the tune he was whistling was 'Run, Rabbit, Run'. He wondered if he would be able to consider its significance with Dr Lemaitre at his session next morning. He reached the end of the drive all too soon and as he did so, a blue Ford Consul drew up and slowed down. The back door opened. He looked up and down the lane: it was deserted, curling in lazy uninhabited loops across the Downs in both directions. The clear calm of morning lay steady on the fields around him. Cows ruminated in detachment, intent on tearing the grass between their big yellow teeth and slobbery sandpaper tongues; the unheeding witnesses of an improbable scene. He looked into the car. The back of it seemed empty. The seats were upholstered in porridgy tweed of the kind known as 'contemporary' and emanating from the designs propagated by the Festival of Britain. A rubber troll with purple hair bobbed in the rear window. It looked tacky in there.

'Get in,' said a harsh voice.

The voice gave Harold a horrible fright. He stopped whistling and his heart started thumping.

'Get in,' said the voice with a rasp that was half a growl.

Harold located its source. A man was wedged into the corner of the seat by the door almost concealed in shadow. With extreme nonchalance, his hands still in his pockets, Harold got in. He stumbled over the man's feet and fell into the seat beside him. He sat back whistling airily under his breath. 'Don't give the farmer his fun, fun, fun'. The door slammed, the car leaped forward and sped down the lane consuming the leagues with extraordinary power.

'What's all the hurry?' said Harold. He felt the hard point of what he supposed might be a gun poking into the soft area of his back just above the kidneys. In front of him, driving, sat a man in a fawn raincoat, the collar turned up to meet a trilby hat with its brim turned down. The man on the seat beside him was similarly dressed, but with his face in some kind of a stockinette tube, black with eye-slits. He felt the fields flash by outside the windows, boundless in the sun, and the sick ache of school cramped his chest.

'What an unusual rig,' he said. 'It must be uncomfortable. Are you members of some club or other?'

Both men ignored him and Harold was engulfed by a feeling of impotent despair that had accompanied him all his life. The circumstances were familiar: a strong sense of menace coming from someone who had power over him; an unidentified misdeed on his part; a suppressed desire to hit out, to feel his fist meet flesh and crunching bone, to draw blood, to wound, to kill. The denial of this physical impulse caused acute discomfort, extreme weariness, hopelessness, depersonalisation, though he

293

could still strike with his tongue. 'Won't you get into trouble for staying out of school?' he said, not expecting any response, and resigned himself to sit it out.

The car seemed to be heading towards London. The familiar landmarks flashed by in reverse. He usually made the journey in this direction at night. Surely a policeman would apprehend them soon; they were travelling at ninety miles an hour. He slouched and turned his face to the window. As the fields and green woods gave way to suburbia – rows of identical houses, net curtains looped at the windows; unlovely rose treelets spiked with giant flesh-coloured blooms; rustic name-plates: The Haven, Shangri-La, Shirleybob – he began to feel sick, not with dizziness but with worry. Maybe they had got him at last. Maybe, after all his prevarication over the years and, just as he had set course firmly in the other direction, they had put an iron hand on him. If it was him or Alice, he would have to go.

Alice! He groaned. Where was she? The man in the black stocking mask leaned over to wind down the window a few inches and a stream of fresh air hit Harold between the eyes. He closed them and raised his face to meet it. He thought of Victoria out there in the quiet sun; of her sturdy perseverance, of her firm flesh and her apricot-coloured skin, and of the spicy, sharp smell of the scent she wore. He kept his eyes closed and breathed in.

When he opened them again they were crossing the Thames at Chelsea Bridge. The car swung right, roared down the Embankment, past the Houses of Parliament and came up towards Soho through Trafalgar Square. Soon after two, they drew up outside his flat.

The man in the driving-seat spoke. Without turning his head he said, 'Get out from the car and go into your flat.

Collect all the letters your father wrote to you in the war. Bring them down here. All of them. We will know. You have ten minutes. The telephone has been disconnected.'

'My old dad's letters?' said Harold. 'What on earth do you want them for? I burned most of them before I came back to England in '45.'

'Now,' said the man.

'What about Alice and Flora? Where are they?' said Harold.

'You will not see them again if you do not hand over the letters. All of them. Now,' said the man.

'You cheap little blackmailer,' said Harold. A sour surge of rage lifted his fist and sent it smashing towards the back of the man's neck. Before it made impact, he felt his arm caught from behind and pinioned high behind his back. The position was acutely painful. He was forced forward, his head over his knees, gasping for breath, immobilised.

'Now,' said the man in the front seat.

The door of the car was opened and Harold stumbled out onto the pavement. A woman shopper with a basket on wheels drew back to avoid him. 'Look where you're going,' she said indignantly. His arm felt as if it had been broken. It hurt like hell.

'Sorry,' he mumbled.

The woman saw his white face. 'Dear, dear, dear, dear,' she said. 'Whatever are things coming to?' She fished in her purse and handed Harold a threepenny bit. 'They're not closed yet and you're quite a gent, aren't you?' she said and bustled on, clicking her tongue and shaking her head.

Harold hung on to the threepenny bit; its chunky twelve-sidedness was a link into everyday life which he now saw was going on with quiet indifference all around him. He longed to embrace it, to sink anonymously into its Englishness.

'Now,' said a hard voice from the pavement behind him.

Excluded for ever, thought Harold. He got his front door keys out of his pocket with his left hand and managed to open the door. He held onto his right shoulder with his left hand. Pain shot through it like a scream. He kept his mind off Alice and Flora. His flat, a metropolitan river-bed at low tide, awaited him, serene in its disorder. He tried the telephone. It was indeed dead. How do they manage such things? he wondered. He took a swig of whisky from the bottle on a bookcase and went upstairs.

My old dad's letters, he thought as he went to the top right-hand drawer of the chest-of-drawers. Some of them *were* rather odd. There were bits he had never been able to make head or tail of. He sat down on the bed and began to laugh. The old boy must have been some unwitting part of a chain of wartime information; an obedient cog in the intricate machinery of espionage and counter-espionage. He had worked part-time in a ministry during the war and been an auxiliary fireman as well. Harold could imagine him sitting at his desk in the black-out, writing with immense seriousness by the low light of a well-draped lamp and inserting incomprehensible phrases for his country, unquestioningly, into his letters to his son; letters whose message was directed – who knows – at the Camp Commandant or some member of his staff censoring PoW mail. Harold was touched – and depressed by this reminder of the futile, bungling nature of man's activities, immutable defects of which he felt himself to be the inheritor.

But a great weight was lifted off his mind: it could not

be his own ridiculous skirmishings on the fringe of the Communist Party in the post-war years that had led to this balls-up. He wondered momentarily what footling scraps of information the old boy could possibly have been required to transmit. He would have been tickled pink at the honour conferred upon him. Inside the drawer among the mess there were fewer letters in the shaky blue writing than he remembered and none of them, as far as he could see, with the flowery phrases he had found so quaint at the time. He gathered them up and made for the stairs.

The pain in his shoulder was beginning to die away and he felt comparatively sanguine. The woman with the shopping basket had been quite right: he had needed a drink. He took another quick swallow and ran down the stairs. The blue Consul was waiting at the kerb. Harold bent down and tapped on the front window. 'Here you are,' he said, as it was lowered a few inches.

'Get in,' said the driver, curtly.

Harold got in, with some misgiving, and felt the hard muzzle of the gun or whatever it was – probably a tube of Smarties – dig into the thin wadding of flesh at his waist.

'Look here,' he said chattily, 'you've got it all wrong. Here's all the letters I've got left. There really can't be anything in them – my father would have told me when it was all over after the war. You're barking up the wrong tree. Tell your chaps at headquarters. There's really nothing to blackmail me about, so please tell me where Alice and Flora are. There's bound to be the most frightful stink soon, if you don't, and you'll all be exposed. This is England, you know.' He was beginning to feel frantic with worry again. Black wisps of horror invaded the corners of his mind. He repelled them and kept up the chat. 'What can I do more for you gentlemen?' he said and felt the pressure at his waist ease off.

'Put the letters on the seat,' said the man in the front, 'get out of the car. Walk back to the house. Don't look behind. Go straight up to your flat and do not leave it. You will be told what to do. There is no hope for your daughter if you do not obey. Go. You are being watched.'

Harold got out of the car and walked back to his front door. He felt eyes watching him and his spine crawled with apprehension. He heard the car start up and drive away. He swivelled his eyes as far as they would go in their sockets to catch a glimpse of the number plate.

'Move,' said a harsh voice from the doorway on his right.

Harold gave a start that shook him to his bowels. The voice was an assault on his equilibrium. He felt as though he had taken a step in the dark and the ground had given way. Holding onto the frame of the door he let himself in and fumbled his way up the stairs. He was taken aback by the weakness of his knees and legs. He went right up to the bedroom, slower and slower. His heart was beating fast and he could hardly get his breath. He took the photograph of Alice out of the drawer that now seemed pathetically empty. He was used to the jumble of papers clamouring at him with claims for his attention and consideration. He stared at the face in the photograph. The solemn child's face stared back at him.

The primary obligation of a parent was to protect one's offspring from predators and he had failed his daughter in this one basic imperative. Desolation welled up in him. He kissed the face in the photograph and bent over it, cradling it to him and tears, immensely painful tears, squeezed from the corners of his eyes and trickled down his cheeks.

# Chapter Thirty-one

For a few seconds Victoria watched Harold walk away under the tall trees. She watched him from a window beside the front porch. He moved with exaggerated indifference. She wished she were at his side. As soon as he was lost to her sight at the end of the drive she would follow him in the grey Bentley – she would handle it somehow. She picked up the telephone to dial 999.

'Put ze telephone down,' said a lisping female voice behind her. Victoria turned to see Heidi and a hefty young man, his fair hair cut *en brosse*, standing behind her.

'I've got to telephone the police, Heidi,' said Victoria breathlessly. She was not quite sure how much of the morning's proceedings Heidi had followed, but she was not altogether surprised at the young man's presence. 'The children are lost – I don't know if you know. I'm going to call the police,' she said and reached out.

The hefty young man stepped swiftly behind Victoria and gripped her arms in a half-nelson, forcing her head painfully down between her shoulders.

'We know, Miss Benjamin,' she heard Heidi's voice say. She gave a kind of snigger.

'What on earth are you doing? How dare you. Let me go!' shouted Victoria, her voice muffled up against her thighs. There must be something more than schoolgirl-story language she could use in her defence. She began to struggle in the young man's arms, wriggling vainly in his iron grasp. The more she struggled the more it hurt. She tried to stamp on his feet. Heidi removed a long scarf from her neck and wound it, giggling, round Victoria's mouth and head. She looked adoringly at her young man now and then. Victoria felt the scarf suffocate her. When she opened her mouth to protest the rough patterned rayon material, smelling sickeningly of hair and scented soap, filled her mouth. She tried to spit it out. The two of them propelled her towards the stairs and manhandled her up them. They paused once or twice and Victoria heard heavy breathing and the sucking sound of long kisses.

This is not happening, she thought in disbelief. She was revolted. Indignation and outrage made her feel her heart was bursting. The names of all the influential people she knew went through her mind: the controller of television, Rosalynn's father, who was a colonel, her brother – not many. She threatened and blustered to herself behind the choking scarf. She was being pushed towards the attic. The impotence of her position was insufferable. She managed to hook a foot round Heidi's ankle, but the hefty young man only jabbed her head down further and she gasped with pain. They dragged and pushed her up the narrow stairs talking in an unknown language above her head.

At the top of the stairs they blundered, an unwieldy Caliban, all legs and arms in opposition, into the room where Alice and Flora had slept. Heidi gave Victoria a shove and the hefty young man let go of her for a second before they both took her by the arms and threw her face down on a bed. 'Come, Ivan,' Victoria heard Heidi's voice

301

say through the dizzy baffle that spun in her head. They left the room, hand in hand, locking the door behind them.

Victoria, sprawling on the bed wrapped in nausea, heard their footsteps on the stairs. She jumped up and hammered on the door, rattling the knob. Wrenching at the scarf, she managed to loosen it and free her mouth. 'Let me out!' she screamed till her voice cracked. Though the attic rooms all led into one another, this door alone led to the stairs. Between her screams, she heard laughter and the sound of voices receding. Then she heard the car start up on the gravel below.

She rushed to the window, the little slanting window before which Alice had stood as Victoria brushed her hair less than twenty-four hour ago, and watched the grey Bentley jerk and then speed away down the drive. She sat down on the bed. Tears of rage and wounded pride choked her throat. Her neck and back ached and her legs felt bashed and bruised. She pulled up her trouser legs and rubbed them tenderly. The house settled down round her and there was utter silence. It stood, as it had stood for hundreds of years through the seasons, a manor house of many rooms, in the afternoon sun of early summer. Victoria felt its space, impersonal and inaccessible, extend round her. I could be here for days, she thought and began to weep.

She wept and sobbed – tears of pain and misery stored up from many months and thick sobs of confusion and fright – until her face was a slobbering, blubbering mess and her eyelids stiff and swollen. She sobbed herself still and then, exhausted, she got up and went into the bathroom next door. A tap dripped its well-worn way down a long, wedge-shaped brown mark into the bath. The children's Tex toothbrushes and a tube of striped toothpaste stood on a glass ledge above the basin. She filled the basin with cold water and plunged her face in, holding it there till her breath ran out, then she cleaned her teeth and as she squeezed the striped toothpaste onto the brush she thought of Florence Smith. Her nanny would never have allowed such vulgar indulgence: Phillips Magnesia was the only toothpaste permitted in the Benjamin nursery. She cleaned her teeth thoroughly and rinsed her mouth well, then she swilled water round the basin and went back to the bedroom. In the still attic room she went over to the window and leaned out as far as she could. She saw the red tiled roofscape round her, trees, their leaves motionless in the kindly warmth of afternoon, and cows grazing in the field beyond the garden. Later in the afternoon, someone would come and fetch them in for milking. She heard the telephone ringing in the hall far below.

She pulled a sheet from the bed and hung it out of the window, then she spread another one on the floor. Strange that her primer in this life-crisis should be the *Girl's Own Paper*. She took the pencil box from Flora's satchel and found a pen and began to write HELP in huge letters. It was slow unsatisfactory work: the sheet kept wrinkling up and the pen ran dry. She tried crayons, rubbing them frantically up and down until the points broke and every now and then she ran to look out of the window.

She had just got to the upright of 'L' when she heard the sound of a car coming down the drive. The *Girl's Own Paper* had never mentioned the extreme discomfort caused by the heart in these situations, lurching horribly between throat and entrails. Far away, crawling like a toy between the trees, was the Hammersleys' old black Riley. She leaned out as far as she could and screamed.

'Help. Help. Help!' she shouted at the top of her voice, waving her arms. She seized the sheet and shook it up and down. She saw Vivien and Clare, pin figures but perfectly distinct, get out of the car and then Guy emerge rather stiffly from the driving-seat. They stood talking beside the car and moved slowly towards the front door.

'Help,' shouted Victoria. 'Help!' She put two fingers into her mouth and whistled. Guy shielded his eyes with his hand and looked upwards, then he moved off after the others. Victoria ran to the door and hammered on it with her fists. She shouted and rattled the handle and took off her shoes and banged. Her strength failed, but she thought of Harold, alone in the blue Ford Consul; of Alice and Flora abroad and unprotected in their pyjamas, and she screamed with all her might. And then, at last, she heard the heavy tread of feet on wooden stairs approaching. She redoubled her screams and battered on the door with all her might.

'Hullo, hullo. What's up?' she heard Guy's voice say.

'Is anyoneth-ey-ah?' enquired Vivien in her elongated syllables.

'Alice? Flora? This is rather a tiresome game,' murmured Clare. 'Do come out. We've had to come all the way upstairs.'

'They've been kidnapped,' shouted Victoria. She found herself sobbing again. 'And I'm locked in,' she said between gulps. 'Please, please do something. Hurry. They've taken Harold too.'

There was a long silence, a very long silence while Victoria leaned sniffing and hiccuping against the door. Then Vivien's voice said, 'My dear, how perfectly frightful.' She rattled the knob and Victoria heard her say, 'It's locked all right.'

Guy put his mouth to the keyhole. Victoria could feel his warm breath coming through the tiny space. It was, as he had intended, both comforting and comic. 'Be a good girl,' he said, 'hang on a mo' . . . what a pickle. We'll find Huggins to set you free.'

Victoria sniffed and laughed and ran her fingers through her hair. Her breath kept catching in her throat in the most inconvenient way. She sat down against the door. Her legs were shaking. 'Don't go away,' she said, 'and please, telephone the police.' Her voice rose to a squeaky scream on the last three words.

She heard footsteps going away down the stairs, and Vivien's voice said, 'I'm here, my dear, on the other side of the door. Calm yourself. It won't be long now. It's maddening getting oneself locked in. I spy with my little eye something beginning with "S".'

'Stairs,' said Victoria.

'Splendid,' said Vivien, 'your turn.'

The Hammersleys and Clare were very kind to Victoria. They patted her on the back and made sympathetic noises half-way between chuckles and clucks. Clare put an arm round her. They took her down to the kitchen and made coffee. Guy disappeared and came back, his face shining with goodwill, and handed her a glass of brandy. They listened to her story, only occasionally glancing at one another above her head.

'My *dear*!' said Vivien from time to time.

'Naughty Heidi,' said Guy.

'They must be in the pyjamas I brought them back from Rinascente. Italian children's clothes are adorable,' said Clare.

Victoria found her voice petering out as she condensed

episodes; she had had to gloss over the scene in the midnight garden, anyway. As she reached the end of her tale she found that embarrassment had replaced the compelling emotions that had exercised her so powerfully earlier in the day. She felt hangdog and sheepish.

'I'm sure they'll be back soon,' said Guy, patting her hand. He went off to telephone a police inspector in Lewes, but Victoria had the impression he was only doing it to placate her. She wondered if he would even lift the receiver. She felt as though her brain had been emasculated.

Silence fell on the cool room.

'Have some more coffee, my dear,' said Vivien. Her tone was solicitous, but Victoria could see the corners of her lips twitch as she bent her head over the coffee pot.

'Rose has got some glorious tarragon growing in the kitchen garden. I think I'll pick some for tonight,' said Clare.

'*Do*,' said Vivien.

Guy came back. His voice was full of surprise. 'They say Clare's car has been found outside the station. One of the doors was wide open. A local bobby telephoned in to report it.'

'How very careless of dear Har— ... How very careless,' said Vivien severely.

'Thank God I've got spare keys,' murmured Clare. 'I think I'll telephone his flat.'

Guy sat down at the kitchen table. 'You've had a most unpleasant experience, dear girl. Drink up. It'll do you good,' he said.

Victoria jumped up. 'We must *do* something,' she said desperately. She felt mad. Her voice sounded harsh and out of place in the peaceful kitchen.

Guy raised his bushy eyebrows and looked at Vivien. 'Perhaps we'd better ask Dr Roberts to call round,' he said in a low voice.

Clare came back into the kitchen. 'His line's dead,' she said, 'they say his telephone's been cut off. I suppose he never paid the bill.'

Vivien turned with a decisive movement towards Victoria. All this had gone on quite long enough, the day would get out of hand soon. 'What would you like to do, my dear,' she said firmly. 'We've got a guest for dinner – that's why we came over. We thought Harold – you both – might like to come. But you didn't answer the telephone. We must get back soon.' She felt she was being more than reasonable. 'I'm sure you don't want to stay here alone in this strange house. Perhaps you'd like to come back with us and lie down. You could take a couple of aspirins and we could bring you up a tray later if you felt like it.'

Victoria looked at the faces round the table. Their expressions of consideration and concern were turning to ones of mild irritation. She felt she had only a few moments of their attention to play on. She stood up. 'Thank you for all your help. Please don't let me keep you any longer,' she said in a carefully controlled voice. 'I shall be perfectly all right. I think it would be better for me to stay here.' Tears pricked the back of her eyeballs at the thought, but she longed for them to go. 'Get out,' she muttered under her breath.

'Atta girl,' said Guy awkwardly. He stood up.

'I'll just get the tarragon while you're turning the car,' said Clare.

'I'm sure Rose has got some aspirins in one of the bathrooms,' said Vivien. 'Do take some, my dear, and be sure to telephone if there's anything you need.' She took

307

Guy's arm. 'Christopher's arriving soon after half past six,' Victoria heard her say to him. 'I should hate him to turn up before we get back.'

Victoria followed them to the door. She stood in the porch and watched them drive slowly away. One by one they leaned out and waved with slightly exaggerated gestures as if to a child. The car edged round the corner into the lane and she was alone. She felt the weight of the house settle on her back and turned to face it, with dread. She walked hesitantly back down the stone passage to the kitchen and drank the brandy. She had only taken a sip to oblige. It burned her aching throat and the fumes expanded the vessels in her brain. My brother, she thought, Leo, steady as a rock. He'll back me up as sure as sunrise. She looked at her watch. He would still be at work, his crinkly hair carefully brushed, his big shoes immaculately polished, his long limbs impeccably clothed in charcoal-grey flannel, an inch of cuff flashing beneath the sleeves. She hurried back into the hall.

'Why aren't you in your office, sis?' said her brother when she explained to him where she was. 'It's Tuesday. They can't be taking a very good view of it on the Programme.'

'Oh please listen, please,' said Victoria. She described to him the events of the past twenty-four hours as fast as she could. She found, with practice, they could be précised into a few sentences: 'We were walking on the lawn in the moonlight when there was this blood-curdling scream from the house. In the morning we couldn't find the children and their clothes were still where I'd put them . . .'

'Hmm,' said her brother when she had finished. 'Hmm. I don't suppose you've got any money?'

'No,' said Victoria. 'I spent it on the train – and presents.'

'What about the police?' said her brother.

'Oh, Leo,' said Victoria, 'I've told you. We can't tell them. I don't know why, really. Harold would be furious, anyway. Please understand.'

'Hmm,' said her brother. After a bit he said, in a measured voice as if dictating to a secretary, 'As I see it, you'd like me to come down in the car and fetch you, or at least, spend the night there.'

'Oh yes,' said Victoria. 'Would you? Oh please. That's just what I'd like.'

'I've got a dinner date,' said her brother, 'but I suppose there's a decent restaurant somewhere round about. You might do some research. I'll come down as soon as I've finished work.'

'Couldn't you come sooner?' said Victoria.

'No,' said her brother shortly, 'and please book a table for three. It so happens I've had a difficult afternoon too.' He rang off.

Victoria sat down in the open doorway under the porch. The sun was beginning to slip lower in the sky and a wonderful luminous light played on the leaves. She leaned her head against the wooden door-frame and closed her eyes. The stone of the step was just warm. The noises in her body quietened down. Soon I'll go and see what I look like, she thought, but she lingered on, her will slack, in the borderland between inside and out. In the stillness a telephone rang. She stumbled to her feet and ran for it, seizing the receiver from its rest.

'Hullo,' said the operator's voice, 'will you accept a reverse charge call from a London 'phone box?'

'Yes,' said Victoria, 'yes, yes, yes.'

'Go ahead please,' said the operator.

There was a click. From far away and very faint came a child's voice. 'Can I speak to Daddy?' said Alice.

Bit by bit through the long, empty day, Alice and Flora in the garage had demolished most of what was on the tray. Flora tried making masks of the thinly buttered squares of floppy bread. She poked eye-holes with her fingers and bit a space for her mouth and loped round the floor on her bare toes holding the corners of the bread up to her ears. 'Your money or your life!' she said, in a squeaky growl. Her face and the ends of her hair were smudged with butter.

'Come here,' said Alice and rubbed at her face with the bottom of her pyjama jacket. Her pyjamas were striped pink, pistachio and yellow; Flora's were white with red rosebuds.

They made patterns with the fruit gums and threw them into each other's mouths. Flora dropped red ones into a cup of cold tea and played at cooking tomatoes and gravy. Alice refused to eat the dish when it was ready. She was even more bored than at school. She let herself be a passenger in one of the cars while Flora drove. The cars – there were three of them altogether – were all blue.

'My dear,' said Flora, 'do you think the children would like to go to the Zoo?'

'I dunno,' said Alice, drooping on the seat beside her. They had a fight and pushed and pulled and kicked and pinched until Flora started crying.

'Serves you right,' said Alice and went back to the bed. Flora curled up beside her as tight as she could. 'I wish Mummy would come,' she said. Alice said nothing; she was used to hours of waiting on boats and benches and the back seats of cars; sitting on stairs, sitting on chairs, leaning against walls while grown-ups talked. She thought, if she had a dog she could play with it whenever she liked.

She was the eldest. She made a tremendous effort. 'You can be my dog,' she said to Flora and patted her head. Flora nodded and put her thumb in her mouth. They lay there for a long time, held in the silence beyond thought or activity but not sleeping. It must be teatime, thought Alice. Probably it was tomorrow. She hated grown-ups, but it was better not to say anything.

They were lying there when the man in the black mask came through the door again. The chain rattled, the padlock clanked, the key creaked and he edged in carrying another tray in his black-gloved hands. Neither of them moved.

'Where's Mummy?' said Flora in a baby voice, as he looked around for a place to put the tray. There were sausages and baked beans on it this time. The man said nothing. He seemed to be in a hurry. He put the tray on the floor and walked away fast, leaving the door open behind him.

When he had gone, Alice sat up. 'Baked beans!' she said. 'We might as well eat them while we're allowed.'

'I'm not hungry,' said Flora, still in the baby voice. Alice shrugged and took a mouthful of beans, all slithery-sweet and pink. She loved them. 'Come on,' she said.

Flora, sucking her thumb, kicked her. 'I want Mummy,' she said.

'I'll eat yours,' said Alice.

Flora sat up and put her fingers into the beans. She put one in her mouth. 'Mmm,' she said, 'you must let me have the recipe, darling.'

They ate in silence, then Flora wriggled down off the

bed. She marched round the room, holding out her stomach. 'I'm full,' she said, 'I'm going to have a baby.' After a bit she said, 'D'you think we're meant to go outside?'

'I suppose so,' said Alice.

The two girls moved cautiously towards the doorway and peeped outside. They saw an overgrown yard with weeds and straggling bushes and red rustling mudguards and bits of iron bed strewn among them. There were fallen lumps of masonry and broken walls at the sides. No one was about. They stepped out of the door and walked across the yard. Flora put her hand in Alice's. On the other side of the yard, they came into a cobbled mews. It was dilapidated and deserted and full of corrugated tin dustbins spilling over with rubbish. At one end was a high blackened brick wall. The other end was open. They walked towards the open end feeling the hard round stones on the soles of their bare feet. They came out into a wide street with houses and trees on either side. Cars thundered up and down, but there were no pedestrians. Flora drew in her breath and clutched Alice's hand. They were never allowed in a main road on their own.

'I expect we're in London,' said Alice.

'Let's go home,' said Flora.

'Silly,' said Alice.

'We could get a taxi,' said Flora.

'Stupid,' said Alice, 'we haven't any money and there's nobody there.'

Flora looked down at her feet. They looked funny there on the pavement at the bottom of her pyjamas. 'Funny,' she said and began to giggle. She tugged Alice's hand. Far away at one end of the street it looked as if there was an open space, green, with trees and sky instead of buildings. 'Let's go and see,' she said.

The two girls walked along the pavement, side by side, in their pyjamas. At the end there were traffic lights and an even bigger road with buses and vans and cars piled up and panting to go. On the other side was a huge common.

'We'd better find a crossing,' said Alice. They walked along until they came to a place where there was an island and a Belisha beacon and stood there, looking carefully right and left.

'Now!' said Alice.

'No, you don't,' said a voice above them. They looked up and saw a policeman. He was frowning down at them under his helmet. 'Never cross a main thoroughfare without an adult,' he said to them sternly. He walked majestically out into the road and held out his arms. The traffic came to an obedient halt at his back. He motioned to the children with his head. Hand in hand they crossed the road. When they got to the other side, the policeman followed them.

'Run along home now before it gets dark,' he said, 'Clapham Common is no place for young ladies after nightfall. And tell your mum to put some proper clothes on you. She'll have the law after her or else.'

Alice and Flora ran. Alice was crying; she wished the policeman had not gone away. The grass felt fine after stone. They came to a pond and watched, for a while, the boys and the man sailing boats on it and, gradually, Alice stopped crying. 'We'd better get on,' she said. On the other side of the common they came to a church. It had a bright blue clock and a round spire. The clock said five past six. Close by was a telephone box.

'I'm going to telephone Daddy,' said Alice.

'Can I come in too?' said Flora.

Inside Alice dialled o. She told the operator the number and asked her to reverse the charges. When she heard Victoria's voice at the other end, she nearly cried again.

'Darling darlings,' said Victoria. 'Are you all right?'

There was a long wait while Alice struggled with her voice. 'Yes,' she said at last.

'D'you know where you are?' said Victoria.

Alice told her.

'Is there a seat nearby?' said Victoria. Alice looked out through the red-framed panes. 'Yes,' she said, 'two – on either side of the path into the church.'

'Sit there,' said Victoria, 'on the one nearest the road and don't move. Don't talk to anyone. A man called Leo Benjamin will come and get you. He's tall with glasses. He's my brother. He'll bring you down in his car. You can tell me all about it when you get here. Can you see a clock?'

'Yes,' said Alice.

'If he doesn't come in half an hour, telephone me again,' said Victoria, 'and, oh, darlings, I am pleased to hear you. How sensible to telephone.'

Alice and Flora went to the churchyard and sat on the bench outside. 'She wasn't cross,' said Alice. They looked up at the sky which was still blue. The seat was warm.

'I spy with my little eye something beginning with "P",' said Alice.

'People,' said Flora.

'Right,' said Alice, 'your turn.'

# Chapter Thirty-two

In Sussex, the Hammersleys and Clare waited for Sir Christopher Sharpe. A delightful evening lay ahead. They sat on the verandah in the golden light of late afternoon, glasses in their hands, watching the play of sun and shadow on the soft line of the Downs, their appreciation sharpened by an agreeable sense of anticipation.

'What a perfect day,' sighed Vivien.

' "*And did those feet . . .*",' mumbled Guy contentedly. He picked up the unlabelled bottle and refilled his glass with Chianti. Clare was drinking whisky. Now that the anxiety consequent upon the disruption of their plans earlier in the day was behind them, dinner safely in the oven and the table laid with the first Mme Alfred Carrière roses in its centre, they felt able to discuss the unusual behaviour of Miss Victoria Benjamin with tolerant amusement.

'Such a strange little creature,' said Vivien.

'I suppose those bad children locked her in and ran away. What a prank!' said Guy. 'Naughty Heidi. She should have more sense of responsibility at her age. But foreign girls are much more advanced – sexually speaking – than our English rosebuds.'

'Little Miss B was quite upset,' said Clare, 'Harold can be very trying. I wonder where he went with them?'

'Harold's *moods*,' said Vivien, shaking her head. They fell silent. They had all experienced aspects of Harold's moods at one time or other; it was one of the things that gave knowing him a special flavour.

'Peppery fellow!' said Guy.

'It's worse than that,' said Clare. She gazed at the Downs with her big, beautiful eyes and stretched out a slow sunburned hand for the whisky bottle.

'Where *can* Christopher have got to?' said Vivien. 'It's not like him to be late.' It was quarter to seven; it would be a pity to rush the convivial hour before dinner.

'I think I'll telephone Rose's and see if the children are back. I haven't spoken to them since yesterday,' said Clare. The old wicker chair creaked as she left it and Guy watched the languorous curve of her narrow back, so deceptively slight in outline, as it disappeared into the hall.

'I do *worry* about Clare,' said Vivien. Guy nodded and took out his pipe. He felt for his tobacco and packed it carefully into the bowl as Vivien watched him, a smile in her heart. ' "*It is a little rift within the lute*",' she said, and reached out her hand.

' "*Unfaith in aught is want of faith in all*",' said Guy, taking it in his. He did not move his eyes from the prospect before him. Theirs was an unblemished partnership and they had trusted one another *all in all* for so many years now that they thought as one.

Clare returned to the verandah. 'What news?' said Guy through the stem of his pipe.

'All well,' said Clare. 'They went off to London, the naughty things. They're on their way back now.'

'What a relief,' said Vivien laughing. 'Is Heidi with them?'

'Apparently not,' said Clare, sighing, 'I suppose she's

316

gone off with her young man. What a terrible bore. I'll have to find another au pair.'

Both Guy and Vivien tutted sympathetically. 'And Harold?' said Vivien.

Clare shook her head and shrugged. She leaned on the weatherbeaten white railing of the balustrade. Flakes of paint adhered to her elbows and Guy thought, for the thousandth time, what shapely little buttocks she had beneath her straight corded cotton skirt.

They chatted away in perfect amity, sitting there, enjoying one another's company and the golden descent of the sun as it condensed into a fiery sphere and dropped slowly into the space above the Downs. A faint grey chill on the air began to hint at nightfall.

'What can have become of Christopher?' said Vivien, a puzzled edge of irritation in her voice.

'I'll put the eggs in the oven,' said Clare. She stood up. She had made a dish of buttered eggs with cream and tarragon for a first course.

'Good girl,' said Guy. He looked at Vivien and observed with dismay signs of gathering agitation. 'No point in telephoning his flat,' he said in a soothing voice. 'D'you think his secretary could still be in the office?'

'I'll try,' said Vivien, pushing back her chair with a disturbingly rough movement. She walked off to the telephone and asked the operator for London. Guy heard her voice rise in surprise and braced himself. He heard her footsteps on the creaky boards of the hall floor.

'He's gone *abroad*,' she said from the doorway, 'can you be*lieve* it?'

'Abroad?' said Clare from behind her. She rested a hand on Vivien's arm.

'The girl said that he came in in the middle of the

317

afternoon and told her he'd been called suddenly abroad,' said Vivien. 'He seemed flustered, very unlike himself and took a few things from his desk and dashed off to catch the boat train. He wouldn't tell her where he was going or when to expect him back. She's been in the office ever since dealing with things. They were organising the return of the Italian Exhibition.'

'Good heavens,' said Guy.

'How frightfully inconsiderate,' said Clare.

Vivien gave her a grateful look. 'I can't imagine what's come over him,' she said, 'the soul of courtesy . . .'

'What a disappointment,' said Guy, 'but I dare say we can entertain ourselves.' There was a silence for a few moments among the three of them.

'These marvellous long evenings,' said Guy.

'June,' said Clare, 'wild roses, cow parsley, night-ingales.'

'I'll have to unlay his place,' said Vivien. She shook her head and sighed. 'One simply can't rely on *any*one these days.' Her creased old face with its fine high cheekbones and bright boot-button eyes looked quite defeated for a moment.

'Dear, dear,' said Guy.

'Fiddledidee,' said Clare.

They looked at each other and smiled and, gathering up the bottles and their glasses, went in to dinner.

Meanwhile, Victoria's brother in his black Citroën slowed down by the church on Clapham Common. A very pretty girl with long brown hair sat in the seat beside him. He had been delayed at the office after a trying day, and it was already nearly seven. He knew his mad sister well enough by now to believe there was something in the

unlikely story she had told him and, sure enough, two
little girls in pyjamas were sitting swinging their legs on a
wooden seat outside the churchyard. He pulled up the car
and got out.

'I'll stay,' said his girl friend. 'It may upset them if
they're only expecting you.'

He walked over to the bench. 'Good evening,' he said
in his deep voice. 'Alice and Flora, I presume? I believe
you're expecting me.' He inclined his long body towards
them.

Alice looked up at him and nodded. She was relieved
to see him because it was well over half an hour since she
had spoken to Victoria and she did not know what to do.
He looked like a very proper grown-up.

Victoria's brother said, 'My car's just there. Perhaps
you'd like to get in?'

Alice nodded again and stood up. Flora stood up, too,
and hid behind her. Their bare feet were black, their pyjamas crumpled and stained, their faces filthy – streaked
with white where tears had made pathways down their
cheeks, the area round their mouths pocked with dried-
up food.

Victoria's brother got a rug from the boot and spread
it on the back seat, carefully tucking in the corners and
removing a speck or two from its woolly surface. He held
the door. 'Do get in,' he said. 'This is Sarah van Doren.
She's coming too.'

The girl in the front seat turned round and smiled. 'We
were just about to get an ice-cream,' she said, gaily.
'Maybe you'd like one too.'

The car rose on its springs and started off. Sarah van
Doren put a hand on Victoria's brother's knee. 'I know
it's beastly having to stop once you've started,' she said,

'but there's a newsagent still open over there and it says "Lyons Maid". Shall we get some choc-ices?'

'No, no, no,' said Victoria's brother, 'something watery. Less messy.' He drew up at the kerb and waited. LATE NIGHT SPECIAL. UNIVERSITY SUICIDE. PROFESSOR TELLS, said the placard on the pavement. Sarah van Doren came back with two orange water-ices and handed them to Alice and Flora. 'We're going to wait for dinner,' she said, 'but you go ahead.' She took a white linen handkerchief out of her handbag, embroidered in maroon silk with her initials and a coronet: 'This is for the drips,' she said, and gave it to Alice.

They set off down the A23, clear of traffic at this time on a weekday evening. 'All right, girls?' said Victoria's brother from time to time, raising his eyes to look at them in the driving-mirror. Sarah van Doren turned round and smiled. She had a lovely wide smile with cherry-red lips and brown eyes.

She must be a princess, thought Flora hazily, as she slid down on the rug and fell asleep, the sticky paper of the Orange Maid crumpled up in her hand. Alice looked out of the window. The first stars pricked the sky as it changed to the colour of bluebells. She sucked her ice as slowly as she could. She felt like crying again and did not want to finish it, but, by and by, she too let her head fall back against the seat and fell asleep.

'What a lovely night. I'm dying to meet your sister,' said Sarah van Doren. She had a touring map spread over her lap and kept a rosy rounded nail on the route. Victoria's brother took his hand from the wheel and closed it briefly over hers. He had had a hellish day and felt he needed the comfort of her small, warm fingers as the car sped on in the gathering dark.

*

320

Ninety minutes later it drew up with a crunch on the gravel outside the old manor house on the Downs. Lights were on in all the downstairs windows and Victoria came running out to meet it.

'Have you got them?' she cried, as her brother got out.

'Good evening, sis,' he said and bent to kiss her. 'Of course I've got them. They're in the back. Rather messy but nothing broken, it appears.' He took a cigarette from his engine-turned cigarette case and blew a smoke ring into the sky. Sarah van Doren got out and took his arm. 'What a heavenly place,' she said. 'What a lovely night to be in the country.'

Victoria opened the back door of the car and threw herself on the sleeping children. 'Alice! Flora!' she cried. 'How wonderful to see you. Are you all right? What happened?' Tears ran down her face as she hugged them. Flora put up her arms and hugged her back.

'A man came in,' said Alice, sleepily.

'We were in a garage,' said Flora. 'He locked us in. He had black on his face.'

'Flora was sick,' said Alice.

'Fibber,' said Flora.

Victoria pulled them out of the car. She held their hands tightly and knelt on the gravel. Putting her arms round their waists she burrowed her face under the thin material of their pyjamas and kissed their stomachs. They smelled of sick and engine oil.

'Come on,' she said, 'you're going to sleep in my bed tonight with all the lights on and the door open. You can have milk and biscuits and I'll tell you the story of Moses in the Bulrushes.'

'Can we have a drink, sis?' said her brother. 'I hope you've booked us in somewhere respectable.'

Victoria let go of the children's hands and held her brother's face between her own. She reached up and kissed him on both cheeks. 'Good old Leo,' she said, 'I don't know how I'd live without you. I've cooked some dinner here. There didn't seem to be anything nearer than the hotel in Lewes.'

Hand in hand, arm in arm, the five of them moved off into the house. 'Quite a place,' said Victoria's brother.

'Isn't it divine to be out of London?' said Sarah van Doren, with a sigh. Victoria settled them in the drawing-room with drinks and took the children up to her bedroom on the first floor.

'Where's Daddy?' said Alice.

'I don't know,' said Victoria sadly. 'I think he may have gone to London. But your mother's at the Hammersleys'. I saw her this afternoon and she knows you're back.'

'We walked in the street without any shoes,' said Flora.

'Is she cross?' said Alice.

Victoria shook her head. 'I'm sure she's not. She didn't sound it,' she said.

The smell of honeysuckle came in through the open window and the moon made a silver path across the fields and up over the Downs. Cows grazed in peace beneath it. Victoria turned on the lights by the bed.

'Once upon a time a poor daughter of Israel left her baby in a basket by the waters of the Nile,' she said, as the two little girls in clean vests slid their grubby limbs between the sheets.

'What's Nile?' said Flora, taking her thumb out of her mouth.

'A river, silly,' said Alice, kicking her. 'It's where the rugs Mummy brought us at home come from.'

\*

322

It was after eleven by the time Victoria, her brother and Sarah van Doren finished dinner by candlelight in the kitchen. Victoria had found some rice and a tin of corned beef and made a dish of it with fried onions and sultanas. First, they had had buttered eggs with cream from the dairy and tarragon from the garden and afterwards, there was still some Camembert left in the larder. She had gone down to the cellar and brought up a bottle of Lady Rose's claret, Ducru-Beaucaillou. She had enough confidence in her to feel she would not mind in the circumstances.

'Hmm,' said her brother, holding his glass up to the light and circling it gently, 'not bad.' He took a sip, let it lie in the front of his mouth and drew air with a whistling sound in between his teeth.

Every ten minutes one of them had gone up to look at the sleeping children, and Victoria had talked until two spots round her cheekbones burned hectic red.

Her brother pushed his chair back from the table and cast his napkin on its scrubbed wooden surface. He lit a small cigar. 'I haven't told you what happened to *me* this afternoon,' he said, placing one grey ribbed ankle on his knee and leaning back.

'Is that why you were – tzt, tzt, tzt – late?' said Sarah van Doren merrily. Victoria's brother put his hand over hers and gave her a long look. 'I'm sorry,' he said, 'I really couldn't help it.'

'What?' said Victoria.

'Well,' said her brother, 'we've been doing an audit at a big news agency in Holborn. I've been working in the Managing Director's office. It's vast. He's a bullying sort of chap, quite difficult to get on with. I came back after lunch at two thirty and saw that he was still at his desk at the other end of the room. I was surprised, because he

323

normally has long lunches and comes back about four with a red face and his neck bulging over his collar. I coughed and said, "Good afternoon". I couldn't see him very well, because the desk's in front of the window, but there seemed to be something funny about the way he was sitting, sort of humped over the desk. He didn't say anything, so I said "Good afternoon" again. Then I went over to have a look at him and he didn't move. The poor chap didn't seem to be breathing. My God, it was awful.'
He held his head in his hands and shook it slowly.

Sarah van Doren leaned over and stroked Victoria's brother's hand, looking at him with her brown eyes wide.

'Yes,' said Victoria, 'go on. How awful.'

Victoria's brother went on: 'I didn't know what to do. There didn't seem to be any secretaries about. I thought he ought to lie down, so I kind of got hold of him in a kind of fireman's lift and staggered over to the sofa with him. He has a big leather sofa against one wall. My God, what a weight and he was completely floppy. I got him down on the sofa – his face was sort of dusky blue – and I felt for his heart but I couldn't find it and I couldn't find his pulse either. It was absolutely terrible. Poor man.'

'What did you do?' said Victoria and Sarah van Doren together.

'Well, I got the operator on the telephone,' said Victoria's brother, 'and I told her to find the Editor-in-Chief. He's a good chap. We sometimes have a drink, and he came and he said he thought he was dead. Well, that's what I was afraid I thought too, and he got the nurse to come down and she said he definitely was. And then the ambulance came and the police. I spent the whole afternoon at the police station. I'd only just got back when you rang, sis. I've never seen anyone dead.'

Victoria's brother looked green. 'I'll get some brandy,' she said and ran off to get it from the drawing-room. When she came back, Sarah van Doren had her arms round his neck. Victoria poured him some brandy.

'What on earth was it?' she said.

'Heart, I suppose,' said her brother and shrugged.

'How dreadful,' said Victoria. 'My God, Leo, what a day you've had. You are a sport.'

'Poor, poor you,' said Sarah van Doren. 'I think you're a saint, a hero. A heroic man.' She rubbed her cheek against his face.

They sat in a tight circle in the candlelight, shaking their heads and making tutting noises. Victoria's brother blew his nose. The kitchen clock whirred and struck twelve. 'Actually, I thought I was going to have a heart attack myself,' he said.

'Let's go to bed,' said Sarah van Doren.

At that moment they heard a hammering on the kitchen door. Victoria drew in her breath. They looked at one another.

'Go on, open it, sis,' said her brother. He grasped the empty bottle by the neck and held it like a truncheon. Victoria went reluctantly away from the table and its warm sphere of candlelight, drew back the bolts and opened the door. A wild figure stood there in the dark.

'Harold!' cried Victoria and threw her arms round him.

Harold shook her off. 'Why the hell are all the doors locked?' he said angrily. He took a step into the room and glared round. 'And who the bloody hell are these people?'

# Chapter Thirty-three

Alone in his flat, Harold had sat a long time on the bed. He leaned the photograph of Alice against the wall on top of the chest of drawers, but he could not bring himself to look at it. Her eyes held an unspoken reproach that he found unbearable. 'I should have been castrated,' he muttered to himself, and held onto his balls with one hand. Everywhere he went in the warren of his mind, he came up against a dead end. The inaction of his situation, mental and physical, set up an intolerable twanging tension inside his head. He ran up and down the stairs and in and out of rooms banging doors, and he opened his mouth and roared out his frustration. The walls of the flat shivered and shook, objects on shelves skipped and skidded and flakes of plaster fell into the kitchen sink, but nothing answered his despair.

He flung himself on the striped ticking sofa and shook his head violently between his two hands. I'll give myself a detached retina, he thought with gloomy satisfaction, and reached out for the telephone. His hand, he noted, was perfectly steady but the telephone was as dead as ever. Would Victoria have taken it upon herself to call the police, he wondered briefly. He rather hoped she would and take the responsibility, thus, out of his hands. He could still be justifiably furious with her if she had.

The implacable silence in the flat, the inanimate indifference of its walls and furniture bore in on him with intolerable pressure. This was what it must be like to be a diver on the sea-bed, only he had no oxygen line. A plan formed, like an eye opening, in his mind. It required extravagant physical action, but he felt himself magnetised by its irrevocable pull. Steadied by resolve, he walked upstairs to the bedroom and, grunting and heaving, squeezed himself out of the window onto the roof. The air there, though flat, was alive and filled with rumours from the city below. He took a long breath of it. With his back to the slates and his hands outstretched against them, he edged along the gully. It seemed quite solid and the slates were warm against his palms. He craned to look over the parapet and his head swam as his eyes took in the drop between his own body and the pavement. He fell onto all fours and clambered on surrounded by chimneypots, puff pipes capped with chicken wire and the odd television aerial. He was surprised at the debris that had found its way up there: old kettles, lengths of timber, bricks and empty paint pots, all scarred with pigeon droppings.

He hoisted himself across to the next house and paused, panting, with his eyes closed. But Alice, white-faced in her striped pyjamas, swam into his mind's eye, and he opened them again.

There were three houses between him and the end of the street where he planned to descend, by drainpipe and window-ledge, to a sunless yard at the back of the street. He thought of his desk – a dining-table, really, strewn with papers; he must get himself a proper one. This would have been an ideal opportunity to pursue his work undisturbed. But he was committed: going back presented as uninviting a prospect as going forward. He pressed on. By the time he got to the last house he was sweating and covered in grime. Prickling with terror, he grasped a drainpipe and swung his legs over the edge of the roof, flailing them wildly in search of the ledge below. The drainpipe swayed sickeningly before his foot found the narrow sill. He crouched there, knees trembling, before he launched himself towards the next window down. There were two more storeys to go. Rotten pointing dislodged itself from between bricks and tumbled onto the cobblestones below. The taste of blood was in his mouth as his heart pounded. At the window of the first floor, clinging desperately to the pipe, he let himself go and made a leap for the ground. The impact jarred his limbs and knocked the breath out of his lungs. He lay there, sprawling, his cheek squashed against the dank stones, his mouth open, his eyes closed.

By and by he pulled himself together and stumbled to his feet. As he raised his head, he realised he was not alone. A few yards away, on the other side of the cobbled yard, stood a policeman. He was accompanied by the Greek restaurant owner from the ground floor of his own house. The three of them regarded one another warily. Harold wondered whether he should run, but he was too tired; besides, it was too late. He had lost the initiative of surprise.

The policeman addressed him: 'May I enquire, sir, what you think you've been doing?' he said, taking out his notebook. The ponderous phrasing he gave to his words reduced Harold's frantic activity of the last twenty minutes to a commonplace infringement of the regulations.

'Good afternoon, Mr Costa,' said Harold. Embarrassment, the most familiar and crippling of all the emotions in his repertory, took him in its grip. He leaned against the wall. 'I'm terribly sorry, officer,' he said to the policeman, 'it's ridiculous, but I locked myself in. I've got to catch a train. I couldn't think what else to do. I didn't want to disturb anyone and the telephone's out of order.' He dropped his eyes.

'Do you understand, sir, that climbing over other people's property is a trespass, whatever the intent?' said the policeman.

'I'm afraid I hadn't thought of it like that,' said Harold, humbly.

Mr Costa looked at the policeman and raised his eyebrows. 'He is good customer,' he said, 'no trouble. Always very nice.'

Oh my God, thought Harold, I'll have to have a filthy dinner in his filthy restaurant. He smiled at Mr Costa.

'You do not wish to proceed?' said the policeman to Mr Costa. Mr Costa shook his head. The policeman put his notebook away. 'In that case,' he said to Harold, 'I shall let you off with a caution. But I must warn you that any attempt to vacate your place of dwelling in a similar manner will be met, in future, with a severe penalty.'

Harold nodded his head. 'Thank you,' he said. There seemed nothing more to be said and he wondered what to do next. Then the policeman spoke. 'What time is your train, sir?' he said in a friendly voice.

Beyond evading the watcher in the doorway, Harold had not really thought of what he was going to do once he escaped. 'Victoria Station, six fifty,' he said at random. They all looked at their watches. Harold's, as was its custom lately, said half past two. It was twenty past six.

'You've had a nasty experience, sir,' said the policeman.

329

'The squad car's round the corner. We could offer you a lift.'

Harold patted his hair. He wished he was wearing a tie. He did up the top button of his shirt. 'Thank you, officer,' he said. He would go anywhere with the solid figure in blue.

They walked out of the yard into the sunlit street. The black Wolseley police car was waiting with its driver. As Harold got in the back he glanced down the street towards his own front door. A man stood in the shadow of the doorway. He was reading a newspaper. Harold grinned to himself. A secret crow of triumph exploded in his chest and filled him with warming fragments of satisfaction. He settled back in his seat.

'Bye-bye,' said Mr Costa from the pavement. He untucked a tea-cloth from the waistband of his trousers and waved.

'Bye-bye,' said Harold.

The drive to the station was an exhilarating experience. Harold found the sensations it imparted of power and impunity as the car drove through red lights and swung round traffic blocks on the wrong side of the road, most agreeable. Life on such terms would be altogether more manageable, he realised.

Alone in the train, he leaned his head back against the patterned plush and jerked it, immediately, up again. My child, my child, he thought. Little pictures like an endless scrapbook of snapshots, swarmed round his brain in torturing profusion: Alice as a baby in Clare's arms, himself as a baby in long ceremonial nightdress and lacy bonnet; Alice's first staggering steps, her first shoes, her first birthday; Alice on the sands with bucket and spade, her chubby legs splashing in a puddle of sea; Alice learning to ride a bicycle with himself running behind, his hand on the saddle; his hand under her chin as he taught her to swim; her hand in his. Alice – his baby, his little girl: the seed of his loins. The ultimate horror presented itself to his brain. Alice – white, bound, abused, in the hands of some sick perverted thug. His mind screeched and skidded through the unbearable images that popped up before it like tableaux in a sadistic fairground. He opened the window and was sick.

Faint and shaken, he sat down again, collapsing on the seat, and remembered Victoria. We'll have a baby, he thought. Staunch little Victoria, she'll be the mother of my child: he corrected himself, of our child. Affection lapped at the raw edges of his sensibility. Why was he so hard on her? Remorse overcame him.

He stared out of the train and began to take in the soft forms and fresh greens of the bracken-filled fields as they flashed by. The sun, slipping lower in the sky, cast a slanting glow on the ferny fronds, brushing them with magical light and the sky had turned white on the horizon where he could see it through the trees. One or two lights began to blink yellow in windows alongside the line. By a level crossing, its wooden gates closed on a patient cluster of pedestrians and cars, a gabled house caught his eye. It sat in a wild overgrown garden, a broad space of grass in front of it leading down to a stream at the edge of a meadow.

We'll get a house like that, thought Harold, and I'll be a writer and I'll make Victoria happy. I'll tell her how pretty she is and we'll have children and a big kitchen and a room for Alice and a room for Flora. He couldn't wait. I'll pick wild flowers for her and we'll go for long walks in the evenings and after supper we'll listen to Beethoven

331

quartets in the lamplight – and I might even tell her that I love her. He tried saying the words under his breath, 'I love you'. It was easy. 'I love you.' Lulled by such notions of sympathetic domesticity, he leaned his head against the cropped patterned prickles of the upholstery and let blurred pictures of order and harmony flit beneath his eyelids. A shift of attitude, a resolution or two made and kept and they could be his in reality. He would make it up to Victoria. He would temper his behaviour. He would buy her a present, when all this – this farce – was over. He would buy her a present now.

The train drew up in Brighton Station and stopped against the terminals with a bump, but Harold sat on, dreaming, in the gathering dark. By and by, the absence of motion caused him to shift in his seat and look up. He saw where he was and pulled himself to his feet. Lord, he was tired! He got down onto the platform and addressed a porter. The next train for Arlington Halt left in half an hour, and he set off in search of something to buy. Typically, nothing was open except for a dimly lit buffet. Damp sausage rolls and packets of Smith's Crisps were all that was available and not what he had in mind. Valiantly suppressing his irritation, he left the station. In a side-street nearby he found a dismal newsagent's where he bought a box of Milk Tray and the *Evening News*. It's the thought that counts, he told himself, squashing down the uneasy memory of Victoria's absurd self-imposed prohibition on fattening food.

He sat down on a bench where he unfolded the newspaper and saw, staring up at him from its front page, the face of her oafish admirer who had gate-crashed his dinner party two weeks before: '*University Suicide*', read the

332

caption beneath, '*Secret torment of leading physicist. Professor tells all. See centre pages . . .*'

The present in all its black unmanageable disquiet displaced the rosy future of his fancy, and he leaped to his feet. He must telephone. But it was nine o'clock and he sprinted, instead, for the little steam train that would bear him, chugging slowly from station to station along the seafront and then, inland, through the Downs.

'Let me introduce myself,' said Victoria's brother. He replaced the bottle on the table and stood up. He was at least three inches taller than Harold. 'I'm Victoria's brother, Leo Benjamin, and this is Lady Sarah van Doren.' He inclined his head gravely.

'Oh my God,' mumbled Harold, 'a family party.' He sat down heavily on the nearest chair and put his head in his hands. Victoria sat down on the edge of the chair next to his. She bent her head and looked up at him: 'He brought Alice and Flora back,' she said, her eyes wide, her forehead creased, a knot at the back of her throat. Harold collapsed his head on to the table and groaned.

'I'm sure you'd like a drink,' said Sarah van Doren.

Victoria's brother poured brandy into a glass and set it in front of Harold. Harold pushed it away. He sat up. 'Alice and Flora!' he said wildly. His eyes darted round the room like a hunted animal. 'What have you done with them?'

'They're upstairs, asleep in my bed,' said Victoria.

'In your *bed*?' said Harold. He pushed his chair back from the table with a harsh scraping noise and rushed from the room. Victoria put out a hand and started from her chair. Then she sat back and closed her eyes. The old clock ticked. Nobody spoke.

333

'We'd better be going, sis. We've got a long drive,' said her brother.

'It'll be fun. Under the stars. In the dark,' said Sarah van Doren, 'and we've got lots to talk about.' She took Victoria's brother's arm and squeezed it.

'Oh stay the night. Please. I've made your beds,' cried Victoria. Shame engulfed her and a kind of melancholy. These two were firm ground in this alien world to which she had become affiliated of unknown customs and unfamiliar moral values.

'You'll be all right now,' said her brother bending to kiss her.

'It was a lovely dinner. What a good cook you are,' said Sarah van Doren.

'Oh,' said Victoria, 'oh, oh, Leo.'

The three of them went out to the circle of gravel in front of the house. The inky heavens were full of stars. Victoria put her arms round her brother and laid the side of her face against the spruce stripes of his Turnbull & Asser shirt.

'Thank you,' she said.

'Not at all, sis,' said he. He moved to open the door of the passenger seat for Sarah van Doren. The two of them got in.

'Let's have a drink at the weekend,' called Sarah van Doren as she waved from the window.

The Citroën, black in the black night, moved away down the drive. Victoria watched the headlights make a path of light under the trees. Then the brake-lights glowed red. The car turned and disappeared from view, though she heard the receding hum of its engine for a few seconds more as it wound its way over the Downs.

Upstairs, inside the house, Harold was sitting on the

stairs outside the bedroom where the children slept. The door was open behind him and their small bodies made shallow humps under the patchwork eiderdown in the yellow light of the bedside lamps. It was very quiet and still.

Victoria approached him. He appeared to her eye smaller, somehow, than usual.

'Hullo,' he said and held out his hand to take hers.

She sat down next to him. His clothes were in a remarkable state of disarray. His breath smelled sour and his underarms, strongly, of sweat. They sat side by side on the stairs, hand in hand, saying nothing. Victoria felt unbearably sad. The events of the day rose in her throat and constricted the muscles there, so she could barely get her breath. Then Harold put out a finger and touched her cheek. He pulled her face towards him and kissed it. His hands were shaking. He kissed her on the forehead between the eyes, he kissed her eyes and he kissed her mouth.

'Let's go to bed,' he said. 'You can tell me all about what happened here and I'll tell you all about what happened to me. It'll be better lying down.' He rose and, tucking Victoria's head under his arm, moved off down the passage. Victoria, inhaling the rich smell of his armpit, felt their hip-bones in conjoint motion as they walked slowly together to his bedroom where a high single bed stood against the red wall in the moonlight. They dropped their clothes on the floor and climbed in.

'You first,' said Harold, putting his arms round Victoria.

'No, you first,' said she.

Harold settled her head into the hollow between his collarbone and his neck. 'No, *you*,' he said. 'I want to hear what happened to *you*. And I'm sorry about your brother. He's a fine fellow.' He put his leg over hers, so that it lay between the two of his and nudged her captive foot lovingly with his toes.

Soon after dawn, Victoria woke. She felt more comfortable than she had ever felt in her life: every joint and muscle in her body was luxuriously accommodated by a reciprocal hollow, protrusion or curve of Harold's body. She disengaged herself reluctantly, kissed him lightly on the forehead and padded along the scratchy matting to the room where the children slept. They were still there, dirty faces grey against the white pillow-cases in the pearly half-light before sunrise, and she tiptoed away again. As if she were slipping into a still warm suit of clothing, she settled back into bed beside Harold. He stirred and put a hand over her breast. Together they drifted in a white world of tranquillity.

They woke again at eight o'clock.

'My God!' said Harold. 'Dr Lemaitre!' He flung himself across Victoria and the bed and started making violent sweeping movements across the carpet in search of socks and shoes. Victoria sat up and the rhythms of the night fell away as if they had been hosed from her. The clear bright light of day filled the room.

The Programme! she thought, and said, 'You can't possibly get to South Kensington by nine.'

Harold glared at her. He already had one leg in his trousers, but Victoria could see that they were going to go on back to front. She threw back the bedclothes and knelt beside him. As if she were lifting a horse's hoof from the ground, she tried to encourage him to move his foot so she could ease the trousers off and onto a more appropriate leg.

'Why don't you cancel it,' she said, her cheek pressed against his hairy leg. 'Or I could telephone and say you're going to be late. What about the children?' She did not mention that she was as determined as he was to get to London that morning.

Harold raised his arm to strike her. 'Don't try to dominate me,' he said. A nameless sense of urgency, a compelling need to act, to gather all the straying pieces together and weld them, by will-power, into one, possessed him. He hopped to the chest-of-drawers and peered at himself in the looking-glass that hung above it.

Victoria sat on the bed and wrapped the eiderdown round her. 'Harold,' she said, 'don't you want to see the children? Who's going to look after them? How are we going to get to London? You need a bath.' Harold came at her and aimed a blow but Victoria anticipated him for once and dived under the bedclothes.

She felt indignant. Here we go again. How stupid he is, she thought. She lay there in the bumpy white cave for a minute before surfacing. She wound a sheet round herself. 'I'll go and make some coffee,' she said with dignity and managed to get to the door without turning her back. From outside and just above her breath she addressed him furiously. 'Don't you dare hit me,' she said and made to flee. But she stopped herself. 'Use your brain,' said a voice in her mind and she walked down the stairs with a firm deliberate tread.

Half an hour later Harold came into the kitchen, clean, shaved, and wearing a suit and tie. He poured coffee and hot milk into a cup. 'I'll get a taxi to the station,' he said, as he put a piece of toast on his plate. 'Perhaps you'd better telephone and say I'm on my way.'

Victoria opened her mouth and shut it again. 'Give me the number,' she said finally.

'It's too embarrassing,' said Harold, putting his head in his hands.

'He won't know who I am,' said Victoria. The notion that Dr Lemaitre might not even know of her existence stung painfully.

'KENsington 1357,' said Harold.

An irresistible impulse overtook Victoria. She picked up a piece of toast and when she got to the door, she threw it at Harold. It missed. 'I despise you,' she said, 'you're pathetic.' It was what she wanted to say, but as soon as the words were out of her mouth she wished she could fish them in again. There they hung, articulated thoughts, anxious objects on the air between them. Victoria was not even sure that Harold had heard them. She stood marooned.

'What was all that about?' he said presently.

Victoria marched to the telephone.

Harold came after her. 'Why on earth did you throw a piece of toast at me?' he enquired. He held a bitten slice of buttered toast in one hand and a napkin in the other.

Carefully censoring her feelings, Victoria said, 'You're behaving like a child . . . a . . . a spoilt child.'

'How dare you call me childish,' said Harold. His face tightened. 'Take it back immediately. I demand you take it back.' He seemed genuinely upset.

'Sorry,' said Victoria, mystified.

They faced one another in the hall, two animals on a raft with spikes. Then Victoria climbed off. 'I'm going to get dressed,' she said, 'and pack. I'm going back to London.' She walked up the stairs slowly waiting for the javelin to strike between her shoulder blades. Harold, restraining himself, watched her with a thoughtful frown on his face.

When she came down again, he was in the kitchen with the children. Their faces were washed, they wore clean shorts and Aertex shirts; only their hair was matted and tangled. Harold was stirring Quaker Oats in a saucepan. He had a table-cloth tied round his waist.

'Morning,' he said. Only the challenging half-smile he flashed her gave any hint of the events of the preceding two hours.

'Morning,' said Victoria smiling with her lipsticked lips, freshly scarlet, at the little family grouped round the scrubbed wooden table. She was wearing tight black trousers and a black cotton shirt with batwing sleeves. A scarlet, black and purple striped scarf was draped round her neck and tied like a cowl.

'I must get on,' she said. 'I'll go and telephone for a taxi.'

Harold handed her a cup of coffee. 'Must you go?' he said. 'We thought we'd take a picnic up on the Downs. It's a glorious day. You like *hot* milk, don't you?'

The little girls said nothing. Alice, her eyes on her plate, stuck a spoon into her porridge. Flora, her face only six inches above the table, gazed at Victoria. 'Ooh, how beautiful,' she said, 'you look like a princess.'

Harold looked at her too. 'You do,' he said, 'you look really stunning. You do dress *well* and I think you've got thinner. I got you a present last night, only I forgot to give it to you. Here . . .' He offered her a small box wrapped in newspaper and tied with tartan hair ribbon.

'Open it,' said Flora. 'It's lovely.'

Victoria looked at them. They were all watching her. She turned the package over in her hands. 'All right,' she said slowly, 'I will.' She undid the ribbon, rolling it carefully up to smooth out the creases, and unwrapped the newspaper. 'Oh,' she said when she saw the chocolates. 'Oh, how . . . however did you manage *yesterday*. Oh, thank you.' She smiled down at the purple box, biting the corners of her lips. It was the funniest present she had ever had.

Alice looked at her and grinned.

Flora rested her chin on the top of the table. 'Can I have strawberry crème?' she said.

Harold laughed. 'It should have been Black Magic and red roses,' he said. He walked over, wooden spoon in hand and put both his hands on her shoulders and kissed her. 'It will be Black Magic and red roses from now on. I promise,' he said and gave her an awkward pat. It was an unfamiliar gesture, rusty from non-use and he tried to turn away. But Victoria held him: 'Will it?' she said and looked him gravely in the eye. 'Good.' She put the box on the table. 'After breakfast we'll all have one – or two or three,' she said. 'I'm going to get Flora a cushion.'

'I'll go,' said Harold. He hurried past her and came back with two big striped ones from the drawing-room. He held Flora up under the arms; Victoria slipped the cushions beneath her.

'What shall we take?' he said. 'I'm making some hard-boiled eggs. Would you mind keeping an eye on them while I go and telephone Dr Lemaitre?'

Left in the kitchen with the little girls, Victoria slipped automatically to thinking of ways to engage them. She would show them how to make paper boats as her nanny had shown her twenty years ago, as they sat at the table in the day nursery, turned schoolroom once breakfast was cleared away, the canary fed and the tortoise nibbling fresh cabbage-leaf in its cage. Harold would find them animated and occupied when he returned and she would have been the instigator. She put out her hand for the newspaper wrapping that lay on the table and let it drop again into her lap. She looked at the two children. Alice was staring at the table and Flora was making bays and islands in her porridge. She left them to it and as she let go of them in her mind, she realised she was quite cross – both with them, irrationally, for the enormous emotional toll they took of her and with the unlikely grown-ups in whose care they were meant to be. Was no one going to talk to them about their experiences? She supposed not; denial and evasion appeared to be the modes by which this clan operated. All their feelings came out sideways. It was very tiring. She turned her face to the window and stared out at the ancient fruit trees espaliered against the old brick wall of the kitchen garden and at the panes of the greenhouses sparkling in the sun. There was no sound in the room save for the bubbling of the pot upon the hotplate and the faint clack and splosh of Flora's spoon.

In the silence Alice spoke. 'We had cornflakes in the garage,' she said tonelessly.

Victoria turned her head to face them. 'Cornflakes? In the garage?'

'And baked beans and fruit gums,' said Flora. 'The man gave us fruit gums.'

'The man gave you fruit gums,' said Victoria. She got up and took the eggs in their pot from the cooker to the sink and let the cold water run on them from the tap. When she turned round she saw that Alice was crying. Tears were running soundlessly down her white cheeks and dripping off her chin. Her face was without expression and she did not move but sat on her chair as slack as a rag-doll.

Flora gave a high, thin squeal and put her head on the table. 'I wanted Mummy,' she wailed and started to weep.

Into this wretched hullabaloo walked Harold, cheerfully smiling. He stopped dead in the doorway and his countenance blackened. He turned on Victoria. 'What the hell's going on,' he said ferociously. 'I leave them here perfectly happy, eating their breakfast and now look what's happened. What have you done to them?'

Victoria wiped her hands. 'You'd better find out,' she said, 'I'm going to telephone my office,' and she walked past him, looking straight ahead, through the doorway, down the stone passage, across the hall to the telephone by the front door.

There was a lot of noise down the other end of the line when she got through to the Programme. 'Who?' shouted Owen. 'Oh, Victoria. Where are you, girl?'

'I'm in the country,' said Victoria. 'And Owen, I'm terribly sorry, but I simply can't get back till this afternoon.'

'That's all right, girl,' said Owen, 'you need a break.' She heard the crisp fizz and flare of a match striking and some grunts and scuffling sounds as he held the receiver under his chin.

'How was Edith Sitwell?' she said when they had subsided.

'Who?' said Owen. 'Oh – the Dame. Fine.' He chuckled. 'Fine. What a face!' He gave a short bark of laughter. 'And . . . Victoria,' he said.

'What?' said Victoria.

There was a silence, then Owen's voice said, 'I thought I ought to tell you, girl – I'm getting engaged.'

'Engaged?' said Victoria. She held the receiver away from her ear and looked at it. Then she put it back. '*You!*' she said.

'Yes,' said Owen, 'I thought I ought to tell you. She's a nice little thing. Works on the Programme as a matter of fact.'

'Well,' said Victoria, 'gosh – well, thanks for telling me. What have we – what have you got for tonight?'

Owen told her, and Victoria said, 'Perhaps that young man with the fair hair who was sitting in my office could look after my items. He seems quite sensible.'

'He's gone,' said Owen. 'Seconded to Bush House. He was only a trainee. We'll manage.'

Victoria walked slowly back to the kitchen. She felt bereaved and ill at ease. When she got to the door her hand rested several seconds on the handle before she let it fall again to her side. Few sounds came from within; low voices, occasional sniffles and then, a loud, dissonant clash.

'Ta-ra-ra BOOM-de-ay,' Harold sang, as he banged two saucepan lids together.

In the cool stone passage, Victoria turned away. She could not tell why but her steps led her, with a momentum of their own, back to the telephone. She dialled the number of the local taxi and asked to be picked up in half an hour. 'Will a cheque be all right?' she asked.

She had her cheque book, she had her overdraft and she had her place on the Programme still, just. But one way or another, she had to move on. She went up to the bedroom on the first floor and made up the bed. The children's dirty pyjamas lay on the floor and she left them there. As she made the bed, she thought with immense tenderness of the loving night she had spent close to Harold in the high, single bed in the red room at the other end of the house. She picked up her two bags and bumped them down the stairs and across the old wooden floorboards to the front door. Then she went back to the kitchen. The children and Harold were playing noughts and crosses among the crumbs. Harold was pulling his face this way and that and winking as he called out, 'Well played!' Flora jumped up and down and Alice sat, pencil in hand, with a solemn white face.

'Come on, Victoria,' cried Harold. 'We're playing noughts and crosses.'

'I'm bored,' said Alice. Harold frowned and shot Victoria a peremptory glance.

'Do you know how to play Boxes?' Victoria started to say. Instead, she found herself saying, 'I've asked for a taxi to take me to the station. It'll be here in fifteen minutes. Would you like me to brush your hair, Alice, before I go?'

'You've what?' said Harold. 'But we're going for a picnic.'

Alice nodded her head and slipped down from her chair.

'Me too,' said Flora, wriggling off her cushions.

The three of them went upstairs to the attics. 'Do you mind going in here again?' said Victoria at the doorway into the bedroom. Alice shook her head. Flora rushed past them. 'My darling Teddy,' she cried.

They stood at the window from which a white sheet still hung, limp in the bright air. Victoria teased and tugged at the two honey-coloured heads in front of her. A smell, the inimitable nursery smell of children's hair mixed with Johnson's Baby Shampoo, came off their heads.

'Teddy too,' said Flora, holding up the threadbare cloth head to be brushed.

A car rounded the corner from the lane into the drive and made its way sedately towards the house.

'There's my taxi,' said Victoria. 'You look lovely, girls. Come on.' She took their hands and walked down the stairs with them into the hall below. Harold sauntered towards them.

'Aha,' he said. 'So it's the Retreat from Moscow, is it?' He held a straggling bouquet of wild roses in his hand and some ragged tendrils of honeysuckle.

'Stay,' said Alice tugging her hand.

'Darling, darling,' said Flora, clasping her thigh.

Harold thrust the flowers at her. 'I suppose you want me to say "I love you",' he said making a face of fearsome distaste, 'or do the roses have to be red?' He stood looking at her, frowning. Then he turned abruptly away and picked up her bags. Victoria followed him to the taxi. The driver held the door. As Victoria got in, Harold seized her and turned her to him. He dug in his pocket and jingled among the coins there: 'You'd better have this,' he said and pressed a £5 note into her hand.

'Oh!' said Victoria. 'Thanks.'

Harold put both hands on her shoulders and gripped them. He kissed her hard on the mouth and long.

Victoria shook herself like a dog coming out of a pond. Harold laughed and put his arm round her shoulder. With his other hand he tilted her head so that it rested, for a moment, in the curve between his neck and his collarbone. He gave her shoulder a long steady squeeze. He felt unaccountably light of heart but serious and free as if he had stepped out of a constricting suit of clothes made for someone whose body was quite another shape.

345

'Oh, Victoria,' he said.

'Oh, Harold,' said Victoria.

She got into the taxi and the door closed behind her. The way ahead seemed clear though she did not know where it would lead.

'You'll just make the eleven forty-five nicely, miss,' said the driver.

The car set off down the drive, under the trees. The fields on either side shone in the sun, the intense green of new summer and overhead the sky enclosed the universe; a steady unbroken infinite blue, the same blue Volnicek had seen when he reached up into his mother's arms the Sunday before. Behind, three figures, a man and two children hand in hand, receded slowly into the distance and were lost from view as the taxi hooted and turned the corner into the lane over the Downs.